One Christmas...to forever

SCARLET WILSON

JENNIFER FAYE

JANICE LYNN

MILLS & BOON

First Published in Great Britain 2022
By Mills & Boon, an imprint of HarperCollins*Publishers* Ltd
1 London Bridge Street, London, SE1 9GF

www.harpercollins.co.uk

HarperCollins*Publishers*
1st Floor, Watermarque Building,
Ringsend Road, Dublin 4, Ireland

ONE CHRISTMAS...TO FOREVER © 2022 Harlequin Enterprises ULC.

A Family Made at Christmas © 2017 Scarlet Wilson
Snowbound with an Heiress © 2017 Jennifer F. Stroka
It Started at Christmas... © 2016 Janice Lynn

ISBN: 978-0-263-31800-5

MIX
Paper | Supporting
responsible forestry
FSC™ C007454

This book is produced from independently certified FSC™ paper to ensure responsible forest management.

For more information visit: www.harpercollins.co.uk/green

Printed and Bound in Spain using 100% Renewable electricity at CPI Black Print, Barcelona

A FAMILY MADE AT CHRISTMAS

SCARLET WILSON

This book is dedicated to Sheila Hodgson, my fabulous editor. Thank you for believing in this story and letting me see it through, and thank you for being the best advocate for Medical Romance in the world!

CHAPTER ONE

'HURRY UP, RILEY. It's your round.' The hard slap on the shoulder nearly ejected him from his chair. Riley laughed and turned around. Frank Cairney, one of the rehab nurses, was standing with his rucksack on his shoulder. The rest of the team were hovering outside near the door. 'Should I go and hold up the bar for us?'

Riley nodded. 'Just a few notes to finish and I'll be there. Thanks, guys.'

He typed quickly on the electronic record, leaving detailed notes on the plan for Jake Ashford, a soldier injured on duty in Afghanistan and now a resident in the army rehab hospital at Waterloo Court.

It was late afternoon on a Friday. Those who could go home had gone home. But some patients wouldn't be able to go home for some time—Jake was one of those.

Working in the rehab hospital hadn't really been on Riley's career plan. But, due to a family crisis, a fellow colleague hadn't been able to start when he should have, meaning the hospital needed someone to fill in. Riley's surgical experience in orthopaedics had been flagged and his deployment had been delayed on a temporary basis for a few weeks.

But today was his last shift. And truth was he was relieved. The staff and support team at Waterloo Court were fantastic, as were the world-class rehab services, but Riley liked the pace of emergencies. On Monday he'd be in Sierra Leone, where another outbreak of Ebola seemed to be emerging.

He finished his notes and walked down the corridor to the in-patient beds. He heard the laughter before he saw her familiar frame.

April Henderson had Jake sitting at the side of his bed. Laughing. Really laughing, as if she'd just told him the funniest joke in the world.

Even from here he knew exactly what she was doing—testing Jake's sitting balance. She was one of the best physiotherapists he'd ever worked with.

She was tireless. She was relentless. She was polite. She was professional.

He'd caught himself on more than one occasion watching that blonde ponytail swishing up the corridor in front of him as she made her way between the ninety patients that were housed in the state-of-the-art unit.

But even now—four weeks later—he really didn't know a thing about her.

April was the quietest co-worker he'd ever met. Every conversation, every communication had been about their patients. When he asked her about life, what she was doing at the weekend or anything other than work she just shut down.

He'd asked other staff a few questions about her, but no one really said much. Apparently she wasn't married and hadn't mentioned a boyfriend. The staff here were a mixture of military and civilian. April was civilian. She'd transferred to the new unit at Waterloo Court. The centre dealt with serious musculoskeletal injuries, neurological injuries and complex trauma, including amputees. The brand-new facility was four times bigger than its predecessor. There were gyms, full of cardiovascular and resistance equipment, two swimming pools, a hydrotherapy pool and a specialist centre where artificial limbs were manufactured on-site and individually tailored to the patients' needs.

'Doc?' Jake caught his eye.

Riley crossed the room, holding out his hand. 'I came to say goodbye.' He paused for a second. 'I'm shipping out again tomorrow.' He had to be truthful, but he could see the momentary pang in the young man's eyes. Jake loved the army. Had wanted to serve since he was five. And now, at the grand old age of twenty-three, would be unlikely to ever ship out again.

Jake took Riley's extended hand. 'Good luck, Doc—it's been short and sweet. Where are you headed?'

Riley gave a shrug. 'At the moment, I think it's Africa. But you know how things can change. By the time Monday comes around it could be somewhere else completely.'

He glanced down at April, who was leaning against a stool at the side of the bed. 'Are you coming to the farewell drinks, April?'

It was obvious he'd caught her off guard because two tiny pink spots flared in her cheeks and she stumbled over her words. 'Wh-what? Er…no…sorry. I don't think I'll manage.'

Jake nudged her with one of his dangling feet. 'Oh, go on, April. When was the last time you could tell me a good night out story?'

The pinkness spread. But the shy demeanour vanished instantly. He'd always found that curious about her. April Henderson knew how to engage with her patients. *Really* engage with her patients. Around them she was relaxed, open and even showed the occasional glimmer of fun. But around any of the staff? She was just April.

'I'm not here to tell you night out stories, Jake. I'm here to help get you back on your feet again.' She leaned forward and put her hands on his bare leg. 'But don't think I didn't notice that deliberate kick.' She looked up and gave Jake a wide smile. 'That's great. That's something we can work on.'

With her bright blue eyes, blonde hair and clear skin, April Henderson could be stunning if she wanted to be. But there was never any make-up on her skin, never any new style with her hair. It was almost as if she used her uniform as a shield.

Riley watched the look on Jake's face. For the first time in weeks he saw something that hadn't been there much before. Hope.

It did weird things to his insides. Jake was a young man who should be filled with hope. His whole life was ahead of him. But there was already a good hint that his injury could be limiting. They still didn't have a clear prognosis for him, and that was why April's work was so vital.

He winked at Jake and folded his arms across his chest. 'I'm completely and utterly offended that you won't come to my farewell drinks. Four long weeks here, all those shifts together, and you can't even say goodbye.'

'He's right, April.' Jake nodded. 'It is shocking. Thank goodness you're not actually in the army. At this point you'd be getting a dishonourable discharge.'

For the briefest of seconds there was a flash of panic behind her eyes, quickly followed by the realisation that they were kidding with her.

She raised her eyebrows. Gave her best smile. The one reserved for patients in trouble. Both of them recognised it instantly.

'Uh-oh,' Riley muttered.

April touched Jake's leg. 'Well, just so you know, Jake,

now that we've established there's some movement and—'
she stood up '—your balance is gradually improving, I
think I'll have a whole new plan for you, starting tomorrow.'

Jake groaned as Riley laughed. He couldn't quite work
out why April could chat easily with patients but could
barely say a word to him on a normal day.

Jake pointed at Riley. 'This is all your fault. You're
abandoning me to this wicked, wicked woman. You know
she'll work me hard and exhaust me.' He said the words
with a twinkle in his eyes.

Riley nodded as he glanced at April. Her blue gaze met
his. For the first time since he'd met her, she didn't look
away instantly. He smiled. 'You're right, Jake. But I'm
leaving you with one of the best physios I've ever met.
She'll push you to your absolute limit—exactly what you
need. If anyone can get you back on your feet again, it's
April Henderson.' He put his hand on Jake's shoulder as
he leaned forward to fake whisper in his ear, 'Even if she
won't have a drink with me.'

There was something about that bright blue gaze. Even
under the harsh hospital lights that seemed to drain the colour from everyone else, April still looked good. The edges
of her mouth gave just the slightest hint of turning upwards. It was the first time he'd wished he wasn't leaving.

Jake reached up and grabbed his hand, giving it a shake.
'Thanks, Lieutenant Callaghan. Good luck with your deployment.' There was a tiny waver in his voice. Almost
as if he knew the likelihood was he'd never make another
deployment himself.

Riley clasped his hand between his. 'I'll look you up
again when I come back.' He started towards the door,
then glanced over his shoulder and gave a warm smile.
'You too, April.'

* * *

Her heart was acting as though she were racing along a beach, rather than sitting at the side of a patient's bed.

Darn it.

Ever since Riley Callaghan had turned up on this ward she'd spent the last four weeks avoiding him. It was everything. The little kink in his dark hair. The smiling green eyes. The cheeky charm. Oh, lots of doctors and servicemen she'd met in the last few years had the talk, the wit, the *lots* of charm.

But she'd had enough to deal with. The diagnosis of her twin sister's ovarian cancer, rapidly followed by her failing treatment, then Mallory's death, had meant that she had found it easier to retreat into herself and seal herself off from the world. Her own genetic testing had floored her. She had decisions to make. Plans for the future.

Her last relationship had been half-hearted. Mallory had got sick and she'd realised quickly that she needed to spend time with her sister. But, since then, the last thing she wanted was a relationship.

After her own testing, she'd spent a day wondering whether she should just find some random guy, try to get pregnant, have a baby quickly and deal with everything else after.

But those thoughts had only lasted a day. She'd met the surgeon. A date for her surgery would be agreed soon. And she needed to do this part of her life alone.

Then Riley Callaghan had appeared on her ward. All cheeky grins and twinkling eyes. It was the first time in a long time she'd actually been aware of every sense in her body. Her surge of adrenaline. Every rapid heartbeat.

That was the reason she didn't engage in small talk. That was the reason she kept to herself. She couldn't afford to let herself be attracted to a guy at such a crucial point in her life. How did you start that conversation anyway? Oh, you want to go on a date? Great. By the way, in a few months' time I'm going to have my ovaries and fallopian tubes removed and maybe later my breasts. What? You don't want to hang around?

It didn't matter that she'd found herself glancing in Riley's direction every time he'd appeared on the ward. She'd hated the way she'd started stumbling over her words around him, or had trouble looking him in the eye.

But as she watched his retreating back her mouth felt dry. Part of her wanted to grab her jacket and join the rest of the staff for a drink. But then she'd be in a pub, where her inhibitions could lower, and she could encourage the gentle flirtation that could go absolutely nowhere.

She shook her head and turned her attention back to Jake. 'Can we get you more comfortable? I'll work on your new programme and we'll start tomorrow.'

Jake gave her a nod and she helped settle him in a comfortable, specially designed chair for those with spinal injuries.

Her shift was finished but it wouldn't take long to write up her notes and make the adjustments needed for tomorrow. It wasn't as if she had anywhere to go, right?

Half an hour later there were a few voices in the corridor behind her. This was a military hospital. When the Colonel appeared, it was never good news.

All the hairs bristled on her arms. She looked around, wondering who was about to get bad news.

'Ms Henderson?'

She spun around in her chair and jumped to her feet. Her? How? What?

A woman with a pinched face and dark grey coat stood next to the Colonel. She didn't even know that he knew her name.

'Y-yes,' she stumbled.

'We're wondering where Lieutenant Callaghan is.'

Her heart plummeted in her chest. Riley? They had bad news for Riley?

She glanced around. 'He's not here. But I know where he is. Can you give me five minutes? I'll get him for you.'

The Colonel nodded and she rushed past, going to the changing room and grabbing her jacket. If she ran, the pub was only five minutes away.

As soon as she stepped outside she realised just how much the temperature had dipped. It was freezing and it was only the middle of November. As she thudded down the dark path a few snowflakes landed on her cheeks. Snow? Already?

She slowed her run. If spots of rain had turned to snow, then there was a chance the damp ground would be slippery.

The pub came into view, warm light spilling from its windows. She stopped running completely, her warm breath steaming in the air around her.

She could hear the noise and laughter coming from the pub already. She closed her eyes for a second. She hated that she was about to do this. To walk into a farewell party and pull Riley away for news he probably wouldn't want. Did his family serve in the military? Did he have a brother? She just didn't know. She hadn't allowed herself to have that kind of conversation with Riley.

She pushed open the door to the pub, the heat hitting her instantly. It was busy. She jostled her way through the people, scanning one way then another. It didn't take long to recognise the laugh. She picked Riley's familiar frame out of the crowd and pushed herself towards him. Her work colleagues were picking up glasses and toasting him. She stumbled as she reached him, her hands coming out and landing square on his chest. His hard, muscular chest.

'April?' He looked completely surprised. 'Oh, wow. You made it. That's great.' His arm had automatically gone around her shoulder. He pulled her a little closer to try to talk above the noise in the pub. 'Can I get you something to drink?'

He frowned as he noticed she hadn't even changed out of her uniform.

She looked up into his green eyes. 'Riley, I'm sorry—I'm not here for the drinks.'

He pulled back a little whilst keeping his arm on her shoulder. 'You aren't?'

Her hands were still on his chest. She really didn't want to move them. 'Riley—' she pressed her lips together for a second '—the Colonel is looking for you. He came to the ward.'

She felt every part of his body tense.

'What?' His voice had changed.

She nodded. 'I said I'd come and get you.'

Riley didn't even say goodbye to anyone around him. He just grabbed hold of her hand and pulled her behind him as he jostled his way through the crowd.

The snow was falling as they reached the main door. Riley spun around to face her, worry etched all over his face. 'What did he say? Is it just the Colonel?'

April shook her head. 'He didn't tell me anything. And there's an older woman with him. I didn't recognise her.'

She reached up and touched his arm. It didn't matter that she'd vowed to keep a distance. This was a completely different set of circumstances. This was a work colleague who was likely to receive some bad news. She'd never leave a workmate alone at a time like this. 'Let me come back with you' was all she said.

And, after the longest few seconds, Riley gave a nod.

* * *

He started walking quickly but eventually just broke into a run. His brother. It had to be his brother. He was on a training exercise right now somewhere in Scotland, flying out to Afghanistan tomorrow. Accidents happened. As a doctor, he knew that more than most. Unless something had happened to his mum and dad. Could they have had an accident?

He was conscious of the footsteps beside him. The ones that broke into a gentle run when he did. He'd been surprised by April's appearance earlier—it had made his heart lurch for a few seconds. But it hadn't taken long to notice the paleness of her complexion. The worry in her bright blue eyes. And she was right by his side. Trouble was, right now he couldn't think straight.

By the time he reached the ward area his brain was spinning completely. He slowed down to a walk, took a few deep breaths and tried to put on his professional face. He was a soldier. He could deal with whatever news he was about to receive.

The Colonel ushered him into a room where a woman in a grey coat was sitting with a file in front of her.

April hovered near the door—she didn't seem to know whether to leave or not—and he was kind of glad she was still around.

'Lieutenant Callaghan. Please take a seat.'

He didn't want to sit. In fact, sitting was the last thing he wanted to do. But if it would get this thing over with quicker then he'd do it.

He sat down and glanced at the woman. She leaned across the table towards him. 'Dr Callaghan, my name is Elizabeth Cummings. I'm a social worker.'

He frowned. A social worker? Why did she need to speak to him?

She flicked open her file. 'I understand that this might seem a little unusual. Can I ask, do you know an Isabel Porter?'

He flinched. This was not what he'd been expecting to hear. He glanced at the Colonel. 'Sir, my parents? My brother?'

The Colonel shook his head and gestured back to Ms Cummings. 'No. They're fine. They're absolutely fine. Please, this is something else entirely.'

Riley shifted in his chair. He glanced behind at April. She looked just as confused as he was.

Now he felt uncomfortable. He looked back at the social worker. 'Isabel Porter, from Birmingham?'

The woman nodded.

'Yes, I know Isabel. At least, I did. Around five years ago. Why are you asking me that?'

Ms Cummings gave a nod. 'I see. Dr Callaghan, I'm sorry to tell you that there was an accident a few days ago. Isabel was killed in a road traffic accident.'

It was like a cold prickle down his spine. Nothing about this seemed right. 'Oh, I see. I'm really sorry to hear that. But I don't understand. Why are you telling me?' He looked from one tight face to the other.

Ms Cummings glanced at the Colonel. 'There is an issue we need to discuss. Ms Porter left a will.'

'Isabel had written a will?' Now that did sound weird. Isabel had been a bit chaotic. Their relationship had barely lasted a few months. And they hadn't kept in touch. He hadn't heard from her at all in the last five years. 'Why on earth are you telling me this?'

Ms Cummings slid an envelope across the desk to him. 'Maybe this will help explain things.' She kept talking. 'Obviously there's been a delay. Isabel had no other family. No next of kin, which is probably why she left a will and wrote this letter for you. It takes time to find out if someone has left a will or not.'

Riley glanced at the letter on the table in front of him. He had no idea what was going on. Nothing about this made sense.

April walked over and put her hand on his shoulder. From the woman who'd seemed so shut off, it was such an unexpected move. But the warm feel of her palm on his shoulder sent a wave of pure comfort through his confused state.

Ms Cummings stared at April for a second then continued. 'It's apparent that your name wasn't on the birth certificate. I'm not quite sure why that was. But because Isabel didn't have you formally named as next of kin, Finn has been in temporary foster care for the last few days.'

Riley shook his head. 'Who?'

She stared at him. 'Finn. Your son.'

For the first time he was glad of the chair. If he hadn't had it, his legs might have made him sway.

'My son?'

Ms Cummings glanced at the Colonel again. 'Yes, Dr Callaghan. That's why I'm here.'

'I have a son?'

She stared at him again. 'Finn. He's five. Isabel never told you?'

He shook his head as his brain just spun. Not a single rational thought would form. 'No. Isabel never told me.'

Ms Cummings pushed the letter towards him again. He noticed it was sealed. The social worker had no idea of the contents. 'Well, maybe that's why she left you the letter.'

Riley looked at the cream envelope in front of him. He picked it up and ripped it open, pulling out a matching cream sheet of paper.

Dear Riley,

I hope you never have to read this. But if you do it's because something's happened. I'm sorry I never told you about Finn. You'd already left for Afghanistan and it just seemed pointless. We already knew our time was over and I didn't need to complicate your life.

I hope I'm not about to spoil things for you. I hope you've managed to meet someone, marry and have a family of your own.

Finn and I have been great. We haven't needed anything at all. He's a funny, quirky little boy and I can see traits of us both in him every single day. I love him more than you can ever know, and I hope you'll feel that way about him too.

He knows who you are. I only had a few pictures, but I put them in his room and told him you worked away and would meet him when he grew up.

Please forgive me, and love my darling boy for both of us.

Isabel

He couldn't speak. He couldn't breathe. His life had just been turned upside down and on its head. He had a child. He had a son.

And he'd never been told. Rage filled his brain, just as April's fingers tightened on his shoulder. She could probably read every word of the letter over his shoulder.

April leaned over and spun the letter around to face the social worker, giving her a few seconds to read it. Her face paled.

Ms Cummings looked at him. 'You didn't even know that Finn existed?'

He shook his head. The firm touch by April was dissipating the rage that was burning inside. Isabel had been quirky. She'd been a little chaotic. This didn't seem completely out of character. He just hadn't had a clue.

'Where is Finn now?' April's voice cut through his thoughts.

Ms Cummings looked up. 'And you are?'

April leaned across and held out her hand. 'I'm April Henderson. I'm a friend and colleague of Dr Callaghan's.' She said the words so easily. A friend. It almost sounded true.

Ms Cummings shuffled some papers. 'Finn's been in temporary foster care in Birmingham.'

Panic started to fill Riley. 'My son is in foster care?' He'd heard about these things. Wasn't foster care bad for kids?

Ms Cummings nodded. 'We have a few things to sort out. As your name isn't on the birth certificate, you may want to arrange a DNA test. However, Ms Porter named you as her son's guardian in her will. Pending a few checks, I'll be happy to release Finn into your custody. You will, of course, be allocated a local social worker to help you with any queries.' She lifted something from her bag. 'As you'll know, in England we have a number of legal procedures. Isabel left everything in trust—via you—for Finn. But probate takes some time. I can only let you have these keys to the house for a day or so—to pick some things up for Finn. Although ultimately it will come to you, the keys have to be returned to the lawyer in the meantime.'

'When do I pick up Finn?'

'Do you have somewhere suitable for him to stay?'

His thoughts went immediately to his temporary army lodgings. He was only supposed to be here four weeks. 'I'm supposed to leave for Sierra Leone on Monday.' The words came out of nowhere.

The Colonel interjected quickly. 'Don't worry. I'll take care of that. You have a family emergency. Your son obviously takes priority here. Do you want me to arrange some other accommodation for you?'

He nodded automatically. He didn't own a property. He had money in the bank but had never got around to buying a place as he'd no idea where he'd eventually end up.

His eyes caught sight of a box in the corner of the room. Red tinsel. It was stuffed full of Christmas decorations. Christmas. It was only six weeks away. His son had lost his mother, six weeks before Christmas.

'I'll give you an address. I can meet you at the foster parents' house tomorrow if that suits.'

'It suits.' The words were automatic.

Ms Cummings gave a nod. 'There's one other thing.'

'What's that?'

She licked her lips. 'As Ms Porter had no other next of kin and you're the only person named in the will, it will be up to you to organise the funeral.'

'What?'

Ms Cummings's eyes narrowed. 'Will that be a problem?'

He shook his head. 'No. Of course not.'

Ms Cummings pushed some papers towards him. 'Here's a copy of the will. A note of Ms Porter's address and her lawyer's address to drop the keys back. And a copy of the address for the foster family tomorrow. Let's say eleven o'clock?'

Business obviously concluded, she gathered her papers and stood up. Riley glanced at the clock. In the space of ten minutes his life had just turned on its head.

'Do you have a picture?'

She looked startled. 'Of Finn?'

He nodded. Of course of Finn. Who did she think he wanted to see a picture of?

She reopened her file and slid out a small photograph. His mouth dried instantly. It was like a blast from the past. That small innocent face. Thirty years ago that had been him. A whole world he didn't even know existed.

He didn't even speak as the Colonel showed Ms Cummings out.

April had an ache deep inside her belly. This was a whole new Riley Callaghan in front of her right now.

He looked almost broken. She'd spent the last four weeks secretly watching his cheeky grin, positive interactions and boundless energy. There had been a few emergencies on the ward and Riley thought and moved quicker than anyone. He was a great doctor. Happy to help others. And always itching to get on to the next thing.

It was the first time she'd ever seen him slumped. He just seemed stunned.

His hand reached up and crumpled the letter on the table in front of him. She moved instinctively, brushing her fingers against his, pulling the paper from his and smoothing the paper back down.

'Don't. In a few years' time you might want to show that to Finn.'

He stood up so quickly the chair flew back and hit the floor. 'She didn't tell me. She didn't tell me about him.' He flung his hands up. 'How could she do that to me? How could she do that to him?'

April's mouth dried. She didn't know what to say. How on earth could she answer that question?

He started pacing, running his hands through his thick dark hair. 'What do I do? I don't know the first thing about children. I don't know how to be a father. What if he doesn't like me? What if I suck at being a dad?' He threw his hands out again. 'I don't have a house. What do I buy for a five-year-old? What does a five-year-old boy need? And what about my job? Will I still work here? What about school? Does Finn even go to school yet? I move about, all over the place. How can that be good for a kid?'

April took a deep breath. It was clear that every thought in his brain was just tumbling straight out of his mouth. She shook her head and stood in front of him. 'Riley, I don't know. I honestly don't know. But there's a foster mother. She'll probably be able to help. You have keys to the house. Everything that a five-year-old boy needs will be there. And it will probably help Finn if you take his own things to help him settle.'

The light in the office was dimmer than the rest of the hospital. But Riley's hurt green eyes were the thing she could see clearest. She was standing right in front of him. Closer than she'd ever wanted to get.

He closed his eyes for a second then nodded. 'You're right. I know you're right. But my son… Finn…he's been in foster care. Isn't that supposed to be terrible?'

She gave a soft smile. 'I think those days are long gone. Foster carers have to go through a mountain of checks these days. Finn will have been well looked after. But the last few days will probably have been a blur.'

He reached out and took her hand in his. It made her catch her breath. It was so unexpected. And more. He just didn't let it go.

She could almost feel his pain. It was palpable. It was right there in the air between them. Riley Callaghan had just had the legs swept from clean under him. And, to his credit, he was still standing. Just the way she would have expected of him.

'Will you help me, April?' He squeezed her hand.

Fear swept through her. 'What do you mean?'

'I don't know. I don't know anything. Will you help me?'

Help. What did that mean? She was all for supporting a colleague in a difficult situation. But this one was probably bigger than anyone could have expected.

'Please? I'm out of my depth, April. I know that already.' His green eyes were pleading with her. Twisting her insides this way and that.

A child. A little boy had just lost a parent. Finn must be feeling lost. He must feel as if his whole world had just ended.

She met Riley's gaze. 'I'll help where I can,' she said cautiously. 'I can help you with the funeral.'

He frowned. 'You will?'

Mallory. She'd organised every tiny detail of the funeral, even though it had ripped her heart out. Who else knew her twin better than her?

She nodded. 'Let's just say I'm good at funerals.'

And she squeezed his hand back.

CHAPTER TWO

WHAT ON EARTH am I doing?

April spent the whole time on the motorway questioning herself. Riley's hands gripped the steering wheel so tightly his knuckles were white. He'd looked pale this morning. As if he hadn't slept a wink.

By the time the satnav took them into the Birmingham street, the tension was so high she felt as if it could propel the car into the sky. As he killed the engine she leaned over and put one of her hands over his. She really didn't want to touch him. Touching Riley did strange things to her senses, but this wasn't about her. This was about a little boy.

'Stop.'

'What?'

'Just…stop.'

He pulled back his hands and sat back in the seat. 'What are you talking about?'

She could see the tension across his shoulders, reaching up into his jaw.

'You can't go in there like this.'

'What?' The anger that had been simmering beneath the surface was threatening to crack through.

'This is the first time Finn will see you. None of this is his fault. He's about to meet his dad—someone he's only seen in a photograph before.'

She lifted up her hand as Riley opened his mouth to speak. 'I thought about this last night. I told you I don't have any experience with kids, but what do I think this little boy needs to hear?' She leaned a little closer to him. 'I think he needs to hear his dad loves him. His dad is going to look after him and stay with him. His dad is his family and you'll always be together.'

He frowned and then his face relaxed and he shook his head. 'I know. I know that's exactly what I should say.' He lifted one hand and ran it through his hair. 'I spoke to my brother last night.'

Her stomach twisted. 'Isn't he in Scotland?'

Riley nodded. 'He's on a training exercise. There's supposed to be radio silence. But the Colonel made some arrangements for me. Dan was blown away. Says he can't wait to meet Finn.'

'Good. That's great. At least you know you'll have the support of your family.' Then she tilted her head to the side. Something seemed just a little off. 'What aren't you saying? Did you speak to your mum and dad?'

He shook his head and put one hand back on the steering wheel. 'That's the one thing Dan actually understands. My mum and dad will be great. They'll be overwhelmed. They've always wanted a grandchild. But—'

'But what? Don't you need all the help you can get?'

Riley hesitated. 'My mum…has the best of intentions. I love her. I really do. But she'll want to take over. She'll pick up her life and sweep right down.'

'Ah…and you don't want that?'

Riley smiled. 'Maybe…eventually. But right now I need to get to know Finn. I need to spend some time with him. Like I said, I have no idea about five-year-old boys.'

April shook her head. 'Well, that's a strange thing to say.'

He shrugged. 'Why?'

She lifted her hands. 'Because you've been one. Your brother has been one. You know all you need to know about five-year-old boys.'

He shifted in his seat and pulled his phone from his pocket. 'Look at this.' He opened an app. 'This is what I bought last night.'

She leaned forward to glance at the screen and couldn't help the little laugh that came out. 'A parenting guide? You bought a parenting guide?' She started shaking her head.

'What? I told you. I don't know anything. Anything at all.'

She leaned back against the seat and looked over at him. Riley Callaghan was just about to change before her eyes. The doctor, the soldier and the cheeky charmer was about to take on a whole new role. She admired him for his fear. She admired him for wanting to get to know Finn without letting his mother take over.

Her mouth dried. This was a whole world that she'd never know. She'd already made the decision. She'd never have kids. Her biological clock would never be allowed to tick. When her sister had died it had almost been like watching herself in a mirror. Mallory hadn't had the information that she had. April's genetic testing had only been approved because of Mallory's diagnosis and a look back through the family history. If she ignored the results she would be disrespecting her sister's memory. She could never do that.

But this time of year was especially hard. Her heart gave a little squeeze as she thought of her parents. Before this—before any of this—her mother had always joked she would like a house filled with grandchildren once she retired. But that would never happen now.

And even though her mum and dad fully supported her

decision, she knew they had a secret ache for the future life they were losing.

'April?'

Riley's voice pulled her from her thoughts. She gave him a soft smile and wrestled in her pocket for her own phone. She turned it around so he could see her Internet search: *Top ten Christmas toys for five-year-old boys.*

Riley groaned. 'Christmas. It's only six weeks away. I made no plans because I thought I'd be in Sierra Leone. I don't even have a Christmas tree.'

'It's the middle of November. You have time.'

He was staring at her with those bright green eyes. There was silence for a few seconds. She shifted in her seat and brought her hand up to wipe her cheek. 'What is it—do I have something on my face?'

'Why wouldn't you talk to me before?'

She was surprised. 'I did. We spoke about patients all the time.'

He gave a gentle shake of his head. 'But you wouldn't talk to me about anything else.' He paused and continued with his curious stare. 'April, why did you tell me you were good at funerals?'

She could sense his wariness in asking the question. But he'd still asked. He was like this at work too. He always asked patients the difficult questions. Always spoke to the surgeons about the risks and possibilities.

This time he reached out and touched her hand. 'April, did you lose someone? Were you married?'

She closed her eyes for a second. Riley had only been there four weeks. Word obviously hadn't reached him. Then again, the turnover of staff at Waterloo Court could be high. Not everyone knew her background and she preferred it that way.

This wasn't normally something she would share. But

she'd just shared a major part of Riley's life. If they'd been on the ward, she would have found a way to dodge the question. But, alone in the confines of the car, there was nowhere to hide. And she didn't want to tell a lie.

'I lost my sister,' she said quietly.

The warmth of his hand was flooding through her system. 'When?'

'Eighteen months ago.'

'Was it an accident?'

She licked her lips. She should have known he would press for more details. This was hard. Probably because she hadn't really shared with anyone before. Probably because she didn't want them to figure out the next step. 'No. It wasn't an accident.' The rest of the words stuck somewhere in the back of her throat. She didn't mention the cancer. She didn't mention the fact they were twins. She didn't mention the genetic tests. These were all things that Riley Callaghan didn't need to know.

By some grace, he didn't ask any more. He didn't ask those details. 'You organised the funeral?'

She nodded. 'She was my sister. My mum and dad were devastated—we all were—but it seemed the one thing I could do that made me feel a little better, a little more in control.' She took a deep breath and met his gaze, trying not to think that his hand was still covering hers. 'So, I can help you with that. If I can find a few of Isabel's friends, talk to some of them, I can make the practical arrangements for you, and you can focus on Finn.'

At the mention of Finn's name again she sensed him tense. 'Riley,' she said warningly.

'What?'

'You're tensing. You're angry. You've been angry the whole drive up here. That's no use. No use at all.' She was talking to him firmly, the way she usually spoke to a patient who was just about ready to give up on their physio.

He snapped. 'What do you expect? I've been cheated out of five years of my son's life. If I'd known about Finn, I would have been there. If Isabel had been involved in an accident, at least my little boy would know he would be with someone who loved and cared about him. He doesn't know any of that. I'm a stranger to him. She did that.'

She shook her head at him. 'Don't you dare.'

'Don't dare what?' He was almost indignant.

She pulled her hand out from under his and pointed her finger at him. 'Don't you dare go in there simmering with resentment at Finn's mother. You're an adult. Deal with it. Deal with the fact that life doesn't always give you the hand of cards that you want. Finn will need you to talk about his mum. If he hears resentment or anger in your voice he'll close off to you. You'll wreck your relationship before it even has a chance to form.'

'I thought you didn't know anything about kids?'

'I don't. But I know enough about people. And so do you. You're a doctor. You deal with families all the time.' She dropped her hand and let her voice soften. 'I know you're angry. And if you are, talk to me. Talk to your brother.' She stared out of the window at the blue sky above them. 'My sister and I used to do a thing.'

'A thing?'

She nodded. 'If either of us was angry or upset—and it happened a lot—we used to hug it out.'

'You what?'

She shrugged. 'Hugging. Physical contact. Scientifically proven to reduce stress and anxiety. To release tension.'

He looked amused. 'You want me to hug it out?'

The expression on his face was incredulous. She unclipped her seat belt and opened her arms. 'Why not? You can't go in there all tense and angry. That doesn't help you. That doesn't help Finn.' She raised her eyebrows. 'And, just so you know, this is a one-time offer.'

His face broke into a smile as he shook his head and unclipped his own belt. 'I must be crazy.'

'I've heard you called worse.'

He leaned forward and wrapped his arms around her. Riley Callaghan knew how to hug. This was no gentle, delicate hug. This was a massive pick-you-up-and-swing-you-round bear hug. Just as well they were in the car.

His emerging stubble brushed against her cheek. The waft of soap and masculinity flooded through her senses. That whole sensation of being held by a man, being comforted by someone who wrapped you in their arms, made her catch her breath. It had been so long. So long since she'd let someone this close.

She was doing this for him. Not for her.

So why did it feel like this?

He couldn't see her face, so she closed her eyes for a few seconds. Letting herself just remember the moment. Feel the heat, the warmth and the comfort.

She'd missed this. Missed this contact more than she'd ever expected to. What she'd done with the best of intentions had turned into something that was kind of overwhelming.

His voice murmured in her ear. 'Thanks, April.'

'No problem,' she replied automatically. Lost in the warm breath near her ear.

After the longest time he pulled back.

'Okay,' he said. 'We're all hugged out.' She could see how nervous he was. 'It's time for me to meet my son.'

In the blink of an eye his life had changed.

He was a father. His first priority was his son.

April was a godsend.

His first sight of Finn, sitting on the edge of his bed in the foster home, ripped his heart clean out of his chest. Finn was his living image. If he'd sat his five-year-old self down next to Finn they would have looked like twins.

He'd never need a DNA test.

He'd wondered about the photo last night—if it was really a good representation of Finn. If they really looked that alike. Now he knew.

The foster carer was possibly the greatest human being he'd ever met. All preconceived ideas were swept out the window in a matter of seconds. She was used to taking kids in crisis situations and was very experienced. She even ran rings around the po-faced Ms Cummings.

She was warm and friendly. She knew Riley and Finn hadn't met before and had already made a little list of things Finn had mentioned in the last few days. That included things from home he wanted, a list of clothing he would need, the contact details of his school and a few names of friends of his mum's.

April stayed in the background, just accepting the lists with a gracious nod and leaving Riley to ask all the questions that he wanted.

It hadn't taken much to notice the slight tremor in Finn's hands. Riley had sat down on the bed next to him and spoke to his son for the first time. He'd never been so terrified in his life. Not when he'd been serving, not when he'd been retrieving military casualties and not when he'd been stranded on a battlefield with virtually no equipment. This was a whole new ball game.

Somehow it felt good that April was there to have his back. She didn't interfere. She just stayed in the background. That hug in the car had done weird things to his mind. Her body pressed against his had sent a quick flash of a few thoughts he'd had about her in the past four weeks. The vanilla scent that had drifted up his nose had taken him to a whole other place. One where April wasn't permanently dressed in her physiotherapist uniform.

Today was the first day he'd seen her in something else. She was wearing a dress. A dress. He hadn't thought of April as a dress sort of girl. It was dark, covered with assorted pink butterflies, finishing just above her knees, which were covered in thick dark tights and knee-high black boots. She'd wrapped a pink scarf around her neck and was wearing a black military-style jacket.

She even looked as if she had a little make-up on. Either that or her lashes were darker than normal and highlighting those blue eyes. He'd never seen April outside the work environment and somehow it felt as if he'd been missing out.

April Henderson looked good. But then he'd always thought that.

And she'd been right. He'd needed to leave his resentment at the door. One look at Finn told him that.

Finn was charming. Polite, well mannered, and the first thing he told him was that he was going to be an astronaut. Riley smiled. He remembered having the same ambition. His little voice shook when he spoke about his mum and Riley wrapped his arm around his shoulder and pulled him close. 'I'm sorry, Finn. I'm sorry about the accident. But I'll look after you now. I'm your dad. I didn't know about you before, but I know about you now.'

He'd pulled Finn up onto his lap. 'If you want to, we'll go and get some of your things. You can bring whatever you want.'

'I can go back home?'

It was like staring into his own green eyes, but these little eyes were laced with uncertainty. Riley tried to keep his voice steady. 'You're going to stay with me now. But your mum's house will stay as it is for now. We can collect your clothes, your toys, some photographs and anything else you want.' He ran his hand over his son's brown hair. Finn had the same little kink in his hair that he did. 'I know some people who will be so happy to meet you. Your uncle Dan has just flown out to Afghanistan. But he's already sent me a message for you. And your gran and granddad will be really happy to meet you too.'

Riley's mouth was running away with him. He could see the tiny tremble in Finn's hands. It made his heart ache. Should he squeeze him harder? He wasn't quite sure.

'I have a gran and granddad?' Finn's eyes widened. 'I never had those before.'

Yes, you did. You just didn't know it.

He resisted the temptation to say the words out loud. 'Well, you do now.'

It wasn't just Finn's hands that were trembling; it was his voice too. Riley had spent his life as a doctor seeing things that affected him deep down. He'd wished a million times he could change things for the patients he worked with. But he'd never wished he could change things more than he did right now. He'd do anything to take away the hurt in Finn's eyes.

Finn looked up shyly across the room, as if he were searching for something. Riley had the oddest sensation.

'Who is the lady?'

Riley shifted on the bed. 'The lady?'

'The pretty one with the blonde hair. Is she your girl-friend?' There was an almost hopeful edge to Finn's voice.

Riley followed Finn's gaze. April was talking quietly with the foster mum, scribbling down a few more notes. He wasn't quite sure what to say.

Something washed over him as he watched the expression on Finn's face. He was right on Riley's knee but it was almost as if he were trying to anchor himself. Finn had spent his whole life brought up by his mum and, from the sound of it, mainly in the company of her friends. His heart squeezed. That was why he was looking at April.

He was used to being with women. Being in the company of a male from this point onwards would be a huge deal for Finn. Riley squeezed his eyes closed for the briefest of seconds as he remembered all the things his mum used to do with him and his brother as kids. Climbing into bed for cuddles, secret cake baking, her patience with homework, and the way one look could let him know that everything would be all right. It was only in the last few years he'd realised that even though she could be overpowering, how central she'd been for him and his brother. Finn had lost that. He'd lost his central point. Could Riley ever hope to become that person for Finn? Or would he always look for a mother figure in his life?

Riley's skin was pale. 'That's April. She's my…friend.' Was she? 'She works with me at the hospital. She's a physiotherapist. She helps people get well again. Sometimes she has to help them walk again.' It seemed the simplest explanation.

Finn frowned. 'If Uncle Dan is in Afghanistan, will you have to go there too?' His voice had a little tremble. 'What will happen to me?'

And, just like that, the thoughts from last night filled his brain again.

He loved his job. He loved the postings. They fired his enthusiasm and ignited his passion. The last four weeks had been fine, but only because he'd known it wouldn't be for long.

His heart twisted in his chest as he said the words he had to out loud. 'It's you and me, Finn. I won't be going away again. I'll be staying here, with you.'

He looked up. April had appeared in the doorway. He could see the expression on her face. She'd heard him in the last few weeks. Being excited about his future plans, talking about all the missions he'd been on.

The Colonel had phoned him this morning. He could stay at Waterloo Court for the next six months. He had temporary family accommodation. This was his life now. Part of him ached. But he pushed it away. He gave April an almost imperceptible nod.

He'd decided. His son would come first. Always.

She could tell he was struggling. And she felt like an intruder, watching two people who were alike in so many ways getting to know each other for the first time.

The visit to the house was the hardest. And she could relate to this. She really could. She'd had to pack up her sister's house and give away some of her belongings. She'd heard other people talk about it in the past, but you could never really appreciate how hard something like this was until you had to do it yourself.

She fingered her necklace as they reached the house. Two intertwined gold hearts. Her parents had given Mallory and April the same thing for their twenty-first birthdays. Mallory had been buried wearing hers.

The first surprise when they reached the house was the tree.

It seemed that Isabel loved Christmas and even though it was only November the tree was already up and covered in decorations.

'We did that last week,' Finn said shakily.

April knelt down and looked at some of the decorations on the tree. She could see instantly they'd been made by a child's hands.

'Will we take some of these too? You made these, didn't you?'

Finn nodded and pointed to a few of them, which April folded into some tissue paper that she found.

She'd done the practical things. She'd found all the clothes and packed them up. She'd helped Finn choose all the toys and books he'd wanted. Then she'd taken a deep breath and thought about all the sentimental things the foster carer had spoken to her about.

'Photos,' she whispered to Riley. 'We need to find some photos for Finn to have of his mum.'

Riley knelt down in front of Finn. 'Should we get some photographs? Pictures of you and Mum we can put in your new bedroom?'

Finn gave a nod and broke into a run. 'This one,' he shouted. 'This is the one I have.'

April glanced at it and her heart gave a little flip. It was a picture of Isabel and Riley together. They were in a pub somewhere. He had his arm around her shoulders and they were looking at each other and laughing. It looked as if it could have been taken yesterday.

It was like a little spear hitting inside her.

Why? She instantly pushed the feeling aside. She'd no right to feel like that. Riley and her weren't anything to each other. Never could be. She wasn't at that point in her life. And he had his hands more than full for the next while.

Riley's face had blanched. The letter had said Finn had a photograph of his dad; he must not have expected Isabel to be in it too.

April bent down and took the photo frame. 'This is a good photo, Finn. I like it a lot. But let's take some other photographs too. Ones of you and your mum together.'

Finn nodded and darted through to the main living room. April followed his lead and took a photograph from the wall he pointed at, and a calendar from the kitchen that had different photographs of them for every month of the year.

'And the stick!' said Finn. He jumped on top of a chair and found something on a shelf. 'My mum has all our pictures on this!'

Riley gave a nod and put the USB stick in his pocket.

He bent back down. 'Finn, do you want to take anything else?'

Finn hesitated. There was clearly something in his mind.

A wave of something came over April. She'd packed up Finn's bedding to take with him. But after her sister had died, when she'd been packing up the house, she'd collapsed onto the bed at some point and been overwhelmed by the familiar scent from her sister's pillow. She'd sobbed for hours.

She brushed her hand against Riley's. 'I think I know,' she whispered.

She reached out with her other hand and touched Finn's head. 'Should we take some other things of your mum's? How about her pillow, or a blanket that she used? Is there a jumper she loved? Do you want to take something like that?'

Riley squeezed her hand. He must know what this was doing to her. But his look was pure gratitude.

Finn sniffed. So April took his hand and gathered up the things he showed her. He buried his face in his mother's pillow for a few seconds and let out a sob. She couldn't help herself. She gathered the little boy into her arms and just held him. 'I know, honey. I know how hard this is. I'm right here with you. And so is your dad.'

The little body crumpled against hers and a tear slid down her cheek.

This wasn't about her. This wasn't about the family of her own that she'd never have. This was about a little boy who was desperately sad. But somehow it felt about both.

Riley seemed choked too. They gathered up the rest of the belongings and he walked Finn out to the car.

'Wait,' she said. Something had just struck her. She pulled out her phone. 'Let's get a picture of the two of you together.'

Finn looked up at his dad. 'Can we?'

Riley seemed surprised at the question. He knelt down and wrapped his arm around Finn's shoulder. 'Absolutely. I'd love a picture of us both together.'

She knew she should capture it. A first picture of father and son together. But the smile Riley plastered on his face didn't quite reach his eyes. They were still full of worry. As for Finn? He just looked a little nervous. As if he didn't quite know what would come next.

She snapped a few. 'Perfect,' she said.

Riley strapped Finn into the car. As she walked around to her side of the car, he pulled her hand and stopped her, spinning her around to face him.

'April, I just wanted to say something.'

Her heartbeat quickened. It was starting to get dark. Collecting the things had taken a little longer than expected. It had been such a big day. One she'd never expected to be part of.

Today was a Saturday. She might have gone into work for a few hours—even though she wasn't on duty. She'd planned on working with Jake today, but when she'd phoned and left a message for him he'd been absolutely fine. The only other thing she would have done was pick up a few things for dinner.

As it was cold she might even have stayed in her pyjamas all day and watched Christmas movies on TV. Part of her knew that if life had gone as planned, she would probably have had a little pang about not going to Riley's drinks last night. She would have had a twinge of regret that she wouldn't see him again. But part of that would have been reassuring.

It would have left her clear to lock away the attraction she'd been trying to ignore for the last four weeks. She could have parcelled it up in a box like a Christmas present and stored it away in a cupboard. That would have been so much simpler than any of this.

Before she had time to think, Riley slid his hand behind her waist and pulled her towards him, resting his forehead against hers.

It was so up close and personal. They were at the back of the car. Finn couldn't see them. The temperature had dropped; their warm breath was visible in the cold air.

A wave of emotions swept through her. She'd seen a whole other side of Riley Callaghan today. There had already been a glimmer of attraction. Now, she'd seen him at his most exposed. She'd been there when he'd got the news about Finn, then met his child for the first time. It felt too big. Too much. More than she could handle right now.

Finn was adorable. He pulled at every heartstring she had. In a way she knew that she'd picked up some things that Riley might have missed. Riley would be a good father; he just had to get to know his little boy first.

Her heart flipped over. That parent relationship. The one she'd never have. The one she'd never even allowed herself to think about since she'd made her decision. For a few seconds today she'd felt…something. Even if it was only tiny. That urge to reach out to help a child in need. She pressed her lips together and tried to push all the emotions away.

She had to think about the surgery. She had to think

about preparing herself. She didn't need her heart tangled up in this mess. She had to keep it somewhere safe.

She hadn't moved. His head was still pressed against hers.

'Thank you,' he whispered. 'Thank you for coming here with me today.'

She gulped and pulled back.

'You're a colleague. No problem.' Her hand brushed against a piece of paper she'd pushed into her pocket. 'I think it's best if you and Finn have some time to yourselves now. I've got a couple of numbers of friends from Isabel's phone book. I'll talk to them to get an idea of what she would have liked. They might want to help with the arrangements.'

A frown furrowed Riley's brow. 'That would be great, thank you.' The words were pleasant but the look on his face told her something different. It was almost as if she'd just abandoned him on a cross-country hike with no provisions.

And he didn't say another word until he dropped her back at her house.

CHAPTER THREE

THE THING ABOUT life throwing you a curveball meant that you didn't always get things right. Finn was the easiest and best part of it all. Riley had heard children were resilient and Finn was still hesitant around him.

But they'd set up his room the way he wanted, hung up his clothes and established a little routine. When he'd heard Finn crying in bed one night, he'd just gone in, wrapped his arms around him and lay with him until he stopped.

He now knew that Finn hated peas, liked chicken in all forms, was also partial to sausages and tomato ketchup, and loved a kids' TV show with spacemen. He had seven DVDs of it and Riley had watched them all with him.

The whirlwind that was Riley's mother was a whole other matter. Thank goodness he hadn't seen her in the flesh when he'd told her about Finn. He was pretty sure she'd had a heart attack at the other end of the phone. Of course she was driving right down. She wanted to meet her grandchild straight away. She'd asked a million questions that Riley didn't know the answers to.

Eventually he'd told her a white lie. He told her that the social worker had recommended that he and Finn spend the first week together on their own to get used to each other. Not to overwhelm him with things. In fact, the social worker had recommended routine as soon as possible. So he'd registered Finn at school and taken him in to say hello. The headmistress had been great, suggesting he bring Finn in for a few hours in the first instance to let him find his feet.

Riley had finally managed to placate his mother by sending the picture that April had taken of them both together. She'd cried at that point. But at least it had given him some time.

What he couldn't work out right now was how to be around April.

Since they'd picked up Finn together, she'd retreated right into herself again. She'd spoken to him about a few funeral arrangements she'd helped put together after talking to Isabel's friends. She'd asked him to speak to Finn about a few things too. But that was it.

No closeness. No real glimmer of friendship.

Maybe it was his fault? If she'd planned her sister's funeral, had she had to deal with other things too? Maybe empty her house, or deal with all her financial affairs. She'd seemed so knowledgeable in Isabel's house—a place he'd felt entirely uncomfortable. She'd seemed to know exactly what Finn needed—even though she said she had no more experience of children than he had. The visit might have revived memories for her that he hadn't considered. Was it any wonder she was keeping her distance?

The rest of the staff had been great. They'd been surprised he was still there. But the news had spread quickly, and everyone was supportive.

Finn had asked to stay at school today until lunchtime. That meant he had three hours. Hours best spent in the hospital.

He'd barely got across the doorway before someone gave him a shout. April.

'Dr Callaghan? Can you come and assess Robert Black

for me, please?' He could see the concern on her face straight away.

He nodded and walked over quickly. Robert had been caught in an explosion. His spinal injury was severe and he was currently in neurogenic shock. This was always a crucial time for patients. Neurogenic shock happened in almost half of patients with a spinal injury above T6 in the first twenty-four hours and didn't go away for between one to three weeks. Patients in neurogenic shock needed continual assessment of their circulation, senses and breathing abilities. Neurogenic shock could lead to organ failure.

Robert Black's blood pressure was low, his heart rate bradycardic. His limbs were flaccid, his skin warm and flushed due to the vasodilation caused by the neurogenic shock.

Riley signalled to the nurse. 'Connie, can you get me some atropine?'

She nodded and handed him a vial from the emergency trolley. April moved automatically to the head of the bed to keep assessing Robert's breathing. The staff here were used to emergencies and good at recognising the symptoms.

Riley kept his voice calm and even as he flushed the atropine through the Venflon in Robert's arm. 'Robert, I'm just giving you something to speed up your heart rate a little. I'm also going to give you something to help your blood pressure.'

He nodded at Connie again. 'Get me some dopamine.' He turned to April. 'Can you put some oxygen on for me, please?'

April nodded and slipped the mask over Robert's face, lowering her head to the bed to monitor the rise and fall of his chest and keeping her eyes on the numbers on the oximeter.

Teamwork was crucial. Neurogenic shock was difficult. It was different from spinal shock or the most common type of shock with injuries—hypovolemic—and had to be treated differently. Often patients could have a respiratory arrest.

Right on cue, April waved her hand. 'Can we call an anaesthetist?'

'No time,' said Riley as he finished administering the dopamine and moved to the head of the bed. It only took a few seconds to tilt Robert's head back, using the laryngoscope to insert an endotracheal tube.

He glanced towards the doorway. 'We need to transfer him to high dependency. Does anyone know if they have a bed?'

April took his cue and ran over to the phone. Riley kept bagging the patient. At this stage, Robert needed to be ventilated. He could only pray this was a temporary setback.

Robert's regular doctor appeared at the door. His eyes widened. 'What the—?'

He stopped himself and held open the ward doors. 'High dependency?'

April put the phone down and nodded. 'They'll be waiting.'

He moved over and grabbed a side of the bed. Between the other doctor, April and the nurse, the transfer was smooth. Riley concentrated on the airway, bagging the whole way, then setting up the ventilators and pressures when they arrived.

'Need anything else?' he asked his colleague.

The doctor shook his head. 'I take it he had just had a rapid deterioration?'

Riley nodded. 'April was working with him. She picked up on it straight away.'

'Thank goodness. This could have been a disaster.'

Riley gave a thoughtful nod and stared back towards the door. April had stopped in the corridor. He gave a brief smile. 'Give me a page if you need any help.'

The other doctor nodded and he headed out into the corridor.

April was dressed in her usual attire of the physios, white tunic and navy trousers, with her hair pulled back in a ponytail. She had her eyes closed and was resting her head and body against the wall.

He touched her arm and her eyes jerked open. 'April, are you okay?'

Their eyes connected for a few moments. Hers were bluer than ever. Maybe it was the bright hospital lights. Or maybe it was the fact he was noticing so much more about her. April had always looked away quickly before, but this time she didn't. This time it felt as if there was more to their gaze.

But she pulled her arm away. 'Of course, I'm fine.' She gave her head a little shake. 'I just got a fright when Robert deteriorated so quickly.'

He nodded. As a doctor, he was used to dealing with emergencies, but other staff didn't have the same exposure as he did. Quite often they did a debrief after things like this.

'Come with me.'

Her eyes widened. 'What?' She shook her head fiercely. 'No, I've got work to do. I need to get back to the ward.'

'Actually, you don't.'

She glared at him and folded her arms across her chest. 'I can't.'

He spoke firmly. 'You can. Get your jacket. I have to pick up Finn at twelve. But we have time for a coffee before I go get him.'

April shifted on her feet. 'I have work to do.'

'You must be due a break, and we need a chance to debrief—to talk about what just happened. We usually do it as a team after any emergency. Let's take some time out.'

She hesitated and took a few breaths. He gestured towards the locker room. 'Go and get your jacket.' He wasn't going to let this go. There was something in that glance. Some kind of connection.

She gave the briefest nod then disappeared for a few seconds while his stomach gave a little roll.

No getting away from it. April Henderson had definitely been avoiding him. He just had to figure out why.

Her hands were still shaking as she opened her locker and grabbed her jacket. The canteen and coffee shop were across the main courtyard. She slid her hands into her puffy winter jacket. Riley was waiting for her at the door.

This was nothing. It was a simple chat. A debrief. She had heard of them before—she'd just never needed one.

So why was her stomach flip flopping around?

She'd spent the last few days avoiding Riley. She'd done the things she'd been asked to do. The funeral arrangements were sorted. She'd arranged the undertaker, the church, the minister and the plot at the cemetery. According to Isabel's friends, she'd been a little unconventional. One had offered to speak. Another had offered to say a poem. She just had to find out what Riley would think appropriate for Finn. She figured he'd want to give Finn the chance to say goodbye to his mum. She just wasn't quite sure how a kid did that.

She lifted her bag. All the paperwork and arrangements were inside. She just had to hand them over.

Riley was holding the door open. Large flakes of snow were falling outside. Even though it was still morning, the sky had a grey tinge.

They started walking across the courtyard. 'Coffee shop or canteen?'

April shrugged. 'Either.'

'How hungry are you? Do you want an early lunch?'

She shook her head.

'Then coffee shop it is.'

They walked over to the coffee shop and he held the door for her again. 'Take a seat. I'll get the coffee.'

She sat down on a red fabric sofa next to the lit fire. There was a garland above the fireplace and red tinsel adorning the walls. November. Another place with dec-orations. The music being piped around the room was a medley of Christmas songs. She smiled. This would have driven Mallory crazy. She used to say that Christmas seemed to begin as soon as Halloween had finished.

A few minutes later Riley appeared, carrying a tray. She looked up as she shrugged her way out of her jacket. The heat from the fire was already reaching her.

He smiled as he set down the two tall latte glasses filled with hot chocolate, with whipped cream and marshmallows spilling over the edges. A plate with shortbread Christmas trees followed.

She looked up. 'Really?'

His eyes twinkled. 'Why not? I love Christmas.'

There was something about that smile. Something about that twinkle in his eye. It had always been there before, and it was part of the reason she'd avoided him. Riley Cal-laghan was too easy to like. He was almost infectious.

She was surprised. 'You do? So do I.'

'At last.' He smiled. 'Something we have in common.'

She frowned. 'I imagined you were always away for Christmas.'

He looked amused. 'You think about me?' He couldn't hide the cheeky gleam in his eyes. Then he shrugged. 'A lot of the time I am. But here's the thing...' He leaned across the table as if he were going to whisper to her.

She followed his lead and bowed her head next to his as his face lit up with a wicked grin. 'Many other places in the world do Christmas too. Sometimes in forty degrees. And if they don't? Well, I can always take it with me.'

She sat back and shook her head, pointing her finger on the table. 'Well, I don't want a sunny Christmas or to be anywhere else. I like Christmas *here*. I like tacky Christmas songs. I *really* like it when it snows. I like Advent calendars, Christmas cards and—' she winked at him '—I really like Christmas food.'

She spooned some of the cream into her mouth.

'So do I,' he said cheekily as he dug his spoon into her cream instead of his.

'Hey!'

She gave his hand a playful slap. 'Watch out, Riley. I bite, you know.'

His gaze met hers for a few seconds. He didn't speak. Just kept staring at her. As if he were contemplating a whole host of things to say. A whole type of discussion she just couldn't think about right now.

She broke their gaze and dug her spoon back into the cream.

'About today,' he started. She looked up. Work. This felt like safe territory.

'You did everything right. There is always a risk of sudden deterioration in patients with neurogenic shock. It can happen at any point. You picked it up well.'

She sighed and leaned her head on her hand. The teasing and fun had finished, but that was fine. This was what they really should be talking about. 'But he's ventilated now. That can't be good.'

Riley nodded. 'It's not great. It is a deterioration. Now,

we need to monitor carefully in case he's going into organ failure. He might not.'

She met his gaze. She felt sad. His emerald-green eyes were saying a whole lot of things that they weren't discussing out loud. They both knew that things for Robert might not be good.

He leaned across and touched her hand. 'You did everything you should.'

She stared down at his blunt cut fingernails. She should pull her hand back. Jerk it away. She wanted to. But somehow after the events earlier she wanted a few seconds of comfort.

She looked up again. 'How is Finn?' It was the question she should have asked immediately. It didn't matter she was trying to step back and detach herself from the situation. She'd spent the last few days worrying about the little guy.

Riley took a long slow breath. 'He's not happy, but he's not sad. He's getting there. He's met some school friends and the teacher says he's fitting in well. They're going to do some bereavement work at school with him because it's still all so new.' He stirred his hot chocolate. 'He was crying in bed the other night.'

Her heart squeezed in her chest. 'What did you do?'

He pressed his lips together. 'I thought about it for about ten seconds. Then I climbed in next to him and just held him. What else could I do? I hate that he's sad. I hate that this has happened to him. I know the upheaval must be awful. And my learning curve is steep.'

'What have you done?'

A smile crept onto his lips. 'Well, my fridge and freezer are now stocked with child-friendly foods. I never knew there were so many yogurts. Potatoes have to be mashed.

Raisins have to be a particular brand and he'll only eat Pink Lady apples.'

April smiled as she spooned marshmallows into her hot chocolate. 'But that all sounds good. It sounds as though he's settling.'

Riley nodded. 'We've put up the pictures you brought from the house. It's weird. Seeing Isabel all around me.'

He dropped his head and stopped speaking.

Something inside her lurched. A horrible feeling. Envy. Why on earth was she feeling that? It was so misplaced. So wrong. But it was definitely there. Maybe there had been more to the relationship than she'd initially thought. 'So…do you miss her?'

He sighed; the pained expression on his face said it all. 'That's just it, April. I didn't really know her that well. We only went out for a couple of months. I don't have a million nice tales I can tell Finn about his mum. I don't have a lot of memories. She was nice.' He shrugged his shoulders. 'How awful is that? That's about as much as I have to say about her. Finn deserves more than that.'

She licked her lips for a second. She could see what he wasn't saying. 'You're still angry.'

He pulled a face. 'Inside, I am. But I hope I don't show that around Finn. It's just when I turn around Isabel seems to be staring me in the face.' He ran his fingers through his hair. 'And the family housing. It's not ideal. You probably already know that. I need to find a place for us. A home.'

The way he said those words sent a little pang through her. Riley wanted to make a home with his son. Would she ever get to make a home with someone? Would anyone want to be in a relationship with a girl who could always have a cancer risk hanging over her head, and couldn't have a family? It wouldn't exactly make for a winning profile on a dating website. She cringed at the thought of it and focused back on Riley.

'You can't just jump out and buy the first thing you see.'

'Can't I? Why not? I can get a mortgage. I have enough money in the bank.'

'But you don't know if you'll always be here. Another move might not be good for Finn.'

'But what if it's a permanent move?'

Riley Callaghan. Here permanently. Working together every day. She'd need to see his smiling face. Avoid his cheeky grins. Four weeks had been manageable—there had been an end date in sight. But for ever? How could she lock away the attraction she felt for him for ever?

She leaned back in her chair. 'It's a lot to think about.' She glanced at the glass in front of her. 'This must be a million calories. You—' she wagged her finger at him '— are a bad influence.'

He leaned forward. 'Just call it a bribe.'

He had that grin on his face again. The one he used time and time again on the ward when he wanted to talk someone into something.

She pointed at the shortbread Christmas trees. 'Am I going to need one of these?'

He pushed the whole plate before her and clasped his hands on the table. It seemed such a formal stance for Riley she almost laughed.

'Thing is,' he started seriously, 'I appreciate all the arrangements you've made for me. I know doing something like that really goes above and beyond.' He pointed at the hot chocolate and shortbread. 'And these don't count for that.' He waved his hand. 'I'll get you something more appropriate.' He leaned a little closer across the table. 'But there's something else.'

She shook her head and ignored the 'more appropriate'

comment. Riley Callaghan was trying to sweet-talk her. 'Don't build it up, Riley. Just hit me with it.'

He did. 'Finn.'

She narrowed her gaze. 'What about Finn?'

He sighed. 'I haven't had that conversation yet—the one about the funeral. And I was hoping you might help me do it.'

She sat back again. But Riley kept going. 'I'm still taking baby steps here. I don't want to do anything wrong. And I could ask my mother, but then—' he shook his head '—that would just open the floodgates for her to bulldoze all over us.'

'Has your mother met Finn yet?'

He shook his head. 'I'm holding her at bay. I've told her the social worker advised to give him a few days to settle.'

She opened her mouth. 'You what?'

He held up his hand. 'You haven't met my mother—yet. Don't judge.'

She folded her arms across her chest. 'What exactly is it you want me to do, Riley? I'm not sure I should be getting involved. This is really something you and Finn should work through together.'

'I'm scared.'

He said the words right out of the blue.

And she couldn't catch her breath.

'What if I make a mess of this, April? Do I say Finn's too young to be at a funeral and everything should go on without him, or do I insist he attends when he really isn't ready for it? Do I ask him what he wants to do? At five, how can he even know?'

Anguish and pain were written all over his face. She understood. What had happened on the ward today had just helped open the door for him. He wasn't grieving for Isabel. He was grieving for his son.

'I get that you're scared, Riley. But this is your son. I think you need to have this conversation with him.'

He didn't look any better. He turned a shortbread tree over and over in his hands before finally looking up through dark lashes and meeting her gaze. 'He's been asking for you.'

'What?'

'Finn. He's asked where you were. I think because we brought him back together he's expected to see you again.'

She gulped. The kid was five. He was confused. It wasn't such a strange thought to have. 'I don't want to give him any mixed messages.'

'What mixed messages? Aren't we friends, April?'

She didn't speak. Her brain was flooded with memories of her hands against his chest, his forehead next to hers. All things she didn't need to remember. But they were annoying; they seemed to have seared their way into her brain and cemented themselves there.

She locked gazes with Riley. He'd asked if they were friends.

No. They weren't. Being around Riley was making her feel things she didn't want to. Didn't need to. Life was hard right now. She was clear about her decision. She knew what her next steps would be. Getting involved with anyone would confuse things. They might want to talk. They might have an opinion. Somehow, already, she knew Riley would have an opinion. And she wasn't ready for any of that. After Christmas her ovaries and fallopian tubes would be removed. It wasn't a complete and utter guarantee that she would remain cancer-free, but when the odds were against her it was as good as it could be.

The image of Finn's face clouded her thoughts. He was so like Riley.

It still made her ache. She was trying to stay so strong.

But being around a kid as adorable as Finn had made all those children she would never have suddenly feel so real. All those grandkids her mum and dad would never have to entertain. She couldn't help but pine for the life that would never be hers. She stared down at the shortbread Christmas tree. And Christmas made it seem just that little bit harder—because Christmas should be all about family.

She sucked in a breath. How dare she feel sorry for herself right now? The person she should be thinking about was Finn.

She met Riley's gaze. Somehow he knew just when to keep quiet.

She took a deep breath. 'I'll come over tomorrow. I still haven't arranged the flowers. I'll ask Finn if he knows what his mum's favourites were. Maybe if he can help pick something it will help that conversation get started.' She pointed to the pile of paperwork. 'The minister at the church is pretty modern. I told him I'd get back to him about music. If there is a particular song that Finn likes, maybe that's the one to use? I asked Isabel's friends. But they all had different ideas.'

Riley nodded. 'Thank you. I mean that.'

She gave him a smile. 'It's okay.'

'Is it? Until a few days ago we'd never really had a proper conversation. You always seemed to avoid me. When I saw you come into the pub the other night I thought…' His voice tailed off.

'You thought what?'

He shrugged. 'I thought you might actually have come in to have a farewell drink. I thought you might have found it in your heart to be nice to me for five minutes.'

He was teasing her. She knew that. But his words seemed to strike a bit of a nerve. She had the feeling some of it might come from a little deeper.

And there was that little twisting feeling again. He might as well sell corkscrews from the way his words, his looks and his touch affected her.

'I like to keep focused at work. These patients, they've been through enough. They need our full attention. They deserve it.'

He shook his head. 'Oh, no. Don't give me that. You engage perfectly with all the patients. It's only me that gets the cold shoulder; don't think I didn't notice.'

There was a surge of heat into her cheeks. 'Maybe you're just hard to be around, Riley?'

She knew it was a deflection, and as he folded his arms and narrowed his gaze she also knew he wasn't about to let her off.

'So what is it? Why no chat? Why no friendly banter? You seem to do it enough with the patients.'

'Maybe I just don't like to mix work with pleasure.'

As soon as the words left her mouth she realised her mistake.

His eyes gleamed. 'Oh, so I could be pleasure, could I?'

She shook her head and waved her hand. 'Don't be ridiculous. Anyway, you servicemen, you come and go so often. You were only supposed to be covering for four weeks. It's exhausting having to befriend new staff all the time. Sometimes I just don't have the energy.'

His grin had spread from one ear to the other. It was clear he wasn't listening any more. 'So I'm exhausting, am I? I kinda like that.'

'I didn't say that.'

He nodded firmly. 'You did.'

She sighed in exasperation. 'It's not all about you, Riley.'

She didn't mean it quite to come out like that. But if he heard he didn't react badly. The smile was still plas-

tered across his face. He must have thought she was jok-
ing with him.

If only that were true. Her heart gave a little squeeze.

If only she could have a different life. If only she could
have a different gene pool. But that would mean that she
and Mallory would never have existed—and she wouldn't
have spent more than twenty years with a sister she'd both
hated at times and adored. Sisterly love could never really
be matched. And the bottom line was: she couldn't change
her genes. She just had to find a way to manage her risk.
For her, right now, that meant finding a way to live her
life. She swallowed the huge lump in her throat. No matter what little strings were tugging at her heart right now,
it was best to ignore them. Best to stay focused on what
she could manage.

He glanced at his watch. 'I'm sorry to cut and run but I
need to go and get Finn. I don't want to be late.' He pulled
his jacket from the back of the chair. 'Thank you for your
help with Finn. I mean it.' Then he gave her a cheeky wink.
'But it looks like I'm here to stay. Better get used to having me around.'

He disappeared out of the door into the snow as her
heart gave a lurch.

Riley Callaghan here on a permanent basis.

This could be trouble.

CHAPTER FOUR

IN A WAY, the funeral went so much better than he ever could have expected.

The horrible conversation with Finn had turned out much easier than he could have hoped for. When April had come over to chat to Finn about flowers, Finn had asked outright if she would come to the funeral too.

It seemed that the thought of not being there hadn't even occurred to Finn.

Isabel's friends and workmates turned out in force. They all wore bright colours and sang along to the pop song that Finn had picked for his mum.

He was thankful they'd all attended. The decision to bury Isabel here instead of Birmingham had been a difficult one. But Riley and Finn would be the ones who tended her grave, and he didn't want to have to travel every time Finn wanted to visit.

April stayed steadily in the background. Finn had drawn her a picture of the flowers his mum liked best and, even though it was nearing the end of November, the church was full of orange gerbera daisies. The room felt bright. And Finn's little hand had gripped his the whole time.

He felt oddly detached about it all. He'd organised a funeral tea afterwards but only vaguely recognised a few of Isabel's friends, even though they all made a point of coming and speaking to Finn. The little guy seemed overwhelmed. April looked even more uncomfortable.

He crossed the room, Finn's hand still in his. He glanced down at Finn. 'I think we've probably stayed long enough. I was thinking we could do something together with Finn right now.'

He could tell she was hesitant but Finn had perked up at the suggestion. 'Can we go and pick a spaceman film?'

He looked at her again. She was pale in the black dress with her blonde hair tied back. The outfit had a severity to it that just didn't seem quite right for April. They'd discussed wearing something bright like Isabel's friends, but somehow it didn't feel quite right for them. April had found a brooch with a bright orange gerbera that matched the church flowers and pinned it to her dress. Riley had relented and worn a bright orange tie with his dark suit. Even though they'd asked Finn if he wanted to wear one of his superhero T-shirts he'd shaken his head; he'd wanted to wear a suit like his dad's.

Riley had been choked. He'd love to wear matching clothes with his son—just not like this. Everything about this was hard. He was questioning every decision he made.

He almost gave a shout when April gave a sigh of relief. 'Let me get my coat,' she said.

As they walked along the icy street together Finn reached out to hold April's hand too. Riley was glad of the cold, fresh air. Finn hadn't said much at all during the service. He'd placed a bunch of orange flowers by the grave and shed a few tears while Riley held him in his arms.

It had been exhausting. Smiling politely and shaking hands with people he really didn't know—all of whom he knew were looking him up and down and wondering about his suitability to bring up Finn.

He'd had a stand-up fight with his mother about attending the funeral. She wanted to offer 'support' to her grandchild. But Riley had been insistent that the event was already too overwhelming for Finn. He'd been clear that she needed to wait a few days. Finn needed some space.

He would be starting full days at school next week and Riley had suggested his mum and dad come down to meet him then. He hadn't told her that Finn had video-chatted with his uncle Dan a few nights ago. It was obvious that Dan was smitten by his nephew straight away, and Finn with him, but Dan being away was actually easier. More manageable.

'Who is your favourite spaceman?' Finn asked April out of the blue.

She looked surprised and he could see her searching her brain. 'Well, it would have to be the one that I met.'

Finn stopped walking, his mouth hanging open. 'You've met a spaceman?'

She nodded. 'I went on holiday to Florida once and visited NASA. I got to have lunch with a spaceman. It was great.'

Finn's eyes were wide. 'Really? Dad, can we do that?'

Riley smiled. He was still getting used to being called Dad. First few times, he'd looked around to make sure it was really him that was being spoken to.

He gave a sort of nod. 'We haven't had a chance to talk about holidays yet. But it's always something we could consider.'

'Could we, Dad, could we?' The excitement on Finn's wide-eyed face made his heart swell. Right now he was tempted to promise the world to Finn, but he wasn't sure that was the best idea. He wanted his son to grow up to appreciate people, things and places. He was still trying to figure out everything in his head.

And that included the woman walking at the other side of his son.

April had been quiet most of the day. She'd agreed to come because Finn had asked her to. Riley wasn't sure she would have come on his invitation alone.

Although he'd been curious about April before, he hadn't pursued things. He'd been due to leave. But that hadn't stopped him trying to engage her constantly in conversation and trying to find out a little more about her.

Her face was serious. She'd told him she was good at funerals. She'd said she'd lost her sister but hadn't elaborated. Had today brought back some bad memories for her?

He was still curious about April. She was fantastic with patients. She'd been supportive to him in the most horrible set of circumstances. Even now, she was holding his son's hand. April Henderson had a good heart. Why didn't she let anyone get close to her?

They walked onto the main street and into one of the local shops. Finn raced over to the large display of DVDs. Riley put his hands in his pockets. 'Are you ready for this?'

She raised her eyebrows. 'You think I can't handle a little sci-fi?'

He gave a playful shrug. 'I thought you might be more of a romance girl.'

'Oh, no.' She shook her head straight away, even though her gaze was locked directly with his. A smile danced across her lips as she brushed past him to join Finn. 'What I don't know about *Star Wars*, *Star Trek* and Buzz Lightyear isn't worth knowing,' she whispered into his ear.

He grinned. Another tiny piece of information about April Henderson. He was just going to keep chipping away at that armour she'd constructed around herself.

After a hard day for him and Finn, April was the brightest light on the horizon. And he'd never been so happy that she was there.

Two hours later Finn was fast asleep against April's shoulder. He might even have been drooling a little. The credits of the sci-fi movie were rolling on the screen. The room had grown dark and it was almost as if Riley read her mind as he crossed the room and flicked the switch on a lamp.

She wasn't quite sure how she'd managed to end up here. She hadn't intended to. But when Finn had asked her to come back she didn't have the heart to say no. Meaning that right now she had a five-year-old draped halfway across her, snoring.

Riley glanced towards her legs. As she'd sat on the sofa with Finn her dress had crept up a little more than it should. She tried to wiggle her dress down but it was nigh impossible with Finn's weight on top of her.

'April, can I get you something else a little more comfortable to wear?'

She almost laughed. It sounded like the old adage, *Do you want to slip into something more comfortable?*

He must have caught the expression on her face. 'I have scrubs,' he said quickly.

'Scrubs would be great,' she said. The black dress had been perfect for a funeral, but as the day had progressed it had started to feel more restrictive.

He disappeared for a second and set down a pale blue set of scrubs next to her, leaning over and adjusting Finn's position to free her up.

She pushed herself from the sofa and looked around. 'Bathroom this way?' she asked.

Riley nodded and she walked through to the hall. It was a typical army house. Adequate. But not perfect. As she wiggled out of her dress in the cramped bathroom she understood why he'd immediately thought about getting a place of his own. Everything in the house was bland. It would be difficult to put a stamp on the place and give it a family feel. It didn't really feel like a home.

By the time she came out of the bathroom, Riley was in the kitchen. 'I thought I'd make us some dinner,' he said simply.

She opened her mouth to refuse straight away, then stopped. Would it really be so bad to share a meal with him? It had been a big day. For him, and for Finn. And, truth be told, for her too. It was the first funeral she'd been to since her sister's. It didn't help that Isabel had only been five years older than Mallory. Mallory's funeral had been full of young people too. And, while it was comforting, there was also a terrible irony about it. Some people were cheated out of the life they should live. If she was honest, she didn't really want to be alone right now.

'Can I help?'

Riley pulled a face. 'That depends.'

'On what?'

'On how fussy you are. I can make lasagne, spaghetti bolognaise or chilli chicken. That's as far as I can go.'

'Three things? I'm impressed. My speciality is chicken or sausage casserole.'

He laughed. 'Okay then, which of the five—' he opened his fridge '—no, sorry, four—I've no sausages—do you want to go for?'

April leaned her head on her hand. She was tired. It had been a long day. And it had been a long time since she'd had a conversation like this. A guy actually offering to make her dinner.

'I think I'm brave enough to try your lasagne. Do I get to watch the chef at work?'

He smiled. 'Sure you do. I'll even give you wine. But, just so you know, I'm a bit of a messy cook.'

He pulled two wine glasses out of the cupboard, held them up to the light and squinted at them. 'I'm just checking that they're clean. I moved in such a rush that I literally just walked from the flat to this house with things in my arms.'

She shook her head. 'Riley Callaghan. So far, you've told me that you only have three recipes, you're messy, and now I'm questioning your housekeeping skills.' She shook her head. 'If this were online dating, you wouldn't get a "like".'

He went into another cupboard and brought out two bottles. 'But I have wine! So I win. Now, white or red?'

'I guess for lasagne it should probably be red but I fancy white. Is that okay?'

He opened the bottle and poured the wine, then started pulling ingredients from the fridge.

She took a sip of the wine and relaxed back a little into the chair. 'I'll cut you a deal. You let me pick dinner—' she raised her eyebrows '—from a limited menu, of course, and you let me pick the wine. How about I do the clearing up?'

He tipped the mince into a pan to start browning it, giving her a wink from the corner of his eye. 'My plan has worked.'

April glanced back through to the living room at the little sleeping boy. 'Will Finn eat this?'

Riley followed her glance. 'Probably not. I'll give him it first, but have some chicken on standby in case he doesn't like it.' He leaned against the doorjamb as the mince began to sizzle in the pan. 'I wonder if he'll wake up at all. It's been a big day.' He picked up his glass and took a sip of his wine. 'Thanks for being there.'

She shrugged. 'It's fine. He's a cute kid.'

She could see the pride on his face. Riley was rapidly turning into a doting dad. He moved back into the kitchen and started chopping an onion.

He was methodical. He added the herbs and tomatoes, then made a quick white sauce. Five minutes later he'd layered up the mix with lasagne sheets, sprinkled with cheese and put it in the oven.

She nodded. 'I'm impressed. You never struck me as the organised type.'

He sat down opposite her. 'I didn't? What's that supposed to mean?' He wrinkled his brow. 'Am I supposed to be offended right now? Because if I am, I'm just too tired.'

She shook her head. 'For the last four weeks you've been racing about the place doing one hundred things at once. The unit isn't normally like that.'

He pulled a face. 'I know.' He sat back a little and looked at her carefully. 'I've been used to working at a frantic pace. I need to step down a gear and get more perspective.'

'Can you actually do that?' she asked softly.

He sighed. 'I hate the way you do that.'

'What?'

He lifted his hand towards her. 'You ask the questions that I don't really want to answer.' He turned his head into the living room again. 'The answer to the question has to be yes. And you can see why. I have to change things. I have to be a father to Finn. I'm all he's got.'

'But…?'

He groaned and leaned forward, putting his head on the table. His real thoughts were written all over him. She touched his dark hair. 'You weren't born to be a rehab doctor, Riley. You want to be where the action is. But if you're going to have Finn on a permanent basis that will be impossible.'

He looked up a little as she shifted her hand, his bright green eyes peeking out from underneath dark lashes. 'I love him. I love him already. Finn comes first.'

She bent forward, her head almost touching his. 'You're allowed to say it, Riley. But maybe just to me. You're allowed to say that this life change gives you twinges of regret.' She licked her lips. 'Maybe I understand that a bit more than most.'

And she did. She was inches away from a guy a few years ago she would have flirted with, enjoyed his company and maybe even dated. There might even have been more possibilities that right now she didn't even dare think about.

His face crumpled and he put his head in his hands for a second. He kept his eyes closed as he spoke. 'Last week I thought I was going on a tour of Sierra Leone. I was looking forward to it. It might sound strange but I love the overseas tours. Always have.' He opened his eyes slowly. 'But last week I didn't know I had a son to come home to. My whole life has changed in the blink of an eye. I'm not sure I was ready for it.'

She spoke carefully, sliding her hand across the table and letting her fingers intertwine with his. 'Promise me that you'll only ever talk to me about this. Don't let Finn know. You've had the legs swept from under you. Mallory and I used to call that being cannonballed. It will take a while to get your head around things. To work out what is best, for you and for him. You can do this, Riley. I know you can.'

He looked at their connected fingers. 'I'd never take out how I'm feeling on Finn. You must know that.'

'I do,' she said simply. 'But I want you to know that it's okay to feel like that. It's complicated. If you're having a bad day you can call me.'

They were touching. Having their fingers intertwined was so much more personal than a brush of the hand. And it was sending a weird stream of little pulses up her arm. Under the bright kitchen lights there was nowhere to hide. Those bright green eyes were even more startling. Last time she'd seen something that green, she and Mallory had been taking a photo of the emerald-tinged sea in Zante at Shipwreck Beach. It was still one of her favourite ever pictures.

The little lines around his eyes gave him character, made her know that he'd seen and done things she never would. There was so much to like about Riley Callaghan, meaning there were so many more reasons to push him away.

So why wasn't she?

He looked at her, the barest hint of a smile quirking his lips. 'You mean you're going to give me your number?'

She frowned. 'Didn't I already when I was helping with the funeral arrangements?'

His fingers tightened around hers. 'Ah, but that was different. That was for practical reasons. This—' his smile broadened '—this sounds like almost *giving* a guy your number.'

She shook her head and pulled her hand back, surprised by how much she didn't want to. 'Don't get the wrong idea, mister.' She picked up her glass. 'You're supplying the wine and—' she nodded towards the oven '—the food. I'm a practical girl; I'm only nice as long as you're feeding me.'

Riley laughed. 'Oh, I have plenty of wine. As long as you're happy with a limited menu, we can be friends for ever.'

Something warm spread through her. It was like the kind of thing kids said to each other. The kind of thing she and Mallory used to say. Her fingers went automatically to her neck. To the pendant their parents had given both girls on their twenty-first birthdays. Two golden hearts linked together. Touching it made her feel closer to her sister. Touching it made her feel that sometimes Mallory wasn't quite as far away as reality told her.

'What's that? It's pretty.' Riley noticed her movement straight away.

She hesitated before letting her fingers fall away to reveal what she was touching. 'It was a gift from my parents.' She didn't add the rest.

Her brain started working overtime. What would Mallory have thought of Riley Callaghan? They'd generally had different taste in men. But somehow she knew Mallory would have loved this guy. It was both a comfort and a regret, that her sister wasn't here to meet him.

Riley leaned his head on his hands and gave her a curious stare. 'Are you going to tell me anything about yourself, April?'

She caught her breath. She hadn't expected him to be so direct. 'What do you mean?'

He counted off on his fingers. 'Well, I know you're a physio. I know you're a good physio—a great one. I'm not quite sure what age you are. Or where you live, although I know it's close. I know you had a sister. And you like spacemen.' He gave her a smile. 'But that's about it.'

She couldn't help but be defensive. 'What exactly do you think you're entitled to know about me?'

He stood up, his wooden chair scraping on the kitchen floor as he turned around, grabbed a tea towel and pulled the steaming-hot lasagne from the oven.

He didn't speak as he handed her a plate, some cutlery and a serving spatula. He didn't seem fazed by her briskness at all; in fact, it almost felt as if he was teasing her now. He sat down opposite and folded his hands on the table. 'I don't *think* I'm entitled to know anything. But I'd *like* it if you shared.' He even grinned. 'For example, my mum and dad are up north. My mother can best be described in terms of weather elements—she goes from snowstorm, sandstorm, whirlwind and tornado. My brother Dan is serving in the army. He's twenty-seven and can't wait to meet Finn. He probably is at the same stage of maturity.'

She wanted to smile. She really did. The waft of the enticing lasagne was winding its way across the table to her. He made everything sound so reasonable. But sharing wasn't the place she wanted to be right now. Sharing about her sister would mean sharing about the disease, and the follow-on questions about genetics. And surgery.

Inside, a little part of her shrivelled up and died. The whole reason she wasn't in a relationship right now was to give herself space to get this part of her life sorted. To not have to explain her thoughts or decisions to another person.

But a tiny part of her also recognised that she'd never actually been in a relationship where she would have been able to have that kind of serious conversation. Perhaps that was why she was trying to wrap Riley Callaghan up and stick him in a box somewhere in her brain before he let loose thoughts she wasn't ready for.

Thoughts like the ones where those perfectly formed lips were on hers.

She choked as Riley started to dish out the lasagne.

He still didn't speak. Just handed her the dish with a raise of his eyebrows.

This guy was too good at this.

'Maybe there's just not much to tell. I'm twenty-seven too. I've worked here for the last eighteen months. Before that I was in a general hospital, specialising in chronic injuries. And before that I did a year with kids who had cystic fibrosis. I've moved around to get a variety of experience.'

Not strictly true. She'd moved to the general hospital to be closer to Mallory when she'd got her diagnosis. And she'd moved to Waterloo Court after Mallory died because she couldn't face all the sympathy and questions from her colleagues. It was easier to be in a place where people didn't know your history.

'Are your mum and dad still around?'

She nodded. 'They moved up to Scotland just over a year ago. My nana was starting to get frail and they wanted to be closer to her.'

Her family felt as if it were falling apart. They'd lost one daughter and knew there was a possibility they could lose the other. And every time she looked at them she could see the pain in their eyes—that this was genetic. A time bomb that no one could have known about—at least not until fairly recently. But their pain had also affected her own decision. Would she want to risk passing faulty genes on to her own child? No. No way. Not when she saw the pain it could cause.

'Do you visit?'

She nodded. 'I visit a lot. Well, whenever I get time.' She looked up from the lasagne. 'I can't believe how good this is. Who taught you how to make it?'

He smiled. 'It's a secret.' His eyes were twinkling.

Was it a woman? She felt a tiny stab of envy.

He topped up her wine glass. 'I worked with an Italian doctor in an infectious disease unit for a while. He gave me his grandma's recipe.'

She kept eating. 'Well, I hate to say it, but it might even beat my sausage casserole.' She glanced through to the living room. 'Do you want a hand to wrestle Finn into his pyjamas? I don't think he's going to wake up now.'

Riley followed her gaze as he kept eating. 'In a minute. Darn it—jammies. I need to put them on the list.'

'Finn doesn't have pyjamas?'

He shook his head. 'He does, but I think he might just have taken a little stretch. Either that or I've shrunk them in the wash. I'll need to get him some new ones.' He looked around the plain kitchen. 'And I need to get some decorations too. I don't even own a Christmas tree. I'm not even sure where to buy one around here.'

'There's a place just a few miles out of town—that's if you want a real one, of course. They can be a little messy, but they smell great.'

'Will you show me?'

She paused. She wanted to say no. She should say no. But a little bit inside of her wanted to say yes. Riley Callaghan was messing with her mind.

'I can give you directions.'

'I didn't ask for directions.' His fork was poised in mid-air and he was looking at her pointedly.

She licked her lips. It didn't matter she'd had plenty of wine; all of a sudden her mouth felt very dry. 'Why don't we just play it by ear? I've got some plans in the next few days. If you let me know when you're going I can see if I'm free.'

His eyes narrowed for a moment. He was a doctor. He could recognise a deflected question easily. It was second nature. But Riley was gracious enough not to push.

They finished dinner and she washed up while he prepared Finn's room. It only took a few minutes to wiggle Finn into his pyjamas, and then Riley carried him up to bed.

She couldn't help but follow him up the stairs as he laid Finn down in his bed adorned with a spaceman duvet. He whispered in his son's ear, put a kiss on his forehead and switched on the nightlight that illuminated stars on the ceiling.

'Oh, wow,' whispered April. 'That's fantastic.' She smiled at him in the dim light. 'I think I want one.'

He raised his eyebrows as he walked back to the doorway, his shoulder touching hers as he bent to whisper, 'I hate to break it to you, but you'll have to sweet-talk my mother. She sent it down yesterday for Finn and I've no idea where she got it.'

April watched the circling stars on the ceiling. It was almost magical. Hypnotic. And by the time she stopped watching she'd forgotten about how close she was to Riley. She could smell his aftershave. Smell the soap powder from the soft T-shirt he'd changed into when they'd got home. Her eyes fixed on the rise and fall of his chest, then the soft pulse at the base of his neck. She was suddenly conscious that the scrubs she was wearing were thin. Thin enough to probably see the outline of her black matching underwear beneath the pale blue fabric.

All of a sudden it felt as though a part of life that was so far out of reach was right before her eyes. A gorgeous man, a beautiful child—things she couldn't even contemplate. Things that seemed so far away and unobtainable. When she and Mallory had been young they'd always joked about who would marry first, and being each other's bridesmaids. They'd both taken it for granted that those things would naturally happen. Right now, she had to concentrate on surgery. Getting through that, gaining a little confidence again and getting some normality back to her life. Pursuing anything with Riley Callaghan wasn't possible. It wasn't fair to her. It wasn't fair to him. It especially wasn't fair to a little boy whose whole world had just been turned upside down.

In the dim light Riley's hand lifted oh-so-slowly towards her. 'April—'

She turned swiftly and walked out of the room, her breath catching somewhere in the back of her throat. She needed to go. She needed to get out of there.

She rushed down the stairs and picked up the bag with her dress in it and her black coat. 'It's getting late. I need to get home. Thanks for dinner.' She said the words far too brightly.

Riley was at her back, but his hands were in his pockets and his eyes were downcast. 'Yeah. No problem. Thanks for coming today. I appreciate it.'

She nodded as she slipped her arms into her jacket and headed for the door. 'Say goodnight to Finn for me. See you at work tomorrow.'

Riley gave the briefest of nods as she hurried out the door. It didn't matter how quickly she walked, she could sense his eyes searing into her back the whole way, as the smell of his aftershave still lingered around her.

He watched as she hurried away like a scalded cat. What had he done? He hadn't *actually* touched her. Yes, he'd meant to. Yes, he'd wanted to.

His lips were still tingling from the fact he'd wanted to kiss her. To let his lips connect with hers. Right now, he almost felt cheated.

But it was clear that something else was going on.

There was a reason he'd been curious about April Henderson. It wasn't the good figure, the blonde hair and cute smile. It was *her*. The way she engaged with the patients. The way he could tell sometimes she was considering things, trying to do what was best. She'd captured his attention in a way he'd never really been caught before.

She'd relaxed a little around him tonight. When she'd

been with Finn she'd been happy. She was so good around
Finn. He seemed to almost sparkle when he was with her
they connected so well.

And it wasn't just Finn. Riley wasn't imagining things.
There was definitely something in the air between them.
Even though she was trying her best to ignore it.

He should probably ignore it too. Finn was his priority. Christmas was coming. His son was about to face his
first Christmas without his mother, but Riley was about
to spend the first Christmas with his son.

He wasn't even sure how to mark the occasion. He
should be overjoyed and happy, but in the circumstances
it wasn't appropriate.

There were obvious times when Finn's childhood innocence shone through. He spoke about his mum. He cried
at times. But children possessed a resilience that adults
couldn't quite comprehend. And he seemed to be settling
in to his new house, his new surroundings.

But for Riley there was something else. Finn seemed
to light up around April. It seemed he'd spent much of his
five years around women, so that didn't seem so unusual.

What was unusual was the way it made Riley's heart
skip a beat.

Or two.

He sighed and closed the door. It was just the wrong
time. He still had to work out his career plans. His house
plans.

His life plans.

It was best that he do it alone.

CHAPTER FIVE

WORK FELT STRANGE. April had spent most of the last few days glancing over her shoulder in an attempt to try to stay out of Riley's way.

What might have happened if she'd stayed longer the other night? It annoyed her that there was almost an ache inside at the mere thought of it. By the time she'd got home that night she'd been resolute. It was best not to get involved with Riley and Finn Callaghan. Things would get busy anyhow. They would forget about her. Riley's parents would visit and Christmas plans would start to be made. She could fade into the background and take care of herself for now.

So why had she spent the last few days with her stomach doing flip flops?

Lucy, the staff nurse in the ward, was waiting for her when she arrived. 'Hi, April. You here to see John Burns?'

April nodded. John had been wounded in action and after a few weeks with an extremely damaged lower leg and a persistent infection they'd taken the decision to perform an amputation. 'How's he doing?'

Lucy pushed his notes over. 'Riley's spent quite a bit of time with him this morning. He's had a lot of phantom pain. He had some analgesia about two hours ago, so he should be fit for you to see.'

She nodded and walked down the corridor towards John's room. She could hear the laughter before she reached the room and her footsteps faltered. Riley. This was where he'd been hiding out. From the way Lucy had spoken she'd assumed that Riley had already left.

She screwed up her face. She couldn't avoid this. It was her job. Physiotherapy was essential for John's recovery and for his confidence. She'd just have to keep her professional face in place.

She fixed on a smile and walked into the room. 'Good morning, John. How are you doing today?'

Riley was sitting on an easy chair in the corner of the room. He looked comfortable. Too comfortable. She gave him a glance. 'We don't want you distracting us, Dr Callaghan. John and I have some work to do.'

John was sitting up on the bed. He waved his hand. 'No, it's fine. Riley wanted to stay to make sure I'm good to go with the painkillers he's given me.' John shook his head. 'I just can't get my head around this phantom pain stuff. How can I feel something that just isn't there?'

April took a deep breath. Riley hadn't spoken; he was just watching her with those green eyes. She turned her full attention to John as she sat beside his bed. 'You're right. It is difficult to understand. And we still don't really know why it happens. Scientists think that the sensations come from the spinal cord and brain. The imprint of the leg has always been there, so it's almost like the brain keeps hold of it.' She licked her lips. 'You're not alone, John. Lots of patients experience phantom pain after this kind of operation. It's our job to manage that pain for you. So you need to tell me if anything we do today is too uncomfortable.'

John let out a sigh. 'I just want to get back on my feet as soon as possible.' Then he realised the irony of his statement. He let out a hollow laugh. 'Well, at least one of them.'

He met April's gaze. 'I just want to get some normality back. The last few months have been terrible. I want to be able to do things for myself.'

April nodded in appreciation. John's mobility had been badly affected by his damaged and infected limb; that had been part of the decision for the amputation. 'And we'll get you there, John. We will.'

She looked at his position. 'How has lying flat worked out for you?'

The first essential procedure for patients who'd had an amputation was to lie flat for at least an hour each day. This helped straighten the hip as much as possible. Any risk of hips tightening could make it more difficult to walk with a prosthesis.

John gave a nod. 'That's been okay.'

She gave him a smile. 'So how do you feel about hitting the gym with me today?'

He grinned. 'I thought you'd never ask. Music to my ears.'

She wheeled in the chair that was parked in the corridor outside, taking care to help him change position and ease into it. Riley stood up.

She gave him a tight smile. 'I take it you have other patients to see? I can leave a report for you about how John does in the gym.'

But it seemed that the more she tried to brush off Riley, the more determined he became. And the most annoying thing about that was how casual he was about it. He didn't act offended. He didn't appear to be angry. He just seemed determined to hang around.

She pushed John down the corridor to the state-of-the-art gym. It was specially designed for patients with spinal cord injuries and amputations. April turned towards Riley. If he was going to hang around, she might as well use him.

'I've looked over John's wound and think it's looking good. Good enough to take part in a walking trial. What do you think?'

Riley nodded. 'It's healing well. No problems. I think it would be useful to see how John manages.'

April gave a nod and took the chair closer to the parallel walking bars. She turned around and picked up what she'd left in preparation for today's session. 'We're going to try one of these,' she said, smiling as she watched the expression on John's face.

'What on earth is that?'

She kept smiling. 'It's called a pam aid. Pneumatic Post-Amputation Mobility Aid. It's basically an inflatable leg. It helps reduce the swelling around your stump and helps you walk again. We need to assess your muscle strength and standing tolerance.' She raised her eyebrows. 'And the big one—your balance.' She gestured behind her. 'We always start with the parallel bars.'

John frowned. 'Can't you just give me one of those prosthetic limbs and let me get on with it?'

Riley stood up alongside as April started to make adjustments to John's stump-shrinker compression sock. 'If you manage well with your walking trial over the next few days then we'll make arrangements to have you fitted with a prosthetic limb. But it has to be made just for you. And we have to wait until your wound is completely healed and any residual swelling has gone down.'

John gave a nod. 'Then let's get started. I want to be out of this wheelchair as soon as I can be.'

It was almost like being under the microscope. Even though she knew Riley was there to observe John, every move she made, every conversation that she started felt a little forced. She hadn't even been this self-conscious when she was a student and was being assessed.

Riley, on the other hand, seemed completely at ease. He cracked jokes with John and kept him distracted while April got things ready.

But she was conscious of the way he watched. It was annoying. Her emotions were heightened.

Eventually she stopped keeping the false smile on her face. 'Are you going to do something to actually help?'

Riley's brow furrowed with a deep frown. Now, finally, he looked annoyed. He glanced around the gym as he positioned himself next to John. 'What would you like me to do?'

April pulled herself into professional mode. It was the safest place to be. Then she wouldn't notice those eyes. Then she wouldn't focus on the fresh smell stretching across the room towards her.

She didn't even look at him. She waved her hand. 'I'll stay on one side of John. You stay on the other.'

She bent forward in front of John. 'First time standing on your own can be difficult. I'm going to let you push yourself up—it's best if you can get a sense of your own balance without us taking your weight. Don't worry. If it's too painful, we can help you sit back down, and we're on either side; we won't let you fall.'

John nodded. Guys who'd served always had a grim determination about every task. They didn't like to fail at anything and John was no different. He placed a hand on either parallel bar and pulled himself up sharply. April kept her hands off but close by, ready to catch him if he swayed. There was a kind of groan. Weight bearing on a stump for the first time would be sending a whole new range of sensations about John's body. She didn't look up at Riley. He had adopted a similar position to herself, ready to take the strain of John's weight if it were necessary.

After around thirty seconds, John's breathing started to

slow a little. 'Okay,' he said gruffly. 'It's not exactly comfortable, but it's bearable.' He turned his head to April. 'Do I get to walk in this thing?'

She nodded. 'Only a few steps at a time. I'm going to pull the wheelchair behind us so it's handy if you need it.'

John shook his head. 'No way. I'm going to make it to the end of these bars.'

She smiled. Somehow she didn't doubt he would.

Riley leaned forward. 'John, just remember. This isn't a military operation. Your wound is healing well. But parts will still hurt. We need to be able to judge how much analgesia you need to be able to take part in your physical therapy. If we give you too much, you could do yourself harm. Push your body to do things it's not quite ready for.'

'Do people normally make it to the end of the bars?' John asked April.

She held up her hands. 'Some people can't weight bear at all the first time. Some people can stand for a few minutes; others manage a few steps. We're all individuals, John. And this is the first day. Your first steps. Let's just take it as it comes.'

He nodded, his hands gripping tightly to the bars, his knuckles blanching.

She could see Riley noticing the same things that she was. Why was he even here? This was her job. Doctors rarely visited the gym. They usually only appeared if their presence was requested.

Suddenly, there was a pang in her stomach and she caught her breath. That had been a few times today. She hoped she wasn't coming down with something.

John took a step forward with his affected leg. She pressed her lips together for the next stage. It was just as she expected. He had his weight on the amputated limb for the briefest of seconds before his weight fell back on his good leg.

That was entirely normal. It was hard for the body to adjust. It was hard for the brain to make sense of the changes. John was starting to sweat. It was amazing how much work just a few steps could take. She stayed right next to him. As did Riley.

It took another ten minutes to reach the end of the parallel bars. By the time John had finished he was thankful to sink back down into the wheelchair. April put her hands on his shoulders. 'Well done, John. That was great.' She walked around to the front to release the pam aid. 'Ideally, we'll do a bit of work in the gym three times a day.' She looked at Riley. 'Dr Callaghan will have a conversation with you about what works best analgesia-wise for you. The more regularly we can get you down to the gym, the more quickly your body and brain will adjust. The nurses will also do regular checks of your wound to make sure there are no problems.'

John gave an exhausted sigh. 'Any chance of a coffee?'

She laughed. 'Absolutely.' She set the pam aid aside. 'I'll take you back down to the ward and we'll set a programme for tomorrow.'

John looked over at Riley. 'She's a hard taskmaster.'

Riley's voice wasn't as relaxed as it had been earlier. 'She is. But it's the only way to get you back on your feet.'

He pushed his hands into his pockets as April finished tidying up. His pager sounded and he glanced at it. The expression on his face changed.

'Sorry, need to go.' He'd already started striding down the corridor in front of them when he turned around and looked back. 'John, I'll be back to talk to you later.'

April watched his retreating back. Part of her wanted

to ask what was wrong. Part of her knew it was none of her business.

Could something be wrong with Finn?

She tried to push things out of her mind. She had a patient to look after. She had work to do. But, as they reached John's room, he said the words she'd dreaded. 'Isn't Ballyclair the local school?'

She nodded.

'Thought so. That's what his pager said. Hope his kid is okay.'

Her footsteps faltered as she took the final steps towards the chair in John's room. 'Oops, sorry!' she said brightly as she bent down to put on the brake. Her heart was thudding against her chest. She moved automatically, helping John into the other chair.

This was none of her business. None of her business at all.

So why did she want to pull her mobile from her pocket and phone Riley right now?

One of the nurses stuck her head around the door. 'April, are you free? I'm wondering if I could steal you to do some chest physio on someone who is sounding a little crackly?'

She nodded straight away. Work—that was what she had to do. That was what she should be concentrating on. She smiled at John. 'Can we coordinate our diaries for around two p.m. and we can go back to the gym again?'

John put his hand on his chin. 'Let me think. There's the afternoon movie. Or the browsing of the dating websites. But I think I can fit you in.'

She laughed and put her hand on his shoulder. 'You did good this morning. Let's keep working hard. See you in a while.'

Her fingers brushed against her phone again and she pulled them from her pocket.

None of her business.

She gritted her teeth and kept walking.

He was trying to be rational. But the words 'Finn's been hurt' had sent a deep-rooted fear through him that he'd never experienced before. His legs had just started walking to the car even with the phone still pressed to his ear.

Apparently it was 'just a little head-knock'. When was any head injury 'just a little head-knock'? Finn had slid in the school playground, fallen backwards, cracked his head on the concrete and been knocked out for a few seconds.

His car was eating up the road in front of him. Finn's school was only a ten-minute drive from the hospital but right now it felt like a million miles away.

His mum and dad had come down for the weekend to meet Finn. He'd told April that his mum was like a whirlwind—truth was she'd been more like a tornado. She'd taken over everything. Cooking. Cleaning. Every conversation with Finn. His dad had been much more thoughtful. But Riley could tell that his father just wanted a chance to have five minutes to sit down with his grandson.

It hadn't helped that his mother kept bursting into tears every now and then. Finn had just seemed a little bewildered by it all. He'd finally whispered to Riley, 'I've never had a gran before,' as he'd watched Riley's mum talk and cook at a hundred miles an hour. Riley had given him a hug.

It had all been exhausting. His mother hadn't wanted to leave, and Riley had been forced to tell her quite pointedly that he needed some time with his son. Right now, he was regretting that decision. What if he needed some help with Finn?

His eyes narrowed as he noticed the traffic slowing in front of him on the motorway. He'd come this way to save a few minutes and to stop wasting time at a hundred sets of traffic lights in the town. Seemed like it hadn't been the best plan.

His foot hit the brake as it became clear that things were much worse than he could ever imagine. Smoke was directly ahead. The cars in front had stopped, but it was clear the accident had only happened around thirty seconds before.

Riley's stomach clenched. Two cars, both totally smashed, facing each other and blocking the motorway completely.

For the first time in his life he was completely torn. His doctor instincts told him to get out of the car and start helping. But his newly honed parental instincts told him to find a way to Finn.

He gulped and looked behind him. It only took a few minutes for the motorway to back up completely. There was no exit nearby. There was no way out of here.

He pulled his phone from his pocket as he climbed out of the car. Someone else had already jumped out and ran to the smoking cars. For the first time he regretted sending his mother back home after her weekend meeting Finn. There was only one other natural person to phone in a situation like this. He pressed her name on the screen as he opened the boot of his car and grabbed the emergency kit that he always kept there.

There was only one other person he'd trust with Finn.

April's stomach plummeted when she saw who was calling. 'Riley? What's wrong? Is it Finn? Is he okay?'

His voice was eerily calm. But she could hear some shouting in the background. 'April? There's an accident on the motorway. I can't get off. And I need to help. The school phoned. Can you get Finn? Can you check he's okay? He's had a head injury. He was knocked out. Don't come this way. You'll have to drive through the town. Check his reactions. Check his pupils. If he's nauseous or sleepy take him to hospital.'

April was stunned. It took a few seconds to find some words.

'Of…of course. Of course I'll get Finn. No problem. Riley, are you okay?'

She could almost physically feel his pause. 'I'm fine. I have to go and help. Just take care of Finn.'

She stared at the phone. Her hand had the slightest shake. April moved into automatic pilot. She wasn't sure if Riley had spoken to anyone when he'd left, so she followed procedures and spoke to her boss, making arrangements for someone to cover her workload, and then left a message for Riley's boss. Waterloo Court was a real family-friendly place. No one had problems about her leaving. It only took fifteen minutes to drive through town and reach the school.

Finn was sitting at the office as she arrived, looking a little pale-faced. He didn't seem surprised to see her as she rushed over to sit next to him and give him a hug.

The head teacher looked at her in surprise. She held out her hand in a way that only a head teacher could. 'I'm Mrs Banks. I don't believe we've met. I was expecting Dr Callaghan.'

April nearly opened her mouth to speak, then had a wave of realisation. She pointed through the doors. 'Can we speak in there, please?' She didn't wait for a reply before she whispered in Finn's ear, 'I'll be just a second, honey.'

Once they'd walked through the doors she held out her hand to the head teacher. 'Apologies. I'm April Henderson. I'm a colleague of Dr Callaghan. He's stuck at a road accident on the motorway. I didn't want to say that in front of Finn, since he lost his mother in an accident.'

The head teacher gave a nod of acknowledgement and shook April's hand. 'Of course. I understand. But we have a problem.'

'We do?'

She nodded. 'I'm afraid Dr Callaghan hasn't named you as an emergency contact. It means I can't let you take Finn away.'

'Oh.' It was all she could say. Her brain filled with distant memories of conversations with colleagues over the years about making things safer for kids at school. Of course they wouldn't just hand Finn over to anyone. But that hadn't even occurred to her on the way there. It must not have occurred to Riley either. They were both treading waters unknown.

'I take it Riley didn't manage to call you and tell you I was coming?' Why did she even ask that? Of course not. She shook her head. 'He's treating people at the accident scene.'

The head teacher gave her best sympathetic look. 'Well, I'm sorry. But we have good reasons for our rules. Until we hear from Dr Callaghan, we can't let you leave with Finn.'

April glanced through the glass panel in the door, where Finn was so white he seemed transparent. She took a deep breath. 'Let me keep trying to get hold of Riley while I keep an eye on Finn.'

Riley surveyed the scene. Two cars—both had their bonnets completed crumpled, one had its side doors crushed inwards. He ran towards the cars, checking in one, then the other. Another man was talking to a lady in the first car.

'I'm Riley Callaghan, a doctor.'

The guy looked up. 'I'm Phil—just Phil. I know a little first aid but that's it.'

Riley gave a nod and took a quick look in the car. It was an elderly couple. The man was unconscious, the woman making a few groans. Both looked trapped by the crumpled front end of the car. Riley tried to pull the door open nearest to him. After a few attempts he put his foot up to get more leverage. The door opened but not completely. He put his hand in and felt for a pulse, watching the rise and fall of the man's chest. He grabbed some gloves from his back pocket—life had taught him to permanently have them handy. He then put his hand down the non-existent footwell. He fumbled around. There was no way to see clearly, but after a few seconds he found a pulse at one ankle, but couldn't get to the other. He pulled out his hand; unsurprisingly the glove was covered in blood. He pulled it off and found another. 'How's she doing?' he asked Phil.

Phil pulled a face. 'I'm not sure.'

Riley was around the car in an instant. 'Mind if I have a look?'

Phil stepped out of the way. Riley was keeping calm; his main aim was to have assessed the occupants of both cars in as short a time as possible. He'd take it from there.

He checked the woman's pulse. She was terribly pale, but that might be her normal colour. He checked her breathing; it was erratic and he put his hand gently at her chest. She'd broken some ribs. He was sure of it. And it could be that one had pierced her lung. He did a quick check of her legs. One was definitely broken; he suspected both tib and fib. The second seemed okay.

'Stay with her,' he said. 'I'm going to check the other car.'

He crossed quickly to the other car. There was a man of a similar age to him, coughing, with a little blood running down his forehead. The airbag had deployed and the air was still a little clouded around him. The man was clearly dazed. In between coughs he spluttered, 'Aaron. How's Aaron?'

Riley felt his heart plummet. He looked into the back of the car. A little boy—around two—was strapped into a car seat. He yanked at the rear car door, pulling it with all his might. It was stiff. Part of the door was buckled, but after some tugging he finally pulled it free. The little boy greeted him with a big smile. He started babbling and wiggling his legs.

Riley's actions were automatic. This car already had smoke coming from the engine. He reached and unclipped the little guy, grabbing him with both hands and pulling him out. He leaned Aaron towards his father. He would never have thought to do something like that before. But he could see that in amongst his confused state the man's first thoughts had been for his son.

Finn. As held the little body next to his, all he could think about was Finn. Was he okay? Had April got to him yet? He should be with him. Not here.

Not stuck at a roadside.

'Aaron looks good; the car seat has kept him protected.' He glanced anxiously at the man as his head slumped forward a little. It was obvious he was still completely dazed. 'What's your name?'

'Ben,' came the mumbled reply.

'Well, Ben, I'm going to hand Aaron over to someone else to keep an eye on him and get him somewhere safe. We need to think about getting you out of this car.'

A woman had appeared from one of the cars stranded in the traffic jam. She arrived just as he turned around. He moved away from the cars. 'Can you hold this little guy for a second?' She held out her hands and Riley thrust Aaron into them. 'Wait a second,' he commanded and he gave Aaron a quick check over. No apparent injuries. Breathing fine. Moving all limbs. No abrasions. He pulled his pen torch from his back pocket, choking back a gulp. He'd meant to use this on Finn. He quickly checked Aaron's pupils. Both equal and reacting to light.

He looked at the woman. 'This is Aaron. Everything looks fine but can you take him over to the side of the road and keep an eye on him for now?'

She nodded quickly, seeming relieved to be of some help. 'No problem.' She started chatting to Aaron as she walked away. Riley's phone rang.

April.

He actually thought he might be sick. Something must be wrong with Finn. It must be something terrible. A subdural haematoma? Skull fracture? Intracranial bleeding? His hand fumbled with the phone. 'April? What's wrong?'

'Riley. Are you okay? Finn looks fine. But the school won't let me take him home. They say they need permission.'

Relief flooded through him, rapidly followed by frustration. 'Let me speak to them.' He turned back to the car. The smoke looked a little worse. He needed to get Aaron's dad out of there.

A stern voice appeared on the phone. 'Dr Callaghan? Mrs Banks, head teacher. I'm afraid you haven't listed Ms Henderson as an emergency contact for Finn. We really need you to sign some paperwork so that, like today, we can release Finn into her care.'

He was instantly annoyed. He knew why Mrs Banks was saying all this, but it felt like a reprimand for an unruly child. As he stood, flames started licking from the silver car holding Aaron's dad. 'Damn it!' He started running back towards the car. He tucked the phone under his chin, put his foot on the car and started pulling at the driver's door with all his might. 'Come on!' he yelled in frustration at the door.

'What?' came a squeak from the phone.

'Mrs Banks,' he said between yanks at the door. 'I'm trying to pull a guy from a burning car. You—' he stopped and pulled again '—have my permission to—' every muscle in his arms was starting to ache '—release Finn into April's custody.' He pushed the phone away from his ear and shouted to some guys who were talking near the front of the traffic jam. 'Can you give me some help over here?' He could feel the heat from the flames near the bare skin on his arms. He pushed the phone back to his ear. 'Could you do that, please?'

He pushed the phone back into his pocket, not bothering to wait for a reply. April was there. She'd seen Finn. She'd said he was okay. Maybe his definition of okay was different from hers, but he had to have faith in his colleague. Had April worked with kids before? Hadn't she mentioned something about kids with cystic fibrosis? Maybe she knew more than he thought.

Three men ran over; one joined him, two tried the opposite side of the car. Why hadn't he thought of that?

The man's hands squished over his at the handle. 'Now,' he grunted at Riley as the two of them pulled in unison. His hands were nearly crushed beneath the guy's vice-like grip but the extra strength gave him what he needed. The car door was finally prised open and they both landed on the ground.

Riley picked himself up and leaned in to check on Ben just as the flames shot up towards the sky. The two men on the other side of the car yelled and leapt backwards. Riley reached forward to check Ben's legs weren't trapped. He knew the rules. A casualty should never be moved from a vehicle without a neck collar in place to protect them.

But threat of imminent death from fire took priority over all the normal rules.

He gestured to the other guy. 'Give me a hand getting him out of here.' There was a sound of sirens in the distance. The other guy looked at the flames. Riley could see the doubt on his face but, to his credit, the guy stood up and came forward. Together, they half pulled, half lifted Ben out of the car, looping arms around his waist and carrying him over to the side of the road.

Ben winced in pain as Riley touched his leg. Riley glanced around. His emergency bag was lying on the ground next to the first car. He ran and picked it up, pulling a swab out to stem the bleeding from Ben's forehead.

He shouted over to Phil, whom he'd left at the side of the first car. 'How's everything?'

Phil looked anxious. 'Her lips look a bit blue,' he shouted back.

Riley looked up. He could see the blue flashing lights now and the sirens were getting louder. The police cars and ambulances were trying to weave their way through the traffic. They would still be a few minutes.

He ran over to the car to check both patients again. A quick glance at the man showed he still hadn't regained consciousness. But his pulse was strong and he was breathing easily. The leg injuries remained but it was likely that he'd need to be cut out of the car. There wasn't much Riley could do for him at the side of the road. He turned his attention back to the woman. He spoke quietly. Her handbag was behind the seat, so he checked her details. 'Elizabeth? Mrs Bennett?' She gave a nod. 'I'm Riley. I'm a doctor. There's an ambulance coming soon.' He put his fingers on her pulse again. It was faster and more thready than before. 'Are you having difficulty breathing?'

She nodded again. He glanced at Phil at the other side of the car. 'Take a run towards the ambulance. Tell them we have a pneumo—' He changed his mind about the language. 'Tell them a possible punctured lung. Tell them I need some oxygen.'

Phil nodded and took off. The cars were doing their best to get out of the way of the police cars and ambulances but there was virtually no room to manoeuvre.

Riley was frustrated. He hated the fact he had little or no equipment. From her colour, Mrs Bennett had either a collapsed lung or a blood-filled one. Both needed rapid treatment. But there was nothing he could do right now. He held her hand and spoke quietly to her, trying to ascertain if she had family and if there was someone to contact, in case she became too unwell to communicate. The thud of boots behind him made him look up. The familiar green overalls of a paramedic. He was carrying as much equipment as he could. His eyes fixed on the car that was now firmly alight.

'Tell me no one is in that?'

Riley shook his head. 'Man and a little boy, both at the side of the road. They'll need to be checked but—' he nodded to the car '—Mr and Mrs Bennett look as if they need attention first.'

The paramedic nodded. 'Eric' was his reply. 'What we got?' He handed over the oxygen cylinder.

'Lieutenant Riley Callaghan, a doctor at Waterloo Court.' He leaned forward. 'Elizabeth, I'm just going to slip an oxygen mask over your face.' He did that quickly. 'Mr and Mrs Bennett. Mr Bennett has been unconscious since I got here. I think he has a fractured tib and fib in the footwell. His pulse has been strong and his breathing fine. Mrs Bennett, I think, may have had some damage from the seat belt and I don't know about her pelvis. She also looks like she has a tib and fib fracture. I think she may have fractured a few ribs and punctured a lung.'

A female paramedic arrived too, shaking her head. 'Still can't get the ambulances through. Where do you want me?'

Eric signalled to the side of the road where Aaron and his dad were sitting and she nodded and ran over. Eric ripped open the large pack he'd brought with him. 'Right, Doc, let's get to work.'

CHAPTER SIX

FINN WAS SLEEPING NOW. April wasn't quite sure what Riley had said to Mrs Banks on the phone, but Finn had been released into her care with a few mutterings of 'exceptional circumstances'.

After she'd realised she didn't have a key to Riley's place, she'd made a quick trip to the shops to let Finn pick something for dinner then brought him back to her flat.

Thank goodness for the TV. There was a whole host of kids' TV channels she'd never known about or watched, but Finn could tell her exactly where to find them. She'd checked him over as best she could and, apart from being a little pale and not wanting to eat much, he seemed fine. As soon as he'd eaten a little dinner, he'd fallen asleep, lying on the sofa with a cover over him.

Part of her had been nervous. Hadn't Riley said something about sleepiness being a sign of head injury? But her gut instincts told her that Finn was simply exhausted. It was after seven; she wasn't sure when he normally went to bed.

She walked through to the kitchen to make herself a drink but when she came back through Finn was awake again with his nose pressed up against the window.

'Hey,' she said gently as she crossed the room and put an arm on his shoulder. 'What are you looking at?'

It took her a second or two to realise his shoulders were shaking a little. She knelt down beside him so she could see his face. 'Finn? What's wrong?'

'I… I heard someone shouting. I heard someone shouting my name…' His voice stalled for a second.

April glanced outside. There was a family directly under her window, laughing and carrying on in the light dusting of snow outside. The woman shouted at the little boy and girl. 'Finn, Jessie, come over here.'

Finn started to shake next to her. 'I thought it was my mum,' he gasped. 'I thought it was her.'

Her actions were instinctive. She gathered the little body as Finn's legs collapsed under him and he started to sob. She pulled him in towards her shoulder and stood up, clutching him tightly. Normally she would have thought a five-year-old might be too big to carry like a toddler. But there was nothing else she could do right now. Finn needed her and she would never let him down.

She rubbed his back as he sobbed and whispered in his ear. 'I'm so sorry, honey. I'm so sorry that your mum isn't here.'

His words came out in gasps. 'I… I…miss…her.'

Tears started to flow down her face. She walked over to the sofa and sat down, keeping Finn firmly in her arms. 'I know you do. Of course you do. And I know that your mum wishes she was still here with you.'

He curled in her arms, pulling up his knees and resting his head on her chest. 'I want my mum.'

She rocked back and forward. His pain was so raw. So real. She wanted to reach out and grab it. To take it away for him. No child should have to go through this.

She stroked his hair. 'It's not the same. But I had a sister who died not long ago. I know how hard it is when you lose someone you love very much. And it is hard, Finn.

I won't tell you lies. You'll miss your mum every single day. And while it's really horrible right now, and you'll think about her all the time, I promise that at some point it won't be quite as bad as it is now.'

Finn shook his head. 'I just want her back. I just want to go home.'

It was almost like a fist reaching inside and twisting around her heart.

She kept rocking. 'I know you do, honey. But you're going to have a new home with your dad. He loves you. He loves you just as much as your mum does. It just takes a little getting used to. For him too.' She gave a little sigh and tried to find the right words. Were there even right words?

'Mum used to do this,' whispered the little voice.

April froze mid-rock.

She'd only done what came naturally. She wasn't trying to be a mum to Finn. She was just doing what she thought she should.

Finn's hand crept up and his finger wound in her hair. Now, it was her turn to almost shake. 'Can we stay like this till I fall asleep?' came the tired voice.

Her brain was screaming silent messages at her. *No! Too close.*

Her body started to rock again, but she couldn't say the words out loud. It was almost like being on automatic pilot. And even though her movements were steady her thoughts weren't.

She was overstepping the mark. This was wrong. It was Riley's job to comfort his son—not hers. She couldn't let Finn rely on her. That would be wrong. That would be *so* wrong. Particularly when she didn't know what might lie ahead.

Finn's little heart had already been broken once. It was

bad enough for a child to experience that once. If things developed...

She pushed the thoughts straight from her head. No. They wouldn't. She couldn't let them. It wasn't good for her. And it really wasn't good for Finn.

Her brain buzzed as she kept rocking until the little finger released its grip on her hair and Finn's head sagged to the side.

Moving carefully, she positioned him on the sofa with a blanket on top as she stood on the other side of the room, leaning against the wall and breathing heavily.

She hadn't meant for this to happen. She was getting too close. She was feeling too much.

A few extra tears slid down her cheeks. She had to get a hold of herself.

But it wasn't how he felt about her that was hardest. It was how she felt about him, and Riley.

For her, they were a perfect combination at a completely imperfect time. A guy who made her heart beat quicker with just one glance, and a little boy with so much love to give.

Her heart ached. She just wasn't ready for this. Not right now.

There was a gentle knock at the door. It startled her and she took a few deep breaths, pushing her hair back from her face and wiping her eyes before she pulled it open.

Riley looked exhausted. He was still wearing his pale blue scrubs from work. They were rumpled and had a number of stains that she really didn't want to question.

'How's Finn?' He almost pushed past her in his rush to get through the door.

She shook her head and stepped completely aside. 'He's fine. He's just tired.' She pointed towards the sofa. She hesitated for a second. 'He had some dinner and he's sleeping now. But he was a little upset earlier.'

'He was? Is he sick?'

Riley turned towards her and she could instantly see his panic. She held up her hand in front of him. 'No, he's not sick. His pupils are equal and reactive. I gave him some kiddie paracetamol that I bought at the pharmacy. Yes, he felt a bit queasy for a while, but was fine after I'd fed him.' She took a deep breath. She was being automatically defensive because she wasn't that experienced with kids. Looking after kids with cystic fibrosis had been a whole different ball game. But she could imagine how Riley must have felt, thinking there was something wrong with Finn and he couldn't get there.

He crossed the room in a few strides and knelt down in front of the sofa. She watched as he gently stroked Finn's hair and whispered to him. 'Hey, buddy, sorry I was so long. I've missed you.'

The truth of every word that he said was etched on his face, and she turned away as tears sprang to her eyes.

This guy was doing crazy things to her heart. His love. His connection to his child. That overwhelming parental urge that she'd never felt—and would never feel.

Or would she? When she'd seen Riley's name on the phone screen today her heart had been in her mouth. She'd been immediately worried about Finn. Seeing him, and knowing he was okay, had relieved her concerns instantly. Spending time with him this afternoon had been a pleasure—even though he'd been a little cranky.

His every move, every gesture had reminded her of Riley. Being with Finn today had made her realise that even though she'd made her decision about the future she still had the ability to love a child as if it were her own.

That had almost seemed like something so far out of her reach she hadn't even thought about it that much.

She'd been focused on making the decision and getting her surgery out of the way before she gave herself a chance to regroup and think about what the future might hold.

But the guy who was currently leaning forward, showing every element of being a doting dad, was wrapping her emotions up in knots and her interaction with Finn earlier had exposed her to some overwhelming feelings.

After a minute he came over and stood next to her. 'What happened?'

She sucked in a breath. All of a sudden she didn't really want to tell him. He was Finn's father. He had a right to know his child had been upset. But she couldn't quite extricate her own feelings from all of this. Not without revealing them to Riley.

She gave her head a shake. 'He misses his mum. He heard a woman outside call his name—her son must be called Finn too. For a few seconds I think he thought it was his mum and he got upset and was crying.'

Riley ran his fingers through his hair and shook his head. On top of the exhaustion that was already there, he almost looked broken. 'How do I deal with this, April? What do I do?'

She gulped at the pleading tone to his words. She wanted to wrap her hands around his neck and pull him close.

This was a conversation she couldn't have. She just couldn't.

Not the way she felt right now. He had no idea what she was preparing herself for. She turned and walked into the kitchen. She had to try to distance herself from this. She couldn't let Finn see her as some sort of mother figure.

She couldn't let this potential relationship with Riley develop any further.

She kept her voice steady as she flicked on the kettle. 'You just be his dad, Riley. That's all you can do.'

She looked at the pained expression on his face and the sag of his shoulders. She'd never seen him look so tired. It was time to try to change the subject. 'What happened?' she asked.

He paused for a second and gave her a quizzical glance. She could almost see the words forming on his lips to ask her why she was pulling away, but in the end he gave a brief shake of his head. 'There was another RTA at another part of town. Turned out A&E also have a sickness bug. I had to travel with one of the patients in the ambulance. When I got there...' He let his voice trail off.

She nodded. 'You couldn't leave. You had to stay and help.'

He sighed. 'I'm a doctor; what else could I do? They didn't have enough staff to deal with two major RTAs. By the time I could hitch a lift back to the scene of the accident to pick up my car half the day had just gone. I'm sorry, April.'

She put her hand on his arm. 'It's fine. Really.'

He wrinkled his nose and squinted back at Finn. 'What is he wearing?'

April shrugged. 'He couldn't lie around in his school uniform. I gave him a T-shirt to wear. He picked it. It's a superhero one. He said it was better than the one with pink sequins.'

They'd laughed about it. Finn had been impressed with her variety of superhero T-shirts. He'd been even more impressed by her collection of superhero socks, especially when she'd whispered, 'I think these are mostly for boys.

But girls need superheroes too. And I always have cold feet. So I need *lots* of socks.'

Riley smiled, shook his head and followed her into the kitchen. He looked around. 'Nice flat. Have you lived here long?'

She shook her head. 'Just since I took the job at Waterloo Court.' She held up her hands in the glossy black kitchen. 'It was brand new when I bought it, and already finished, so I didn't have much say. Hence, the wooden floors throughout and the black kitchen.' She shrugged. 'I think they do up most new places the same these days. White walls, white bathrooms and very little personality.'

He pointed towards a large cardboard box tucked in the corner of the kitchen. 'What's that?'

She lifted a cup out of the cupboard. 'Oh, that's the Christmas tree. I just pulled it down from the loft last night. I have a little loft space because I'm the top floor flat. It's good. I'm secretly a hoarder, so I can hide all my junk up there.'

Riley stood up and lifted the edge of the cardboard box. His eyebrows shot up. 'A black Christmas tree? I thought you loved Christmas? This seems kinda weird.'

She smiled. 'Yeah, well. It fitted with the flat. It has purple baubles, though. I'm sure Finn will approve.' She wagged her finger. 'And, believe me, you have no idea just how many other Christmas decorations I actually have. Now, tea or coffee?' She held up both in her hands.

'What, no wine?'

She shook her head. 'Not on a school night. It seems like there's no dinner either. I bought something for Finn but forgot about myself. I can make you chicken nuggets if you want? Or cheese on toast.'

Riley let out a groan. 'Coffee, please. Just black since

you don't have a fancy cappuccino maker. And I'd kill for some cheese on toast.'

She smiled as she opened the grill. 'I'm glad you appreciate my cooking talents.'

It only took a few minutes to start toasting the bread under the grill and to grate some cheese. Riley nursed his coffee as he watched.

'How was the accident? Was everyone okay?'

He sighed. 'Hopefully, yes. There was an elderly couple. The man has a broken tibia and fibula. He was pinned in the car and I waited until the fire brigade could cut him out. He was unconscious while I was there, but came around when he got transferred into the ambulance. The woman had a pneumothorax and a fractured tib and fib too. She needed a chest tube when she reached A&E and then had to go to emergency theatre. It took about three hours for the anaesthetist to agree to take her. The other two were a father and son. The little boy was unharmed and the father just had a head lac, and some burns from the airbag.'

'What happened?'

He shook his head. 'Apparently a deer ran across the road. Who knows where it came from.'

April turned around and bent down to watch the cheese on toast as it started to bubble. A few seconds later she slid the grill pan out and lifted the toast onto plates.

Riley was watching her carefully as she sat down opposite him. She could tell straight away that something was bothering him.

'Thank you,' he said. 'Thank you for picking up Finn and looking after him.' His bright green eyes were fixed on hers with an intensity she hadn't expected.

'No problem.' She looked at the cheese on toast. He hadn't started eating yet.

She could see his tongue pressed into the side of his cheek, as if he were contemplating saying something.

'What?'

He met her gaze with those green eyes. 'I didn't have anyone else to call.'

She shifted in her chair. 'So?'

He was still nursing the coffee cup in his hand. 'That's just it. I didn't have someone else to call for Finn.'

She wasn't quite sure where this was going but her skin prickled. 'But you called me, I picked him up, everything was fine.'

He shook his head. 'But it's not right. Finn should have more family than me. I should have more people around him.'

Her stomach started to churn. 'But you have your mum and dad. Didn't you say your mum wanted to move closer?'

He ran his fingers through his hair. She took a bite of her cheese on toast. She wasn't going to wait any longer.

'That's just it. I made a decision today.'

Uh-oh. This sounded serious. She swallowed quickly. 'What?'

He shook his head. 'I can't leave Finn. I just can't. Today, when I couldn't get to him, it made me re-evaluate everything. I'm going to speak to the Colonel. He's arranged things for me on a temporary basis. But I need to plan ahead.'

She gave a slow nod. 'You got a fright, Riley. That's understandable. It was unusual circumstances.' She gave him a smile. 'It's your first time in this situation as a dad. It will feel different.'

Riley was staring at his cheese on toast. It was as if it were easier to look at that than to look at April. 'Being a doctor, being in the army. It's all been about me. That has to stop. That has to change. I can't take an overseas posting again. Those days are gone. What happened if I was in Sierra Leone and Finn took ill? Who would take care of him?'

April had been about to take another bite and she froze, not quite sure where he was going next. Was he about to suggest her?

Please don't suggest me.

But Riley shook his head again. 'No. That's it. I'm done. I have to look for something else. Something that will suit Finn.'

She frowned, part of her brain so mixed up about this whole conversation. 'It doesn't matter what you do, Riley. There will always be days when you're not available. Maybe you just need to set up some kind of contingency plan?'

'Maybe I just need to have a look at my life and wonder how I got here.'

His tone had changed and she jerked her head up.

'What does that mean?'

'What kind of guy am I, that a girl I went out with for two months fell pregnant and didn't feel the urge to let me know? She didn't even seem to want my name on the birth certificate. No financial support. Nothing.'

These thoughts had already shot through her brain. But she shook her head. 'I can't speak for Isabel. I have no idea what she was thinking about. But she did leave a will. And she named you as the person to have Finn. If she thought so badly of you, she would never have done that.'

'Maybe she didn't have any other options? Isabel didn't have siblings, and her mum and dad were dead.' He said the words bitterly.

But April could think a bit clearer. 'No. She did have other options. One of her friends at the funeral said they'd offered to take Finn if something had happened. They'd had a drunken conversation once. But apparently Isabel said she'd made plans for Finn and she knew it was the right thing. She did have confidence in you, Riley. Even if you never had that conversation.'

There was silence for a few seconds. Then he kept going. 'April, how well do we know each other?'

He was jumping all over the place. She was going from confused to bewildered. 'Well...not very.' She hated saying that. It seemed odd. She'd been there when he'd found out about his child. She'd gone with him to his first meeting with his son. And now today, she'd been the person to cradle and hold Finn while he'd cried about his mother.

He set down the cup and drummed his fingers on the table. 'That's just it. How well did I know Isabel?'

She choked. 'Somehow I don't think it's the same thing.'

He gave the slightest shake of his head. 'But it is. What am I going to be able to tell Finn about his mum? I hear what you're saying but it still seems unreal. Why didn't she tell me about Finn? Did she think I was some kind of deadbeat? Some kind of unreliable guy that wouldn't pull his weight?'

She didn't even know how to start to answer that question. She shook her head gently. 'Maybe she was just an independent woman. Maybe getting pregnant was accidental; maybe it wasn't. Maybe she'd reached a stage in her life where she wanted to have a child and didn't want any complications.'

His gaze completely narrowed. He looked horrified. 'A complication? That's what I am? I'm his father!' His voice had risen in pitch and she shook her head and glanced through to Finn's sleeping form on the sofa.

'Shh. I know that. You're asking me to make guesses about someone I never even met. How can I do that? I have no idea what was going through Isabel's mind. How can I?' She took a deep breath. 'Somehow I don't think she'd write you off as a deadbeat. You're a doctor, Riley. It's hardly a deadbeat career. But maybe she thought if she told you that you might be angry with her. You said you were focused on your career. Maybe she knew that?'

He ran his fingers through his hair and closed his eyes. 'But I've missed five years of my son's life. I've missed so much. I didn't hear his first word. I didn't see his first steps.' He shook his head again. 'I wasn't bad to Isabel. Why wouldn't she tell me?'

April ran her tongue along her lips. She could see his anguish. See how distraught he was about all this. The tiny fleeting thought she'd had a few months back entered her mind again. She'd considered going out and trying to get pregnant. It had been the briefest thought. A moment of madness. She could have done to some random stranger what Isabel had done to Riley.

'I have no idea about any of this, Riley. It's horrible. I know that. But this isn't about you. This is about Finn. You have to put all this aside. You can't let Finn know that you're angry at his mother. You can't let him see this resentment. Isabel obviously didn't need financial support from you.' She paused; something he'd said had just struck her. 'Your name—it isn't on Finn's birth certificate, is it?'

There was a real sadness, a weariness about him. 'No. I had a discussion with the social worker. The will was clear. That's why Finn is with me. But if I want to get my name on his birth certificate, there will need to be a DNA test and it will go through court. It's just a formality. But it will also help if I want to change Finn's name. Right now he's still Finn Porter. He should be Finn Callaghan.' He pushed the coffee cup away from him. 'This is such a mess, April. I want to do everything right. But I can't make up for five lost years. And the truth is I'm never going to get over that.'

She ached for him—she really did. Riley was a good man. The kind of man she'd spent part of her life searching for. But now that she'd found him?

It wasn't the right time. For either of them. And that made her sad. If she blinked she could imagine meeting him five years ago—when Isabel had. Before she'd known about her genetic heritage, before she'd lost her sister. When the world had still looked bright and shiny. Riley would have fitted in well.

If Finn was their child, would she have told him?

Of course she would have. She knew that with certainty.

But today she'd been overwhelmed by her motherly feelings towards Finn. They'd made her realise exactly what she was missing. Exactly what she would never be. And she wasn't ready for that. Not right now.

'You have to stop thinking about what you've lost, Riley.' She reached across the table and let her fingers brush against his. 'You have to start thinking about what you've gained. And that's the best little boy in the world.' She licked her lips again and prayed her voice wouldn't shake. Because she meant that—she truly did. 'Some people don't ever get that far. They never get that chance, no matter how much they want it. Count your blessings.'

He looked up sharply, his gaze melding with hers. She knew she'd revealed part of herself that she hadn't meant to. It was only words. And she hadn't actually told him anything. But Riley was a doctor. A good doctor. He would pick up on the words she wasn't saying.

He spoke carefully. 'You're right. Of course you're right. If someone had told me a few weeks ago how much my life could change…' His voice tailed off as he looked through at Finn.

Her heart swelled against her chest. A few weeks ago she would have said that Riley Callaghan was a cheeky charmer—a flirt, with good looks to match. It was part of the reason she'd kept her distance. She didn't want the pull; she didn't want the attraction. She had enough going on in her life.

But there was so much more to him. He was changing before her eyes. Watching him take these first few steps as a parent was enlightening. It was revealing more and more of the man to her. Was she really prepared for this?

'I need to sort things out. I need to make plans. Get things in place.' His voice cut through her thoughts.

She gave him a smile but his face was serious. 'And that starts with you, April.'

'What?' She sat forward in her chair.

He gestured towards her. 'You did me an enormous favour today. And there's always a chance I might ask it of you again. If that's okay with you, of course.'

She nodded automatically before she really had time to think about it. Her brain was screaming *No* at her. But her heart had overruled her head in milliseconds.

Caution still niggled at her. Once she agreed a surgery date she'd be in hospital for a few days. She might not be able to drive for a few weeks after. She chose her words carefully. 'Do you really think that's a good idea? It's really important right now that you and Finn get a chance to bond. I think me being around could complicate matters.' She was trying to steal herself away in the easiest way possible.

Riley didn't seem to pick up on her cautionary words.

He held up his hands and looked around. 'I'm only asking you to be a second contact for Finn in case of emergency. Situations like today are unlikely to happen again. I just need a second number. You can do that, can't you? I think it's most important for Finn right now to be around people he can trust. Isn't it?'

She swallowed. When he said it out loud it made perfect sense. If she argued now it would make her look petty and small, and it might mean that Riley would ask more difficult questions. She gave a brief nod. 'Okay, fine. You've got my number. You can use it.'

He smiled. 'Perfect, thank you.' Then he looked around. 'Since I'm trusting you with my son, I think we should get to know each other a little better. I've never been in here before. I only knew where you live because you came with me to pick up Finn. I feel as if I'm doing this all back to front.'

She shook her head. 'What are you talking about?'

'Okay. Tell me something about yourself. You picked up Finn today because you were the one person I could think of to phone—to trust with my child. But are we really even friends?'

Her stomach coiled. He was right. How well did they really know each other? What kind of movies did he like? What kind of food? Instinctively she felt as if Riley needed a giant bear hug. A simple show of affection because he'd had a bad day and was feeling so confused about things. That was the kind of thing you would do for a loved one— or for a friend.

But there was a prickliness to him. An edge. As if he just didn't know where he was in this life.

She recognised it because she'd worn it herself for so long.

It was almost like staring into a mirror and it made her heart flip over. Because, no matter how hard she tried to convince herself, she didn't think of Riley as a friend. It felt like so much more.

'I... I...think we're friends,' she said hesitantly, almost

as if she were trying the word out for size. Why was that? Was it because saying she was Riley's 'friend' out loud didn't seem quite adequate?

He gave a nod. 'I would say so too. But we have gaps. We have bits missing.' He gave the tiniest wince. He already knew she hadn't talked about her sister much. Was he going to try to push her to talk more?

But he didn't. He just held up his hand towards her. 'Tell me something—' he paused '—not related to work. For example—' he frowned, as if trying to think of something himself '—tell me something most people wouldn't know about you. Like when I was a kid—' he put his hand on his chest and looked a bit sheepish '—I caused a panic on a beach once by saying I'd seen a shark. Truth was, I didn't want to swim in the sea but didn't want my brother to know.'

Her mouth fell open. 'What?' She wrinkled her brow and leaned forward. 'Riley Callaghan, were you scared?'

He winked. 'My lips are sealed. I'll never tell. Now, your turn.'

She racked her brain for something equally odd. It was hard being put on the spot. After a few seconds something came to mind. 'Okay, I once tried to steal a chocolate bar from a shop. But I chickened out when my sister saw me.'

From the expression on his face that was the last thing he'd expected. He leaned forward. 'You? Really?'

Now she felt ridiculous. Where on earth had that come from?

She just nodded.

'Why?'

She threw up her hands. 'I don't know. I just wanted it, I suppose.'

Riley shook his head. 'What age were you?' He wasn't going to let this go.

'Five,' she snapped.

Now, he laughed. 'Okay, that was random…and unexpected.' His hand crept towards the now cold cheese on toast. 'Tell me about your sister?'

Her skin prickled. 'What about her?'

'Let's start with her name.'

She wanted to change the subject. Her brain started thinking of random questions to throw at him.

Who was the first girl you slept with? was the one that danced around inside her head. But she didn't want to ask that. She didn't want to *know* that.

She imagined herself pulling on her big-girl pants.

'Mallory' was what she finally said.

He looked thoughtful. 'April and Mallory. Nice names, quite unusual.'

She nodded. 'My mother thought so. She picked April and my dad picked Mallory.'

'Ah, so they took turns? Interesting.'

She opened her mouth to say no. Then stopped. She hadn't told him Mallory was her twin. And she didn't want to. Not when she could guess where this conversation might lead.

'So you said that Mallory died eighteen months ago. I'm sorry. What happened?'

This was the second time he'd asked her. She tried not to let her voice shake, but she certainly couldn't meet his gaze. 'Mallory had cancer.'

'Oh. That's terrible. What kind?'

He hadn't missed a beat. She squeezed her eyes closed, just for a millisecond. He couldn't know the rest of what was going on in her head. He couldn't know the connections.

'Ovarian cancer,' she said quickly. 'She was unlucky.'

He pulled back a little. 'She was young.'

'Lots of people die young. It's a fact of life. Look at Isabel.'

It was a little bit cruel to turn it back around. But she needed to. She didn't want to have this conversation at all.

All it was doing was reinforcing the gulf that was between them. How far apart they really were.

The dreams of motherhood she'd felt earlier while looking at Finn? She had to push them away for now. Her stomach gave another twinge.

That was a few times that had happened now. What if it was…*something*?

It was as if the temperature had just plummeted in her flat to freezing. One hand went automatically to her arm, rubbing up and down.

She was being ridiculous. It was nothing. Surgery was to be scheduled in the New Year. She always experienced painful periods. She often experienced ovulation pain too. It was just that. It must be.

Riley tilted his head and looked at her curiously—maybe even with a little disappointment. 'I guess you're right. It's still sad. For all parties.'

'I know.' It was a blunt response. But she just didn't want to go down this road.

He sucked in a deep breath. 'I'm going to be staying. I'm going to be staying at Waterloo Court for now and thinking about other options. We could be working together for a long time.'

His hands pressed together for a second on the table. Then he seemed to regain his focus. 'How do you feel about that?'

He wasn't looking at her. Her heart missed a beat, then started doing somersaults in her chest. Part of her was praying he wasn't about to suggest something more between them, part of her wishing that he would.

'What do you mean?' Her mouth seemed to go into overdrive. 'That will be fine. You staying is what's best for Finn. It will give you a chance to get to know each other more.' She held up her hands casually. 'And work? That's just work.' She narrowed her gaze. 'We get on well at work, don't we?'

He looked a bit amused. 'I just wondered what you'd say.' He gave her a playful wink. 'Unless I'm buying you hot chocolate you seem to avoid me. Now that you're my emergency contact for Finn...' He let his voice tail off as he kept smiling at her. 'Thank you for saying yes. It means a lot. He knows you. He trusts you. *I* trust you.'

She blinked. It almost felt like diving off one of those high Greek cliffs over the perfect sea. That sensational plummet. There was nothing romantic about this. No promises or intentions. But there seemed to be a huge amount of unspoken words hanging in the air between them.

She'd thought he was attractive from the start. She'd deliberately tried to keep him at arm's length. And her instincts had been right, because being around Riley Callaghan was tougher than she had ever imagined.

Just being in his company made her wonder about the brush of his skin next to hers. It sparked memories of the hug—that she'd initiated—and the reminder of what it was like to be close to someone.

She missed it. But it felt amplified around Riley. Because his company was so much more appealing than anyone else's.

And it was ridiculous, but an icy glove had just wrapped around her heart. After her feelings earlier around Finn it all seemed too much.

Her mouth was dry. She stood up, picking up her plate and cup. 'It's fine, providing I'm free and available.'

He smiled. 'Planning any month-long holidays in the near future?'

She shrugged. 'You never know. Things can come up.'

She kept her back to him and started washing up. The *I trust you* statement wasn't giving her the warm glow it probably should. And this wasn't about Finn. None of this was about Finn.

This was about her and how mixed up she was about everything.

This was about the fact that for the first time in a long time she'd started to feel attraction and a pull towards another human being. And it wasn't just that it didn't fit in with her plans.

This was all about Finn. Just like it should be. The only reason Riley was staying in one place now was because of the unexpected arrival of Finn.

He wouldn't have stayed here for her. No, he would have been on that plane to Sierra Leone, probably with a sigh of relief and a smile on his face. Riley Callaghan would just have been a doctor she'd briefly worked with at some point.

But was that really what she wanted?

Riley appeared at her side with his cup and plate. It seemed he'd managed to eat the cold cheese on toast after all. 'I'll take Finn home now,' he said quickly. 'Thanks for looking after him. I appreciate it. How about I pick you up on Saturday and you can help us pick a Christmas tree? I think it would be good for him. He's already said he wants you to come with us.' He let out a short laugh and looked at her cardboard box. 'Maybe you want to trade yours in? Or buy some new decorations for your hidden stash?'

He had no idea. No idea of the crazy thoughts that had just pinged about her head and her heart. She moved into self-protection mode. She could do this. She could make completely inane conversation. She could find a way to make a suitable excuse.

'Oh, I'm not sure. I was going to do some Christmas shopping. Try and get a head start on things.'

Riley had already walked through to the main room. 'Well, that's perfect. You love Christmas. I love Christmas,' he said easily. 'You can do your shopping at the garden centre.'

For a second she was stunned. She hadn't quite been ready for that one.

He pulled his jacket over Finn, picked him up and walked over to the front door. 'See you later,' he said as he opened the door and walked out into the foyer.

April was a bit stunned. Her plan was to say no. Her plan was to create some distance between herself and Riley.

She closed her door and sagged against it.

She was becoming more confused by the second.

He'd almost said something. He'd almost hinted to her that maybe they should reconsider their relationship. What relationship? He wasn't even capable of having a relationship. At least, that was what Isabel must have assumed since she hadn't even told him about his son. He was still struggling with that.

It was just, for a few minutes today, he'd looked at April sitting across the table from him and been overwhelmed by the sadness in her eyes. That was why he'd pressed her. That was why he'd been quite pointed.

He liked her. He more than liked her. If he was being truthful, he might actually care. She was a good person. She was the only person he'd considered when he'd realised he couldn't get to Finn.

But even before Finn, even before he'd realised the enormity of being a dad, there had still been something about April. He could remember, as clear as day, that overwhelming lift he'd felt when she'd appeared in the pub and he'd thought, for just a second, she might actually have come to see him.

And she had. Just not in the way he had hoped for.

When he watched her with Finn it was like a little clenched-up part of him just started to unfurl.

He knew he should only concentrate on his son. Finn had lost the person that he knew best. Riley was playing rapid catch-up. And sometimes feeling like a poor replacement.

But April was constantly around the edges of his thoughts. And she had a shell of her own. He knew that. He could tell. She was doing her best to keep him at arm's length.

It was almost as if they were doing a dance around each other. He liked her. She liked him. Sometimes when their gazes connected he could see the sparks fly. Other times he could almost see her retreat into herself.

And she'd hinted at something today. As if she might be going somewhere in the future. At least that was what he thought. Was she considering another job? Would that mean she wouldn't be around?

That thought sent a wave of cool air over his skin.

He just didn't know what to do next.

The more time he spent with April Henderson, the more time he *wanted* to spend with her. She was infectious. And being in her company made him happy. Made Finn happy. He wanted to act on the pull between them—but did she?

He already knew he wouldn't sleep tonight. He'd be too busy watching over his son. It didn't matter that, as a doctor, he would say it wasn't necessary. Right now he wasn't a doctor; he was a parent.

He also knew that April was going to haunt his thoughts tonight.

He'd watched her try to make an excuse for Saturday but he'd already decided he wouldn't listen.

Chipping away at April Henderson's armour was helping him chip away at his own. He just wasn't quite sure where it would lead.

CHAPTER SEVEN

EVEN THOUGH IT was early afternoon, the sky was already darkening and the lights from the garden centre twinkled in greeting to them. Finn pressed his nose up against the window of the car, sending steamy breaths up that smoked his view. 'Is this where we get the Christmas tree?'

April nodded. She'd spent the last few days trying to make up an excuse not to be around Finn and Riley—each of them more pathetic than the one before. Her stomach had been in a permanent knot for the last few days. Finally, she'd realised it was almost like being a teenager going on a first date. Mallory used to tease her relentlessly about it. April had nearly always been sick before a first date, whereas Mallory had walked about the house singing.

And as soon as she'd had that thought, she knew she was going to go.

She smiled at Finn. 'They have lots to choose from. You'll find the perfect one.'

Riley opened the door of the car for Finn so he could climb out. The car park was busy; a group of children were crowded around the outside display—Santa's sleigh being pulled by reindeers.

'Look!' gasped Finn as he wriggled free of Riley's grasp and ran over to lean on the barrier. He stretched to touch the carved wooden reindeers. The largest one was just out of his reach. April looked around and gave him a bump up, so his fingertips could brush against the roughened wood. 'I touched him!' Finn squealed excitedly. 'I touched Rudolph!' April laughed as she let him down. Sure enough, someone in the garden centre had painted the nose of this reindeer bright red. Finn pulled her down towards him and whispered in her ear, his eyes sparkling, 'Are these the real reindeers? Do they come to life on Christmas Eve so they can deliver all the presents?'

April glanced conspiratorially around her. 'What do you think?' she whispered back. Finn's smile spread from ear to ear. Riley was standing behind them with his hands in his pockets.

'Come on, you guys. Let's go pick a tree.'

April nodded; she slipped her hand into Finn's and he took it without question. As they walked through the main entrance she gestured to a blacked-out area to the left. 'All the neon trees are in here. The real trees are on the other side. I wasn't quite sure what you would want.'

Riley bent down to Finn. 'Should we take a look at them all?'

Finn nodded excitedly. The area was encased by a giant black tent and, as soon as they pushed the curtain aside, Finn gasped. The tent was full of trees, all different sizes, all pre-lit, some multi-coloured, others with just white lights. Some of the lights were programmed, twinkling intermittently, or staying bright the whole time. Finn walked slowly from one tree to the other, stopping in front of one tree that was covered in bright blue lights. 'I like this one, Dad,' he breathed.

Riley glanced at April, then bent forward and lifted the price tag. His face gave a twisted look. He turned the tag towards her and mouthed, 'How much?'

She laughed. 'Come on, Finn.' She gave his hand a tug. 'Let's look at them all before we make a decision.'

They walked out of the tent, past all the rope lights for decorating the front of houses, and an array of illuminated parcels, Santas and white reindeers. The back of the tent led out into the middle of the garden centre, with tinsel and tree decorations as far as the eye could see.

Riley blinked. He turned and put his hand on April's waist. 'Boy, Christmas is really a big production, isn't it?'

'And you want to buy a house?' she quipped. 'By the time we leave here, you won't be able to afford a house.'

The decorations were all organised by colour. Finn made his way over to the red ones, his little fingers touching everything that was hanging on the wall in front of him. April laughed at Riley flinching every time Finn stretched for something delicate-looking. 'Let him look,' she said quietly. 'It's part of the fun.'

Riley rolled his eyes. 'I can see me leaving here with an enormous bill and not a single thing to show for it.'

She shook her head. 'Don't worry; they're used to children.'

They spent nearly an hour, Finn running between the coloured displays then back into the tented area. Finally, April pointed to outside. 'Do you want to go and see the real Christmas trees?'

Finn nodded and slipped his hand into hers. Her heart swelled. It was ridiculous—it didn't mean anything. But the warmth of that little hand in hers sent a whole wave of emotions circling around her body.

Riley held the door and they headed outside. In the space of an hour, the last elements of light had gone, leaving the perfect backdrop for viewing the real Christmas trees, which were planted in lines and all currently topped with a dusting of snow.

April sucked in a breath. 'Well, this is definitely the place to pick a Christmas tree.'

Riley brushed against her. 'I think you could be right.'

Finn's hand slipped from hers and he ran yelling down the middle of the path. 'This is great!' he shouted, holding out his hands to brush against the trees.

'Eek!' April took off after him and swept her arms around him. 'Watch out—you might damage some of the trees. And you've not picked your own yet.'

He looked a little disappointed, his head turning from side to side. 'But how do you pick a tree?' He wrinkled his nose. 'What's the strange smell?'

Riley laughed. 'It's all the trees. Haven't you had a real one before?'

Finn shook his head, so Riley knelt down in front of him. 'Well, now is the time to decide. Do you want a light-up tree from inside, or a real one from outside?'

Finn looked confused. 'Does the real one go in the garden, or go in the house?'

'It goes in the house.'

He touched the nearest tree. 'But if we pick one of these does that mean our Christmas tree has no lights?'

Riley shook his head. 'We just buy some lights separately. We need to buy some Christmas baubles too.'

Finn looked thoughtful. He started to walk in amongst the row of trees again. April and Riley exchanged glances and followed him around. There were plenty of other families at the garden centre picking Christmas trees. April realised that people would assume the same about them—that they were a family. Her heart gave a squeeze as she realised how much she'd wished for something like this.

Riley was confusing. It was clear he was trying his best with Finn. It was clear he was learning along the way. And so was she.

She couldn't work out in her head how she felt about all this. She'd been attracted to Riley from the start, but he was only there for a short time and she hadn't been in a place to begin a relationship.

Now, he was staying. And she wasn't entirely sure how happy he was about it. It was clear he loved his son. But his career plans had just been halted abruptly.

And the constant lingering looks made her wonder what else there could be between them. Riley was flirtatious. He hadn't mentioned any significant long-term relationships in the past. Who knew what he'd want in the future?

She hadn't even revealed her health issues to him. It was quite likely that Riley might see his future with more children in it. That couldn't happen with her.

She had surgery to go through. There would always be that threat of cancer somewhere in the background.

That could be true for a lot of people. She was well aware that one in three adults in the UK would develop cancer at some point in their lives. But, even with surgery, chances were her odds would be higher.

The long and short of it was that she was a risk.

Finn had already lost a parent. Was it fair she might even consider being a part of his life—even as a friend?

As for Riley… She squeezed her eyes closed for a second. Finn was running around a Christmas tree now. He seemed to have picked his favourite. And Riley was joining in and chasing him around.

Her heart ached. She liked this man far more than she should. He was a charmer. Last thing he needed in his life was a woman with a potential ticking cancer and no ability to have children.

There was a real pang deep inside as she watched Finn. Another woman was standing to her side with a small curly-haired girl, and her stomach swollen. April turned away quickly. She didn't want to get emotional. Since she'd made her decision about the surgery it seemed as if the world was full of pregnant women.

It felt as if the number of female staff she worked with who'd announced they were pregnant recently had doubled. It could be that there was something in the air. Or it could be that she was noticing more, and becoming more sensitive to it.

She gritted her teeth. Her decision would give her a better chance at *life*. A life she should embrace. A life she would live on behalf of herself, and her sister.

'Okay?' Riley came up behind her, his breath visible in the cold air, his cheeks tinged red and his eyes shining. He caught the expression on her face. 'What's wrong?'

She shook her head. 'Nothing. Nothing at all. Are you done?'

He gestured with his hand towards the tree Finn was still dancing around. 'We've picked our tree. I've spoken to the sales guy. They'll deliver it. We just need to pick some decorations.'

For a second she thought she might have to paste a smile on her face. But she didn't. The warm feeling of being around Riley and Finn was spreading through her stomach and up towards other parts.

'Great. Let's get back inside.' She rubbed her hands together.

Riley looked down and closed his hands over hers, rubbing them with his own. 'Are you cold? Sorry, I didn't think.'

The gentle heat from his hands was so personal. So unexpected. He smiled as he did it for a few seconds. 'I should buy you some gloves.' He pulled his hands away and turned back to Finn. 'Come on, Finn. April's getting cold. Come and pick some lights.'

Finn turned at his father's shout and ran straight to them. 'What colour? What colour will we get?'

Riley slid his hand around Finn's shoulders. 'Well, you get to pick. I don't have any decorations yet, so you can pick your favourite.'

She followed them back into the darkened area. The lights twinkled all around them. It wasn't just lights. There was a whole array of illuminated animals at their feet, and a whole Christmas village on a table too. April wandered over. She knew as soon as Riley was at her back as she could smell his woody aftershave. 'What are you looking at?' he whispered.

She bent down to get a closer look. 'This village. I just love it. Look, there's a schoolroom. A bakery. Santa's workshop. A church. A shop. There's even a skating rink.'

Riley was right behind her and, instead of stepping around her, he just slid his hand forward, brushing against her hip as he turned one of the price tags over. His cheek was almost touching hers. 'They're not too expensive.' Then he gave a low laugh. 'That's if you only buy one. If you buy the whole village...'

She laughed too, leaning back a little, her body coming into direct contact with his. Neither moved. It was as if both of them just paused, and sucked in a breath.

After the longest time Riley spoke, his warm breath at her neck. 'Which is your favourite?'

She looked over the village again. There were tiny characters in every scene, packages on shelves, mounds of snow at doorways, each one gently lit. Everything was so detailed. She sighed. 'I don't know. I think I love them all. I want the whole village.'

She reached down and picked up the toyshop. 'This is like the kind of thing where you could buy one every year, build up your collection and keep them for ever.'

He was smiling at her, only inches from her face. He reached and brushed a strand of hair away from her eyes, his hand covering hers as she held the shop. 'So how about you let me buy you your first one? As a thank you,' he added, 'for coming here with us today.'

The twinkling lights were behind them, but even though his face was in shadow his green eyes seemed brighter than ever. And they were focused totally on her.

She held her breath. Her hand itched to reach up and touch his dark hair that glistened with moisture from the snow outside. His cheeks were tinged with pink. Those green eyes were still, just locked with hers, and as she watched he licked his lips. Every nerve in her body was on fire. Every sense on overload.

He reached up again, this time his finger touching her cheek. 'Let me do something for you, April.'

The rush of emotion tumbled through her in waves. When was the last time someone had spoken to her like that? When was the last time she'd wanted someone to get this close? It felt like for ever. It felt like a whole lifetime ago.

A lifetime before her sister's vague symptoms. Shock diagnosis. Frantic treatment attempts. And the life just slowly draining from her body.

He made the smallest move. His cheek touched hers as his lips brushed against her ear. 'A toyshop. Along with the superhero T-shirts, I think you might secretly be a *Peter Pan* kind of girl.'

She could sense he was smiling.

Her eyes were closed, the toyshop held in front of her chest. She turned towards him just as his head pulled back from her ear.

Every part of her literally ached. Ached for his lips to touch hers.

Then, before she had time to think any more, his lips brushed against hers. The sensation was just as sweet as she'd imagined. Every bit as magical.

His hand tangled in her hair as the gentlest pressure increased.

She wanted this. She wanted this more than she'd ever imagined.

But just this—the slightest kiss—put her sensations into overload. Every part of her brain fired. She was starting something she might not be able to continue. She was taking what could not be hers. She was kissing a man she hadn't been entirely truthful with.

She trembled as the feelings threatened to overwhelm her and her eyes filled with tears. She pulled back.

Riley rested his head against hers. 'April? What's wrong? Did I do something wrong?'

She shook her head quickly. 'No. Of course you didn't.'

'But—' he started.

She placed her hand on his chest and gave him a regretful smile. Everything about the kiss had been right.

And everything about the kiss had been wrong.

'It's just not the right time,' she said as she looked around.

For a brief second she could see the flash of confusion, but then he glanced around and gave a nod.

Her heart squeezed in her chest. He thought she meant here, in the garden centre, was the wrong time. But she meant so much more than that.

Riley looked around and spotted Finn racing around a Christmas tree. He gave an approving smile and dropped to his knees, looking under the table and emerging with a box in his hand. 'Look. The toyshop. You can take it home.'

She felt a pang inside.

Home. She wasn't quite sure what that meant for her any more.

Her flat had seemed so empty the other night after Finn and Riley had left. Her footsteps had echoed around the place. She'd never noticed that before.

Before it had been her haven. Her quiet place. Now, she was just conscious of the fact it had seemed so full with the two of them in it.

'Dad! I want these ones!' Both of them jerked at the sound of Finn's voice. He'd found blue twinkling stars wrapped around one of the trees.

Riley nodded in approval. He gave her a wink. 'Come on then. We've got more shopping to do.'

He walked off towards Finn and her stomach clenched. Riley had the box with the toyshop tucked under his arm. He was going to buy it for her.

As a thank you.

But when she'd thought about buying a piece of the village every year, she'd never really imagined just doing it for herself. She'd imagined it with a family around her.

Finn squealed as his dad threw him up in the air. 'April, I've picked the blue ones! Come and see.'

Her lips tingled. Riley's aftershave still filled her senses.

She glanced around. Christmas surrounded her. Both the best and worst time of year for some people. She could almost hear Mallory's voice in her head urging her on.

One kiss. That was all it had been. But she wanted so much more.

Right now, it just didn't feel honest, and she hated that more than anything. She licked her lips and looked around.

Was it wrong to want to enjoy this time with Riley and Finn? Was it wrong to join in with their celebrations? Mallory was whispering in her ear again. *Go on.*

Riley caught her eye. 'Okay?' he mouthed.

She nodded and walked over to join them. It was time to stop brooding about things and start enjoying life. 'Come on, guys.' She looked at the toyshop box and the Christmas lights. 'Oh, no, we're not finished yet. Someone grab a basket. We're going to shop till we drop.'

CHAPTER EIGHT

PLANS SEEMED TO be bursting from his head. Riley was buzzing. He couldn't wait to find April and tell her.

For the first time since all this had happened, things seemed to be falling into place.

He'd kissed her. He'd finally kissed her and it just felt so right. And all he could think about was kissing her again.

Okay, so she'd pulled back. Maybe April was more private than most. Maybe she didn't like being kissed in a public place. But that was okay. He could handle that. He could deal with that.

As long as he could kiss her again.

And even though he was currently bursting with excitement there was a tiny part of him that wondered if there could be something else—something else going on with April. He was sure it wasn't another man. April would never have let their spark and attraction grow if there was another man in the background.

She still hadn't really talked that much about her sister. Maybe it was just Christmas and the time of year? It just felt as if there was something he couldn't quite put his finger on yet. But he had to give her space. If he wanted to have some kind of relationship with April, he had to trust her to tell him the things he needed to know. Right now he should be concentrating on Finn.

His mother had stopped calling ten times a day. April had shown him a Top Ten list of Christmas toys for boys and it had been the biggest blessing in disguise. Finn seemed to like a whole range of things, so he'd handed the list over to his mother and asked her to track down what she could.

She'd been delighted. It had been a brilliant idea and he could hug April for it. Gran was over the moon to have a task related to her grandson and was tackling the list like a seasoned pro.

Finn seemed to be settling well. The crying at night had stopped after the first week. He was still wistful at times, and Riley encouraged him to talk about his mum as often as he liked.

Riley was finally making peace with the pictures of Isabel around the place. April had been right. It was good for Finn and that was what mattered. And, if all went to plan, they would have a place to permanently call home soon.

Work was still something he had to sort out, but he had plans for that too.

But he still didn't really have plans in his head for April.

He liked her. He more than liked her. He wanted to move things on. As soon as he set foot on the ward in the morning, the first thing he did was look for the swing of her blonde ponytail. Last night he'd nearly texted her around five or six times. He'd had to dial back in and only text twice. And it was all nonsense. Nothing that couldn't wait until the next time he saw her. But that had just seemed too far away.

If the phone buzzed and the screen lit up with her name he could feel the smile on his face before he'd even pressed the phone to his ear.

And it was ridiculous. Because sometimes it was actually about work.

He knew he should only be concentrating on Finn. Of course he should be. But there was something about April Henderson. The way she sometimes caught his gaze and gave him a quiet smile. The expression on her face when they'd been in the garden centre and she'd looked at all the Christmas decorations. But, more importantly, it was how he *felt* around her. It had been a long time since his heart had skipped a few beats at the sight of a woman. It had been a long time since he'd met someone he'd felt a real connection to. But even though it had been the briefest kiss, even though they hadn't really acted yet on the growing bond between them, Riley knew that at some stage he would take things further.

He knew there was more. Her sister had died of ovarian cancer. That must have been tough. It must have been a shock for her family. Maybe she was just quiet right now because it was the lead-up to Christmas. Tomorrow would be the first day of December. Finn would get to open the first door on his Advent calendar, though Riley was almost sure it wouldn't last that long.

In the meantime, Riley had to find April. He wanted to share his news. Maybe when she knew for sure that he and Finn planned on staying around it might take them to the next stage. He'd told her he was staying, but she'd looked as if she hadn't really been convinced.

His plans had changed. He'd found what he had been looking for, but the funny thing was, when he'd seen the house he hadn't just imagined Finn and himself being in it. If someone had told him this a few months ago, that he could see himself staying in one place and settling down, he wouldn't have believed them. But April was making those plans seem real. They weren't even dating yet. But he planned on remedying that soon.

Maybe proving he planned on staying around could be the key to opening her heart.

'Come here—I want to show you something.'

April looked over her shoulder. No one else was around. 'Are you talking to me?' She couldn't stop the little pang she felt as soon as she heard his voice.

Riley glanced around. 'Who else would I be talking to? Here—' he spun the laptop around '—look at this.'

She bent down to see what he'd pulled up. Her eyebrows shot up. 'A house?'

He nodded. The excitement was written all over his face as his fingers moved over the keyboard.

She wasn't quite sure what to say. 'But Finn has just moved here. You can't want to move him again?' She'd phrased it as a question, but she hoped he'd get the hint.

He looked at her in surprise. 'But where we're staying is only temporary. It won't do. Not long-term.'

She licked her lips. 'So…your long-term is here?'

He shrugged. 'I told you it was. Where else would it be?'

This was going to take longer than she'd thought. She hitched her hip up onto the desk. 'Have you spoken to the Colonel?'

He shook his head. 'But I did try and get an appointment. Why?'

She wasn't part of the forces but had been here long enough to know how things usually worked. 'I thought he just let you stay here as a temporary measure? Won't you maybe have to change regiment or posting to get a permanent headquarters?'

What she really wanted to say was, *Are you crazy for considering buying a house right now?*

But she didn't. She kept her thoughts in her head. Riley flicked through the pictures. It was a large grey Georgian sandstone semi. The house was full of character. Original doors, large sash windows with internal shutters. A huge fireplace. A large drawing room, separate dining room and a smaller room at the back they could make into a snug. A kitchen that had been renovated with a Belfast sink. Two bathrooms. The wide entranceway and sweeping staircase gave her a pang of envy. Long-term, she'd always wanted to own a house like this. The bedrooms. Three of them. And a large garden at the back of the house—big enough for a kid to play football in.

Riley couldn't stop smiling and she wasn't quite sure what to say. It was ideal—a family home and something like that seemed so far out of her grasp right now.

She could almost picture the perfect woman who'd be standing next to him in a few years with a new baby in a pram to complete the family. And that hurt in a way she could never have imagined.

'It's for sale, but I could temporarily rent it for a few months—try it out for size—with a view to buying it. It's even in the right catchment area for Finn's school.' He gave her a nudge with his elbow. 'See? I'm learning.'

He was. Riley was getting the hang of things quicker than she'd given him credit for. He had no idea about the fact she could barely breathe right now.

Since when had she started having such irrational thoughts?

'When could you start renting?' she managed to ask.

'This week,' he answered quickly. 'The owner has moved to Japan. He just really wants someone to either buy the house or move in and take care of it.'

April thudded backwards in her seat. She still wasn't sure what to say. Riley hadn't seemed to notice. He was either too excited or too swept up in the idea to figure out she'd stopped talking.

He sat back too. 'So, if I sign the agreement tomorrow, Finn and I can move in the next few days.' He pointed at some of the décor. 'It maybe isn't perfect but it's in good condition. I can give the place a lick of paint. That's all it really needs.'

The thoughts jumbling around in April's mind started to sort themselves into some kind of order. Practical things. That was what she could think of. At least they were the kind of things she could say out loud. 'You'll need furniture. You don't have a sofa or a dining room table. Or beds. It's only a few weeks until Christmas. Riley, do you have any idea how much stuff you'll need?' She started to shake her head.

The smile had faded a little. 'Well, just the stuff you've said. A sofa, a table and some beds. What else is there?'

April leaned forward and pulled a piece of paper from the printer. 'Here, let me get you started.' She wrote down the things they'd just mentioned, then started adding more. 'Cushions, cutlery, dishes, lamps, towels, bedding…' She frowned and turned the computer towards her. 'What comes with the kitchen? Do you need a washer, dryer and fridge freezer?'

Riley looked pale. 'You're beginning to sound like my mother.'

'Does your mother think you need a reality check?' She sighed and put down the pen. 'What happens if they move your base?'

He pressed his lips together and looked around. 'I might not be in the army much longer.'

'What?' She couldn't help it—she said the word much louder than she meant to.

'Shh—' he put his finger to his lips '—I haven't decided yet. I've just started to look into other options.'

'Like what?' A strange feeling was spreading through

her. Like any serviceman, there was always a chance he would get moved. But she hadn't expected him to consider other options like this.

'I've looked at a few things. I could go into one of the training schemes at the local general hospital. I have a lot of experience. The most natural places would be accident and emergency, general surgery or orthopaedics.' He held up his hands. 'I could even look into infectious diseases, but the nearest place for that is around thirty miles away. Or...' His voice tailed off.

'Or what?' She was incredulous. When had he had a chance to think about any of this—his career plans or the house?

'I could think about training as a GP. It takes a year, and would have better hours for me.'

'You could still work here.' Where had that come from? And even she could hear the edge of desperation in her voice. 'Not all the staff here are service personnel. There's a mix of NHS and army personnel throughout Waterloo Court.'

He met her gaze. It was the first time since they'd sat down. 'I don't know if rehab is for me, April.'

It was like a spear into her heart. She gulped. He wasn't talking directly about her, but he might as well have. This was the place she'd chosen to work. This was the career path she wanted. It didn't matter that only a few weeks ago she'd known in her heart that he wasn't really a rehab doctor. It was all right for her to think those things. It felt entirely different when *he* said them to her.

It was almost as if Riley was saying it wasn't good enough for him.

She stood up, letting the chair roll away behind her. 'Well, I guess that's all up to you, isn't it? I have patients to see in the other ward. Good luck.'

She stalked off, picking up her blue coat and shoving her arms into it, all the while trying to figure out why she really just wanted to cry.

Riley stared at April's retreating back. He wasn't quite sure what he'd just done.

He was only being honest. What was so wrong with that?

But part of him was uncomfortable. He hadn't meant to say anything that offended. But he was disappointed. He'd thought she'd be excited for him. Thought she might suggest talking over career plans with him. Maybe even suggest dinner. Instead she'd acted as if he'd just said he had the most infectious disease on the planet and made a run for it.

He shook his head. Since when had he got so bad at all the woman stuff?

Riley had never had problems getting dates. Never had problems with dating for a few months at a time. He might have had the odd few issues when he'd broken things off. But that had all been about his career. He didn't want long-term when he knew he was going to be away for months at a time.

He hadn't even got to the date stage with April.

Though there was no denying that was where he'd like to go.

In fact, he'd like to go a whole lot further.

He sighed, leaned back and put his hands behind his head.

What was he doing?

Was he crazy? She was gorgeous. She was fun when she wanted to be. She was sexy. She was sweet. She was great with Finn. But, most importantly, he'd found himself gravitating towards her more and more. He wasn't imagining things. There was a definite tug between them. April Henderson had well and truly buried her way under his skin.

And up until a few seconds ago that had made him happy.

For too long he'd focused his life on his job. Training as a doctor had taken all his energy; serving in the army had helped him focus. Moving around every six months had meant he was constantly meeting new faces and always learning to adapt. The medical situations were frequently frantic. Setting up in emergency situations was exhausting, and the long hours were draining. But for a long time Riley had thrived in that environment. He'd frequently been praised for his clinical care and cool head in a storm.

Thinking about a new career path was daunting. But since finding out about Finn he was just so anxious to get things right.

April pushed the door open, letting an icy blast sweep past him as she vanished out into the snow, and his heart gave a little tug. He liked her. He *more* than liked her. And that was so different from being attracted to her. At least it was in his head. Because that was the way he'd lived his life for the last twelve years.

So many things were changing. Was he changing too?

Finn flashed into his head. His laugh, his smile, the way he said the word *Dad*. All his energy right now should be focused on the little boy who needed him most. He didn't have room for anything else. But when he closed his eyes for a second Finn's face was replaced by the hurt expression on April's.

In an ideal world he would have liked it if she'd told him she loved the house and thought it was perfect. His stomach coiled. Perfect for whom?

'Stuff it!' he said out loud as he grabbed his jacket from the chair beside him.

The snow had picked up as he ran outside. The other ward was based on the other side of the courtyard, but right now he couldn't even see that.

He stopped. April hadn't made it to the other ward. She was standing in the middle of the courtyard, snow falling all around her. His footsteps slowed as he pulled on his jacket and walked over to her.

It was bitter cold. The snow was falling in thick flakes all around them. April had her hands at her throat, fingering her necklace, with hot, angry tears spilling down her face.

He cringed. No. He'd made her cry. And he didn't even really understand why.

'April? What's wrong? What is it?' He put his hands on her upper arms.

She tried to shake him off but he stayed firm. She shook her head. 'Nothing. Everything. I don't know!'

Her hair had loosened from her bobble and was straggling around her face. She looked so hurt. So desperate. This couldn't just be about him.

He took in a deep breath of the icy air. 'Talk to me, April. I'm right here. Just talk to me.'

She was shaking. She was actually shaking. He looked from side to side. 'Let's get inside. Let's get somewhere warm.'

She shook her head again. 'No. I don't want to. I need air. I need fresh air. I need to think straight.'

'What do you need to think about, April?'

This was killing him. He could see how upset she was, how much pain she was in. But he couldn't understand it.

'The house,' she breathed.

'You don't like the house?' He was confused.

Tears were still spilling down her cheeks. 'I love it.'

Now it was Riley who shook his head. 'April, you have

to help me out here. I don't understand what's wrong. I don't understand what you're so upset about.' His insides were churning.

His grip tightened on her arms. 'Why won't you talk to me? Why do you keep pushing me away?'

Her face crumpled and he couldn't stop the stream of thoughts in his head. 'Is it me? Is it Finn? Don't you like being around kids?'

She shook her head.

Exasperation was building.

'April, you're gorgeous. And even though you try to pretend you're not, you're a people person. Why don't you have a husband? Why isn't there a boyfriend? I bet you could have a string of dates if you wanted.' Now he'd started he couldn't stop. 'And don't tell me you're not interested.' He moved over to her so he was only inches from her face. 'I see it, April. I sense it. We don't need electricity for Christmas lights. There's enough between us to light up the whole house—a whole street. What's happened to you, April? What's happened that you won't let anyone get close to you? What's happened that you won't let *me* get close to you?'

She shook her head. He could sense her frustration. It almost equalled his. But she just seemed so determined to keep him shut out. 'Don't ask. Just don't. I don't want to talk about it.' The blue of her coat seemed to make her eyes even brighter. It didn't matter how cold it was out here, or how cold she pretended her heart was, he wouldn't move away from her. He couldn't move away from her. He'd never felt so connected to—and yet so far away from—someone.

He couldn't hide the wave of concern that swept over him, feeling instantly protective towards her. 'Are you hurt? Has someone done something to you?'

He reached up and touched her cheek. 'April? Tell me—I want to help you.'

She blinked. Several heavy snowflakes had landed on her eyelashes. Those blue eyes fixed on his. He'd never seen anyone look so beautiful. So vulnerable. So exquisite.

The urge that had been simmering beneath the surface since the first time he'd seen her, the one that had spent the last few weeks threatening to bubble over at any point, just couldn't stay hidden any more. Riley had always been an action kind of guy.

She wouldn't speak to him. She wouldn't tell him what was wrong and that meant he didn't know how to support her—what to say to make things better.

But sometimes actions spoke louder than words.

'April,' he whispered, 'please tell me you don't have a husband, fiancé or boyfriend hidden away somewhere.'

Her eyes widened. She shook her head. 'No. Why?'

'Because I have to do this again. I have to show you how I feel about you.'

He bent his head and kissed her. Her lips were cold. Her cheeks were cold. But it only took a few seconds to heat them up. April tasted exactly the way he remembered. Sweet. Pure. Exciting. Like a world of possibilities. And the perfect fit for him.

At first she didn't move. Then her lips gradually opened, her head tilting to allow their mouths to meld against each other.

He couldn't remember ever feeling a kiss like this. The tingles. The flip flops in his stomach. His hand slid from her soft cheek, tangling through her messy hair and anchoring at the back of her head. Her hands moved too. Sliding up around his neck. Her body moved closer to his.

It didn't matter that they were both covered by thick jackets. He could still feel her curves against his, sense the tilt of her hips towards him as her light floral scent drifted up around them.

In a way, being out in the snow was the perfect place for this kiss. They both loved Christmas. And there was nothing more Christmassy than snow.

Their kiss was deepening. It was almost as if he couldn't get close enough to her. To get enough of April Henderson. His brain was going to a million different places right now. Of course he wanted to know what was really going on with April. But kissing her had just seemed like the right thing to do.

The only thing that made sense to him. Her cold nose touched his cheek and he laughed, their lips finally parting. But he didn't want to part. And it seemed neither did she.

They stood for a few seconds with their foreheads pressing together as the snow continued to fall all around them. Their warm breath instantly steamed in the freezing air.

Riley couldn't help but smile. 'Should I apologise for kissing you?'

'Don't you dare' was the prompt reply, but after a second she gave a little shudder.

'What's wrong? Are you cold?'

She pulled back a little. 'I'm sorry, Riley. I can't do this.'

She was saying the words, but he could see the look in her eyes. It was almost as if she felt she *had* to say it, instead of wanting to say it.

'Why, April? Why can't you do this? This is the second time I've kissed you and the second time you've pulled back.'

She bit her lip. She lifted her hand to her necklace again. What was it about that charm?

'Is this about Finn?' Guilt started to swamp him. He was just coming to terms with being a father. His head was telling him he had to concentrate all his time and energy on that. And he would. Finn needed stability. Riley knew that. But April? She was just… April. How could he ignore what was happening between them?

She shook her head firmly. Sadness almost emanated from her pores. 'Oh, no. This could never be about Finn.' Tears glazed her eyes. 'He's perfect, Riley. He just is.'

'So what is it, then?'

She pulled a face. 'I'm going to say the corniest thing in the world. But, right now, it's just so true.'

He didn't speak. This was confusing him more by the second.

'It's not you, Riley. It's me.'

He let out an exasperated gasp. 'Oh, no. I'm not taking that.'

'There's so much you don't know.'

'Then tell me.' His voice was firm.

She was staring at him with those big blue eyes. 'My si-sister died,' she stuttered.

He stopped. It seemed an odd thing to say. 'I know that,' he said steadily. 'And I know this time of year is hard for everyone.'

She shook her head. 'My *twin* sister died.' Her hand was clasped around that charm.

It took him a few seconds. 'Your twin sister?'

She nodded.

'Identical twin?'

She nodded again.

It was cold out here—freezing. But Riley had the horrible sensation that he'd just been plunged into icy depths. Ovarian cancer. That was what she'd said Mallory died from. She'd mentioned she was young. She'd used the term 'unlucky'.

Twins. How much did he know about twins? How similar were their genes? Something clicked in his head. Her necklace. Two hearts linked together. He felt a wave of panic. 'April, do you have cancer?'

She shook her head. 'No. Well, I don't think so. Not yet.' Her voice sounded detached.

Thoughts were flooding through his brain. He'd seen the reports. It might not be his speciality but he couldn't miss the headlines from a few years ago about the famous actress. They were making discoveries about cancer all the time. But this was the one that had been given the most news coverage. 'April, do you have the gene?'

She let out a sob and he pulled her towards him. His brain was doing overtime. Trying to remember everything he'd ever heard. He could already guess that her statistics wouldn't be great.

There were thick flakes of snow on her blue coat. The outside of her was freezing. But he didn't care. He could feel her trembling against him. He hugged her even tighter and bent his lips to her ear. 'There's things that can be done. Have you seen someone? Have you spoken to a counsellor?'

Her words were low. 'I've done all that. I know my chances. My surgery will happen in the New Year.'

He pulled back, surprised, and put both hands on her face. He couldn't believe she'd been helping him so much while going through something like this.

'January? April, I had no idea. I'm so sorry. Why didn't you tell me?'

Another tear slid down her face. 'How do I tell someone that? How do I say, *Nice to meet you, but I'm a carrier of a potentially deadly gene, I'm going for surgery soon and I won't be able to have children.* I'm never going to get to be a mum. And maybe I won't even be here. The surgery isn't a guarantee. I might still go on and develop cancer at some stage. And yes, I have looked at all my options. It's all I've thought about for months.'

He lifted his thumb and wiped away her warm tear. He couldn't even begin to comprehend what she'd been going through. He'd been so focused on himself, and on Finn. He hadn't really left room for anything else. He hated himself right now. He'd known there was something he couldn't put his finger on. He should have pressed her. He should have pushed harder and let her share the burden, let her talk things over.

Her head was against his chest. 'I'm sorry. I didn't want to tell you. I didn't want to tell anyone. I need to get this over with. I need to have my surgery, get out the other side, then see what comes next. I just needed some time. I just needed a chance to—'

He pulled her back again. 'A chance to what? To be alone?' He shook his head. 'You don't need to do that. You don't need to be on your own, April.'

She sucked in a deep breath as she pulled herself free of his grasp. But he wasn't quite ready to let her go. He put his hands on her shoulders. 'But I do, Riley. This is hard. This—' she held up her hand '—whatever it could be, it just isn't the right time.' She met his gaze. 'And it isn't for you either. You have Finn to think of. You have to concentrate on him.'

'I know I do,' he had to stop himself from snapping. 'But Finn likes you. I like you. I don't want this to go away, April. I want to see what *this* is. I want to know.'

Her lips were trembling. She lifted her hand and put it over his. 'We both work in the medical profession. Let's be clear about this. I think I'm well right now. I hope I'm well. But until I have my surgery, and until I have my pathology report, we just don't know. What if I'm not okay? What if I'm riddled with cancer? You've just introduced me to Finn. He's lost his mum. He's a five-year-old kid who just had to stand at his mother's funeral. What kind of person would I be if I didn't consider Finn here?'

It was like a fist closing around Riley's heart. Protect. That should be his first parental responsibility. As much as he hated every word, she was making sense.

'I could be in an accident tomorrow, just like Isabel was.' They were the first words that came into his brain. He knew they sounded desperate. But that was how he was feeling right now.

She shook her head. 'I know that. But it's a cop-out. You need to give me some space. You need to spend time with Finn and leave me out of the equation.' She tipped back her head and let out an ironic laugh. 'I knew from the first second that I saw you that you'd be trouble. I tried so hard to stay out of your way—and it almost worked.'

Something swelled inside his chest. 'You did? You deliberately kept away from me?'

'Of course I did.' She was smiling as she shook her head.

'Darn it. I thought my spider sense had stopped working. I thought you didn't like me at all.' The pathetic thing was that her words gave his male sensibilities a real sense of pride. He hadn't imagined things. She'd felt the attraction as much as he had.

Her hand was still over his and he gave her shoulders a squeeze. His stomach was churning. He didn't know enough about this condition. He only knew the bare basics and statistics he'd heard in casual conversations with other professionals. All of a sudden he wanted to know so much more.

'I don't want you to be alone through all of this, April. Let me be your friend.'

Her voice was shaky. 'I don't even know if we should do that.'

'Why?'

She winced. 'Riley, you're buying a house. A beautiful family home. In a few years, once you and Finn are settled, you'll want to fill that house with more children. I can already see what a good dad you are. It's a steep learning curve. But you're getting there. And you will thrive doing this, Riley. You will.'

'And?' He didn't get where she was going with this.

Another tear slid down her face. 'And once I have the surgery, my ovaries are removed. My fallopian tubes are gone. I can't have kids of my own. I can't have kids with you. The option is gone. And I'm not going to change my mind about this. The disease is such a silent killer they haven't really found any reliable way to monitor for it yet. I can't live with a perpetual cancer cloud over my head. I won't. But I also don't want to take the chance of children away from you. Finn should have the chance to have brothers and sisters. At some point you'll want to fill that house with children, Riley, and I can't do that with you.'

He shook his head. 'You…we don't know any of that yet. And you must have thought about this. There's other ways to have kids. You must have considered that in your future.'

She pressed her hand over her heart. 'There is. And that's the option for me.' She lifted her hand and pressed it against his chest. 'But it doesn't have to be the option for you.'

There was so much swirling around in his head right now. He'd just had the best kiss of his life. A kiss that seemed perfect. A kiss that told him everything he thought he needed to know.

And now it seemed that kiss could result in a life he couldn't quite add up in his head. Finn had been a big enough shock. Families and kids had always seemed in his distant future. Filling a house with kids seemed a bit Neanderthal, but was he really willing to write all that off after a kiss? And what if April was sick or did get sick? What could that do to Finn? How much could one kid take?

April must have read all the confusion on his face. It was like watching a shield come down. A protective barrier.

'Concentrate on Christmas. Concentrate on Finn.' Her voice sounded tight.

He reached up to touch her cheek again but she stepped back. Her hair was coated with snow. She must be freezing right now. And even though his brain was telling him to take some time, to think about things, his heart was telling him something else entirely.

'And give me a little space at work,' she added.

His mouth opened to respond. He didn't want to give her space. But she held up her hand. 'Please, Riley.' She pressed her lips together. 'Now, I have work to do.'

She turned and headed off through the heavily falling snow to the other ward.

And left his broken heart somewhere out in the snow.

CHAPTER NINE

IT HAD FELT like the longest day in the world. She'd held it together as long as she could but as April walked into her flat and turned on the side lamp she felt exhaustion overwhelm her.

The mask she'd worn all day on her face finally slipped and the pent-up tears started to fall again.

Her Christmas tree was in the corner of the room. It was black with purple baubles and lights. When she'd bought it a few years ago black trees had been very avant-garde. But those days were long gone, and now it just felt a bit pretentious.

She sagged down onto the sofa. She'd loved this flat since she'd bought it after getting the job at Waterloo Court. But as she sat in the dimly lit room, watching the flickering purple lights and staring out into the dark night outside, for the first time it seemed so empty.

She'd always unconsciously smiled when she got back home. She'd felt warmth walking into her own place. She quite liked staying on her own. It was nice not to have to wrestle the duvet off someone else, or fight over the remote control.

Or was it?

A tear prickled in the corner of her eye. She'd been a twin. She *was* a twin. Mallory had been an integral part of

her. When they'd reached their teenage years both had chosen separate university and career paths. Both had created
their own circle of friends. But they'd still had each other.

That teenage resentment which had flared for around
five minutes had rapidly disappeared. They'd started to
appreciate each other more. Their university campuses had
been two hundred miles apart but April had spent more
time speaking to her sister on the phone than they'd spoken in the last few years sharing a room at home.

There were still mornings when she woke and, for a few
brief seconds, she thought her sister was still alive. Then
realisation hit all over again.

She couldn't pick up the phone and hear Mallory's voice
at the other end. She couldn't hear about her latest date.
The latest fight at work.

Mallory had left this life as she'd entered. With April
by her side.

April had climbed into the hospice bed alongside her
sister and just held her as her mother and father had sat
on either side.

April wiped the tear from her eye. She rested her head
back against the sofa. If only she could talk to her sister
about the genetic tests. The surgery. The family that she'd
always hoped for but would now never have.

Today, everything she'd kept tightly locked inside, everything she hadn't talked about to anyone but her parents,
had come bubbling to the surface.

Her finger touched her lips and she closed her eyes.

That kiss. For a few moments, a few seconds, things
had been perfect.

Life had been what it should be.

The gorgeous, sexy guy who had flirted with her and
teased her, tangled his way around her heart, had kissed

her in a way that had made every single part of her feel alive again.

Every nerve ending had sparked, lit up by the sensation of his lips on hers. It was better than she'd ever even imagined. And she might have imagined quite a bit.

But it had broken her heart more than she ever could have contemplated.

Her actions felt selfish. But she wasn't being selfish.

She didn't want to make promises to Riley that she couldn't keep. She had to be upfront. She had to be honest. She didn't want to form a relationship with the gorgeous man and little boy that could ultimately hurt them all.

She wanted him to be happy. She wanted Finn to be happy.

But ever since she'd met him she'd been so confused. Living in her own little box had seemed to simplify things for her. Gene testing. Decision. Surgery.

Then…

She pulled her knees up to her chest and hugged them tight.

She'd never felt so alone.

First Mallory. Then Riley. Now Finn.

Her stomach twinged again and she rubbed it to ease the pain.

Her mind was as foggy as the weather outside. And she just couldn't see a way through.

Finn was sleeping by seven o'clock. He'd said school was busy and he was tired.

Riley was distracted. He couldn't concentrate. His mind had been full of what April had told him.

He set up his computer and began researching.

He read and read and read. Everything he could find out about BRCA1 and BRCA2. Finding out the risks for twins was much more difficult. There was limited research.

BRCA1 genetic mutation was scary. April had mentioned something about a strong family history and, considering her sister had already died, he had to assume there had been some other ovarian cancer cases in her family too. There was also the added risk of breast cancers—although she hadn't mentioned that. At least for breast cancer, there was an evidence-based screening programme that could pick up early signs. Ovarian cancer was much more difficult.

The hours just seemed to meld together, his concentration only broken by some mumbles from Finn's room. He walked through. Finn seemed restless and Riley sat at the edge of the bed and stroked his hair. 'Hey, little guy, it's okay. Go back to sleep.'

'Dad,' came the muffled voice. He smiled at that. It warmed his heart. There would always be that tiny sense of resentment that he hadn't seen Finn get to this stage. When his mother had visited she'd voiced her opinion about Isabel's decision over and over once Finn had gone to bed. And he did understand, but it also made him appreciate how unhelpful that was.

'Is April here?'

Riley was jerked from his thoughts. He lowered his head down next to Finn's. 'What?'

Finn still looked as if he were sleeping. 'I miss April,' he murmured.

It was as if the little voice tugged directly on his heart. 'I miss her too' was his immediate response. He'd seen her today. He'd kissed her today. He'd held her today. And she'd revealed the deepest, darkest secret that she'd been keeping for so long.

It felt as if he'd failed her. Completely and utterly failed her.

The conversation kept playing back in his head but each time with different scenarios. He'd said something different; he'd done something different. He'd told her how much she meant to him. He'd told her he wanted to help her through all this.

His stomach curled again as he looked at his sleeping son. He was so peaceful. So settled. This might be the honeymoon period. The social worker had told him that Isabel's death could affect him in a whole host of different ways that might manifest over time.

He squeezed his eyes closed. What if the surgery wasn't soon enough for April? What if she was already sick and just didn't know it yet?

His hand kept stroking Finn's head. He felt physically sick now. Her risk of particular cancers was still higher. Getting rid of her ovaries and fallopian tubes would not be the all-clear. But it would reduce her risk of dying of ovarian cancer by eighty per cent. That was massive. After surgery, it would be about learning to manage the risks.

He wanted to be by her side. He didn't want her to go through any of this alone.

But what about his son?

He would be making a decision that could leave his son vulnerable. They could both put their hearts on the line, loving someone who could possibly be sick at some point.

It was a risk he was willing to take for himself, but could he really do that for his son?

He sighed and lay down next to Finn. There wasn't a parenting book in the world that would cover this one.

CHAPTER TEN

'IS THAT OUR new house?' Finn's voice echoed from the back of the car as they pulled up outside.

Riley wanted to smile. He did. Even from here he had a good feeling about this place. 'Yes, it is.'

Finn waved something from the back of the car. 'We still have to give this to April, Dad.'

Riley nodded. Finn had made a card at school for April yesterday. It had melted his heart and he just wasn't sure what to do with it.

'No problem. We'll do that later.'

He glanced down at the keys in his hand as his mobile sounded.

His mother had organised things with military precision. The sofa, beds, TV, fridge freezer, washing machine and dryer were all arriving in the next few hours. Money just seemed to have haemorrhaged from his bank account in the last few days. He looked down at the message. It seemed that the engineer would be here in the next hour to connect the Internet and cable TV.

He jumped out of the car and unclipped Finn's seat belt. 'Come on, little guy. Let's go pick a bedroom.'

The rest of the car was jam-packed with bedding, towels and kitchen paraphernalia. He hadn't even started trying to get their clothes together.

Finn skipped up the path. This was odd. In his head he'd sort of imagined April being next to them when this happened. The key turned easily in the lock and he pushed the door open.

He'd rented this place without even setting foot in it. But it seemed his instincts had been spot on. People always said you knew within thirty seconds if a house was for you or not; Riley didn't need that long.

They walked from room to room. After army housing the space just seemed enormous. Two people could never fill this place.

His stomach rolled. April's eyes appeared in his head. The sorrow in them when she'd mentioned this place and how she could imagine it filled in the future.

But although he could see it in a few years, filled with his touches and decorated the way he wanted, he couldn't imagine the anonymous wife that April could, or the nameless children. The only person he could see here was April.

She'd avoided him the last few days. He knew that. Of course he knew that. And even though she'd insisted he give her some space, his heart wouldn't really let him comply. He'd sent her a text. And left a phone message. Just saying he was thinking about her. Because he was. And Finn was too. Even if she didn't want to know that right now.

He didn't like this distance between them. Every cell in his body told him that it was wrong. But he wanted to respect her request. He didn't want to force himself and Finn on her if that wasn't something she could cope with right now.

Because this wasn't all about him.

The thought sent a memory shooting through him. April, saying almost those exact words to him when they'd sat in the coffee shop together. He hadn't understood at the time. He'd still been at that jokey, flirty stage then. It seemed like a lifetime ago.

Then there had been that kiss in the garden centre. The one where she'd told him it wasn't the right time.

She hadn't been talking about the garden centre at all. She'd been talking about now. Now was not the right time for April. Now he understood—even if he didn't really agree.

Finn ran up the stairs, darting from room to room. 'This one—no, this one. No, this one!'

Riley smiled. Finn could have any room he wanted. He walked through to the dining room that looked out over the back garden. A football goal—that was what he could put out there for Finn. The garden was much longer than he'd anticipated. A lawnmower—he'd need to get one. Something he'd never owned and never even considered. Thank goodness it was winter and the grass wasn't growing. The whole place was covered in snow and ice; it looked like something from a kid's book.

Somehow things just didn't feel right. He'd imagined April somewhere in this picture. But she'd made it clear she wasn't ready for that—and he was trying so hard to respect her wishes right now.

He sighed and turned back to the living room. The large sash windows with internal shutters were exactly what he'd expected in a house like this. His mother had even ordered blinds for the windows, but they wouldn't arrive until tomorrow.

His mother was doing better than he'd anticipated. He knew she wanted to be here—he knew she wanted to smother Finn. But, for once, she was listening. And giving her a range of tasks to do that would benefit Finn seemed to have played to her strengths. He was starting to appreciate her tenaciousness in a way he'd never imagined.

The previous owner had left a pile of wood next to the fireplace. It made him laugh as the 'living flame' fire was actually gas. He walked over and bent down to light it. It didn't matter that it was the middle of the day and the house was warm enough already. He needed some more heat. He wanted the place to seem more cosy. Because right now the emptiness echoed around him.

A white van with green writing pulled up outside. He smiled. Perfect. The most ridiculous thing to do first in the new house. He couldn't have planned it better.

'Finn, come on down! The Christmas tree is here,' he shouted. He'd persuaded the garden centre to delay their delivery until they arrived at the house. Sure enough, the guys were already bringing the boxes with the decorations to the door.

Finn squealed and ran down the stairs, throwing the front door wide to the world and letting the icy-cold air blast in around them.

Riley gave a nod to the delivery guys. 'Welcome to the mad house,' he said.

This was going to be a long, long day.

It was later than she expected. But the last few days April hadn't been in a hurry to get home from work. So she'd taken a few of the patients down to the gym for an extra session after dinner. They'd started an impromptu game of wheelchair basketball and she'd been dumped out of her chair on at least three occasions.

She knew she was safe. Riley wasn't working today. This was the day he got the keys to the house. The place that he and Finn would call home.

She wanted to be happy for him. It was a gorgeous

house. A perfect place. Her own flat paled in comparison. And she hated that, because she used to love it.

Her stomach gave yet another twinge as she righted the chair and shook herself down. 'That's it for me, guys. You've finished me.'

They laughed. The camaraderie in here was one of the best parts of the job. Everyone looking out for each other. She was sure if she shared with her colleagues her plans for surgery they would be more than supportive. Of course they would. But it was coming up to Christmas. She didn't want to have those kinds of chats. Maybe in the New Year when she knew her surgery date she'd start to tell a few people.

The guys left and she finished tidying up the gym before turning the lights out, grabbing her coat and heading for home.

The snow seemed to be heavier yet again. She pulled her hat down over her ears and fastened the top button on her coat.

Her stomach growled. Food. There was little in the fridge. Maybe she should get a takeaway? She groaned. She'd forgotten her purse today. She'd have to go home first and pick it up.

As she pushed her front door open, she almost trod on an envelope that was bright red with squiggly writing on the front. She picked it up. *ApRiL*. Her heart lurched. It was obviously a child's writing, a mixture of upper- and lowercase letters, and she could almost imagine Finn's tongue sticking out at the side of his mouth as he'd tried his hardest at writing. It couldn't possibly be from anyone else.

She blinked back tears as she pulled the handmade card out of the envelope. There were a few things stuck on the card. A silver foil star. A green, badly cut out tree along with something else in yellow she couldn't quite distinguish. Baubles were drawn at the edges of the tree in red pencil, and another wiggly blue pencil line snaked up the tree, representing the lights or the tinsel. Her heart gave a tug as she remembered the blue lights that he'd picked.

She opened the card.

To my fiend.
Love Finn

She laughed. She couldn't help it. She loved the fact he'd missed the R.

It was beautiful. It was sorrowful. She could imagine how long he'd taken to make this for her. But it was also joyful. She hugged the card against her chest, wishing it was both Riley and Finn.

She blinked back the tears as she walked over to her shelf and put Finn's Christmas card in front of all the others. It had pride of place for her. She wanted to look at it and remind herself what could be out there when she was ready.

Her stomach growled loudly again and she grabbed her purse, which was lying on her sofa. The walk to the main street only took a few minutes.

She loved the winter time—especially when the pavements were glistening and the trees were dusted with snow. The lamp posts glowed orange, bathing the rest of the street in a warm hue. Even though it was after seven, the hustle and bustle of Christmas shopping was alive and well on the high street. All of the shops had started opening late, enticing people to shop more and more.

Some of the takeaways already had queues but her eyes were drawn to the soft yellow lights from the old church. She smiled. From here it looked like the church from the Christmas village in the garden centre. There were sandwich boards on the pavement outside. *Christmas Cheer Dinner.* She'd forgotten about that.

She rubbed her hands together as she glanced at the queue outside the pizza shop. She'd been introduced to the Christmas Cheer Dinner last year by a colleague. The church members chose one night to make a proper Christmas dinner that everyone could attend and pay what they wished. It was really a charity fundraiser, allowing them to use the proceeds from that night to make an actual Christmas dinner for those in the homeless hostels on Christmas Day. She'd planned on eating at home, alone. It might be nice to eat amongst some other people and donate to the cause.

Her feet carried her into the church hall automatically. She smiled at a few familiar faces and joined the queue of people waiting for dinner. There was a choir from the local school singing some carols in a corner of the room, with a few playing instruments. She couldn't help but smile. Christmas was always all about the kids. The biggest tree she'd ever seen was in another corner, adorned with red and gold decorations, and small tea lights were on the window ledges beneath the stained-glass windows, sending streams of red, blue and green across the room.

The line moved quickly and she soon had a plate with a steaming-hot Christmas dinner and she stuffed a few notes into the collection pot next to the cutlery.

She looked around. There was a low hum of chatter amongst the people already eating dinner. Most of the tables were full, with only a few spaces here and there. The lights at the food dispensary were bright, but the lights in the hall were dim; the tables had flickering candles lining them, creating a more Christmas-like atmosphere.

She walked over to the table nearest the choir. It would be nice to hear the children sing as she ate.

'April!' came the shout.

She recognised the voice instantly. Finn was in the front line of the choir—how had she missed that cheeky face?—and he looked as proud as Punch dressed in his uniform of grey trousers and a red jumper. 'There's a space next to Dad. You can see me!'

April gulped and looked to where an excited Finn was pointing. Riley glanced up from his plate of turkey and gave her a half-smile and shrug. He'd texted and left her a message a few days ago but she hadn't responded. She'd spent the last two days timing her visits to wards to ensure they didn't coincide with his. But she couldn't keep doing this.

Her heart gave a lurch as she sat down next to him.

'Sorry,' he murmured.

'It's fine,' she said, giving Finn a wave. 'I had no idea he was singing with the choir.'

'Neither had I,' sighed Riley. 'I found the note in his school bag about five minutes after the last delivery guy left.' He gave a wry smile. 'Remind me in future that I need to check the school bag every day. There were four notes in there.'

April smiled as she tried not to look into those green eyes. It had only been a few days and she missed them—no matter how much she'd tried not to.

She picked up her knife and fork. 'I'd forgotten about the Christmas Cheer Dinner. I came last year too. Couldn't eat for about three days after it because the portions here are huge.' She glanced sideways. Riley's eyes were locked on hers.

'How are you?' he said quietly.

She broke their gaze and looked down at her food. 'I'm fine,' she said automatically. She paused. 'Thank you for the card. It was lovely. It was so thoughtful.' She looked up at Finn, who automatically gave her another wave.

'He missed you.' Riley's voice was hoarse. 'I miss you too.'

As she stared at her dinner her appetite started to leave her. She moved her knife and fork; it would be a shame to waste this lovely dinner. She didn't want to get upset. She'd come in here tonight because it felt like the right place to be. She wanted to help the charitable cause, and she wanted to surround herself with people who loved Christmas as much as she did.

She started eating. People around them were chatting easily. The kids started another song. One of the helpers came around and filled up all their glasses.

The words *I miss you both too* reverberated around her brain. She really, really wanted to say them. It felt honest to say them. But something still stopped her.

'How was the house move?' she asked quickly.

For a second it seemed as if Riley's face fell, as if he'd been waiting for her to say something else. But he gave a brief nod. 'Exhausting. I didn't know I could plumb in a washing machine, but apparently I can. I had to go and knock on a neighbour's door to get him to help me lift the TV onto the wall.'

'You bought one of those giant TVs?' She was smiling. She couldn't help it.

'Of course I did.' He gestured towards Finn. 'The cable and Internet guy arrived this morning. It's the first time I've ever paid for cable TV in my life. I was living in hope of endless nights of watching the sports channels, but it seems Finn has other plans entirely.'

She swallowed her food. 'He found the cartoon channels, didn't he?'

Riley raised his eyebrows and nodded, folding his arms

across his chest. 'Boy, did he. Do you have any idea how many kids' TV channels there are?'

She laughed. 'Oh, yes. I had an introduction the other night. We should compare lists.'

He met her smile. 'We should, shouldn't we?'

Their gazes meshed again. It was almost as if the world fell silent around them. The hum of voices blocked out. It was just him. And her. In the flickering candlelight.

Riley. The guy who had well and truly captured her heart. She couldn't deny it a second longer. She hadn't meant to fall in love. She absolutely hadn't. But it seemed that fate had other ideas for her.

And it wasn't just Riley she'd fallen in love with. It was Finn too. They were a package deal.

She'd never hated her genes more than she hated them now. Not even when they'd stolen her sister from her. The thought made her catch her breath.

She wanted to move on with her life. She wanted to feel as if she could plan for the future. Her fingers actually itched to pull her phone from her pocket and demand a surgery date right now. Once she'd had the surgery she might feel as if she could take stock. To sit down with Riley and talk about the possibility of a future together—if he still wanted that.

She'd seen the fleeting worry on his face when she'd mentioned Finn the other day. Maybe that worry had planted seeds and grown? If it had, there was nothing she could do. She'd never do anything to hurt Riley and Finn.

But, if that was the case, why was he telling her that he missed her?

She couldn't pull her gaze away from his. She wanted to stay right here, in this moment, for the rest of her life.

It was like being in a bubble. A place where no one was

under threat of being sick. Christmas was captured, Finn was happy and there was time just for the two of them. Why couldn't she just stay here?

Riley's hand closed over hers, sending a wave of tingles up her arm. 'This won't ever go away, will it?' she breathed, half questioning, half hopeful.

He lifted one hand and put it behind her head, pulling her closer to him. 'I don't want it to,' he whispered as his lips met hers.

It didn't matter that they were in the middle of the church hall. It didn't matter that people were on either side of them. It was just the simplest and sweetest of kisses. Nothing more. Nothing less. But it filled her with a warmer glow than any fire or candle could.

The music changed around them, a more modern tune bellowing from the speakers. Riley pulled back, smiling. 'Since when is "Jingle Bell Rock" a Christmas carol?' he asked.

She laughed and put her head on his shoulder, just taking a few seconds to breathe in his scent and remind herself what she was doing. Their little bubble had vanished. But she didn't mind. The kids had all been handed out tambourines and were banging away to their own beat. Riley pulled out his phone to video Finn for his mum. 'If I send her this it will keep her happy. She's coming down in a few days to apparently "sort the house out". I might come and hide at yours.'

He slid his arm around her shoulders as they watched Finn and his classmates singing. Tears glistened in her eyes. 'He's doing so well, Riley. He really is.'

'He'll do even better if he thinks you'll be around,' Riley replied. 'We both will.' He sounded so determined. So sure.

Her heart skipped a few beats. This was what she

wanted. It had just seemed so far away. So impossible right now.

She closed her eyes for a second and sent a silent prayer upwards.

Please let this be for real. Please.

CHAPTER ELEVEN

EVERYTHING FELT GOOD. Everything felt right.

It didn't matter that the house was still organised chaos. It didn't matter that he'd spent twenty minutes this morning trying to find one of Finn's school shoes. All that mattered was that he finally felt as if things were on the right track with April.

He'd made a few more casual enquiries about jobs. It seemed that the GP track would be the most viable for him, and the more he considered it, the more interested he became. All the clinics that he'd ever done in settings overseas had been walk-ins. It meant he'd had to deal with a wide range of different issues—a bit like GPs did here. Sure, there had been a whole host of area-specific complications, but it wouldn't be as big a jump as he'd first thought.

Finn had been so animated last night. He'd been so happy that April had watched him sing with the choir and when he'd finished she'd made a fuss of him. She hadn't gone home with them last night, but they'd walked her back to her flat and she'd given them both a kiss on the cheek.

It might not have seemed like enough. But it was enough for right now.

He looked around the ward again. April hadn't appeared yet today. He glanced at his watch. It was coming up to lunchtime. She must be at the other ward. He would go and find her and see if he could interest her in some lunch.

April hadn't walked home last night—she'd glided. At least that was what it felt like. When she'd finally gone to bed she thought it was just nervous excitement that meant she couldn't sleep. It didn't take long to realise it was more than that.

For the last few weeks she'd had weird occasional grumblings in her stomach. Sometimes it felt like indigestion, leaving her feeling nauseous and sick. She was used to having painful periods. Her doctor had put her on the oral contraceptive pill to help reduce her risk of ovarian cancer and also to help with her painful periods. But the period pain had continued. But this type of pain felt different.

She'd shifted around in bed all night, finally getting up to take some painkillers, then getting up an hour later to try to drink some tea.

It hadn't helped. She'd finally pulled on her uniform and gone into work as normal. But as the morning progressed, so did her pain.

John Burns had even commented on her colour as she worked with him. 'Hope you're not coming down with something. Last thing I need is a sickness bug. You're a terrible colour.'

She'd made her excuses and left, going to the ladies' bathroom and retching in the sink.

Her skin broke out in beads of sweat. But the beads of sweat were cold. She shivered as the pain swept through her abdomen again. She ran into the cubicle and sat down, bolting the door.

The sweating wouldn't stop. She could feel it running between her shoulder blades. But it was the waves of pain that were worse.

She put her head against the side of the cubicle as she doubled over in pain. Horror swept through her. Her stomach felt rigid.

Mallory's had been bloated. But she'd had a whole host of other symptoms. Unusual bleeding. Nausea. Pain in her abdomen, pelvis, back and legs. Indigestion. And a complete and utter feeling of exhaustion.

Now, she thought she might be sick again. Her stomach wasn't bloated. She hadn't had any strange bleeding, or pain in her back or legs. But she had felt nauseous a number of times over the last few weeks. There had also been niggling pains—nothing like today, of course.

But now she felt gripped with panic. She'd been so distracted these last few weeks. All because of Riley and Finn. They'd captured her attention. Made her less vigilant.

She'd had a few tiny thoughts when she'd felt the niggles of pain. But she'd been used to painful periods and just put it down to that. She hadn't been tired, or bloated, so it had seemed over the top to start panicking.

But right now she'd never felt pain like it.

She should never have kissed Riley. She should never have started to feel attached to Finn. What if she was sick? Riley had enough to cope with, learning to be a father. Finn didn't need someone to enter his life, then leave him alone again. He was just a kid. He didn't deserve that. A hot, angry tear spilled down her cheek.

She pushed herself up and opened the cubicle door again.

This was a hospital. It might not have an accident and emergency department, but it had enough doctors that someone would be able to take a look at her.

She tried to straighten up, but her abdomen didn't really agree.

Catching sight of herself in the mirror didn't help. There

were black circles under her eyes, only highlighted by the paleness of her skin.

She opened the door back into the corridor.

Riley was standing directly opposite, talking to someone in the corridor and showing them his phone. 'The pictures are great—the house looks fabulous.' The nurse smiled and gave him a nudge. 'And big. I take it at some point you'll be planning on using all those rooms?'

April froze and Riley gave a casual response. 'Yeah... maybe.'

She already knew it was time to walk away. She didn't want Riley and Finn to see her sick. But that? That was just the extra push that she needed.

Riley looked up. 'Hey, there you are. I've been looking for you. Want to go and get some lunch?'

She shook her head and did her best to walk in the opposite direction. She didn't even want to have this conversation. Her brain was so mixed up. Last night she'd been so happy. Things that had seemed out of her reach were right in front of her. She should have known it was too good to be true.

Why should she get to live the life that Mallory didn't? They'd come into this world together—maybe they should have gone out of it together.

Her head was swimming. She couldn't think straight. Irrational thoughts were filling her head.

'Hey—' Riley stepped in front of her '—is something wrong?'

He seemed to blur in her vision. His voice seemed far away, even though he was right in front of her. 'Go away, Riley. Go away. This isn't going to work. It was never going to work. I asked you to give me some space.' She stopped. The wave of pain made her want to double over again.

'April—' this time his voice was directly in her ear '—April, what's wrong?'

She shook her head. She couldn't do this. If she was ill, she didn't want Riley to feel as if he had to be around her. There was enough going on in his life. He didn't need a sick girlfriend, and she couldn't bear for him to see her the way her sister had ended up. A shadow of her former self, weak, emaciated, in constant pain and finally wishing her life away. It had broken April's heart. It had broken her mum's and dad's hearts. She didn't want him to stay with her out of duty or some kind of responsibility.

But, more importantly, she didn't want him to stay with her out of love.

That would break her heart as much as his and Finn's.

She had to walk away. She had to be strong and determined.

She pulled herself straight, willing herself to forget the waves of pain just for a few seconds.

'I'm sorry, Riley. We should never have got involved. It was wrong of me. It was wrong of you. Finn needs your full attention.' She took a deep breath. 'And I'm not sure if I could ever love someone else's son the way I should.' She hated those words. Every single one of them was a lie. But pushing Riley away now was so much more important than him feeling indebted to her when she finally got the diagnosis she was dreading.

Why hadn't her last lot of bloods shown the CA125 antigen? Why hadn't she acted sooner? Why had she wasted time?

Right now she was angry with herself. But she still cared about Riley and Finn. She didn't want them to have to take this path with her.

Riley's face was pale. 'April, what on earth are you talking about? What's changed between now and last night? Have I missed something?'

'No,' she answered abruptly. 'But I have. Let's just leave it. Let's just not take things any further.'

She was trying her absolute best to hold things together. She could see the hurt in his eyes. She knew this was really what neither of them wanted.

He grabbed hold of her arm. 'Wait a minute. You don't mean this.'

She met his gaze. 'You were just a distraction for me, Riley. A chance to not think about things. And, let's face it, I was just a distraction for you too. I can't give you what you want. We both know that.' She couldn't pretend that she hadn't heard those words he'd just said to the nurse.

Confusion swept over his face. He looked as if she'd just punched him in the chest. 'Finn,' he stuttered. 'You think you can't love Finn?' The cruel words had obviously stuck in his head. He looked shell-shocked.

'No. I can't.'

She pushed past him. She had to get out of here. She had to get away from him and find someone who could help her get to the bottom of this pain.

She walked as quickly as she could, her whole body shaking. Riley would hate her now, almost as much as she hated herself.

Maybe that was for the best.

She pushed open the door to the courtyard. The cold wind took the breath from her body just as another wave of pain hit.

The last thing she remembered was the white snow coming up to greet her.

Riley was stunned. At first he'd thought April was unwell. Her colour was terrible and she'd looked in pain.

But maybe he'd imagined it? Because when she looked directly into his eyes and told him she'd made a mistake and she couldn't love Finn it had felt like a knife stabbing through his heart.

This wasn't the woman that he knew. This wasn't the caring, compassionate and supportive woman that he'd spent time with over the last few weeks. The woman who had stolen his heart and helped him reassess his life. Nothing about this felt right. He loved her. He just hadn't told her that yet.

And it looked as if he wouldn't be telling her that now.

How on earth could he be with someone who proclaimed they didn't have the ability to love his son? They were a package. Nothing would come between them. He couldn't let it.

His feet were rooted to the spot as she walked away.

Finn. He had to focus on Finn. Maybe he just hadn't taken the time to get to know April properly. He'd been so caught up in being a good father to Finn, and acting on the attraction between them both, that he hadn't really taken time to step back and think about the future.

His breath caught in his throat. That was a lie. He *had* thought about the future. He'd contemplated the words that April had said to him about the possibility of being sick. He'd sat next to Finn and wondered if he should take things forward.

Guilt swept over him. Of course he had. But surely it was his duty to Finn to consider these things and how they might affect him? Was that really why he hadn't told April that he loved her?

It didn't matter that he'd pushed those thoughts aside. It didn't matter that even though he'd still been worried, the thought of not having April in their lives had seemed like a much more difficult concept than dealing with the fact she could get sick.

The truth was any one of them could get sick. Riley, Finn or April. Life was about taking risks. Taking the safe route could mean that he and Finn would miss out on so much more.

That was what he'd believed. That was what he'd thought after a long and sleepless night.

So why hadn't he just told her? That he and Finn wanted April in their lives full stop.

'Help!' The shout came from down the corridor. Riley started running. It was one of the domestic staff—she was holding the door open to the courtyard. Two of the nurses came running from the other direction. And then he saw her.

April. Her body crumpled in the snow.

And he didn't think he could breathe again.

CHAPTER TWELVE

EVERYTHING WAS WHITE. Everything was too white.

Fear gripped her. Was this it?

Then she heard a noise. A shuffle of feet.

She turned her head. A nurse gave her a smile as she pressed a button and made a BP cuff inflate around April's arm. April grimaced. She'd seen this done a hundred times but she hadn't realised it made your arm feel as if it were going to fall off.

After a few uncomfortable minutes the cuff released. She looked around. She didn't recognise this place. 'Where am I?'

'Arlington General.' The nurse gave her another smile. 'I think you managed to give your work colleagues quite a fright. They've all been camped outside.' She checked the monitor once more. 'I'm going to go and tell the surgeon you're awake. He'll want to come and chat to you.' The nurse went to leave then pointed to something on the bedside table. 'Oh, someone left a present for you.' She gave an amused smile. 'Apparently it's very important.'

The nurse seemed relaxed as she left the room. April tried to move in bed, letting out a yelp. Her right side was still sore, but this was a different kind of pain.

Had the surgeon removed her ovary? She let her hand slip under the covers to feel her abdomen. She had some kind of dressing on her right side. Why would he remove one, and not the other? Surely it was better to do both at once?

She looked from side to side. Her mouth was dry and she couldn't see any water. There was a buzzer at the side of the bed but she didn't want to press it. The nurse had just been in; surely she would come back soon?

Her eyes fell on the parcel. She frowned. It didn't have the neatest wrapping she'd ever seen. But at least it was close enough to reach.

Yip. It looked like recycled wrapped paper, along with half a roll of sticky tape. She peeled away at a small piece of the paper that had managed to escape the sticky tape frenzy. It was something soft—very soft—and pink that was inside.

Now she was intrigued. What on earth was that?

There was a noise at the door.

She looked up. Riley. He was nervously hanging around the door. He looked pale. He looked as if he might have been crying.

Tears welled in her eyes. What she really wanted was a bear hug. But she couldn't ask for that. She wanted to hug it out like she and Mallory used to.

'The surgeon is coming,' she said hoarsely. 'I'm not sure that you should be here.'

He glanced over his shoulder and stepped inside. 'I know that. But I had to see you. I had to know if you were okay.'

She pressed her hand on her stomach. 'I don't know, Riley. I have no idea if I'm okay.'

He nodded and hovered around the side of the bed. 'They wouldn't tell me anything. I mean, of course they wouldn't tell me anything. I know they've phoned your mum and dad. They're on their way.'

'They are?' Now she was scared. She was truly scared. They'd be coming down from Scotland in snowy weather. It probably wasn't the best idea, but if they were on their way, surely it only meant one thing.

The paper from the present crinkled in her other hand as it tightened around the parcel.

Riley glanced at the door again. 'It's from Finn. He said you needed it. He said it was important.' She looked down. She had no idea what it was.

'Riley, I...'

'Stop.' He moved forward and grabbed hold of her hand. 'I don't want you to talk. I just want you to listen.' She'd never seen him look so pale. 'I don't care what the surgeon tells you. Well, of course I care. But it won't change how I feel, and it won't change what I want to do.' He took a deep breath and paused. 'What I want *us* to do.'

She didn't even get a chance to respond.

'You're part of me, April. Whether you want to be or not. I know you said you need space. I know you said the timing isn't good for you. I didn't expect to find out I was a father and meet the woman I want to marry all in the space of a few weeks.' He held up one hand as he said the words. 'But too late. It's happened. And it's good. It's great. I can't pretend that it's anything else. I should have told you the other night. I should have told you at the Christmas Dinner. I don't know why I didn't. But I love you, April. Finn and I love you. Yes, things may be hard at times. Yes, we might take some time to get used to being a family. But I didn't believe you when you said you can't love Finn. I've seen it, April. I've seen it in your eyes. It's in every action you take, every move you make around him. You're good for him. And you're good for me.' He stopped talking for a second to catch his breath. 'Don't push us away. Don't. I am choosing to be part of your life. I am choosing for us to be part of your future. Whatever happens next, I want to be by your side. All you have to do is say yes.'

She couldn't breathe. How could this be happening?

Didn't he know what could lie ahead?

'You can't, Riley. You can't hang around. It's not fair.'

His voice became strong. 'What's not fair is meeting someone that you love and not being able to be with them. I want this, April.' He held up his hands. 'Whatever this may be, I want it.'

Tears pooled in her eyes.

He leaned closer. 'Tell me. Tell me if you love me and Finn. Be honest. If you don't, I can walk away. But I still won't leave you alone. I'll still be your friend. I'll still be around. But look me in the eye and tell me you don't feel the same way that I do.'

She felt her heart swell in her chest. Those green eyes were fixed straight on her. She could see the sincerity. She could see the strength. It was right there before her. His hand was still on hers. But he wasn't gripping her tightly. He was holding her gently, letting his thumb nuzzle into her palm.

She blinked back tears. 'I do love you, Riley. And of course I love Finn. But I just don't feel I've any right to. Not when I don't know what lies ahead.'

He bent forward and kissed her on the forehead then looked at their hands. 'Your hand in mine, April. That's the way we go forward. That's the way it's supposed to be.'

There was a noise at the door behind them. The surgeon cleared his throat and walked in. 'Everything okay in here?'

April nodded. Her mouth couldn't be any drier. She just wanted this part over with.

But as she waited to hear him speak she realised he didn't look the way she'd expected. He seemed almost jolly. The nurse came in too, holding a glass of water in her hand that she set on the bedside table.

He waved his hand. 'Chris Potter. I was the surgeon on call. You gave us quite a scare, lady.'

April swallowed. 'I did?'

He nodded and pointed to Riley. 'Okay to discuss things in front of your friend?'

Riley's grip tightened around her hand. 'Her fiancé,' he said quickly.

What? He'd just said what?

The surgeon didn't notice her surprise. He just carried on. 'It seems that you have quite a high pain threshold. Most people would have been at their GP's days ago with a grumbling appendix. You must have tolerated that for quite a few weeks. Unfortunately, you're one of the few that has gone on to develop acute appendicitis. Your appendix actually ruptured and you currently have peritonitis. You'll need to stay with us a few days for IV antibiotics. We need to ensure there's no chance of sepsis.'

It was like having an out-of-body experience. April was tempted to turn around to see if he was talking to someone else. Trouble was, she already knew the only thing behind her was a wall. There were no other patients in this room.

'My appendix?' she said quietly. Her brain was trying to process. And it was struggling. She hadn't imagined anything so...so—ordinary. Her mind had immediately gone to the worst-case scenario. There hadn't been room for anything else.

'Her appendix?' Riley said the words like a shout of joy. Then he must have realised how it looked and he tried to look serious again. 'So, that's it. Nothing else?'

The surgeon narrowed his eyes for a second, then nodded. 'I've seen your notes, Ms Henderson. I'm assuming you thought it might be something else?'

She nodded weakly.

He shook his head. 'Had we known about the grumbling appendix, then your gynaecologist and I could have arranged to do surgery together. Unfortunately, as it was an emergency, we didn't have your consent for any other procedure and your gynaecologist was unavailable. I'm afraid your other surgery will have to be scheduled as planned in the New Year. Another anaesthetic isn't ideal, but I didn't have any other option.'

'But…but you didn't notice anything suspicious?'

The surgeon sighed. It was obvious he understood her question. 'I'm not a gynaecologist. I'm a general surgeon, so it's not my speciality. But no, at the time, on the right side I didn't notice anything of concern. Nothing obvious, at least.'

It was amazing, the temporary relief she felt. Of course she knew things happened at a cellular level, but even the simple words 'nothing obvious' were almost like a balm. That, and the hand firmly connected to hers.

The surgeon gave a nod. 'So, at least another twenty-four hours of IV antibiotics. Then we can discharge you home on oral. I think you'll still be sore for a few days and, as I know you're a physio, I'd recommend you stay off work for at least six to eight weeks.' He raised his eyebrows. 'I know you healthcare personnel. Itchy feet. Always want to go back too soon.' He gave them both a wink. 'But those transverse abdominal muscles take a while to heal properly. I'm sure you both know that.'

He picked up her case notes and left. The nurse with him gave them a smile. 'I'll give you some time alone. April, your mum phoned. They're stuck in traffic but should be here in around an hour.' She picked up the observation chart and left too.

For a few seconds neither of them spoke. It was as if they were still trying to take the news in—to process it.

Riley's hand squeezed hers again. 'When can we breathe again?' he whispered.

She laughed, instantly regretting it as her stomach muscles spasmed in protest. She didn't quite know what to say. 'I guess now would be good,' she finally said.

Riley didn't hesitate. He leaned over the bed and gathered April firmly but gently, slipping his arms under her shoulders and hugging her loosely.

She was taken aback, but after a second slid her arms around his neck and whispered in his ear, 'What are we doing?'

He pulled back with a smile, resting his forehead against hers. 'We're doing something that a good friend taught me. And we're doing it in honour of someone else. We're hugging it out.'

Her eyes instantly filled with tears. 'Oh.' Now she really was lost for words. He'd remembered. He'd remembered the one thing she always did with her sister.

He moved and the paper on the gift crackled—it had been caught between them.

Riley picked it up. 'You haven't managed to open this yet. I think you should or I know a little guy who'll be immensely offended.'

She nodded, pulling at the paper again to try to uncover what the pink fluffy thing was. It took some tugging, finally revealing her prize. She pulled it free. 'Bed socks?' she asked in surprise.

Riley nodded. 'Finn said you have cold feet. He was very insistent.' He raised his eyebrows. 'I'm beginning to wonder if my son knows you better than I do.'

She laughed as she shook her head, struck that Finn had remembered. Then she frowned. 'You had bed socks?'

He shook his head. 'No, I had money. I just had to hand it over to Finn and let him spend it in a shop on the way here.'

She tried to push herself up the bed. 'Finn is here too?'

Riley nodded. 'Of course he is. Where else would he be?' He met her gaze again. 'We're family,' he said simply.

A tear slid down her cheek. Riley was proving again and again that he meant what he said. He was here. And she knew he'd still be here if she'd had a bad diagnosis instead of a good one.

Why was she trying to walk away from the two men who'd captured her heart?

She licked her lips and he lifted a glass of water with a straw, almost as if he'd read her mind. 'Here, the nurse left this for you. Take a sip.'

She took a sip of the water and closed her hand over his. 'We need to talk.'

He raised his eyebrows. 'Why do I feel as if I'm about to get into trouble?'

She smiled. 'Oh, because you are.'

He perched at the edge of the bed. 'Hit me with it.'

'You called yourself something when the surgeon was in. I don't think we've had a chance to talk about it.'

He nodded. 'Fiancé.' Then he bit his lip.

Riley Callaghan was actually nervous. It was the moment that she actually loved him most.

'I know it's soon. We can have a long engagement if you want. We can wait until after your surgery, and make sure that Finn is doing well, before we plan the wedding.' He squeezed her hand. 'But I want to let you know that this is it. This is it for me and Finn. We're yours, April Henderson. A package deal. And we'd like you to join our package. I love you, April. What do you say?'

She swallowed as a million thoughts swamped her head. Her heart so wanted to say yes. But she was still nervous.

'They think I'm clear, Riley. But what if I'm not? What if they find something—maybe not now, but later? What then, Riley? I don't want to put you in that position. I don't want to do that to you, or to Finn.'

Riley ran his fingers through his hair. 'How many times, April? How many times do you need me to tell you that I love you? That I accept the risks along with you. No one knows how long they have in this life. You don't know that, and neither do I. But I do know who I love, and who I want to spend the time I have on this earth with. That's you, April. It will only ever be you.'

She gulped as her eyes filled with tears.

He leaned his face close to hers. She could see every part of his green eyes. 'Tell me that you don't love me. Tell me that you don't love Finn. Tell me that you don't wonder about the life we could all have together.'

'Of course I do, Riley,' she whispered. She couldn't lie. Not when he was looking at her like that. Not when his love seemed to envelop every part of her.

He slid his hand into hers. 'We have a life. Let's live it, April. Let's live it together. You, me and Finn. This Christmas will be hard for Finn. But let's get through it together. You, me and him. Let's start something new. Let's create some memories together. As a family.'

She hesitated for the briefest of seconds as her heart swelled.

His eyes widened. 'Is that a yes?' Then he muttered under his breath, 'Please let that be a yes.'

She gave the surest nod she'd ever given. 'It's a yes,' she managed before his lips met hers.

EPILOGUE

It had taken hours, but Finn was finally sleeping. He'd crept back downstairs four times, asking if Santa had been yet, and each time Riley and April had laughed and chased him back upstairs.

But she'd just checked. He was now slightly snoring in bed, wearing his superhero onesie.

'At last,' groaned Riley as they flopped down on the sofa in front of the flickering fire. The tree with blue lights was in front of the main window, decorated with a mishmash of coloured baubles and topped with a golden star. April thought it was the most magnificent tree she'd ever seen. The decorations that they'd brought from Isabel's house had joined the new ones on the tree. It was just the way it should be—a mixture of the past and the present.

It had been a big day. She'd lived here since her discharge from hospital. Riley had insisted, and it had felt right. But today Finn had experienced a bit of a meltdown. She'd found him crying in the morning as the whole momentum of Christmas just seemed to overwhelm him. 'I miss my mum,' he'd whispered.

'I know, honey,' she'd said as she hugged him. 'I miss my sister too. But I think I know something we can do today that will help.'

Riley had been in complete agreement and they'd all gone shopping together in order to find something appropriate for Finn to take to his mother's grave. In the end he'd picked an ornament in the shape of a robin with a bright red breast. It was perfect. And they'd taken him to the cemetery and let him talk to his mother for a while and leave her the gift.

His mood had seemed easier after that, and April had gone and bought flowers to leave at her sister's grave too. 'We need to make this a tradition,' Riley had said quietly in her ear. 'Not a sad one for Christmas Eve, more like a chance to take five minutes to acknowledge the people who aren't here and are missed.'

And she agreed completely. It was something they would do together every year.

Now, it was finally time to relax. The presents were wrapped and under the tree, along with a tray with carrots, milk and mince pie for Santa. 'Better remember to eat that or there will be questions asked in the morning.'

April sighed. 'I've never been fond of carrots. Maybe we can hide it back in the fridge?'

Riley looked a bit odd. He stood up and walked over and picked up the littie tray. 'I think Finn counted them earlier; we'd get found out.'

He sat back down on the sofa next to her and put the tray on her lap. He then knelt under the tree and added a couple of small red parcels. April tilted her head and looked at the tray. 'I think in future years, if I'm consuming what's on the tray for Santa, we'll have to negotiate its contents.'

'What does that mean?'

She grinned. 'It means that I think Santa might prefer a glass of wine and some chocolate cake.'

He nodded slowly. 'Why don't we just take things as they are right now?' He nudged her. 'Open your presents.'

She lifted the first one and tugged at the gold ribbon around the red glossy paper. She let out a gasp. It was the most perfect Christmas ornament she'd ever seen. A replica of her necklace. Two golden hearts joined together.

'Where on earth did you get this?' Her voice cracked slightly.

He smiled. 'I got it made for you. Do you like it?'

She nodded as she tried not to cry. 'I think it's perfect,' she sniffed.

He nudged her again. 'Open the next one.'

She smiled. 'I thought I was supposed to wait until Santa visited?'

He sighed. 'I'm far too impatient to wait for Santa.'

She pulled the ribbon on the second present. The paper fell away to reveal the church from the Christmas village. She felt her heart swell in her chest.

'I bought it for you after the Christmas Cheer Dinner. I wanted to remember how perfect that night was. And I thought we could add it to our collection.'

She hugged him. The way he said *our collection* just seemed perfect.

His face looked serious for a second. 'Now, other traditions. It's time to eat the contents of the Christmas tray.'

She looked at him strangely and picked up the mince pie, taking a nibble. He kept watching her with those green eyes. When she finally finished she licked her fingers then picked up the carrot with her other hand. 'So what am I supposed to do with this?'

The carrot gave a wobble in mid-air then fell apart, one part bouncing onto the floor, the other part staying in her hand with something glistening at its core.

'What…?' she said as she turned it towards her.

She wasn't seeing things. There, somehow stuck inside

the carrot, was a gold band and a rather large sparkly diamond. She turned back. Riley was sitting with the biggest grin on his face.

'Oh,' he said quickly. 'This is my cue to move.' And he did, moving off the sofa and onto the floor in front of her.

He took the carrot from her hand and gave the ring a little tug. 'Just so you know, the story is that Finn thinks Rudolph will leave the ring for you once he finds it.'

'He will?' She was mesmerised. She hadn't expected it at all. Sure, he'd called himself her fiancé in the hospital. But he'd talked about next year, after her surgery was completed, for making future plans.

Riley held it out towards her. The diamond caught the flickering light from the yellow flames of the fire, sending streams of light around the room. 'April, I love you with my whole heart. Even though you tried to avoid me, time and time again, I felt the pull from the first time we met. I know I haven't sorted out my job yet. I know we've still to get through your surgery. But I can't imagine a future with anyone but you. I don't *want* to have a future with anyone but you. I know it's soon. I know some people might think we are crazy. But will you marry us, April?'

Her heart gave a pitter-patter against her chest. Could she ask for any more?

She bent forward and slid her hands up around his neck. 'Now, this is what I call a proposal.'

He pulled her down onto his knee. 'Can I take that as a yes?'

She put her lips on his. 'You absolutely can.'

And there it was. The best Christmas *ever*.

* * * * *

SNOWBOUND WITH
AN HEIRESS

JENNIFER FAYE

For Tonya.

Thanks for being there from the beginning…
I am thankful for our friendship and your
unending encouragement. :)

CHAPTER ONE

PEACE AT LAST...

Serena Winston paused along the snowy path. Out here in the beauty of the Alps, it was so quiet. She lifted her face up to the warmth of the sun just seconds before it disappeared behind a dark cloud. Shadows quickly spread over the mountainous region of Austria.

She sighed. The sunshine had been so nice while it lasted, but the snow was starting to fall again. But she had to admit that the snowflakes had their own charm as they fluttered to the ground. It was so different from her home in sunny Hollywood.

"Arff! Arff!"

"Okay, Gizmo." Serena glanced down at her recently adopted puppy. "You're right. We better keep moving."

There was already plenty of snow on the ground. Serena's fondest wish had always been to learn to ski, but for one reason or another, she'd kept putting it off. First, it was due to the worry of injuring herself before filming a movie. Being an actress did have its drawbacks. And then, there just wasn't time to jet off to Tahoe for a long weekend of skiing—especially now that she'd inherited her legendary father's vast estate. Selling off some of his holdings was more complicated than she had anticipated.

Realizing the direction of her thoughts, she halted them.

She drew in a deep, calming breath. This holiday excursion was meant for escaping her daily pressures and refocusing her Hollywood career. There was yet another reason for this spur-of-the-moment trip, but she didn't want to think about it, either. There'd be time for problem-solving later.

When she glanced back down at her teddy bear dog, she found he'd wrapped his lead around a bush. The easiest way to fix the situation was to release Gizmo from his lead. It was no big deal. Gizmo was not one to wander off.

Serena unhooked the lead. "Stay," she said firmly.

Gizmo gazed at her as though understanding what she'd said. He didn't move a paw.

"Good boy."

Serena set to work untangling the leash from the prickly shrubbery. It wasn't an easy task. What had Gizmo been doing? Chasing something?

At last, she freed the leash. She'd have to be more careful about letting him out on the full length of the lead in the areas with rougher terrain.

"Arff! Arff!"

She watched as her little dog took off in hot pursuit after a brown-haired creature. "Gizmo! Stop!"

Serena ran after the dog. She continued calling his name, but he paid her no heed. For a little guy with short legs, Gizmo could move swiftly when he was motivated enough. And right now, he was very motivated.

Serena wasn't familiar with the terrain, as this was her first visit to the small village nestled in the Austrian Alps. This area had been on her bucket list to visit right after Fiji and right before Tasmania. With her rush to leave Hollywood, it seemed like the right time to scratch another adventure off her list.

The snow grew heavier. Between the snowflakes and trees, she spotted a road ahead. And though it appeared to be a quiet road, the thought of little Gizmo being anywhere near it had Serena pumping her legs harder and faster.

"Gizmo—"

Serena's foot struck a tree root. Down she went. *Oomph!*

The collision of her chest with the hard, frozen ground knocked the air from her lungs. She didn't have a chance to regroup before she heard the sound of an approaching vehicle. With each heartbeat, the sound was growing closer.

Ignoring her discomfort, Serena scrambled to her feet. "Gizmo! Here, boy."

She continued after the little furbaby who'd captured her heart a few months ago. At first, she hadn't been so sure about owning a dog. Gizmo was full of puppy energy and in need of lots of love.

But now she couldn't imagine her life without him. Gizmo made her smile when she was sad and he made her laugh when she angry. Not to mention, he got her up and moving when she thought she was too tired to take another step. He was there for her unlike anyone else in her life.

It wasn't like Gizmo to take off and not listen to her. She supposed that between the long flight from the States and then the intermittent snow showers that they'd been cooped up inside for too long.

The blast of a horn shattered the silence.

It was followed by the sound of skidding tires.

A high-pitched squeal confirmed Serena's worst fears.

Her heart leaped into her throat as she came to a stop.

A loud thud reverberated through the air. And then the crunch of metal sent Serena's heart plummeting down to her new snow boots.

A whole host of frantic thoughts sprang to mind. They jumbled together. The immobilizing shock quickly passed and she put one foot in front of the other. All the while, she struggled to make sense of the tragedy that undoubt-edly awaited her.

As if on autopilot, she cleared the overgrown path. She scanned the quiet road. Her gaze latched on to the back end of a dark sedan. Inwardly she cringed.

And to make things worse, there was no sign of Gizmo.

Or maybe that was a good thing. She was desperate to cling to any sense of hope. She held her breath and lis-tened for a bark—a whimper—anything. There were no puppy sounds.

Please let Gizmo be safe.

Steam poured out from the engine compartment of the crashed vehicle. The driver's side was bent around a clus-ter of trees. Serena's mouth gaped. Was that the reason Gizmo didn't respond? A sob rose in her throat. Was he pinned in the wreckage?

Tears pricked the back of her eyes. *Please, say it isn't so.*

Moisture dampened her cheeks. She swiped at the tears. For a normally reserved person who only cried on a di-rector's cue, Serena wasn't used to a spontaneous rush of emotions. Realizing she couldn't just stand there, she swallowed hard and then moved forward, wondering what she would find.

On legs that felt like gelatin, she moved across the road. Realizing the driver's-side door was pinned by a tree trunk, she approached the passenger side and yanked open the door.

A snapping and popping sound emanated from the car. Serena didn't even want to imagine what that might be. Still, she glanced around for any sign of fire.

Not finding any flames, Serena knelt down to get a bet-ter look. There in the driver's seat was a man with dark brown hair. His head was leaned back against the seat. His eyes were shut. His dark lashes and brows gave his face a distinctive look. There was something familiar about him, but in her frantic state, she couldn't make any connections. Right now, she had to get this man to safety in case his car went up in flames.

Even though she'd played a nurse once in a movie, she didn't know much about first aid. The movie had been a stalker/thriller type. The medical aspects were minimal. She reached for the cell phone in her back pocket. She pulled it out, but there was no signal. This wasn't good— not good at all.

"There…there was a dog…"

The deep male voice startled Serena. His voice wobbled as though he was still dazed. She glanced up to find a pair of dark brown eyes staring back at her. Her heart lodged in her throat. Was it wrong that she found his eyes intriguing? And dare she say it, they were quite attractive. They were eyes that you couldn't help staring into and losing yourself.

The man's gaze darted around as though trying to figure out what had happened. And then he started to move. A groan of pain immediately followed.

"Stop," Serena called out. "Stay still."

The man's confused gaze met hers. "Why? Is there something the matter with me?"

She could feel the panic swelling between them. "I'm not sure." She drew in a calming breath. Getting worked up wouldn't help either of them. She drew on her lifetime of acting. "I don't know the extent of your injuries. Until we know more, you shouldn't move." Which was all well and good until the car caught fire. But she could only deal with one catastrophe at a time. "I'm going to call for help."

"You already tried that. It didn't work." His voice was less frantic and more matter-of-fact.

She swallowed hard. So he'd seen that. *Okay. Don't*

freak out or he'll panic. Without a cell signal, their choices were diminishing. And the car was still popping and fizzing. She didn't want to tell this injured man any of this. Nor did she want to admit that the dog that created this horrific event was hers. The backs of her eyes burned with unshed tears. And that her poor sweet puppy could very well be—

No. Don't go there. Focus on getting this man help.

The man released his seat belt. The only way out for him was to crawl over the passenger seat. But he shouldn't be moving around until a professional looked at him.

"Don't move," she said as he pushed aside the seat belt. "I'll go and get help."

"I'm fine." His voice took on a firm tone.

He was sounding better, but it could just be shock. What if he got out of the car and collapsed in the middle of the road? She certainly couldn't lift him, much less carry him. Even with him being seated, she could see that he was over six feet tall and solidly built. Why did he have to be so stubborn?

The man leaned toward the passenger seat.

"I'm serious. You shouldn't be moving." She swiped her hair out of her face. It was wet from melting snowflakes. It was coming down so hard that she couldn't see much past the other side of the road. "You could make your injuries worse."

As though transforming her concerns into reality, he groaned in pain. Serena's heart lurched. She automatically leaned forward, placing a hand against the man's biceps, helping to support him.

"What is it? What hurts?" Her gaze scanned his body looking for blood or any possible injury, but she didn't spot any.

His breathing was labored. "It's my leg."

"What's wrong with it?"

"I can't move it."

Not good. Not good at all.

And as if matters weren't bad enough, a white cloud billowed out from under the hood. Her heart pounded. What was she supposed to do now?

CHAPTER TWO

SERENA CRAWLED OVER the passenger seat, making her way to the driver's side. "We have to get you out of here. Quickly."

"Don't worry," the man said. "It's just steam."

She wanted to believe him. She really did. But she wasn't sure if the man was totally lucid. For all she knew, he could have a head injury or be in shock or both.

She refused to abandon him. She prayed the car didn't explode into flames before she freed him. With the man slouched over, he was in her way.

With her hand still on his shoulder, she pushed with all her might. He didn't budge. The man was built like a solid rock wall.

"I need you to sit up," she said.

"What?" His voice was a bit groggy. His gaze zeroed in on her. "What are you doing?"

"I need you to move so I can see what's going on with your leg."

"You don't know what you're doing. You're going to make it worse. Go away!"

His harsh words propelled her back out of the car. What was up with this guy? Maybe it was the shock talking.

"I'm trying to help you. Now quit being difficult."

She took a calming breath and knelt down again. "Move! Now!"

The man's dark brows rose.

It appeared her brusque words had finally gained his full attention. The man muttered something under his breath. At last, he started to move. He was almost upright when he let out a grunt of pain.

"Is it your leg?"

He nodded as he drew in one deep breath after the other.

She glanced between him and the dash. There just might be enough room for her to wiggle in there. It'd help if she had a flashlight. And then remembering her cell phone, she grabbed it from her pocket and turned on the light.

Her gaze met his. "I'm going to try not to hurt you, but we have to free your leg. Can you work with me on this?"

The man's eyes reflected his uncertainty, but then he relented with a curt nod. "Just do it. And quickly. I smell gas."

He didn't have to tell her twice. On her stomach, she moved across the butter-soft leather upholstery. When she got to the man's body, she did her best to focus on the task at hand and not the fact that when she placed a hand on his thigh, it was rock hard. The man was all muscle and— and she had work to do. At last, she was wedged between him and the dashboard with barely any room for her to move her arms.

"Can you move the seat back?"

His body shifted. "It's not working. The electrical system must have shorted out."

"Okay. I've got this."

She had to get this man free of the car and then find out what had happened to Gizmo. Her poor sweet furbaby could be hurt or worse—

Stop. Deal with one problem at a time.

Hands first, she repositioned herself. She flashed the light around. The side of the car had been smashed inward. His ankle was pinned between the car door and the brake pedal. It looked bad—real bad.

Serena drew in an unsteady breath, willing herself to remain calm when all she wanted to do was run away and find someone else to help this man. But there wasn't time for that. She could do this. She could. Serena placed her hand gently on his leg and paused. When he didn't cry out in pain, she proceeded to examine the situation. She ran her hand down his leg, checking for any major injuries. She didn't feel any. There was no wiggle room on either side. The brake pedal was digging into his flesh.

Knowing that she was going to need two hands, she held up the phone to him. "Can you hold this for me?"

He took the phone. The light was angled too high.

"Tilt it a little lower. I'm going to try to move the brake pedal. Are you ready?"

"Yes. Just do what you need to do."

Serena pressed on the brake. The pedal became stuck on his black leather dress shoe. She tried moving his foot, but it wouldn't budge.

She felt his body stiffen. Serena released his foot. He was really pinned in there. And it frightened her to know that she might not be able to free him before the car went up in flames.

She swallowed hard. "I'm going to take off your shoe and see if that will help."

"Do what you need to do. You don't have to keep updating me."

Just then she inhaled the scent of smoke. Her pulse quickened. They were almost out of time. And this wasn't the way she planned to leave this world.

Her fingers moved quickly. The shoe tie pulled loose.

He cursed under his breath.

She stopped moving. "Sorry."

"Don't be sorry. Keep going."

"But I'm hurting you."

"It's going to hurt a lot more when that fire reaches us."

"Okay. Okay. I've got it. I'll try to do this as quickly as possible."

"Do it!"

The melting snow on the top of her head dripped onto her nose. With her arm, she brushed it off. All her focus needed to be on freeing this man, and in essence herself, from this smashed-up, gasoline-leaking, smoldering car.

Serena once again worked to free his shoe from his foot. It didn't move easily and she suspected he had a lot of swelling going on. She reminded herself to focus on one problem at a time. However, at this moment the problems were mounting faster than she could deal with them.

The smoke caused her to let out a string of coughs.

"Are you okay?" Not even waiting for her answer, he said, "You should get out of here."

"Not without you."

When she moved his foot again, she heard the distinct hiss of his breath. He didn't say anything and so she continued moving his foot. At last, his foot slipped past the brake pedal.

She pulled back. "You're free."

There was perspiration beading on the man's forehead. It definitely wasn't hot in the car. It was more like freezing. Her maneuvering his foot must have hurt him more than he'd let on. She felt really bad adding to his discomfort, but she had no other way to free him.

"Now," she said, "let's get you out of here."

She eased out of the car and attempted to help him, but he brushed her off. The smoke was getting heavier.

"I've got it," he said. "Just move away from the car."

"Not without you." She stood just outside the car.

"Quit saying that. Take care of yourself."

She wasn't backing away. If he needed her, she would be there. The popping and fizzing sounds continued. Her gaze darted to the hood where the smoke was the heaviest. Her attention returned to the man.

Hurry. Please hurry.

She wondered how bad the damage was to his left leg. It suddenly dawned on her that he most likely wouldn't be able to walk on it. But what choice did they have as they were stuck in the middle of nowhere. It was becoming increasingly obvious that no one used this road—at least not in the middle of a snowstorm. And who could blame them, she thought, glancing around at the snow-covered roadway.

Right now, she just wanted to find Gizmo and head back to the cabin. *Gizmo.* Where was he? Her heart clenched with fear. *Please let him be safe.*

It took her assistance to get the man to his feet. Or in his case, his one good foot. He'd finally had to relent and lean on her shoulder. Between hopping and a bit of hobbling, she got him to the other side of the road, a safe distance from the car.

"Thank you," he said. "I don't know what I'd have done if you hadn't come along."

"You're welcome."

"My name's Jackson. What's yours?"

In the daylight, she recognized him. The breath hitched in her throat. He was trouble. Make that trouble with a capital *T* and an exclamation point. He was Jackson Bennett— the god of morning news. She turned away.

He was on the airwaves for three hours each morning in American homes from coast to coast. People quoted him. And quite often his name trended after a particularly stunning interview.

The producers of his show had been in contact with her agent a few times to set up an on-air interview, but each time the logistics hadn't worked for one of them. She couldn't be more grateful about that now. Still, she couldn't breathe. There was a definite possibility that he'd recognize her.

This was not good. Not good at all.

In her mind, he was the enemy—the press. All of her carefully laid plans were in jeopardy. She was surprised he hadn't recognized her already. Would her different hair color and lack of makeup make that much of a difference? She could only hope. After all, who came to the Alps and expected to run across an award-winning movie star from the States?

Regardless, there was no way she was voluntarily outing herself. She'd worked too hard to flee the paparazzi and everything else related to Hollywood, including her agent. It was best that she kept their encounter brief. Not only was she over men, but Jackson was a professional newsman. With enough time, he was bound to sniff out her story.

"Mae. My name's Mae." It wasn't a lie. It was her middle name.

"Mae?" He gazed at her as though studying her face. "You don't look like a Mae."

Oh, no!

"Who do I look like?" The words were out before she could stop them. She wanted to kick herself for indulging in this conversation that had a distinct possibility of blowing up in her face.

He continued to study her. "Hmm… I'll have to give that some thought."

There was a large rock nearby. She brushed off some

of the freshly fallen snow. "Sit here and wait. I'll be right back."

"Where are you going?"

Gizmo's name clogged in her throat. She'd never be able to get the words out. She swallowed hard. "I... I have to check on something."

"It's too late to save the car."

She turned to find fire engulfing the hood. If Gizmo was there—if he was trapped—she had to help him. Serena quickly set off for the car, before she could talk herself out of her plan.

Jackson was shouting at her to stop, but she kept going. She would be careful—as careful as she could be. She could feel Jackson's gaze following her. She didn't care what he thought. If Gizmo was hurt and needed her, she had to help him.

Serena rushed through the thickening snow to the car. She carefully made her way down over the small embankment. All the while, she kept an eye out for any sign of her buddy. Between the snow and the wind, there was no sign of his little footprints.

With great trepidation, she turned toward the place where the car was smashed against the trees. Could he be in there?

She rushed over and bent down. She reached out to sweep away the snow from around the front tire, but for the briefest moment, she hesitated. Her whole body tensed as she imagined the ghastly scene awaiting her.

She gave herself a mental shake. With trembling hands, she set to work. And then at last, most of the snow had been swept away. There was no Gizmo. She took her first full breath. It didn't mean he was safe, but it was a good sign. And right about now, she'd take any positive sign possible.

She turned in a full circle, searching for him. She even

ventured the rest of the way down the embankment. There was no sign of him. The crash must have spooked him. How far had he run? And how long would he last in the extreme conditions? She repeatedly called his name.

Between the thickening clouds and the heavy snow, visibility wasn't great. With the deepest, most painful regret, she realized she couldn't help Gizmo. A sob caught in her throat. The backs of her eyes stung. She couldn't fall apart—not yet. She had to get Jackson to safety and then she'd return to continue her search for Gizmo. The car continued to smoke and smolder, so she scooped up some armfuls of snow and heaped them on the hood, hoping to douse the flames. She then moved to the side of the car and, catching sight of a bag in the back seat, she retrieved the large duffel bag.

She returned to the rock where the man was still sitting. "I need to get you out of this weather."

"What were you doing?"

"What are you talking about?"

"Just now. You were searching for something." And then his eyes widened. "That dog. He's yours."

Once more her eyesight blurred with unshed tears. She blinked repeatedly. She nodded.

"It almost killed me." The man's deep voice rumbled.

Serena's chin lifted and her gaze narrowed in on him. "And you might have very well killed him."

As though her pointed words had deflated him, the man had the decency to glance away. His anger immediately dissipated as the gravity of the situation sunk in.

"Are you sure?" he asked. "I tried to miss him."

"I called him and I searched around, but I didn't find any sign of him."

"And just now, when you returned to the car, were you looking under it for your dog?"

She struggled to keep her emotions in check. She nodded. It was the best she could do.

"I'm sorry." His tone softened. "I'd never intentionally hurt an animal."

"It's not your fault. It's mine. I let him off his leash. I should have known better."

"Maybe he's okay. Maybe he got lost."

She shook her head, wishing Jackson would be quiet. He was attempting to comfort her, but it wasn't working. Aside from seeing Gizmo alive and healthy, nothing would soothe her pain and guilt.

She couldn't let herself think about Gizmo any longer. She had to take care of Jackson. And the way he was favoring his leg, there was no way she would be able to get him back to her cabin without a little help. Her cabin was a ways from here. And it was situated in a secluded area. That was why she'd chosen it. It was far from prying eyes and, most important, the press.

But now, well, the location wasn't ideal to obtain medical aid. But she was certain that once she got ahold of the rescue services, they'd send someone to get Jackson medical treatment.

With her thoughts focused on getting help, she turned to Jackson. "I have a place. But I think you're going to need some help getting there."

"I'll make it." He stood upright. He'd barely touched the ground with his injured leg when his face creased with obvious pain.

"Are you ready to concede now?"

His gaze didn't meet hers. "What do you have in mind?"

"I'm going to look for a tree branch that you can use as a cane. Between my shoulder and the tree branch, hopefully we'll be able to limp you back to the cabin."

"Cabin?"

"Uh-huh. Is that a problem?"

"Um. No. I won't be there long."

A smile pulled at her lips at Jackson Bennett's obvious disapproval of staying in a cabin. He had absolutely no idea that it was a two-story log home with just about every creature comfort you could imagine. But Jackson was right about one thing: he wouldn't be staying with her for long. Once she had phone service, he'd be on his way to the hospital and out of her life.

CHAPTER THREE

"ARFF!"

Jackson Bennett glanced around. Was it possible that the dog the woman was so worried about had been un-harmed? He hoped so.

He squinted through the heavy falling snow. Where was the dog? Maybe if he caught it, he'd be able to pay the woman back. They could part on even terms. He hated feeling indebted to anyone. If only he could locate the source of the barking.

"Arff! Arff!"

He glanced around for some sign of Mae. Maybe she could find the dog. But it appeared she was still off in search of a makeshift cane for him.

Jackson got to his feet. With difficulty, he turned around. There beneath a tree, where the snow wasn't so deep, stood a little gray-and-white dog. It looked cold and scared. Jackson could sympathize.

"Come here," he said in his most congenial tone. "I won't hurt you."

There was another bark, but it didn't move. The dog continued to stare at Jackson as though trying to decide if Jackson could be trusted or not. Jackson kept calling to the dog, but the little thing wouldn't come near him.

Jackson smothered a frustrated sigh. How did he gain the dog's trust?

He again glanced around for Mae. How far had she gone for the walking stick? A town on the other side of the Alps? Italy perhaps?

He considered shouting for her, but then he changed his mind. If he frightened the dog, they'd never catch it. And it wasn't fit for man or beast in this snowstorm.

Jackson turned back to the dog. If only he had a way to coax him over, but he didn't have any dog treats. And then he thought of something. He'd missed his lunch and had grabbed a pack of crackers to eat in the car. Would a dog eat a cracker?

Jackson had no idea. His experience with a dog consisted of exactly seven days. And it hadn't gone well at all.

Once the dog had made a mess on the floor, chewed one of his mother's favorite shoes and howled when his mother put him in the backyard for the night, she'd taken the dog back to the shelter. Jackson remembered how crushed he'd been. He'd begged and pleaded for his mother to change her mind. His mother had told him that it was for the best and sent Jackson to his room.

He banished the memories to the back of his mind. Those days were best forgotten. His life was so much different now—so much better. He didn't have a dog and, for all intents and purposes, he didn't have a mother, either. It was for the best.

He pulled the crackers from his dress shirt pocket. He undid the cellophane and removed one. It consisted of two crackers with cheese spread between them. He hoped this would work.

"Here, boy."

The dog's ears perked up. That had to be a good sign.

The pup took a few steps forward. His nose wiggled. Then his tail started to wag.

"That's it. Come on."

The dog's hesitant gaze met his and then returned to the cracker. The pup took a few more steps. He was almost to Jackson.

Jackson lowered his voice. "That's a good boy." He laid the cracker flat on his hand and took a wobbly step forward. The dog watched his every move but held his ground. Jackson stretched out his arm as far as it'd go.

And then the dog came closer. After a few seconds of hesitation, he grabbed the cracker. Jackson caught sight of the blue sparkly collar on the dog's neck. Something told him that this was most definitely the woman's dog. The flashy collar was in line with the woman's rhinestone encrusted cell phone and her perfectly manicured nails.

As the dog devoured the cracker, Jackson knew this was his moment to make his move. Balancing his weight on one foot, he bent down. He lunged forward to wrap his hands around the little dog.

The dog jumped back and Jackson lost his balance. He reached out to regain his balance, but he'd moved too far from the large rock. He instinctively put his weight on his injured leg. Wrong move. He swore under his breath.

"What in the world!" came the beautiful stranger's voice.

It was too late. She couldn't help him. His injured leg couldn't take the pressure of his weight. It gave way. He fell face-first into the snow.

Jackson sat up with snow coating him from head to toe. He blew the snow from his mouth and nose. Then he ran a hand over his face. At that moment, he felt something wet on his cheek. He opened his eyes to find the dog licking him. *Ugh!*

"Aww…you found him." A big smile bloomed on the woman's face. If he thought that she was beautiful before, she was even more of a knockout when she smiled. "You're such a naughty boy for running off. Come here, Gizmo."

"Gizmo? What kind of name is that?" Jackson attempted to get to his feet. He failed.

The woman's brows drew together, but she didn't move to help him. "What's wrong with his name?"

Jackson sighed. "It's a bit cutesy for a boy, don't you think?"

"Cutesy?" Her green eyes darkened to a shade of deep jade.

"Never mind." What did he care what she named her dog? If his head wasn't pounding, he would have kept his thoughts to himself. He would have to make a mental note to tread carefully going forward. Without Mae's help, he hefted himself to his feet.

In the meantime, she picked up the dog and brushed snow from Gizmo. "We need to get you home and in front of a fire. You poor baby."

As Jackson brushed himself off, he couldn't help but watch how the woman oohed and aahed over the dog. What amazed him the most was how the dog was eating up the attention as though it knew exactly what she was saying.

Mae turned to Jackson as though an afterthought, holding out a stick. "Here you go."

He accepted the sturdy-looking branch. Somehow it made him feel like some sort of Paul Bunyan figure. Although his suit and dress shoes would definitely suggest otherwise.

"How in the world did you find Gizmo?" she asked.

Jackson couldn't actually admit to having done much of anything, but if she wanted to give him partial credit, who was he to reject it. After all, if he hadn't thought of the crackers in his pocket, the dog might have run off again.

"We sort of found each other. And he likes the same crackers as I do."

"Crackers?"

"Yes. I have some in my pocket. They were supposed to replace my lunch, but I got distracted when I turned on the wrong road and my GPS wouldn't work out here. Anyway, I forgot about them."

She nodded as though she understood, but there were still unspoken questions in her eyes. "I hate to say it, but the snow's not letting up. If anything, it's getting heavier." She frowned as she glanced upward. "I threw a bunch of snow on the fire when I was looking for Gizmo. I think it doused it. If not, this heavy snow should take care of it." She turned to him. "Are you ready to hike out of here?"

"I don't see where I have a choice."

"I've got to carry Gizmo because the snow is starting to get too deep for his short legs. And I'll take your bag as you'll need all your energy to move on your good leg. But you can put your arm over my shoulder to balance yourself. Hopefully between that and the cane, you'll be able to make it back to the cabin."

"Sounds like a plan."

He got a firm grip on the stick and placed an arm over her shoulders, trying not to put too much pressure on her. He felt guilty that he couldn't even relieve her of his bag, but she was right, anything more would unbalance him. His ankle was really starting to throb now that the adrenaline was wearing off.

She glanced over at him. "Thank you for finding Gizmo."

"You're welcome."

Were those unshed tears shimmering in her eyes? But in

a blink, they were gone. And he wasn't sure if he'd imagined them after all.

At least, they were now even. He glanced over at his snow angel. She was the most beautiful woman he'd ever laid his eyes on. It was hard to miss her stunning green eyes. They were unforgettable and strangely familiar. But that was impossible, right? After all, she was here in Austria and he was from New York City.

But the more he thought about it, he realized that she spoke with an American accent. Now, that he found interesting. What was an American woman doing in Austria at Christmastime? Did she have family here? Or was it something else? Perhaps it was the journalist in him, but he was curious about her story. And then he wondered if she might have an interesting story—something to humanize the holiday segment that he'd flown here to film.

He assured himself that it was professional interest—nothing more. After all, he was off the market. Ever since his wife passed away, he'd kept to himself. No one could ever fill the empty spot in his heart and he had no desire to replace his wife, not now—not ever.

Their progress was slow but steady. He felt bad for holding her back. "Why don't you go on ahead?" he suggested. "You've got to be cold."

"No colder than you. And I'm not leaving you out here. You don't even know where my cabin is."

"I can follow your tracks—"

"No. We're in this together."

Boy, was she stubborn. Even though it irked him that Mae was out here in the frigid air on his account, a small part of him admired her assertiveness. She would certainly be a tough nut to crack during an interview. Those were the interviews he enjoyed most. The ones where he had to work hard to get the interviewee to open up—to get to the heart of the matter.

A lot of his peers would disagree and say that an interview should flow smoothly. But he wasn't afraid of confrontation—of setting matters straight. But being stuck on the morning news cycle, he didn't get to do many meaty interviews—certainly not as many as he would like.

They continued on in silence. And that was quite all right with Jackson. His head hurt. No, it pounded. But that pain was nothing compared to his ankle. However, he refused to let any of that stop him.

He clenched his jaw as he forced himself to keep moving. It was very slow progress, but one step at a time, he was moving over the snow-laden ground. The snow had seeped into his dress shoes. At first, his feet had grown cold. Then they had begun to hurt. Now they were numb.

He sure hoped they got to their destination soon. Freezing to death might make a big news story—but he wasn't that desperate for headlines.

He glanced once more at Mae, but she'd pulled up her hood with the fluffy white fur trim, blocking the view of her beautiful face. "Is it much farther?"

"It's just over that rise." She turned her head, sending him a concerned look. "Do you need to rest?"

"No." If he stopped now, he doubted he'd be able to move again. "I can make it."

"Are you sure?" There was a distinct note of doubt in her voice.

"I'm sure." His teeth started to chatter, so he clenched his jaw together.

Attempting to keep his thoughts on anything but the unending cold, he glanced at the woman next to him. He was torn between being angry at her for causing the accident by letting her dog loose and being grateful that she was some sort of angel sent to rescue him.

Then guilt settled in. How could he be upset with someone who was so concerned for him? She may have been irresponsible with the dog, but she'd cared enough to help him. He couldn't forget that. Perhaps this was the twist in the story he'd come to Austria to tell. Perhaps he could attribute her actions to the holiday spirit. Maybe that was stretching things, but he liked the sound of it. He knew that angle would tug on the heartstrings of his viewers. But it wouldn't be enough to garner the attention of the television executives—the same people who had passed him over for the evening news anchor role.

He stared straight ahead. There indeed was a slight hill. In his condition, it seemed more like Mont Blanc. But between the thick tree limb that Mae had located for him and her slim shoulders, he would make it.

Hopefully this cabin came equipped with a landline. He had to get out of here. This wasn't a vacation for him. He was on assignment and his film crew was due to arrive tomorrow. He'd arrived early to scout out some special settings for his Christmas-around-the-world series. This accident would definitely put a crimp in his plans, but by tomorrow he'd be back on track. He refused to let his ankle and various minor injuries hold him back—not when there was work to be done.

He didn't know how much time had passed when the cabin at last came into sight. He paused for a moment, catching his breath. But only for a moment and then he was moving again—pushing through the pain. Between the snow and his injured leg, this walk was a bigger workout than he normally experienced at the gym.

His body was giving in to the cold and he stumbled. "We need to stop."

She narrowed her gaze. "Are you quitting on me? Are you a quitter?"

"I'm not a quitter." What was wrong with her? "Can't you see that I'm injured?"

"I think you're being a wimp."

"Wimp?" He glared at her. Anger warmed his veins. He'd been wrong about her. This woman wasn't an angel—not even close. She was rude and mean.

He'd show her.

He kept going.

One slow, agonizing step after the other.

CHAPTER FOUR

AT LAST.

Serena's gaze zeroed in on the large log cabin. Any other time, she'd stop to admire how picturesque it looked with the snow-covered roof and the icicles hanging around the edges. But not this afternoon. With the thickening snow and the added weight from supporting Jackson, her back ached and her legs were exhausted. Still, her minor discomforts were nothing compared to Jackson's injuries.

She felt bad for being so mean to him back there. But angering him enough for him to prove her wrong was the only way she knew how to keep him going—how to save his life.

If he'd stopped, she'd have never gotten him moving again. Pain and fatigue were deeply etched on his handsome face. And there was no way she was letting her favorite morning news show anchor become a human Popsicle.

Still, she had to temper her sympathy. If she let herself become too involved with this man, she'd end up paying a steep price. Her last romance had cost her dearly.

Her thoughts turned to Shawn McNolty—Hollywood's rising star. He'd also costarred in Serena's latest movie, which was set to release over the holidays. During the filming, their agents had contrived for them to be seen together to get the public buzzing about a potential romance. But as time went on, Shawn had convinced Serena that instead of putting on a show they could start a genuine romance. He had been so charming and attentive that she'd convinced herself that taking their romance from the big screen to real life could work.

And everything had been all right, or so she'd thought, until she overheard Shawn talking to one of his friends. They'd been out to dinner and she was just returning from the ladies' room while they were standing in the waiting area. Shawn was telling his friend that his arrangement with Serena was working out much better than he'd planned. The longer he spent escorting Serena around town, the more promo he got. The more headlines he received, the more movie scripts came his way. And the best part was Serena didn't even have a clue. He prided himself on being that good of an actor. The memory still stung.

He wasn't the first man to date her in order to further his acting career, but she'd soon realized with those other men that the relationship was one-sided at best. But there was something about Shawn that had caught her off guard. Maybe it was his dark, mysterious eyes or his warm laugh that made her stomach quiver or the way he looked at her like she was the only woman in the world for him. Whatever it was, she'd convinced herself to let go of the past. She'd been sure Shawn was different—that he'd truly cared about her.

Maybe that was why she hadn't suspected something was up when he continually demanded that they go out instead of chilling at her Beverly Hills mansion. He always insisted that they stop and pose for the paparazzi, saying that it was good publicity for their upcoming film. The list of suspicious activities went on—activities that at the time she'd refused to see, but later it had all made sense. The pieces had all fallen into place when she overheard his words at the restaurant. Shawn McNolty had used her for his personal gain.

But he wasn't the only actor in this relationship. Not wanting a public confrontation, she swallowed her heated words and pretended that she hadn't heard a word he'd said about her. Serena didn't even remember what she'd ordered for dinner that last night or how she made it through the meal before she pleaded a headache and took a cab home. The rest of the evening was a blur.

Finding out that her romantic relationship was nothing but a sham was followed by a voice mail from her agent telling her that she'd been turned down for not one but two serious award-contending roles. At that point, she had nothing keeping her in California. She'd needed some downtime. A chance to unplug and regroup. That was the moment when her plan to go off the grid had been born.

With the aid of some temporary hair dye left over from Halloween, she'd switched her honey-blond hair to red. She'd been told by her housekeeper that she was practically unrecognizable without her distinctive eye makeup. Add a ball cap and nondescript jeans, and her disguise had been complete. She'd marched right out the door and jumped in a cab bound for the airport.

And now, even though she had the best of intentions, she knew taking this journalist into her home would end up decimating her serene escape from reality. Jackson may not be on the same level as the paparazzi who would climb the trees outside her Hollywood home, but as soon as he recovered, he'd want something from her—just like Shawn.

Unless she drove Jackson directly to the hospital. It would be what was best for all of them. And her rented all-terrain vehicle was sitting in the driveway. If she could make it to the road, the rest would be slow going, but she was confident she could make it, at least to the nearby village. It may not have a hospital, but there should at least be a doctor. Right?

When they reached the vehicle, she stopped. "Just give me a second."

"What are you doing?"

"Looking for my keys." She pulled off her glove and reached in her coat pocket. Her fingers wrapped around the keys. "Okay. Let's get you seated." She brushed some of the snow from around the door. When she pulled it open, the man sent her a puzzled look. "Come on. We have to get going before the snow gets worse."

His gaze narrowed. "You know how to drive in this much snow?"

Not really. A few times, she'd driven when she was in Tahoe, but it hadn't been in a snowstorm. Still, these weren't normal circumstances.

"I... I've done it before."

He looked at her, then the vehicle and finally at the rise up to the road. He shook his head. "No way. I'll wait here until the authorities can get me."

"But—"

"Arff! Arff!"

Gizmo started to wiggle in her arm. "Okay, boy."

"I think he agrees with me. We should go inside."

"We can't." When the man's eyebrows rose, she added, "I mean, you need medical attention."

"I'll be fine. Unless we get in the vehicle and end up in another accident."

She worried her lip. She was out of reasons not to take this journalist into her home. She quickly inventoried the cabin's contents to make sure there wasn't anything lying about that would give away her true identity. There were the contents of her wallet, but he wouldn't see that unless she gave him reason to be suspicious of her—like standing here in the snow, making him wonder why she didn't just take him straight inside.

Serena inwardly groaned.

Stubborn man.

"I know I'm a stranger," he said. "But I promise you no harm."

She wasn't afraid of him. At least, not in the manner that he thought. But at this point, he was either an excellent actor or he hadn't figured out her true identity. Perhaps the hair dye, Strawberry Temptation, and lack of makeup worked as well as her housekeeper had said.

"Arff! Arff!"

She couldn't fight them both. "Well, don't just stand there. Let's go inside."

Serena again let Jackson lean on her shoulder. Trying to get him up the snowy, icy steps was quite a challenge. She wasn't sure her shoulders would ever be the same again. But at last, they made it.

She helped him into the warm cabin and shut the door on the cold. She normally loved snow. But not this much, this fast. And not when it left her snowbound with a member of the press.

She helped him take off his gloves and wool dress coat. He was totally soaked. And ice-cold. His teeth chattered. The only way to warm him up was to strip him down. She started to loosen his tie.

His hand covered hers. "I… I think you're pretty and all, but…but I don't move this fast."

He thought she was coming on to him? She lifted her chin to set him straight when beyond his bluish lips and chattering teeth, she noticed a glint of merriment in his eyes. He was teasing her. That had to be a good sign, right?

"I'm glad to see your sense of humor is still intact, but if you don't get out of these wet clothes, you're going to get severe hypothermia." She attempted to move his hand, but he wouldn't budge.

"I know how to undress myself."

"Fine. Take everything off. I'll get you some blankets." Seeing him standing there leaning all of his weight on his good leg, she knew he was close to falling over from pain and exhaustion. "Let's move you closer to the fire."

She once again lent him her shoulder. Lucky for both of them, the couch was close by. Once he was seated and loosening his tie, she worked on getting a fire started.

A few minutes later, she returned to the great room with her arms piled high with blankets. Jackson sat on the couch in nothing but his blue boxers and socks. Heat immediately rushed to her cheeks. She was being silly. This was an emergency and it wasn't like she was a virgin.

"Something wrong?" he asked.

She knew she was blushing and there was nothing she could do to stop it. She averted her gaze. "Here you go."

She set the blankets beside him. One by one, she draped them over him. That was better. But she couldn't get the image of his very lean, very muscular body out of her mind.

She swallowed hard. "You forgot your socks and they're soaked. I'll get them—"

"No. I can do it." There was obvious weariness in his voice and his eyes drooped closed. "Stop…"

She ignored his protest and set to work. She removed the sock from his good leg. His foot was scary cold. She held it between her hands, trying to get the circulation going. It didn't work.

She glanced up at her unexpected guest. His eyes were still closed. Next, she worked the sock from his injured leg. His ankle was swollen and an angry mess of red and purple bruises.

"Is something the matter?"

His voice startled her. "Um, no." She had to tell him something. "It's just that your feet are so cold."

"They'll be fine."

"It could be frostbite. You weren't exactly dressed to hike through a blizzard. Can you feel your toes? They are awfully pale."

"They have that pins-and-needles sensation."

Holding his feet in her hands wasn't going to be enough help. She grabbed a basin of lukewarm water for him to soak his feet in. He put up a fuss, but eventually he gave in to her ministrations.

When Jackson's feet had sufficiently warmed up, he settled back on the couch. "How does it look?"

The horrible purple-and-red bruise was on both sides of his ankle. The inside wasn't as bad as the outside, but the ankle was a mess. And it was swollen to the point that she couldn't see his ankle bone.

"I think it's broken," she said as though she had any clue about medicine.

"Are you a doctor?" he asked.

"Me? No." Heat swirled in her chest and rushed up to her face. She knew where this conversation was headed.

He arched a brow as he studied her face. "I have the strangest feeling that we've met before. Have we? Met before, that is?"

"No. I don't believe we have."

She knew for a fact that they'd never crossed paths. For the most part, her life was limited to Los Angeles while she knew his work kept him based in New York City. And if they had met, she wouldn't have forgotten. The man was drop-dead gorgeous, and he had the sexiest deep voice. He was the only reason she tuned into the morning news show.

And now he was here, in her cabin, in nothing but his

underwear. But it couldn't be further from a romantic interlude. He was a member of the press and she was a Hollywood star in hiding. Once he figured out who she was, he'd broadcast it to the world. The thought made her stomach roil, especially after the mess she'd left behind in California.

"Hmm… I don't know where I've seen you, but I'm good with faces. It'll come to me."

Not if she could help it.

She retrieved a towel that she'd grabbed while gathering the blankets for Jackson. She called Gizmo over and dried him off. Then she situated him on a chair near the fire with an extra blanket. The puppy immediately settled down. With one eye closed and one partially open, he looked at her as though to make sure she didn't go anywhere.

"I won't leave you." She petted him and then kissed the top of his fuzzy head.

She got to her feet and turned to Jackson. "I'll call emergency services. They'll be out in no time to take you to the hospital and deal with your car."

"I'm sorry to be such a bother."

"It was my fault, or rather my dog's. Anyway, everything turned out okay. Except for your ankle…and your car." She moved to the phone on the desk.

When she'd checked in at the leasing office, they'd warned her that cell service was spotty in the mountains so they'd installed a landline. She picked it up and held the cordless phone to her ear. There was no sound. She pressed the power button on and off a few times, but there was still no dial tone. *Great!*

She could only hope she'd get a signal with her cell phone. She hadn't in the couple of days she'd been here, so why would today be any different? But she refused to give up hope.

With her cell phone in hand, she headed for the door. She paused to slip on her boots.

"Where are you going without a coat?" Jackson asked.

"Out on the porch. The phone lines must be down due to the storm, so I'm going to see if I can get a cell signal outside."

He didn't say anything more. She noticed this was the first time she'd headed for the door without Gizmo hot on her heels. Today's adventure had wiped him out. He hadn't budged from the chair. In fact, at one point she'd heard Gizmo snoring. He was so sweet and she felt so blessed that he was safe.

She paced from end to end of the large porch. There was no signal at all. She held it above her head and craned her neck to see if that helped. It didn't.

She lifted on her tiptoes and waved it around. Nothing. She leaned out over the large wooden banister. Snow fell on her phone and her arm, but there was still no signal. There had to be something she could do.

Her gaze moved to her rented all-terrain vehicle. Maybe she could go get help. But then she noticed how the snow was piled up around the tires. She glanced into the distance and she couldn't even see the line of trees at the end of the smallish yard. Who was she kidding? She'd never even get out of the driveway.

With a heavy sigh, she turned back toward the door. Chilled to the bone, she rushed back inside. She brushed the snow from her arm.

"Well?" Jackson's weary voice greeted her.

"Do you want the bad news? Or the bad news?"

He arched a dark brow. "Is that a trick question?"

"Not at all. So which shall it be?"

Was that the beginning of a smile pulling at his lips? Serena couldn't quite be sure. And then she conjured up the image of him smiling like he did each morning on television when he greeted the viewers. He was so devastatingly sexy when he smiled—

"Did you hear me?" Jackson sent her a funny look.

She'd lost track of the conversation, but she knew that he was waiting on her news. "The bad news is that there's no phone service whatsoever."

"And the other bad news?"

"We're stuck here. Together."

His handsome face creased with frown lines. "And exactly how long do you think we'll be snowbound?"

She shrugged. "Your guess is as good as mine. They did warn me when I rented this place that should there be a snowstorm, it would be quite a while until they dug me out considering I'm off the beaten path."

"Just great." He raked his fingers through his thick brown hair. "I can't be stuck here. I have a job to do."

Did he mean reporting that he'd found her? Serena didn't want to believe he was like the paparazzi. She wanted to believe that Jackson Bennett had integrity and honor. But she couldn't trust him. She couldn't trust anyone—including her own judgment. She always wanted to see the best in people. And that had gotten her into trouble more times than she cared to admit.

Still, she didn't want him to worry. "I promise you that as soon as possible, I'll get you medical attention. And I'm sure soon people will be looking for you."

His eyes widened. "Do you know who I am?"

What was the point in keeping it a secret? "You are Jackson Bennett. You're the face of *Hello America*."

A pleased look came over his face. "And I'm here on assignment. I have a camera crew flying in to help me film some Christmas segments."

It was on the tip of her tongue to ask him if she was to

be included in one of those segments, but she caught herself just in time. If he could be believed, he didn't recognize her. "I can promise you, they aren't getting through the storm."

"Is it getting worse?"

She nodded.

He muttered under his breath. "I can't just sit here."

He went to stand up. As soon as his injured foot touched the ground, his face reflected the pain he felt.

"Sit back down. First, I think I should bandage your ankle and then you can sleep. When you wake up, help should be here." She sincerely hoped so, for both of their sakes.

This luxury cabin may come with a fully stocked pantry and fridge, but something told her it would be lacking on first-aid items. She'd have to be inventive.

CHAPTER FIVE

JACKSON BLINKED.

It took him a moment to gain his bearings. That hike had taken more out of him than he'd expected. After Mae had bandaged his ankle, she'd helped him into a pair of sweatpants and a long-sleeved T-shirt he'd packed in his bag, her cheeks pinking prettily all the while, and settled him on the couch with pillows and blankets. She'd then insisted that he get some rest.

As time went by, there were very few spots on his body that didn't hurt. He didn't want to think of what would have happened to him if it wasn't for Mae. The mental image of his car going up in flames sent cold fingers of apprehension trailing down his spine.

Mae tried to act tough, but he'd watched how she fussed over her dog. She was a softy on the inside. In fact, he was willing to bet there was a whole lot more to Mae than being an angel of mercy. So what exactly was her story?

And what was she doing in this isolated cabin?

Jackson's gaze followed the stone chimney of the fireplace up, up and up until he reached the impressive cathedral ceiling. He took in the balcony and could only imagine what the second story must be like. Okay, this place was much more than a cabin. It was a luxury log home at the least and more like a mansion.

Was Mae staying here all by herself?

The place was much too big for just one person. Oh, and her dog. How could he forget Gizmo? She'd be lucky if the dog didn't get lost in here.

He gave himself a mental shake to clear his thoughts. He had a lot more important things to worry about than this woman's extravagance. He had to find a way to salvage his career—his stagnant career.

Ever since his wife passed away, his job was what got him up in the morning and helped him through the days. The nights were a different matter. He was left with nothing but memories of the only woman that he would ever love. When she'd died, he didn't know how he'd go on. In the beginning, breathing had taken effort. His existence had been an hour-to-hour proposition. And then he'd progressed to day by day. That was when he'd sought refuge in his work—going above and beyond for a good story.

His work was the sole reason he was in Austria. It was the second Christmas since he'd lost his wife, and he couldn't stay in New York City. He didn't want to be invited to friends' holiday celebrations. He didn't want tickets to Christmas programs in theatres. He wanted to be alone, but no one seemed to understand.

He may not be able to totally escape the holiday, but at least in Austria it would be on his terms. Jackson took in the towering pine tree in front of the two-story windows. And when his gaze landed on the boxes of decorations, he realized that he'd been taken in by a Christmas zealot. He sighed. This was just his luck. The sooner he got out of there, the better.

Speaking of his beautiful hostess, where had she gone? He paused and listened. Nothing. Was she napping? If so, he couldn't blame her. The afternoon had been horrific and stressful, not to mention the hike over mountainous terrain with him hanging on her shoulder. He'd tried not to lean on her too much, but at times, she was the only thing keeping him from falling face-first in the mounting snow.

He glanced to the spot where the dog had been lying on a blanket. Even he was gone. That was strange. He was just there a moment ago—right before Jackson had closed his eyes to rest them.

Jackson decided it was best that he go check on things. He saw his makeshift cane close by and grabbed it. His gaze moved to his bandaged ankle. He'd be lucky if it wasn't broken, but he wasn't going to think about that now.

With a firm grip on the cane, he lifted himself up on his good leg. What he wouldn't give now for a set of crutches. He turned himself around, finding the cabin even larger than he'd originally imagined. This place could easily fit three or four families.

Just then Mae appeared with her arms full of clothes. "What are you doing up?"

"I was wondering where you'd slipped off to."

"Well, when you fell asleep, I decided I should move my things out of the master suite to one of the upstairs rooms."

"Upstairs? But why? I'll be out of here in no time."

Mae moved to an armchair and laid her clothes across the back of it. "About that, I don't think either of us is going anywhere anytime soon."

"What? But why?"

"The snow hasn't stopped."

He half hopped, half limped his way to the door and looked out. The sun was setting, not that it was visible with the snow clouds blanketing the sky. But evening was definitely settling in. And Mae was right. The snow, if anything, had gotten worse. There were several new inches out there since they'd arrived at the cabin.

"It doesn't look good," he grudgingly conceded.

"Don't worry. I have plenty of food."

She might be sure of that fact, but he wasn't. It wasn't like they were in a cabin in a highly populated ski resort. This place was miles from the closest village, and from what he could tell, there were no neighbors close by.

He settled on the edge of the couch. "Um, thanks." He wasn't sure what else to say. "But I don't want to put you out. I can take the room upstairs."

From across the room, she sent him an I-don't-believe-you look. "On that leg? I don't think so." She started to pick up the clothes again. "I have dinner under control."

Come to think of it, he was hungry. Jackson sniffed the air, but he didn't smell anything. "What is it?"

"I hope chili will do."

Chili sounded good on such a cold evening. "Sounds great. Do you need help in the kitchen?"

She shook her head. "There's nothing to do but open a couple of cans and warm them up."

Open cans? Was she serious? He did his best to eat healthy. When your career involved standing before the cameras—cameras that picked up every shadow and wrinkle—you learned to drink lots of water and avoid food out of a can.

"Is that a problem?" her voice drew him from his thoughts.

"No. Thanks for taking me in and feeding me. I will pay you back."

She shook her head. "That's not necessary."

She had a point. Anyone who could afford a place this extravagant didn't need a handout. Far from it.

"Are you staying in this massive log home by yourself?" He vocalized his thoughts before he could register how that might sound.

Her brows arched. "I am." She paused as though trying to decide what to say next. "It's all they had left when I arrived."

So this trip was spur-of-the-moment. He found that interesting. To his surprise, he was finding most everything about this woman interesting. That hadn't happened to him since…since he'd met his wife.

Not that his interest in Mae was remotely similar to the way he felt about June. He supposed that it was only natural to feel some sort of indebtedness to the person who saved your life. That had to be it. For all he knew, he'd hit his head in the accident. It sure hurt enough to have struck something.

"Sorry. I didn't mean to be nosy," he said. "I guess it's just the nature of my job."

Just then Gizmo came running into the room.

"Gizmo, stop." Mae had a horrified look on her face.

Jackson couldn't help but wonder what had put that look on her face until the little dog stopped in front of him with something pink hanging from its mouth.

"Gizmo!" Mae rushed forward.

The dog dropped a pink lacy bra at Jackson's feet. He glanced up to find Mae's face the same shade as the delicate bra. Jackson couldn't help himself. On one leg, he carefully maneuvered himself closer to the floor so he could pick up the piece of lingerie.

He straightened just as Mae reached him. A smile pulled at his lips as he held out the bra. "I believe this is yours."

"Quit smiling." She snatched the very alluring bra from him. "It isn't funny."

"Your dog has an interesting sense of humor."

"He's a klepto. That's all." And then realizing that she was still holding the bra in front of him, she moved it behind her back.

"You have good taste." He knew he shouldn't have said it, but he couldn't resist a bit of teasing.

The color heightened in her face. "If you're done critiquing my lingerie, I'll take my clothes upstairs."

She turned promptly. With her head held high and her shoulders rigid, she moved to the armchair. For some reason, he didn't think she would be so easily embarrassed. After all, earlier today she was not afraid to call the shots, including stripping him down to his boxers and then dressing him. But just now, he'd witnessed a vulnerable side of her. *Most intriguing.*

"Pink looks good on you," he called out.

She turned and gave him a dirty look. It was at that point that he burst out laughing. In that moment, he forgot about all his aches and pains. He couldn't remember the last time he'd laughed without it being on cue. It felt good. Real good.

Mae gathered her clothes and strode over to the steps leading to the second floor. A smile lingered on his face as he settled back on the couch. He figured he'd be less of a bother here as opposed to anywhere else.

Gizmo returned to the room. He hefted himself onto the couch. He settled against Jackson's thigh and put his head down. Jackson never bothered with dogs, but maybe Gizmo wasn't so bad after all. He ran his hand over the dog's soft fur. At least, Gizmo had a sense of humor. Unlike his human counterpart.

This was not the quiet solitude that she'd imagined.

Serena busied herself in the kitchen, trying to put together dinner. But all the while, her thoughts were on Jackson. He was not what she'd expected. He was more down-to-earth. And his eyes, they were—dare she say it—dreamy. She could get lost in them. And his laugh, it was deep and rich like dark French roast coffee.

Realizing that she was in dangerous territory, she halted

her thoughts. Maybe she had fantasized about him being the perfect man one too many times while watching his morning show. And now that he was here in her cabin, she was having a hard time separating fantasy from reality.

And her reality right now was preparing an acceptable dinner. For someone who spent very little time in the kitchen because of a constant string of diets, she was pretty pleased with the appearance of dinner. Even Jackson couldn't complain. She hoped...

She glanced down at his tray to make sure she hadn't missed anything. There was a freshly warmed bowl of chili straight out of the can. A spoon and napkin. A glass of water because she didn't know what he liked to drink. But there was something missing. A man his size that had been through so much that day would have a big appetite. Should she add a salad? Nah, it would take too long. And then she decided to add some buttered bread.

When it was all arranged on the tray, she turned toward the door. She just hoped he still had his leg propped up on a pillow. If she could get him moved to the bedroom, she wouldn't have to trip over him in the living room. And maybe then she'd be able to get back to the quiet time so she could do some more work on her screenplay.

Since she'd arrived in Austria, the words had been flowing. Well, maybe not flowing, but they'd been coming in spurts. Sometimes those spurts consisted of an entire scene or two. But other times, she struggled to write a sentence, much less a paragraph. She wondered if that was how it worked for all writers or if it was just because this was her first script.

Serena paused at the doorway. Recalling her monthly indulgence of visiting the local drive-through for a bowl of chili, she realized they would top the bowl with diced onion and cheese. Perhaps she should do the same. The chili did look a little blah. Serena returned to the kitchen island.

By the time she chopped up the onion, her eyes were misty. Maybe the onion wasn't the best idea, but she wasn't wasting it, so she tossed it on. And then she topped it off with a handful of sharp cheddar. She returned the remaining onion and cheese to the fridge. It was then she noticed some fresh parsley.

Gizmo strolled into the kitchen. He came right up to her. He still had a sleepy look on his face.

She knelt down to fuss over him. Her fingers ran over his downy soft fur. "Hey, sleepyhead, you finally woke up."

"Arff!"

She loved the fact that he spoke to her as though he actually understood what she was saying to him. Sometimes she wondered if he understood more than they said dogs could understand. It was almost as though he could read her mind.

Serena washed her hands before rinsing off the parsley. Then she began to chop it up. She glanced over to find Gizmo lying in front of the stove with his head tilted to the side and staring at her.

"What are you looking at?"

"Arff! Arff!"

"I'm not making a big deal out of this. I would do this for anyone who was injured and needed my help." It didn't matter that Jackson was drop-dead gorgeous and when he laughed, he made her stomach dip like she was on a roller coaster.

She assured herself that she wasn't going out of her way to impress Jackson. She wouldn't do that. After all, she was Serena Winston. Daughter of two Hollywood legends. Heiress to the Winston fortune and an award-winning actress. She didn't need to work to impress any man.

Except that Jackson didn't have a clue who she was. That should be a relief, but it made her wonder if she wasn't pretty without her normal layer of makeup. Or perhaps the strawberry blonde hair didn't work for her. Maybe it was true what they said about blondes having more fun.

What was she doing? She yanked her thoughts to a stop.

Now, because she liked the looks of the parsley and not because she was trying to impress the influential reporter, she sprinkled it over the bowl.

She caught Gizmo continuing to stare at her with those dark brown eyes. "Would you stop looking at me like that?"

Gizmo whined, stretched out on the rug and put his head down. That was better.

Serena again grabbed the tray and headed for the door. Time to go wait on Jackson. She assured herself that no matter if he smiled at her or not, she would drop off the food and leave. After all, he was enemy number one—the press.

CHAPTER SIX

He was so comfortable—so relaxed.

And, best of all, he was no longer alone.

Mae was right there, next to him. So close. So temptingly close that he could smell her sexy and flirty perfume. It was the perfect mix of spice and floral scents. As though it had cast a spell over him, he gazed deep into her eyes.

He reached out, pulling her toward him. He ached to feel her lips pressed to his. There was just something about her—about her strawberry blonde hair that turned him on.

"Jackson," she called out to him.

He loved the way she said his name. It was all soft and sultry. He moaned in eager anticipation of where this evening was going to go.

"Jackson."

"Mae." He couldn't bring himself to say more. Why waste time on words when he could show her exactly how he was feeling—

Suddenly, he was jostled.

"Hey, Jackson. Wake up."

His eyes flew open. The bright light from the lamp on the end table caused him to blink. Wait. What was she doing standing there with a tray of food? They had just been snuggled together on the couch.

He blinked, trying to make sense of everything. And

then it all came crashing in on him. He'd dozed off again. Fragmented images of his dream came rushing back to him. Not only had he been dreaming, but he'd been dreaming about Mae. He uttered a groan.

A worried look came over her face. "What's the matter? Is it your ankle?"

He hurried to subdue his frustration. What was wrong with him? He had absolutely no interest in Mae. None whatsoever!

He glanced up at her. The look on her face said that with each passing moment she was becoming more concerned about him. What did he say? His still half-asleep mind struggled to find the right words.

"Um… I just moved the wrong way. It's no big deal."

She consulted the clock on the mantel. "You can have some more painkillers. I'll go get you a couple."

Mae set the tray down on the coffee table and rushed out of the room. He didn't argue, because he needed a moment or two to pull himself together. He shifted until he was sitting sideways on the couch, keeping his foot propped up. Realizing he hadn't eaten since breakfast, he reached for the plate of bread.

At that moment, there was a shuffling sound. And then a fuzzy head popped up over the edge of the couch. Without invitation, Gizmo hopped up on the couch. This time he didn't immediately settle down for a nap. His tail swished back and forth.

So the little guy wanted to make friends? Jackson smiled. It'd been a long time since he'd briefly had a dog. And nowadays, his life wasn't conducive to keeping a pet. But that didn't mean he and Gizmo couldn't be friends.

He sat still as the dog paused and sniffed the bandage on his leg. And then the pup continued up the edge of the couch. Jackson was all ready to pet him when the dog became distracted by the food. Before Jackson could move the plate, Gizmo snatched a slice of buttered bread. For a dog with short legs, he sure could move swiftly.

"Hey. Stop."

Gizmo didn't slow down. He jumped off the couch. Just as Mae returned, Gizmo rushed past her. The dog was a blur of gray-and-white fur.

A frown settled on Mae's face. "What did you do to Gizmo?"

"Me?" Jackson pressed a hand to his chest. "Why do you think I did anything?"

"Because I know you don't really like him."

He didn't like Gizmo? Was that really how he came across? Maybe that was why the dog chose the bread over him. The thought didn't sit well with Jackson. He would have to try harder with the little guy—even if he was a bread thief.

Mae crossed her arms, waiting for an answer to her question.

Jackson's gaze met her accusing stare. "I promise you that I didn't do anything to him."

"Then why was he running out of here?"

Obviously she'd missed the piece of bread hanging from the little guy's mouth. Well, who was he to rat Gizmo out? It wasn't like it was going to score him any points with his very protective owner.

"I don't know. Maybe he heard something." Jackson shrugged. And then he held up three fingers. "Scout's honor."

Her stance eased. "You were a Boy Scout?"

"I was." He studied her, surprised by the glint of approval in her eyes. "I take it you approve?"

"I... I guess. I'm just surprised, is all."

For that moment, he wanted to gain her approval. "I was in the Scouts for a number of years."

"You must have enjoyed it."

"I don't know about that. Some of it, sure. But as I got older, I wasn't that into it. But my mother, she insisted I remain a member."

"Your mother? But why?" And then Mae pressed her lips together as though she hadn't meant to utter that question. "Sorry. You don't have to answer that."

He didn't normally open up to people about his past. He glossed over the important parts and left everything else unsaid. But for some reason, he felt like he could open up to Mae. "I was just six when my parents divorced. My father moved on, remarried and had another family. And so he wasn't around much. My mother felt that I needed a male role model. She worried that she wasn't enough for me. And so she enrolled me in Scouts so I could learn to whittle wood and make campfires. You know, all of the stuff that turns a boy into a strong, responsible adult." Now, it was time to turn the tables on her. "And were you a Girl Scout?"

She shook her head. "My, um, parents, they weren't much into me taking part in group functions."

He arched a brow. "I thought all parents wanted their kids to interact with others."

Mae glanced down. "They…they were overprotective."

"Oh. I see. Well, it appears you didn't miss out on anything by not learning how to build a fire. And think of all the calories you saved by not eating all those s'mores and roasted marshmallows."

He was attempting to make her smile, but she was still avoiding his gaze and she definitely wasn't smiling. There was more to her childhood than she was willing to share.

Something told him she hadn't had it easy—even if this luxury log home said otherwise.

"You better eat before it's cold," Mae said.

"What about you? Where's your food?"

"Oh, I'll eat in the kitchen." Her gaze strayed across the plate on his lap. "I see you already ate some of the bread."

"I guess I was hungrier than I thought. Thanks for this."

"It's no big deal. I'm sure your wife did things like this for you all of the time."

"Actually, she didn't. She came from old money and never learned to cook. By the time we met, she had her life the way she wanted it, and so for us to work, I had to fit into her life."

Mae's mouth gaped and then as though catching herself, she quickly forced her jaw closed.

"I see I surprised you with that admission." He sighed. "I guess I surprised myself in a way. My mother was a lot like my late wife. She had her life and I had to fit into it— but I didn't do a very good job. I always thought when I grew up that I would end up with someone who was the exact opposite of my mother. And I convinced myself that June was different. After all, she had money. She didn't need mine. And she was cultured. My mother was anything but cultured." Why was he rambling on? He never opened up about his private life with anyone. "But you don't want to hear all of that."

"Actually, it's nice to know that my life isn't the only one that isn't picture-perfect."

So he was right. She had skeletons in her closet. He wondered what they might be, but he didn't venture to ask. They'd shared enough for one evening.

His steady gaze met hers. "You've been great. I don't know what I'd have done without you. I won't forget it."

Her cheeks filled with color. "It's not that big of a deal."

"I promise that I'll find a way to pay you back." When she went to protest, he said, "I was thinking that once I'm mobile I could treat you to dinner in the village."

This time her gaze did meet his. "I… I don't think that would be a good idea."

Okay. He may have been out of the dating scene for a number of years, but he was pretty sure that wasn't how the conversation was supposed to have gone. Perhaps he hadn't stated it properly.

"I know this place is really nice, but you can't spend all of your time here alone. And I'll be staying in the area until after Christmas, so I'd like to pay you back in some manner. I just thought a friendly dinner might be nice. If you change your mind before I leave tomorrow, I'll give you my phone number."

There, that was much clearer. Surely she wouldn't object now. Would she?

"Thank you." She sent him a small smile. "That's a really nice offer, but you don't have to feel like you owe me anything. After all, if it wasn't for Gizmo, we wouldn't be here."

She did have a point, but he had a feeling she was just using that as an excuse. Did she really find him that repulsive? He wasn't used to a woman rejecting his offer for dinner—not that he dated, but he did have business dinners and he was never without female companionship for those.

Mae was different. Very different. And that made him all the more curious about her. If only they had phone reception, he'd do an internet search on her. After all, he was a reporter. Research was a part of his daily routine. Sure, he had people to do it, but he liked to do a lot of his own research. He liked learning all sorts of new things.

There was only one problem. He didn't know her last

name. Was that just an oversight on her part? Or had she purposely withheld it?

"Well, I'll let you eat. I need to go check on Gizmo. He's being suspiciously quiet." She turned to walk away.

"Hey, you never said what your last name is."

"I didn't, huh?" And with that she continued toward the kitchen.

He was staying with a mystery woman who had no lack of funds but guarded her privacy above all else. What had happened to make her so secretive? Or had she always been that way?

The bed started to vibrate.

Serena's eyes opened to find that morning was upon them. But for the life of her, she couldn't figure out what was causing the vibration and it was getting stronger. Was it an earthquake?

Gizmo started to whine. She couldn't blame him. She was used to earthquakes, or rather she was as used to them as you could be when you were a California native. The truth was they always put her on edge. But she hadn't expected to encounter them in Austria. Unless this was something else entirely. Whatever was happening, it wasn't good.

She hugged Gizmo close. "It's okay, buddy. We'll be okay."

Serena scrambled out of bed. She threw on her fuzzy purple robe and headed out the door. Her feet barely touched the staircase.

By the time she reached the first floor, the vibration had stopped. She found Jackson out of bed. He wasn't wearing a shirt, giving her an ample view of his bare back with his broad shoulders and tapered waist. A pair of navy pajama bottoms completed the sexy look. She mentally urged him to turn around.

Instead, he remained with his back to her. His hand was gripped firmly to his makeshift cane as he gazed out the window next to the front door.

Perhaps he hadn't heard her enter the room. "What was that?"

He at last turned, giving her a full view of his muscular chest with a splattering of hair. "I'm not sure, but I'd hazard a guess that it was an avalanche."

Realizing that she was staring at his impressive six-pack abs, she forced her gaze to meet his. "That…that was way too close for my comfort."

"Mine, too," Jackson said matter-of-factly.

She was impressed that he was willing to make such a confession. In her experience, men never admitted to a weakness—least of all her ex-boyfriend. Men were all about putting on a show of how macho they were.

And somehow she'd imagined Jackson, with his bigger-than-life personality, to be full of bravado. Instead, she found him relatable. In that moment, she liked him a little bit more—probably more than was wise considering his means of making a living.

"How far away do you think it was?" she asked, trying to keep her attention on something besides Jackson's temping, naked chest.

"I don't know. The power is out, too."

"Don't worry, we have a generator. The realty people showed me how it works."

He glanced down at his leg. "I'd like to get out there and take a look around, but I'm not as mobile as I'd like to be."

"Speaking of which, you should be in that bed, resting your leg."

He shook his head. "I was going stir-crazy."

"I take it you're not one to sit around."

"Only if I'm doing research for a news story. But seeing as how there's no internet and no phone service, that idea is out."

She was thanking her lucky stars for the lack of communication with the outside world. "I'm sure we'll be able to get you out of here today. Your first stop should be the doctor's or the hospital to have your leg checked."

Jackson glanced back out the window. "The snow is getting lighter, but there's got to be at least three feet of it out there. If not more."

"What?" It wasn't nearly that bad when she'd taken Gizmo outside last night, but it was more than her pampered pooch could appreciate. He definitely enjoyed his California sunshine. But then again, a lot of hours had passed since then.

Serena rushed over to the window to have a look. Jackson wasn't exaggerating. There were no signs of their footsteps from the prior evening. Between the snow and wind, any trace of them had been swept away.

She turned back to Jackson to find him staring at her instead of the snow. Heat swirled in her chest. She was used to having men stare at her, so why was she having such a reaction to Jackson looking at her now?

And then she realized that in her hurry to find out what had caused the massive tremors, she'd rushed downstairs without running a brush through her hair. Unlike his sexy appearance, she must look quite a mess.

How did men wake up looking good? It was frustrating because her hair was always going in far too many directions and sticking straight out in other places. And then she started to wonder if she had drool in the corners of her mouth. A groan started deep inside, but she stifled it. But the heat rushing to her face was unstoppable.

Just then Gizmo moved to the door and started to bark. She made a point of turning away from Jackson as though to talk to the dog. With one hand, she petted Gizmo. With the other hand, she ran her fingers around her mouth. She finally breathed a little easier.

"It's okay, boy. I'll take you out in a minute."

"Out? Where?"

"Lucky for me this cabin is fully prepared for anything. There's a snow shovel on the side of the porch."

Serena dressed quickly and then fired up the generator. She stuffed her feet in a pair of snow boots that she'd picked up in the nearby village upon hearing the forecast. And then she put on her coat and pulled a white knit cap over her mussed-up hair.

After attaching Gizmo's leash, she turned back to Jackson. "After I take him out and shovel for a bit, I'll get you some breakfast."

"You don't have to."

She shrugged. "I'm going to need some breakfast after I shovel out the driveway. Or at least start on it. Suddenly that driveway looks very long."

Jackson's face creased with frown lines. "You shouldn't do all of that shoveling."

"Really? I don't see anyone else around here to help dig us out."

A distinct frown formed on his handsome face. "I should be doing it."

"And how exactly would you manage to shovel snow on one leg?"

"Maybe the sun will melt it."

"When? A month from now?"

He sighed. "Okay. I'll help you."

"No, you won't." She glared at him, hoping he'd understand her level of seriousness. "You'll stay right here."

Not about to continue this pointless argument, she let herself out the door. The snow was light but the wind was still gusting. She could imagine that many of the mountain roads would be impassable and she didn't even want to think of how the avalanche would delay Jackson's departure.

At least if she got the vehicle and the driveway dug out, once the roads were opened, she could get him to the village. She just had to hope that would happen sometime today. The longer they spent together, the harder it was to keep her true identity a secret.

CHAPTER SEVEN

HE FELT LIKE a caged tiger.

Moving between the window and the couch was making his ankle throb. His conscience wouldn't allow him any peace. He shouldn't be inside this cozy cabin while Mae was outside doing all of the hard work. He felt awful. He'd never had a woman take care of him—not even his wife.

When he'd first met June, she'd been a model and he'd been at the fashion show to do an interview. It was back when he just did spotlight interviews for an evening entertainment show. She was delicate and spoke with a soft voice. She was kind and thoughtful—the exact opposite of his mother.

And in no time, he'd fallen for her. In just a few short months, they'd been married amid her family's protests. With both of them driven by their passion for life and work, their futures were on the rise. Fueled by his determination and June's encouragement, he'd taken on the anchor chair of *Hello America* within six months of their marriage. It appeared that nothing could stop them.

And then a few years later, she'd received the life-altering diagnosis—she had cancer. He clearly remembered that day at the doctor's office with an overhead light flickering, the slight sent of antiseptic in the air and June's muffled cry. Jackson's gut knotted as the memories washed over him.

That day was when all their dreams and plans had fallen to the white tiled floor and shattered into a million sharp, jagged pieces.

He'd dropped everything as they'd embarked on the fight of their lives. He'd needed to make sure she was always taken care of, whether it be surgery, a treatment or just being at home recovering from the side effects of her treatments. He'd turned his life upside down and inside out—not because he had to but rather because he wanted to be there for June.

He had her favorite magazines on hand for her to thumb through, her favorite flavored water, chicken broth and movies. He'd never minded. He would have done anything for her. Just the memory of everything she'd endured because of that horrible disease made his stomach turn.

And as much as he'd loved June, he could see now that she was so different from Mae. June never would have waited on him like Mae had the night before. But that was not exactly fair. Because June didn't know how to cook, she would have called for delivery service.

As for shoveling snow, June hadn't believed in physical labor. It was the way she'd been raised, with a silver spoon in her mouth. And as luxurious as this cabin may be, June wouldn't have voluntarily come here. She liked touring the small villages, but she preferred staying in the city or at the ski resorts. He'd never had a problem with her choices because when she had been happy, he'd been happy.

But maybe there was more to life. A different way of being. Maybe happiness didn't have to be a one-sided venture. A bit of give-and-take sounded appealing—

Stop! What was he going on about this for? It wasn't like he would ever see Mae and her glorious strawberry blonde hair after he got away from here. It still bothered him that he couldn't place her face. You'd think that a knockout like Mae would stick out in his memory. Maybe it was the accident. He didn't say anything to Mae because he didn't want to worry her, but that had to be the source of his headaches and his fascination with her.

In the three years, five months and eleven days that he'd been with June, he'd never willed her to be anything other than what she was—the woman that loved him. When she'd looked at him, the love had shone in her eyes. No one had ever looked at him that way. Their relationship may not have been perfect, but they'd found a way to make it work.

He jerked his thoughts to a halt. What was the matter with him? Why was he comparing June to Mae?

While Mae was nothing like June, there was something about her—a vulnerability that drew him near. She'd been wounded in the past and was leery of trusting him. They had that in common—the lack of trust. After having loved with all his heart and losing June so quickly, he was wary of letting anyone get close to him. Until now, he hadn't given much thought to how he kept people at arm's length. Maybe it was something they both needed to work on.

Jackson made his way to the kitchen. He may not be any help outside, but he could still whip up a mean breakfast. He pulled open the fridge door to find the shelves loaded with food. Wow! This place was certainly well stocked, or else his beautiful hostess had bought a lot of food for just herself and her dog.

Leaning on one leg tired him quickly, but he refused to give in. He would have a lovely meal ready for Mae. She deserved it. He just wished it would ease his guilty conscience, but preparing breakfast with bacon, eggs, hash browns and pancakes did not even come close to the task of shoveling all that snow.

But thanks to Mae's efforts, he'd soon be getting out of here. The storm was almost over and the road would be opened. And none too soon because he still had to film the segments for the holiday special. He had no idea where his crew was, but they were resilient. He was certain they would have hunkered down for the storm. And as soon as the cell phone service was reestablished, they'd make contact.

However, the holiday special was bothering him. He was better than puff pieces. He wanted to do more substantial segments—the type of investigative reporting that they featured on the evening news. But before he could do that, he had to get a story that would grab the network bigwigs' attention.

He thought of the avalanche. That was a story, but without something more like hikers or skiers trapped, it wouldn't go anywhere. Instead of playing where-in-the-world-is-Jackson? he needed to be tracking down a headline-making story—

"What smells so good?"

He turned from his place at the stove to find Mae standing in the doorway. But she was frowning, not smiling like he'd envisioned. "What's the matter? Did you hurt yourself?"

"The problem is you. You shouldn't be in here hobbling around."

"I figured you'd work up an appetite."

"I told you I would make food when I came inside."

"And I thought I would surprise you. So…surprise." He grinned brightly, hoping to lighten the mood.

And still there was no smile on her face. It bothered him because she was so gorgeous when she smiled. He remembered how hard it used to be to make June smile when she got in one of her moods. But he'd always persevered until he won out and eventually June would smile at him. Because when he'd said his wedding vows, he'd meant every single word. He would not get a divorce like his parents. He would not fail.

But Mae was not June. Why should he care if she smiled or not?

"Go sit down. I'll finish this," she said.

"It's done. I just have to put this last pancake on the plate. By the way, your fridge was well stocked. I hope you don't mind that I helped myself."

She washed up and then followed him to the kitchen table. "No. I was worried that it would all go bad. So thanks for helping me to put it to good use."

Once they were seated at the table next to a bank of windows, Mae's gaze skimmed over all the serving dishes heaped with food. "Who's going to eat all of this?"

"Arff! Arff!"

They both laughed at Gizmo's quick response.

"It appears that Gizmo worked up an appetite, too," Jackson said.

"I don't know how that could be when he spent the entire time sitting on the porch. He refused to get off it, even after I shoveled out an area in the yard just for him."

Gizmo yawned and whined at the same time.

They both smiled at the animated pooch. Maybe Gizmo wasn't so bad—at least when he wasn't running loose and causing car accidents.

As they each filled their plate, Mae asked, "So what had you so distracted when I walked in?"

"Distracted?" It took him a moment to recall what she was talking about.

"You had a very serious look on your face."

"Oh, I was thinking about work."

"Aren't you supposed to relax? Isn't this a vacation?"

He shook his head. "I came here to work."

Was it his imagination or did Mae's face visibly drain of

color. "Um, what's your assignment?" And then as though she realized that she might be prying, she said, "Sorry. I don't mean to be pushy."

"It's okay. I'm doing a Christmas special. You know, a sort of Christmas around the world. I already did one in Ireland, Japan and now Austria. Well, that depends on if I ever find my camera crew after this storm." He glanced out the window. "Hey, the snow is just flurries now."

"That's good, because let me tell you, there's a ton of snow out there." She sighed. "You know, I've worked up such an appetite that I could eat all of this food."

"Go ahead."

She shook her head. "I can't."

"Sure you can. In fact, I can make more."

"Don't tempt me. But really, I can't."

"Don't tell me that you're dieting."

She shrugged. "Okay. I won't tell you."

"What does someone as beautiful as you have to diet for?" He wanted to tell her that she could stand to put on a few pounds, but he didn't dare. He didn't want her to take it the wrong way.

"So I fit in my clothes. But I think I can squeeze in a little more after that exercise this morning." Her gaze met his. "You're a really good cook."

He continued to stare into her green eyes. "I've had a lot of experience."

He didn't bother to add that after his parents divorced, his mother wasn't around much as she had to bounce between two and sometimes three jobs to make ends meet. And so he did the bulk of the cooking. And then with June, she didn't know how to cook and so he'd taken on the role as he enjoyed creating delicious meals that were healthy and nutritious.

"If your job on television ever falls through, you could become a chef."

He smiled at the compliment. "Thanks. I'll keep that in mind. It might come in handy."

Now what was she supposed to do?

Serena stared out the window at the snowy landscape. They still hadn't plowed open the road and there was no way that she could drive through three feet plus of snow. She would have to have a monster truck with chains on the tires and even then she doubted that she'd make it out of the driveway.

With a heavy sigh, she accepted that there was nothing she could do for now. Instead of wasting her energy worrying about Jackson's presence, she needed to concentrate on writing a screenplay.

This was her chance to make a name for herself that had nothing to do with her looks or the legacy her two famous parents had left her. And time was running out because sooner than she'd like, she had to return to Hollywood to begin filming her next movie. The contract had been inked months ago and to back out at this late date would tarnish her name in the industry, not to mention the penalties she'd be subjected to for failure to perform.

But most of all, she took pride in standing by her word. When she said she'd do something, she did it. So not only would she do the movie, but she would also get this screenplay written over the holiday break—before she went back and faced the public scandal of her life.

She wanted to find a place on the second floor to write—away from Jackson. But she was still worried about him. His injury was serious, and he was overdoing things. Try as she might to keep him in bed, he never stayed more than five minutes at a time.

There was a desk with a lamp in the corner of the great room and that was where Serena took a seat with her laptop. This was one of those five-minute periods where Jackson was in the bedroom with his foot up. Gizmo was lying on a padded bench next to the window, watching the snow blow around in between snoozes. Now was her chance to get some work done.

She opened her laptop and after she logged in, her script popped up on the screen. She quickly read over what she'd written last night before she went to sleep. It didn't sound too bad, but something was missing. She just couldn't put her finger on what it was. Perhaps if she kept going, it would come to her. She hoped.

Serena's fingers moved rapidly over the keyboard. This screenplay might not be a serious drama, but it wasn't slapstick comedy, either. It was filled with heart. For now, writing about a warm family with a central love story and a happily-ever-after made her happy. It was about a loving but complicated family that she wished she'd been a part of. In the future, she intended to work on screenplays with more serious scenarios.

She paused and smiled. Perhaps writing an award-worthy screenplay wasn't as important as writing the story of her heart. Who knew, maybe it'd be prize-worthy after all. It might be a little zealous, but wasn't that what dreams were meant for?

For now, she'd chosen a shopaholic heroine and her large, boisterous family. Her ex-boyfriend needed a wife to keep his wealthy grandmother from writing him out of her will and leaving it all to her favorite pet charity. The hero was all about getting the money and pretending to be what his grandmother wanted him to be that he missed the point that money couldn't make you happy. And the heroine had to learn that a bigger wardrobe and a larger apartment wouldn't change who she was and that she has-dto accept herself, blemishes and all.

The more Serena typed, the more she worried whether she was going in the right direction with the plotline. Still, she kept pushing forward one word at a time—one sentence after the next—

Knock. Knock.

She jumped. She'd been so involved in her script that she hadn't heard anyone approach the door. Gizmo must have been sound asleep, too, because it wasn't until the knock that he starting barking as he scrambled to the door.

Serena jumped to her feet. "Gizmo, quiet."

The pup paused to look at her as though to ask why in the world he would want to be quiet when there was obviously an intruder on the premises. Immediately he went to his growl-bark, growl-bark stance.

"Who is it?" Jackson asked from behind her.

"I'm just about to find out—if I can get Gizmo to settle down." She bent down and picked up the dog.

The pup gave her a wide-eyed stare but at least he quieted down. With him securely in one arm, she opened the door. She couldn't help but wonder if it was another stranded person. "Can I help you?"

It was a man in a red snowsuit with a white cross on the left side. "I stopped to make sure you are okay." He spoke English with a heavy German accent.

"We are." She noticed how Jackson limped over to stand behind her. "Are you with the leasing company?"

"I'm not. I'm with the emergency crew working on clearing the avalanche, but they let us know that an American woman was staying here, and that you are by yourself, which I see you're not."

Jackson cleared his throat. "They must have cleared the road."

Serena peered past the man, looking for his vehicle in the freshly shoveled driveway. There was no vehicle. Maybe he left it on the road, but she didn't see it there, either. Surely the man didn't walk here. This cabin was in the middle of nowhere and this wasn't the weather for walking.

The man lifted his sunglasses and rested them on the top of his head. "Actually, I'm getting around on my snowmobile."

As the wind kicked up, Serena said, "Why don't you come inside?"

They moved back and let the man in the door. The man stepped forward just enough to close the door against the cold air. He was shorter than Jackson and had a much more stocky build. His face was tan, as though he spent a lot of time outside, and his eyes were kind.

The man cleared his throat. "The avalanche was bad. It has a stretch of road shut down until we can get equipment in to clear it." The man glanced around. "I see they got the power fixed."

"Not yet," Serena said. "It's a generator."

The man nodded in understanding. "They are hoping to get the power restored to this area sometime today."

Since this man seemed quite knowledgeable about their situation, she asked, "Do you know how long it will be until the road is open?"

He shook his head. "I have no idea."

"The thing is, Mr. Bennett here was in a car accident and I need to get him to the doctor—"

"I'm fine," Jackson interjected.

A concerned look came over the emergency worker's face as he turned to Jackson. His gaze scanned him. "I'm trained in first aid. Why don't you sit down on the couch and let me look at you. We can call in an emergency helicopter if we need to. It'll be tricky under these conditions but not impossible."

Jackson frowned. "I told you I'm fine."

"And I would like to see this for myself." The emergency worker gave him a pointed look.

They continued to stare at each other in that stubborn male fashion. It was really quite ridiculous. Why did Jackson have to be so stubborn?

Serena stepped forward. "Jackson." When he didn't look at her, she tried again. "Jackson, let him look at you. I'd feel much better if he did."

At last, Jackson turned to her. "I told you not to worry."

It was on the tip of her tongue to tell him that she did worry about him, but she stopped herself just in time. What in the world had gotten into her? She barely even knew this man. He might be amazingly handsome and she might be able to listen to his rich, deep voice for hours on end, but she had sworn off men. So she would be fine admiring Mr. Jackson Bennett via her television because that was as close as she planned to get to him once they could get away from this cabin.

Serena could feel both men staring at her. Heat swirled in her chest, but she refused to let that stop her from being honest—or at least partially honest. "I'd feel a lot better if someone who knew something about medicine would have a look at you. That was a bad accident. You have a lot of bruising. And your ankle doesn't look good."

Jackson sighed. "All right. If it's really that important to you."

"It is."

Jackson limped toward the couch.

"I'll be right back," the emergency worker said. "I have medical supplies on my snowmobile."

Serena followed Jackson. He sat on the couch and put

his injured leg up on the coffee table. She knelt down on the floor and set Gizmo next to her. Finally, the pup had settled down. She didn't know what had gotten into him. He was usually friendlier. After all, he'd taken to Jackson.

She reached for the makeshift bandage.

"What are you doing?" Jackson asked.

"Taking off the bandage so he can have a look at you."

"I can do it."

She'd already started undoing the knot that she'd made to hold everything in place. "Just relax." She continued to struggle with the bandage. "I almost have it."

"It might be easier if you use scissors."

She didn't respond. The truth was that he was right, but when she was around him, her thoughts became jumbled. And when she touched him, her heart raced. What was it about this man that had her reacting like she was once again a schoolgirl with a crush on Jeremy Jones, the school's up-and-coming rock band singer?

She'd never felt this rush of emotions when she had been with Shawn. Sure, she'd enjoyed their time together, but she hadn't felt like it was anything special. Maybe she should have realized it was a sign that things weren't right. But she'd never been in love before, so she didn't know how it should feel. And now she never would know, because she was avoiding men—unless they unexpectedly crashed into her life.

Finally, the knot gave way. She made quick work of undoing the bandage. As much as she'd wished his ankle had healed quickly, it remained a kaleidoscope of colors from purplish black to red and some pink. What a mess.

Just then the door opened and Gizmo once more went into guard dog mode. Serena followed him to the doorway, where he had the emergency worker pinned to the door. Serena rushed over to pick up Gizmo.

The man had his hands full of medical supplies. If she were to go by looks, it appeared this man knew what he was doing. And that would be good for all of them because she was so far removed from a nurse that it wasn't even funny.

"I'm sorry," she said. "He's not normally like this." When Gizmo started barking again, she said firmly, "Gizmo, stop." The dog didn't even bother to look at her as he kept a close eye on the stranger. "I'll just go put him in the bedroom."

Fifteen minutes later, Jackson had been all checked out. The emergency worker said that he didn't believe Jackson's injuries were life-threatening, but he was certainly banged up. If Jackson wanted to be evacuated, he'd call in a chopper. Jackson adamantly declined, saying that with the avalanche there were others in more need than him. And Serena promised to keep a close eye on him.

With Jackson in a proper bandage, the emergency worker packed up his stuff and walked away. Just as he opened the door, the light bulbs brightened, signaling that the electricity had been restored.

"Thank goodness," Serena said. "Things are starting to look up."

"I'll be back to check on you tomorrow." And with that the man left.

Serena closed the door. "Sounds like I better let Gizmo out before he scratches the door. I don't know what's up with him."

"He's just protective of you."

"Then how do you explain him taking to you?"

"Oh, that's easy, I bribed him." An easy smile pulled at Jackson's lips.

Serena's stomach dipped. Okay, it was official, he was much cuter in person than he was on television. And if she didn't get him out of here soon, he might worm his way past her defenses. But would that be so bad?

After all, they were on two different coasts. Surely with all those states between them and their busy schedules, they'd never lay eyes on each other again.

She shook her head. Obviously she wasn't used to the solitude. Everything would be fine. She would stick to her resolution of no men. Soon the plows would open up the road and Jackson would be on his way out of here.

"What?" Jackson's eyes filled with confusion.

"Hmm…"

"You shook your head. Why?"

"Nothing." She hunted for a legitimate answer to his question. "I should have figured that you would resort to bribing."

"It wasn't my idea." Jackson said it as though it were the undeniable truth. "Gizmo stole my bread last night and well, I didn't rat him out and we've been friends since."

"And it only cost you a slice of bread?"

Jackson smiled and her stomach once again did that funny dipping thing. "Yeah, I guess it was worth sacrificing part of my dinner."

"And that would explain why he wasn't very interested in his." She planted her hands on her hips. "I don't want him eating human food so if you could refrain from feeding him in the future, I would appreciate it."

"I'll try, but no promises." When she arched a brow, he added, "Hey, he's sneaky."

"Uh-huh." Was it possible that this journalist was truly a big softy at heart?

The thought stuck with her as she went to turn off the generator. She really wanted to dislike Jackson. It would make this arrangement so much easier, but the more time she spent with him, the more she liked him.

CHAPTER EIGHT

THE DAY SLIPPED by very slowly.

Jackson didn't know what to do with himself. He wasn't good at sitting still and yet his ankle, though most likely not broken, was still severely bruised and swollen.

He picked up his cell phone from the coffee table. He put in his passcode only to find that there was still no signal. So much for them getting the cell tower fixed today...or whatever was causing the disruption in service. He knew he shouldn't complain. With the avalanche, everyone had much larger concerns.

He tossed the phone back on the coffee table and sighed.

Mae glanced up from her laptop. "Do you need something?"

"Yes. I mean, no."

"So which is it?"

He limped over to her desk. "I'm just bored, is all. I'm not used to having time on my hands. Usually I don't have enough hours in the day to get things done. Today I don't have enough things to do."

"I understand. My life is usually very hectic. That's one thing I love about being here. No one can bother me and I can make my own schedule."

"So what has you so busy on the computer for hours on end?"

"This, oh, well…it's nothing."

Was it his imagination or did her cheeks take on a shade of pink? His curiosity grew. She closed the laptop and stood. He couldn't take his eyes off her as she stretched.

"You don't strike me as a shy woman. So what has you blushing when I asked about what you were working on?"

Her fine brows drew together. "And you are not on the job. I'm not one of your stories. You don't have to keep pushing until you get all of the answers."

Realizing that he'd overstepped, he held up both hands. "Sorry. I guess this sitting around is really starting to get to me. I think I've read every magazine on the coffee table at least twice."

"Then I can put you to work." Her eyes lit up as though she'd come up with the perfect answer.

He was intrigued. He'd love to spend some productive time with Mae. Perhaps his abundance of enthusiasm should bother him, but he chose to ignore the telling sign. "What do you have in mind?"

"I'll be right back." She took off upstairs.

Gizmo got up from where he'd been napping on the couch. When he yawned, he let out a little squeak. Jackson found himself smiling. Gizmo walked over to him. Jackson petted him and scratched behind his ears.

"You're not so bad. In fact, you're kind of cute."

"Arff!"

Jackson couldn't help but laugh. "You know, if I didn't know better, I'd say you knew what I was saying."

"Arff! Arff!"

"Sounds like you two are having quite a conversation," Mae said as she descended the stairs with her hands full of bags.

"And what is all of that?" He had a feeling he didn't want to know, but the reporter in him needed the answer.

"This is what we're going to do this evening. And if you do a good job, I'll let you roast some marshmallows over the fire tonight."

He couldn't help but laugh again. He tried to remember the last time he'd laughed this much and failed. Was there such a time?

He didn't think so, as June had been more reserved. She was quiet in public. She would say that it was the way she was raised, but he knew the truth—she was painfully shy. Still, she hadn't let it stop her as a fashion model. Each day she did what was expected of her. And although it took a lot out of her to get in front of the cameras, she'd pasted on a smile and never missed a photo shoot.

But there had been times when she'd let her hair down and unwind when they were in bed. Then she'd been all his. And there had been nothing shy about her then. He could make her laugh, moan and make all sorts of unladylike sounds—

Jackson squelched the memories. He wanted to be present in this moment. He took in Mae's smile. It lit up her face and made her eyes sparkle, but it was more than that. How did he say it? It was like when she smiled the world was brighter. It filled him with a warmth, and he never wanted to let that feeling go. It healed the cracks in his broken heart, making him feel whole again.

"Can you make your way over here?" she asked as she set the bags down in front of the Christmas tree.

And then he put it all together. He shook his head. "I don't do Christmas trees."

Her eyes widened. "You don't celebrate Christmas?"

"No. Not that. I celebrate it—or I used to. But I never did the decorating." The truth was, with busy work schedules that often conflicted, neither he nor June were home long enough to worry about it. Instead, June would hire professionals to come in and decorate their tree. It was always different each year. Different color. Different theme.

Mae stood there with a puzzled look on her face. "Why wouldn't you decorate your tree? Doesn't it look rather sad and pathetic without ornaments?"

"It had ornaments. I just didn't put them on."

"Why not?"

"There wasn't enough time." That seemed to be the theme of his life. There were so many things that had been skipped over or missed because there wasn't enough time. And now time had run out for him and June.

"You have to make time for the important things in life. My father used to always put off things and then he died." There was a slight pause, but before Jackson could say a word, she continued. "I don't want to miss the good things in life because I'm too busy. Life is too short."

It was as though she understood exactly what he'd been through, but that was impossible. He kept his private life private. "I'm glad you're taking advantage of life. You're right, it is too short."

She reached into the bag and pulled out a box of ornaments. She proceeded to attach a hook and hang it on the tree. "See. Nothing to it. Come on. Decorate it with me. I already strung the lights the other night."

But it was more than the fact that he didn't have experience at trimming a Christmas tree—everything about the season would remind him of June. It would be a painful reminder of all that he'd lost. Christmastime was the time of year June loved the most. It was when she was at her best—when they had been at their best.

"Jackson?" Mae's voice jerked him from his thoughts.

He shook his head. "I don't think this is a good idea."

"Sure, it is. After all, it's almost Christmas."

"But this is your tree, not mine." He knew it was a lame

excuse, but he just couldn't bring himself to admit the truth—he felt guilty celebrating without June.

"For as long as you're here with me, it's our tree. Yours, mine and Gizmo's." At that point, the dog's ears perked up. Mae turned to her pup and said, "Isn't that right, boy?"

As if on cue, Gizmo barked. Spontaneous laughter erupted in Jackson. These two seemed determined to cheer him up. And it was working.

He normally wasn't that easily amused, but being around Mae and her dog was bringing out a whole new side in him. And he honestly didn't know what to make of it—what to make of the way Mae made him feel.

This isn't a good idea.
It'll be fine.

The conflicting thoughts piled one on top of the other. But it came down to the fact that Serena felt sorry for Jackson. How could a man who appeared to have everything miss out on the spirit of Christmas?

To her, Christmastime was going beyond your normal comfort zone in order to lend others a helping hand. She tried to do it year-round, but filming schedules usually upended her best efforts to visit the soup kitchen during the rest of the year.

She'd been doing it for years now. At first, she'd done it in defiance of her father, who'd said that no Winston should be pandering to others. How she was related to that man was beyond her. They disagreed about most everything. When she was young, she used to wonder if they'd mixed up the babies in the hospital nursery. She'd even said it once to her father—he hadn't taken it well, at all.

But the more time she spent at the soup kitchen, the more she liked the people there. She soon learned that her attendance wasn't so much about what she could give them but rather what they gave her. They reminded her that there was so much more to life than money and contracts. Because in the end, it was about love and kindness.

Of course, none of those people knew her true identity, either. She'd always wear a wig and dress in baggy T-shirts and faded jeans that she'd picked up at a secondhand store. She'd quickly learned just how comfortable those casual clothes could be—

"And what are you thinking about?" Jackson asked as he placed a hook on a glass ornament.

What would it hurt to share her thoughts? After all, they were living here together for the foreseeable future. It wasn't like she was going to open up and spill her whole life story.

"I was thinking about what I would be doing now if I were at home."

"Let me guess, shopping at the mall. Your arms would be full of shopping bags with gifts for your family."

She shook her head. "Not even close."

He blinked as though shocked by her denial. "Hmm… let's see. You'd be on holiday on a cruise ship."

"Although I like the way you think, that's not it."

He shrugged. "Okay. I give up. What would you be doing?"

"Working in a soup kitchen."

He didn't say anything, but the shock was quite vivid in his eyes. And he wouldn't stop staring. He made her want to squirm, but she held her ground.

"Why are you looking like I joined the circus?"

He visibly swallowed. "I'm sorry. I think what you do is great. It's just that I'm not used to people around me being so giving with their time. Everything in my world is rush-rush."

Surely he couldn't be that impressed. She'd watched his

show regularly and knew that he attended fund-raisers. "And if you were in New York, what would you be doing?"

He shrugged. "Not much."

"But it's the holidays. Come on. Maybe you'd be attending some prestigious event."

He shook his head. She glanced into his eyes and noticed how the light in them had dimmed. And then it dawned on her that the look in his eyes was one of pain and loss. His wife had died a while back. And now that she thought about it, she hadn't glimpsed any photos of him at the various gala events since his wife had passed away.

So he knew what it was like to lose someone close—just like she'd lost her father. Even though her parental relationship had been complicated, it didn't mean that she hadn't loved him.

"My...my wife," Jackson said, drawing Serena from her thoughts, "she was always busy with one charity group or another. I don't attend the fund-raising events now—not without her."

The way his voice cracked with emotion didn't get past Serena. She recalled how he and his wife had appeared inseparable. It seemed like every Monday morning there were photos of them on *Hello America*. Serena recalled how they always looked so happy—so in love. It was obvious that he was still in love with her.

Serena's gaze immediately sought out his left hand. No ring. And then realizing what she was doing, she glanced away. There may no longer be a physical link to his wife, but in his heart, he would always love her. The proof was in the pain reflected in his eyes and the catch in his voice when he spoke of her.

"I'm sorry for your loss." And now she understood why he wasn't anxious to decorate the Christmas tree. It probably reminded him of his wife and their holidays together.

"If you don't want to help me, that's okay. I'm sure celebrating Christmas alone isn't easy."

He continued putting hooks on the ornaments. "I lost her a couple of years ago." He paused as though that was all he was going to say. "At first, after she died, I didn't know how I was going to go on. We did everything together. She even traveled with me when I did travel segments for the morning show."

"Did you two make it to Austria? Is that why you're here?"

He shook his head. "She didn't like snow. I had the option of picking the places for the Christmas segment. And I wanted something different—a place without memories."

Serena was surprised that he was opening up to her. It made her feel guilty for keeping so much of herself a secret. But a part of her liked having him treat her like a normal human being and not like a superstar or a part of Hollywood royalty.

Her parents had had the most notorious, glamorous love story on- and off-screen. There was even a movie about their stormy, passionate relationship. Serena had never watched it and never planned to. She'd been there for the real thing and that had been enough for her. Real life was never like the lives portrayed on the big screen. In fact, in her case, reality was as far from glamorous as you could get.

Serena was lost in the past when Jackson spoke.

"What about you? Why aren't you with your family?"

This was her moment to solidify whatever this was growing between them. Dare she call it a friendship? She glanced at him. At that moment, he looked up and their gaze caught and held. Her heart beat wildly. Friendship wasn't exactly the only thing she was feeling where he was concerned.

No other man had ever made her feel this way. Sure there were gorgeous on-screen heroes. But she never let herself get caught in those romances. Growing up in a Hollywood family, she knew that love was fleeting at best. And then she'd met Shawn. It'd been after her father's death and perhaps her defenses had been down. Whatever the reason, she'd let him into her life. And what a mistake that had been.

But she wasn't going to repeat that mistake by making another one with a world-renowned television journalist. With all her effort, she glanced away. She turned to climb the ladder to place the ornament high up on the tree.

"Aren't you going to share?" he asked.

She did owe him an answer. It wasn't fair to expect him to open up when she wasn't prepared to do the same. "My father died last year. I don't have a reason to be home."

"I'm sorry." There was a pause as though he was considering what to say next. "What about your mother?"

"She's off on a Caribbean cruise with her latest boyfriend." She didn't bother to add that the aforementioned boyfriend was Serena's age. "My mother was never very maternal or traditional."

Jackson didn't say anything. He probably didn't know what to say because he'd had the idyllic childhood and the picture-perfect family. She was happy for him, but sad for herself. Some would say that it made her a stronger person, but she just thought it made her more cynical about life.

Jackson moved to the ladder to hand her another ornament. "Mae, I'm sorry."

She turned to tell him that he didn't have to be sorry. But before she could tell him, she dropped the Christmas ball. It fell to the floor and Gizmo let out an excited bark. He'd been waiting all this time for something to play with.

"No, Gizmo."

But it was too late. The dog chased the ball under the ladder. She moved too quickly. She'd never know if it was her sudden shift in weight or Gizmo running into the ladder, but the old wooden ladder swayed. Serena reached out, but there was nothing to grab onto. The ladder tilted to one side.

Serena started to fall. A shriek tore from her lungs.

And then her body crashed into Jackson's.

His strong arms wrapped around her. "It's okay. I've got you."

"Gizmo?"

"Is fine."

She turned her head to thank Jackson and that was when she realized just how close they were. She breathed in his scent—a mix of soap and pure masculinity. It was quite a heady combo.

For a moment, neither spoke. They didn't move as they stared deep into each other's eyes. It was just as well that he didn't say a word, because she'd have never heard him over the pounding of her heart. In fact, it was so loud that it drowned out any common sense.

She was in the arms of Jackson Bennett—her morning eye candy. He was the man that she had had a secret crush on for years now. How was it possible that it took them both traveling to Europe for their paths to cross? When people said that life was stranger than fiction, they were right.

And then his gaze dipped down to her lips. He was going to kiss her. The breath caught in her throat. She'd always wondered what it would be like to be kissed by him. And this was her one and only chance to answer that question.

With the Christmas lights twinkling in the background, Serena's eyes drifted closed. Letting go completely of the ramifications of her actions and just giving in to what she wanted, she leaned forward. His lips pressed to hers.

The kiss was slow and tender. After being unceremoniously groped in the past by eager suitors, this cautious approach caught her off guard. As the kiss progressed, she realized that Jackson was unlike any of the other men in her past.

She wondered what it would be like to have a real relationship with a mature, self-assured man like Jackson. While she could never picture herself long term with Shawn, she could envision a life with Jackson—marriage, kids, the whole nine yards!

The image was so real—so vivid that it startled her.

She pulled back. Her eyes fluttered open. As soon as his gaze met hers, heat rushed to her face. She felt exposed and vulnerable.

She knew that there was no way he could read her thoughts, but that didn't ease her discomfort. Of all the men to imagine a future with, Jackson wasn't the right one. He still loved his late wife.

Jackson didn't say a word as he lowered her legs to the floor. He went to straighten the ladder before he retrieved the Christmas ornament from Gizmo. And all that time, Serena stood there trying to make sense of what had just happened.

That kiss had been like a window into the future. But how was that possible? She immediately dismissed the ludicrous thought.

But she was left with one question. Now that they'd kissed, how did they go back to that easy, friendly co-existence? Because every time her gaze strayed to him, she'd be fantasizing about what would have happened if she hadn't pulled away.

CHAPTER NINE

THE NEXT MORNING, Jackson made his way to the kitchen. He yawned. He'd been restless most of the night. All the while, he'd been plagued by memories of the kiss. It had been an amazing kiss. The kind of kiss that could make a man forget his pledge of solitude—forget the risk he'd be taking with his heart if he were to let someone get close.

Even knowing the risks, there was a part of him that wished it hadn't ended. Chemistry like that didn't happen every day. In fact, he'd be willing to bet that it only happened once in a lifetime.

His thoughts had circled around all night, from how much he wanted to seek out Mae and pull her close to continue that kiss to wondering why he'd let his resolve weaken. What had he been thinking to kiss Mae? And what did that say about his devotion to June?

He still loved June. He always would. That acknowledgment only compounded his guilt.

And now what must Mae be thinking? She hadn't seemed interested in him. In fact, in the beginning he wasn't even certain that she was going to let him seek shelter from the storm in her cabin. But had that kiss complicated their relationship?

He paused at the kitchen doorway, not sure what to say to her. Perhaps it was best to act as though the kiss had never happened. With that thought, he pushed open the door.

An array of cereal boxes sat on the table next to an empty bowl and fresh orange slices. It appeared Mae had been up early that morning. He wondered if she'd had problems sleeping, too. He scanned the kitchen but didn't find any sign of her.

Gizmo came wandering into the kitchen.

"Hey, little guy, where's your momma?"

For once, the pup didn't say anything. Instead, Gizmo yawned. It appeared no one in the cabin had slept well. Maybe it was just from being cooped up for so long. But he knew that wasn't the case. It was the kiss…

Every time he'd closed his eyes, Mae's image had been there. It wasn't right. He shouldn't have done it. He shouldn't have gotten caught up in the moment.

He knew that June was gone and was never coming back, but he'd promised to love her forever. He also re-called how June had made him promise to move on with his life—to love again. The painful memories came flood-ing back.

June had been so unwell and yet her last thought had been of him. He hadn't kept his promise—at least not until now. Not that he was going to pursue Mae. He just couldn't move on as though June had never been a huge part of his life. How could he put his heart on the line again?

The grief of losing June had cost him dearly. The thought of being so vulnerable again had him withdrawing from friends and social settings. Until Mae…

She made him remember how things used to be—think of how things could be if he'd let himself go. She made him feel alive again. He shook his head to clear his thoughts, but it didn't work. Mae was still there in the front of his mind.

With a sigh, he sat down at the table and filled the bowl with corn flakes. He didn't really have an appetite, but his stomach growled in protest. Perhaps some food would help his attitude.

He glanced down to find Gizmo had wandered off, leaving Jackson alone with his thoughts. The cabin was quiet. As he stared out the window, he was pleased to find the sun was out. Today would be the day when he was able to get on with his life. He knew the thought of leaving here should bring him a sense of relief but it didn't.

The truth was, he'd really enjoyed the time he'd spent with Mae. She had a way about her that put him at ease. Maybe it was because they'd each shared a recent loss or the fact that neither had a loving, devoted mother. Whatever you wanted to say, they shared a special connection. One he wouldn't soon forget.

But Christmas was only a week away and if he didn't get this last segment shot, it'd be too late to air. The slot would get filled and everyone would move on.

If only he could put a special spin on this segment, something more than Christmas in a quaint village in Austria. He knew what they'd already planned would pull on the viewers' nostalgic heartstrings, but his thoughts needed to be on the head honchos in the front office. He only had until the first of the year to prove that he was the man for the evening news slot.

Jackson heard the kitchen door creak open. He turned expecting to find Mae, but instead it was once again Gizmo. He strolled back into the kitchen with something in his mouth. Jackson smiled and shook his head. That dog was forever stealing things. He wondered if Mae would find everything the dog had stolen before she left here. Well, he could help her out this time.

He got up and approached Gizmo. "Hey, boy, what do you have there?"

The dog tried to get around him, but Jackson blocked him. That definitely wasn't a dog toy in his mouth, and this time it wasn't a pink lacy bra, either. The memory of that piece of lingerie combined with the kiss last night heated his veins—

No. Don't go there. It was a onetime thing. Let it go.

He knelt down to pet the dog. Luckily his ankle was starting to feel a bit better with the aid of over-the-counter painkillers. Still, he kept his weight on his good leg.

His fingers wrapped around what appeared to be Mae's wallet. "Give it to me."

Gizmo clenched tighter and started to pull back. He gave a little growl, all the while wagging his tail. Gizmo's head shook back and forth as he tried to work the wallet away from Jackson.

"You're a strong little guy, aren't you?"

Gizmo let out another little growl as his tail continued to swish back and forth.

Well, this was one game of tug-of-war Jackson didn't want to lose.

"Let go." No such luck. "Gizmo! Stop."

Suddenly, Gizmo let go.

Not prepared for the dog's sudden release, Jackson fell backward. He lost his grip on the wallet as he tried to catch himself. He landed squarely on his backside.

Gizmo didn't tarry. He turned to make his escape. Jackson sat on the floor and watched as the dog pushed the swinging door open with his nose.

Jackson couldn't help but smile and shake his head. He wondered if this was what it was like having small children. He would never know since he and June were never blessed with any. It was yet another thing that they'd put off too long—another dream that would never be fulfilled.

He went to pick up Mae's wallet when he realized that it had come open and some of the cards had scattered across the tile floor. He picked them up and started putting them in the wallet when he noticed the name on them: Serena Winston.

He immediately recognized the name. How could he not? Serena Winston came from a legendary family. He'd tried repeatedly to interview her, but for one reason or another, it had never worked out.

This had to be some sort of mix-up. The Serena Winston on these cards couldn't be the famous actress. But if that was the case, why did Mae have them? He held the California driver's license closer. He studied the similarities. If Mae were to be a blonde and add makeup—

His mouth gaped.

It was her. The driver's license read: *Serena M. Winston. Serena Mae Winston?*

Jackson sat there stunned. He'd thought that they'd formed a friendship. He'd trusted her with intimate details of his life, but she hadn't even been honest about her name—at least not her whole name.

Everything started to fall in place, such as her ability to lease this luxury cabin for herself and her dog. She'd been hiding in plain sight with her strawberry blonde hair and lack of makeup. He'd never seen any photos of Serena Winston with reddish hair. She was known far and wide for her honey-blond strands. And it explained what had happened to her—how she was able to drop off the radar.

His thoughts circled back to how he'd believed that they were beginning to trust each other. Then there was that kiss—the kiss he hadn't been able to forget no matter how hard he tried. Well, he no longer had to worry about it. Obviously, it had been all one-sided. All the time, she'd been playing him for a fool.

Anger warmed his veins. He didn't like to be lied to. His gut knotted at the thought of her laughing behind his back. He wished this was some sort of dream because he'd liked Mae—a woman who didn't even exist. Why couldn't just one thing in his life go his way?

He stuffed her cards back in the wallet. He got to his feet. With the breakfast dishes and food long forgotten, he headed out of the kitchen to find his hostess. The jig was up and he intended to tell her.

He'd just reached the living room when his cell phone rang. At last, the cell tower had been fixed. But it couldn't have been worse timing. The only person he wanted to speak to was Mae—erm, Serena. But he didn't see her at the desk working on her laptop. Nor was she on the couch. He could only guess that she was upstairs. And he wasn't sure his ankle was up for that particular challenge.

The buzzing of his phone would not stop. He withdrew it from his pants pocket and checked the caller ID. It was his agent. And it wasn't the first time Fred had called. There was a long list of missed calls. He must be worried about Jackson disappearing, especially at such a pivotal time in his career.

Jackson's gaze returned to the grand stairs leading to the second floor. The phone vibrated in his hand. He sighed and accepted the call.

"Jackson, thank goodness. What happened to you?"

"I was involved in a car accident."

"Accident? Are you hurt? Did you injure your face?"

Leave it to Fred to get to the heart of his concern—Jackson's marketability. "My face is fine."

"You're sure?"

"Yes."

"Well, where are you? The crew has been looking for you. They aren't sure what to do."

"I'm snowed in." He headed for Mae...erm...Serena's desk in the great room to drop off the wallet. "And you'll never believe who rescued me..."

CHAPTER TEN

THE KISS MEANT NOTHING.

Nothing at all.

That was what Serena had been telling herself ever since last night, when she'd fallen into Jackson's more-than-capable arms. What had she been thinking to kiss the enemy?

Who was she kidding? Jackson wasn't the enemy, even if he was part of the news media. Maybe at first she hadn't trusted him—with her background, who could blame her? But during the time they'd spent together, she'd learned that there was so much more to him than his dashing looks and his day job.

He was a man who'd loved and lost. He was kind and generous. He went out of his way for others, even when he'd rather be doing anything else. And he had a sense of humor. The memory of his deep laugh still sent goose bumps down her arms. That was a sound she could listen to for the rest of her life—

Whoa! Slow down.

She knew that this moment of playing house would end soon—just as soon as the avalanche was cleared and they were able to plow the roads. Then they would return to reality, but for now, they lived within their own little world with their own rules and she intended to enjoy it as long as it lasted.

And if that should include some more kisses?

Well, she wouldn't complain. An impish smile pulled at her lips.

She'd been kissed by a lot of leading men, but none of them could come close to Jackson. That man was made for kissing. Just the memory of his lips pressed to hers had her sighing. It hadn't lasted long enough, not even close.

And now, instead of kissing that handsome man, she was doing his laundry. Something wasn't right about that. But she was proud of herself for being able to take care of herself. Neither of her parents knew how to work a washing machine much less the dryer. They'd always been dependent on domestic help.

Serena learned early on that if she wanted true privacy, she had to be self-sufficient. And to be honest, she was never quite comfortable with people waiting on her. Maybe it was the time she'd spent serving food at the soup kitchen—seeing people who barely made it day to day—that had opened her eyes to the extravagances that her parents took for granted.

Whatever it was, she'd learned to do everything for herself except cooking. She had yet to master it. But she could clean the bathroom and iron her clothes.

It was only recently when her filming schedule became so out of control that she'd taken on a housekeeper. It was only supposed to be temporary, but Mrs. Martinez was so sweet and in desperate need of work that Serena kept her on.

Sometimes Serena missed doing the laundry. She found it relaxing. But doing Jackson's laundry had extra benefits, like the lingering hint of his cologne on his laundered shirts. She stood in the master suite next to the closet sniffing his shirt. If he were to walk in now and catch her, she would die of mortification. She was acting like some teenager—

There were footsteps followed by Jackson's voice. Was he talking to Gizmo? But she didn't have time to contemplate the answer as she was still clenching his shirt.

Not about to be caught acting like a lovesick puppy, she stepped into the closet and slid the door shut. She had to hunch over in order to fit. Why couldn't this closet be a walk-in? But no, it had to be long and skinny. And there was a hanger digging into her shoulder blade. She started to move when the metal hangers jingled together. She froze in place.

What was she doing in here?

Plain and simple, she'd panicked.

What was it about Jackson's presence that short-circuited her thought process? She never had this problem with any other man in her life. Jackson was unique.

She was about to open the door and step out when she heard her name mentioned. The breath caught in her throat as she strained to catch what he was saying about her.

"I'm serious. Serena Winston saved my life."

There was a pause. He must be talking on the phone. That meant the cell service and internet were back online. She didn't know if that was a blessing or a curse. She supposed she would soon find out.

"Don't you dare say a word. I told you that as my friend, not my agent." A pause ensued. "Because I told you not to. Just leave it be."

Serena smiled. Jackson was protecting her privacy. He was a bona fide hero in her book.

"Hey, Gizmo." Pause. "No. I was talking to the dog."

Oh, no. If Gizmo realized she was in the closet, he would put up a fuss. No sooner had the thought passed through her mind than there was the sound of pawing at the door. Serena didn't move. She didn't so much as take a breath. She just prayed that Gizmo would get bored and move on.

"Arff! Arff!"

"Are you serious? She's all over the headlines?" Another pause. "I don't need to check it out." Pause. "Yes. I know this scoop could make a difference in my career, but it's not worth it to me."

Serena smiled broadly and pumped her fist, banging her hand into more hangers. *Jingle. Jingle.* She reached up, silencing the hangers. The last thing she needed was for him to catch her lurking in his closet. She didn't even want to imagine what she must look like. This was easily the most embarrassing moment of her life—and if Jackson caught her, it would be even worse.

"Arff! Arff!"

Scratch. Scratch. Scratch.

"Stop…No, not you. I was talking to the dog. Listen, I've got to go take the dog out." Pause. "I don't know." Pause. "As soon as they plow open the roads."

Jackson's footsteps could be heard approaching the closet. "There's nothing in there, boy. Come on. I'll take you out."

Jackson's footsteps faded away.

Serena cautiously exhaled a pent-up breath. She opened the closet door a crack to make sure the coast was clear. It was. She quickly exited and stretched. Her muscles did not like being hunched over for so long.

Not wasting too much time, she hung up the shirt, closed the closet and exited Jackson's bedroom. She glanced toward the front porch, where she saw him through the window. His ankle must be feeling a lot better if he could put on a boot and go out in the snow. That was good, right?

For some reason, the thought of Jackson being mobile didn't make her happy. Soon he'd be leaving her. And now that she knew she could trust him, she wanted him to stay.

The only question she had was whether he'd known who she was all along. If not, what had tipped him off?

She carried the now-empty laundry basket back to the laundry room just off the kitchen. As she placed it on the floor next to the dryer for another load, she realized that this place, even though it was quite large, was very homey. She'd never felt relaxed at her home in Hollywood.

And then she realized that perhaps it wasn't the structure around her but rather the people in it. Gizmo was new to her life and they'd immediately bonded. And now there was Jackson. She felt guilty for not trusting him sooner. Perhaps it wasn't too late to make it up to him.

She returned to the great room and was about to sit down at her laptop when she noticed her wallet sitting on the corner of her desk. How in the world had it gotten here? And then she noticed the distinct bite marks in the black leather. Gizmo. He was the one who'd given her away. *That dog.*

Just then the front door swung open. Gizmo raced into the room as though he were being chased. He stopped and shook himself off. Serena couldn't help but smile. This dog did not like snow.

"What's so amusing?" Jackson asked.

"Gizmo. He doesn't like the snow. At all."

"Give him time. It might grow on him."

Somehow she didn't think that would be the case. She glanced down at the wallet with bite marks. She supposed it was a little late to come clean considering Jackson knew the truth about her.

"I see you found the wallet," Jackson said. "I rescued it from Gizmo. I think he was planning to hide it."

"He is a bit of a thief. You better watch your stuff." How did she say this? Did she just apologize for keeping her true identity a secret? Would he understand?

Jackson said something.

"Hmm…" She'd been lost in her thoughts and hadn't caught all he'd said.

"I said your secret is safe with me."

It wasn't until her gaze met his dark, pointed stare that she knew she was in trouble. He was angry with her for keeping her identity from him. She didn't know what to say to undo things.

"I… I'm sorry," she said, but the words didn't seem to faze him. "I have a hard time trusting people."

"Do you know that there's a search on for you? It appears that your fiancé is heading it up. His face is all over the media sites begging for information about your whereabouts."

Her hands balled up at her sides. How dare Shawn act like he cared? It was all a show—just another way for him to benefit by linking himself to her.

"He's not my fiancé. We were never engaged—not even close."

Jackson's brows rose. "That's not what all of the tabloids are saying."

"Shawn would do anything for headlines, including feeding false information to the press. He doesn't like me, much less love me. I'm just a stepping-stone to his goals."

"Really?" Jackson sounded skeptical. "Why don't you tell people the truth about him?"

"Do you think they'd believe me? Anything I say will be twisted and blown up into an even bigger scandal. I just want it to all die down and go away. I want him to go away. I wish I'd never met him."

Jackson wore a puzzled expression. "And that's what you're doing here—hiding until the story dies?"

"In a manner of speaking." She didn't actually consider it hiding, but she wasn't going to argue semantics with him.

"From what my agent was telling me, the story is growing with every day you're gone." He raked his fingers through his hair. "It might be good to let someone know that you're alive and safe. Some tabloids have even surmised that you're dead. Others think you've been kidnapped."

"Seriously?" She shook her head and sat down at the desk. "Can't people mind their own business?"

"Is there anything I can do to help? Perhaps my agent could release a statement to put everyone at ease—"

"No. No statement."

"Okay. So what? You're just going to suddenly reappear one day?"

"Something like that."

She pulled up the tabloids on her laptop. The headlines were ridiculous. And below the headlines was a photo of a distraught Shawn. Her stomach churned. When was that guy going to get on with his life? She would give him this much, he was a great actor. Because if she didn't know that he was lying, she might have believed his show.

Unable to take any more of the lies and sensational journalism, she closed the laptop. "Listen, I'm sorry I wasn't up-front with you."

"I understand. At least now I do. When your driver's license fell on the floor, I wasn't very happy with you."

"I… I don't know what to say. I came here to be alone and then I thought—oh, I don't know what I thought. I should have told you, but I hadn't worked up the courage. It isn't easy for me to let people into my life."

He nodded as though he understood. "You've lived your

entire life in front of the cameras. You don't know who you can trust. And with my occupation, I'm sure that didn't help things."

"You're right. It didn't. I was afraid that once you found out who I was, you would make me a headline on your morning news show."

When frown lines bracketed his eyes, she knew that she'd said too much. That was the thing about letting people get close. She wasn't sure how much to say and how much to hold back. At least when she was acting in front of the camera, she had printed lines to follow. She didn't have to figure out what to say, how much to say and when to say it.

That was another problem that kept her from seeking the spotlight. She was awkward in public. It would seem odd to most considering who her parents were and what she did for a living. But when she was in front of the cameras, she got to pretend that she was someone else—someone brave and ready to say their piece. However, Serena Mae Winston was a private person who struggled with the fame that her family lineage and job brought her.

Jackson cleared his throat. "I know we haven't known each other for long, but do I strike you as someone who would go behind someone's back to make a headline?"

"No." The look on his face said that he didn't believe her. "I mean it. I know we haven't known each other for long, but I… I trust you." He had no idea how hard that was for her to say.

His stance eased, as did the frown lines on his face. "Then maybe we should start over."

"Start over?"

He nodded. Then he approached her and held out his hand. "Hi. I'm Jackson Bennett. The face of *Hello America*."

She placed her hand in his and a warm sensation zinged

up her arm. Her heart palpitated faster than normal. "Hi. I'm Serena Winston. I'm an actress who is trying to have a normal, quiet holiday."

"I'm happy to meet you, Serena—"

Just then there was a loud rumbling sound. It woke Gizmo from his nap on the couch. He started to bark as he ran to the door. Jackson and Serena followed.

"What do you think it is this time?" she asked.

"It's definitely not another avalanche. This is a much different sound." Jackson listened for a moment. "I think they are opening up the road."

"Really? We can get out of here?"

"You're that anxious to get rid of me?"

"I didn't say that, but we need to get you to the doctor to see if you did any serious damage to your leg."

"Do you really think I could walk on it if I had?"

"Is that what you call the motion you make?"

"Hey, I'm trying here."

"I know. I just worry that you're trying too hard and that you're going to do permanent damage to yourself."

As they were standing there next to the window talking, a red-and-black snowmobile cut across the front of the yard.

"Looks like that guy from the emergency crew is back to check on you," Serena said.

"I'm fine. You all need to quit worrying about me."

"If you were fine, you would walk normal."

Jackson grunted and limped over to the couch while Serena waited for their visitor to make it to the door.

CHAPTER ELEVEN

SHE WAS RIGHT.

But that knowledge didn't make Serena happy.

The official diagnosis was in. Jackson's ankle was fractured. Even the doctor was surprised that Jackson was able to get around as well as he had been. As it was, the doctor had set him up with a walking boot.

"We shouldn't be here," she said as they stood at the edge of the town square. "You should be at home resting your leg."

Jackson turned and stared into her eyes. "Have you ever been to a Christmas market?"

"Arff!"

Jackson smiled and gazed down at Gizmo. "I wasn't talking to you, boy." Jackson's gaze rose until it met Serena's again. "I was talking to you."

"Um, well, um…no. But I'm not exactly dressed for it."

His gaze skimmed over her white coat, red scarf and faded jeans. "There's nothing wrong with what you're wearing."

She lifted a hand to her hair. "But I didn't do anything with my hair."

"You look cute with a ponytail. It suits you. You worry too much. You're beautiful just the way you are."

The way Jackson stared so deeply into her eyes made

the rest of the world fade away. In that moment, it was as if just the two of them existed. He was staring at her like— like he wanted to kiss her.

Her gaze lowered, taking in his very tempting mouth. The thought of once again being held in his very capable arms and feeling his mouth pressed to hers was quite tempting. Was it possible that he was the first man to like her just the way she was?

Her father had always been disappointed in her. It didn't matter if it was her choice in movie roles or if it was the style of her haircut. She'd never gained his approval and then he'd died on her before anything could be resolved between them. One minute he was giving her a hard time about not aligning her romantic relationship with her career. And the next, he was lying on the floor, dead, from a massive heart attack. That was it. No time for "I love yous" or "goodbyes." It was just over—in a heartbeat.

Maybe that was why she let herself become involved with her leading man. Shawn was great-looking and he could say all the right things, but she soon learned that it was all a show. He was constantly acting, being whoever he needed to be to impress people—to get a leg up in the Hollywood world.

But Jackson didn't want anything from her. Not even an interview. He was the first man who'd ever been comfortable with who he was without having to put on a show for the public, which surprised her. After all, Jackson's career was about projecting a certain image for the public, but here he was with scruff on his jaw and his hair a little ruffled by the breeze and he wasn't the least bit worried about his appearance.

She liked being treated like a real person instead of a star. A smile lifted her lips. She liked Jackson. He was so different from the other men who had passed through her life.

"I don't know what's going through your mind," Jackson said, "but whatever it is, I approve. You should smile more often."

Just then Gizmo saw another dog. Being the friendly sort, he wanted to go visit. He started to run, but after walking in a circle, his leash was now wrapped around Jackson and herself. So when Gizmo ran out of length, the leash yanked them together.

Her hands pressed upon Jackson's very firm chest. She had to crane her neck to look into his eyes. It was then that his gaze moved to her lips. He lowered his head and immediately claimed her lips.

His kiss was gentle and sweet. It made her wish that they were back at the cabin where the kiss didn't have to end—where they could see where it would lead. Because she realized that their time together was almost at an end. Jackson would have to get back to the project that he'd flown to Austria to do, and she needed to add some serious word count to her screenplay if she wanted it ready for her agent when she returned to Hollywood. It would hopefully give the paparazzi something to talk about besides her scandalous love life.

"Arff! Arff!"

Their lips parted and they turned to Gizmo. He jumped up, placing his front paws on Jackson's good leg.

"I think someone wants to be picked up," Serena said.

"That might be easier if he hadn't wrapped us up in his leash."

"Maybe someone shouldn't have released so much of his leash."

Jackson's eyes widened. "You're blaming me for this?"

"I'm not blaming anyone. I certainly don't mind being tied up with you."

His brows rose. "Oh. You don't, huh?"

When Jackson leaned in for another kiss, Serena pressed her hand to his chest. "How about you hold that thought until later?"

"Later?" He started to frown but then his eyes widened as he caught her true intention. A broad smile lit up his face. "I think that can be arranged."

More and more people continued to arrive at the market. No wonder Gizmo had changed his mind about wandering off and instead wanted to be held. He was not used to such a crowd. The Christmas market really drew in the people. But who could blame them? This was the most wonderful time of the year.

Jackson quickly untangled all three of them. "There. Now shall we go explore?"

"Are you sure you're up for this? The doctor did say that your leg will tire quickly with that boot on."

"Stop worrying. I'm fine. I'll let you know when I get tired."

"You promise."

"I do."

"What about Gizmo?"

"Let him walk for a bit. That pup has more energy than anyone I know. And then when we get home, he'll sleep instead of getting into more mischief."

"That sounds like a good plan." She smiled up at him. "I like the way you think."

"Well, if you like that wait until you find out what I have planned for later."

She couldn't help but laugh at his outrageous flirting. Things between them were so much different now—so much easier since he knew the truth about her. If only she had known how good it could be between them, she would have told him sooner.

They strolled through the Christmas market locally known as Christkindlmarkt. The thing Serena loved most was sampling all of the local delicacies—from sipping mulled wine to devouring *kiachl*, somewhat like a donut with cranberry jam. Serena had never tasted anything so delightful. Jackson enjoyed the *raclette brot*, a type of bread with warm cheese. And of course Gizmo had to sample most everything, too. So much for her rule about not feeding him human food. After all, it was the holidays. Everyone deserved a treat.

"Are you enjoying yourself?" Jackson asked.

"I am." In the background a brass band played holiday tunes. And overhead, strands of white twinkle lights brightened the night sky. "This place is amazing. And I can't bring myself to stop sampling all of the delicacies."

"I know what you mean. I'm full, but I just have to try one more thing."

They both laughed. The evening was perfect. No one recognized her with her strawberry blonde hair pulled up in a ponytail and lack of makeup. Here in Austria, she was just another person on the arm of a very handsome gentleman.

And then he reached out and took her hand in his. His fingers threaded through hers quickly and naturally as though they'd been doing it for years. Her heart leaped in her chest.

This man, he was something extraordinary.

And Serena knew in that moment, in the middle of the Christmas market, that her life would never be the same.

He couldn't stop smiling.

Jackson sat in the passenger seat as Serena pulled into

the driveway of the cabin. She'd chatted the whole way home from the Christmas market. He was glad he'd suggested they go. Not only was it a scouting mission for his segment for his morning news show, but it also had been their first official date.

Serena put the vehicle in Park and turned off the engine. "And we're home."

"Hey, what happened to your smile?"

She shrugged. "It's just that all of the magic of the evening disappeared."

"Ouch." He grasped at his chest.

"What's the matter? What hurts?"

"My ego. You just pierced it. I'm wounded."

"Oh." She smacked his shoulder. "You had me worried. I thought something was seriously wrong with you."

"There is. You just said the magic has ended."

"You know what I meant. The music. The festive mood. The amazing food. I loved the evening."

"And you don't think my company can compare?"

Serena's green eyes widened. "What exactly are you implying?"

"Forget twinkle lights, I'm thinking of setting off some fireworks tonight."

Her mouth lifted into a smile that made her eyes sparkle. "I don't know. Do you think you're up to it?"

"Let me give you a preview." He leaned forward and pressed his lips to hers.

His kiss was gentle and restrained. He wouldn't push her, but he needed to extend the invitation. It'd been a very long time since he was with a woman. His gut tightened at the thought of living up to Serena's expectations.

But he didn't have long to contemplate because she kissed him back with undeniable desire, which soothed his worries. As their kiss deepened, a warmth flooded his chest. The cracks and crevices in his heart filled in. In that moment, he no longer felt like a shell of a man. He felt complete and eager to step into the next stage of his life. Whatever that may be.

Serena pulled back. "We should go inside. It's getting cold out here."

They both turned to find out why Gizmo wasn't whining to go inside. The pup was sound asleep in the back seat. Jackson couldn't help but smile.

"So he really does run out of energy once in a while."

"It's hard to believe, but it does happen. Isn't he so cute?"

"He is…when he's sleeping."

"Hey." She swatted at Jackson's arm. Then a worried look crossed over her face. "You do like Gizmo, don't you?"

He knew by the serious tone of her voice that him bonding with her dog was nonnegotiable. Someday she'd make a good mother. Unlike his mother who'd taken his dog away from him.

"Oh, no," she said. "You don't like him."

"What? No. I mean, yes, I do."

"But you frowned when I asked you about it."

"That wasn't why I was frowning. I swear. I didn't even realize I was frowning."

He was going to have to do better to keep his thoughts from being so obvious on his face. Considering his job, he was normally quite adept at it. But either Serena could read him better than most or he felt so at ease around her that he didn't think to hide anything.

And now he had no choice but to share with Serena that painful moment in his childhood. He'd never told anyone about it—not even his wife. It was a part of his life that he'd blocked out—until he'd met Serena and Gizmo.

"I was just thinking about the past. I had a dog once. He was rambunctious and I was young, about seven years old. Long story short, he got in lots of trouble and a week later, my mother took him back to the pound."

He remembered clearly how his mother had told him to stop crying. He wasn't a sniveling wimp. If he was strong, if he was a man—unlike his father who ran off at the first sign of trouble—then Jackson would be fine. He didn't need a dog.

He'd been so young at the time that his priority was not letting his mother down. He wanted her to be proud of him more than anything else in the world—even more than having his puppy.

"I can't believe it," Serena said. "Your mom took your dog away."

He nodded. "But it's okay."

"What's okay about it? She got it for you, but seven days later she took it back to the shelter."

"It was my fault. I didn't take care of Rover like I'd promised."

"You were only seven. How responsible can a seven-year-old be?"

Jackson shrugged, realizing that even after all this time he was protecting his mother. "It doesn't matter. It was a long time ago."

"But it still bothers you, so it matters."

He pulled back and reached for the door handle. "I don't want to talk about this."

Serena didn't say anything as he walked away. By the rigid line of his shoulders, she knew the evening had been ruined. And it had held such promise.

CHAPTER TWELVE

WHAT HAD HAPPENED?

Serena had been trying to make sense of what had happened to their perfect evening ever since Jackson had withdrawn from her. That had been last night and now, not quite twenty-four hours later, he was still unusually quiet.

Had she misread everything last night?

Impossible. There was no way she'd misread his kisses—his very stirring kisses. Those kisses had left promises of more to come. Oh, he had been into her just as much as she had been into him. So where had it all gone so wrong?

Or was it for the best to put a halt to their desires? After all, every man that she'd let get close had hurt her. Why should Jackson be any different?

But the truth was, she wanted him to be different. She wanted him to be the exception to everything she knew about men—that they were critical, careless with their words and didn't believe in love for love's sake but rather for what it could do for them and their careers.

"Hey, what has you so deep in thought?" Jackson's deep voice stirred her.

At last he was talking to her. A smile came to her face. Maybe she was making too big a deal of things. Perhaps he'd just been tired last night. After all, the doctor did say that the boot on his ankle would tire him out.

"I was just thinking about what I'm working on."

"I'm sorry to interrupt." Jackson had a mug in each hand and held one out to her. "I just thought you might like this."

"Oh, coffee. I always like coffee."

"It's not coffee."

"It isn't?" She accepted the mug and glanced into it to find little marshmallows and hot chocolate. "Thank you."

"I just thought that with it snowing again this might be fitting."

"It is." She took a sip of the milky chocolate. It was perfect. "This is the best hot chocolate I've ever had."

He smiled proudly. "Thank you."

"Is this from a packet? If so, I have to make a note to buy some when I get back to the States."

He shook his head. "It isn't from a box. I made it."

She took another sip and moaned in pleasure. "How did you make it?"

He eyed her up as though trying to decide if he should divulge the information. "Can you keep a secret?"

"Definitely. I just have to be able to make this again. It's that good."

"Well, while we were at the Christmas market yesterday, I bought some chocolate."

"Why don't I remember this?"

"Because you and Gizmo were at the stall with the gourmet dog biscuits. Anyway, that's my secret."

"So you melted chocolate into milk."

"Not just any chocolate but dark chocolate. However, you can't tell anyone. It's our secret."

She smiled, liking the idea that they shared confidences. "I can't believe you are so good in the kitchen." And then she realized that he might not take her words as a compliment. "It's just that you are so busy. I don't know how you find the time."

"I don't have a busy social calendar, not anymore. Anyway, once you learn how to cook, it's like riding a bike, you never forget."

"I wouldn't know."

"You mean you can't ride a bike?" The look on his face was one of unimaginable horror.

"No. I mean, yes, I can ride a bike. It's the cooking that I never conquered."

"Did you ever try?"

She nodded. "I've attempted to teach myself without success. My mother can't cook, so she obviously didn't show me. And my father thought that cooking was a waste of time. That's what he paid people to do. So he forbade me from spending time in the kitchen when instead I could spend the time taking voice lessons as well as dance and acting classes."

"Sounds like you had a very busy and educational childhood."

She shrugged. "It was what it was." Her childhood was a mixed bag of extravagance and neglect. She was certain she wasn't the only Hollywood child to have the same experience. "How did you become so good in the kitchen?"

"Come to the kitchen with me and I'll tell you."

"The kitchen, but why?"

"Because you're going to have your first cooking lesson."

She struggled to keep her mouth from gaping. After she recovered from her surprise, she said, "You don't want to do this. I'm pretty sure I can burn water if left alone."

He smiled. "I think you're better than you give yourself credit for."

"I wouldn't be so certain."

"Come on." He reached out and took her free hand. He tugged until she got to her feet. "After all, you can make chili."

"You know that it was out of a can."

"Still, you didn't burn it. That's a start."

"I must admit that I can handle a microwave."

"Good." They moved to the kitchen. "Now you have to pick—red or white?"

"Wine?"

"No. Sauce."

She liked them both. "Paired with what?"

"Pasta and…" He opened the freezer and searched inside. "How do you feel about shrimp?"

"I love it." She was so thankful that he'd given up on the idea of teaching her to cook. She was hopeless. But with Jackson cooking, this was going to be a delicious dinner.

"Good. Now what sauce would you prefer?"

"White." She couldn't help but smile. She'd never been in the kitchen with a man where his sole interest was in preparing her dinner. In fact, no man had ever cooked her dinner. Her smile broadened.

"Well, what are you doing standing over there. Put your hot cocoa down and wash up. You have work to do."

"Me? Cook?" This was not a good idea. Not at all.

"Uh-huh. In fact, you can do it all yourself. I'll supervise."

Her stomach plummeted. So much for the delicious dinner that she'd been envisioning. "Are you sure you want to ruin dinner? I'm good with watching."

"You'll never learn to cook that way. Trust me. This will work."

She had absolutely no illusions about this cooking adventure turning out to be anything but a disaster. Still, it was sweet that Jackson wanted to help her. She just hated the thought of disappointing him.

Why exactly did he elect himself to teach Serena to cook?

Because it was easier than discussing his background. That was one thing about June, she never prodded him for answers. But Serena was the exact opposite. She was most definitely the curious sort. He wasn't sure how to deal with her.

For so long now, he'd been fine with leaving the past alone. But being around Serena had him reexamining his life. It all made him uncomfortable. The more he thought about things, the more he questioned his choices.

He didn't like the uneasiness filling him. Before he'd arrived in Austria, he'd had a plan—a focus. His life was to revolve around his work. Now he didn't know if that was the right path for him.

What he needed now was to get away from here—away from Serena. He'd be able to think clearly and he could go back to—to what? His lonely condo in New York? His workaholic tendencies?

No matter what his life may be lacking, it was better than the alternative—loving and losing. Once down that road was enough for him. He was better off alone.

He shoved all these thoughts and questions into the box at the back of his mind. Tomorrow his camera crew would arrive. And he doubted that his life would ever intersect Serena's again. Although, the thought of not seeing her again settled heavy in his chest.

"Where do I start?" Serena's voice jarred him from his thoughts.

"You'll need to rinse the shrimp under some water and remove the tails. And while you do that, I'll put on a pot of water for the pasta."

He couldn't believe that no one had ever taken the time to teach her to cook. He felt bad for her. It made him wonder what kind of a childhood she'd had.

"Were you left alone a lot as a child?" The question was out of his mouth before he realized that it was none of his business. He placed the pot on the burner and turned the heat to high. "Never mind, you don't have to answer that."

She glanced over at him. "Is this my friend Jackson asking or is it Jackson Bennett, king of the morning shows, who wants to know?"

Ouch! That comment hurt more than he was expecting. "I promise nothing you share with me will show up on my show or in the press. I'd like to be your friend."

She rinsed off another handful of colossal shrimp and set them aside before she turned back to him. "I'd like that. It's just that I never had anyone in my life that I could completely trust."

"That must have been rough."

She shrugged. "I dealt with it. I learned pretty quick that I could only count on myself."

"Still, that's not right. A kid should have someone to turn to—someone to rely on."

Serena arched a brow. "Are we talking about me or you?"

Jackson realized that he'd let his emotions get away from him. It was just that he felt a strong connection with Serena. It was something that he'd never felt with June or anyone else in his life.

He cleared his throat. "Why don't I give you a hand?"

He moved next to her at the sink and started removing the tails of the shrimp. Why did he keep opening himself up to her? He knew better. The real Jackson Bennett was a man with flaws and scars. He would never add up to the vision she gained from watching him on television.

Serena was used to men who had it all together—looks, careers and charisma. He was the shell of the man he used to be. Cancer had more victims than those carrying the disease. It could suck life right out of the people around it—grinding hopes and dreams into smithereens. And sometimes leaving in its wake a broken person.

"Do you cook a lot?" Serena asked.

He shrugged as he swallowed hard. "As much as I can. It's the only way I've found to make sure that I fit into my suits." He reached for a couple cloves of garlic. "Eating out is tempting, but then I start putting on the pounds that I can't lose even when I go to the gym."

"I totally get that. They say the camera puts on ten pounds but that was before high definition. Now it adds fifteen pounds and amplifies any wrinkles or blemishes. So if you can show me an easier way to watch the scale, I'm all for it."

Jackson placed a clove of garlic on a cutting board. He showed her how to put the flat side of a chef's knife on the clove and with her palm press down on it to remove the skin. She did the same with the other clove. Then Serena minced the garlic before chopping some fresh parsley and tomatoes that they'd picked up at the market.

"Jackson?"

He'd just added butter to the skillet. "Yes?"

"I thought I was supposed to cook the meal."

She was right. He'd just gotten so caught up in his thoughts of the past that he'd been moving around the kitchen on automatic. "You're right. Sorry. It's just habit." He stepped to the side of the stove. "Okay, then. Here. Take the handle. You'll want to swish it so the butter coats the bottom of the pan."

She did as he said.

"Now add the garlic." He talked her through the process of adding the shrimp, the fresh parsley and a little seasoning. Jackson inhaled the savory aroma. "Smells wonderful."

He added the angel-hair pasta to the pot of boiling water, gave it a stir and lowered the temperature.

"You're cheating," Serena said.

And then he realized he should have let her do all the steps. "But it's so much easier when we work as a team. Trust me, you're doing the hard part."

"What do I do next?"

"Turn the shrimp."

He hovered just over her shoulder, watching her every move. He told himself that he was just trying to be an attentive mentor, but the truth was he was drawn to Serena like a magnet. There was something so appealing about her and it went far deeper than her natural beauty. There was a tenderness—a vulnerability—about her. And she made him feel as though he were her equal—as though they were perfectly matched for each other.

"Jackson." Serena waved a hand in front of him to gain his attention. "The shrimp's pink."

Pulled back from his thoughts, he blinked and quickly took stock of where dinner stood. He told her to drain the shrimp and set them aside. Then they added more butter, flour, milk, chicken broth and seasoning to the pan. Then the most important part—the cheese. She added lots of mozzarella and Parmesan. In the meantime, Jackson drained the pasta.

They worked well together. Really well. It was like they'd been doing it all their lives. And he wasn't sure what to make of it. Perhaps he'd isolated himself too much since his wife's death and now he was overreacting to Serena's presence.

Oh, who was he kidding? He was falling for this woman—

this award-winning actress. And he had no idea what to do about it.

"Do I add the tomatoes now?" she asked.

"Yes. And the shrimp. And make sure you remove it from the heat."

He wasn't sure where this evening was headed, but he sure was hungry now. And his hunger had absolutely nothing to do with the amazing Alfredo shrimp pasta they'd just created.

CHAPTER THIRTEEN

DINNER HAD BEEN PERFECT.

The company was amazing.

Jackson couldn't recall the last time he'd had such a wonderful evening. And now Serena leaned back on the couch with Gizmo on one side of her and Jackson on the other. The glow of the fireplace added a romantic ambience to the room. And when Jackson settled his arm around her, she didn't resist.

Was it wrong that he wanted this night with her? He knew that it would be a fleeting moment. After all, he was going to head back to New York as soon as his work was completed.

But there was something special between them. He wasn't ready to put a label on it. Not yet.

"And what has you so deep in thought?" Jackson asked, noticing he wasn't the only one staring reflectively into the fire.

"I don't know."

"It wouldn't happen to be that masterpiece you've been working on every spare moment you get, would it?"

"You'll laugh if I tell you."

Jackson pulled back so he could look at her. "Why do you think I would do that?"

She shrugged. "It's what has happened in the past."

"Not by me."

"True." Serena worried her bottom lip. "I shouldn't have said that. You've been so kind to me, helping me in the kitchen and visiting the Christmas market even though you really didn't feel up to it. Those are things other men in my life would never have done. I shouldn't have made such a thoughtless remark."

"It's okay." He once again settled next to her.

"Can I have a do-over?" When he nodded, she said, "I was thinking about my script."

"You're writing a television show?" He wanted to know more about her. Everything about her fascinated him. "Have you always been a writer?"

Serena didn't say anything. He willed her to open up to him because she was like a mystery. The more he knew about her, the more he wanted to learn.

Her gaze met his. "I've always been a reader. When I was younger, I would write, but then my father found out and told me that I was wasting my time."

"I'm sorry he smashed your dreams."

She shrugged. "I shouldn't have let him. But I was young and easily swayed."

"I take it you're not so easily swayed these days."

"I'd like to think not. Time and experience have a way of changing a person."

"And in your case, I think you've made the most of your experiences."

She arched a brow at him. "You think you know me that well?"

A small smile teased his lips. "I think you are an amazing woman with a big heart. You love your puppy and you take in injured strangers."

Color rushed to her face. He couldn't believe someone as beautiful as her hadn't been complimented on a regular basis. But he couldn't deny that she was adorable with the rosy hue in her cheeks. Not that he was thinking of starting anything serious with her.

It was time he changed the subject before he said too much and made them both uncomfortable. "So what are you writing? A family saga? Or a paranormal series?"

"No…ah, actually, it's a big-screen movie." She paused as though expecting him to say something, but he quietly waited for her to finish. "A family saga with a central romance."

"That's great."

"You're just saying that."

"No. I'm not. I read some every day. Mostly biographies but I also enjoy some suspense. I think anyone that writes has a precious gift."

This time she shifted on the couch until she could look him in the eyes. "Do you mean that?"

"I do. I'd like to read it, if you'd let me."

She shook her head and sat back on the couch. "You can't. It's not finished."

"How about when it's finished?"

"That's the thing. I'm stuck. I've tried different endings but nothing I've tried seems to work."

"Give it time. Don't force yourself. If you relax, the answer will come to you."

"Do you really believe that?"

"I do. It works for me. When I'm working on a segment. I like to do a lot of my own writing."

"Thanks." She turned her head and smiled at him. "I really appreciate your support."

He lowered his voice. "Just know that you can always talk to me—about anything. I care about you."

Serena's heart jumped into her throat. She turned her head to say something, but words failed her. Her gaze met his dark eyes. He wanted her. It was right there in his eyes. They were filled with desire.

When he lowered his head, she found her lips were just inches from his. Her heart beat faster. Should she do it? Should she make the next move? Meet him halfway?

Perhaps actions did actually speak louder than words. She leaned forward, claiming his lips with her own. They were smooth, warm and oh, so inviting.

Jackson shifted on the couch so that he was cupping her face. Her arms instinctively wrapped around his neck. The kiss deepened. There was no hesitation—no tentativeness. There was only passion and desire.

It seemed so right for them to be together. It was like she'd been looking for him all of her life. He accepted her as she was and he hadn't tried to change her.

Jackson leaned back on the couch, pulling her on top of him. Her hands shifted to his chest. Beneath her fingers she felt his strapping muscles. Her heart fluttered in her chest as her body tingled all over. She'd never felt this way with a man before—not even close.

Thoughts of Jackson's approaching departure crowded into her head, but she forcefully shoved them away. If all she had after this vacation were memories, she wanted them to be good ones. She wanted them to be so good that she would recall them with a smile when she was a little old lady.

She was beginning to realize the greatest gifts in life were the good memories. She wanted to make exceptional memories with Jackson. She needed him to remember her, because she would never ever forget him. Not a chance.

Jackson took the lead with their kiss. Exploring, taunting and teasing. Her body pulsed with lust and desire. Beneath her palm, his heart beat hard and fast. Oh, yeah, this was going to be an unforgettable night—

Something cold and wet pressed to her cheek. *What in the world?*

Serena pulled back to find Gizmo standing up on his back legs with his nose next to hers. A curious look reflected in his eyes as though he was thinking: *What did I miss? Huh? Huh?*

Simultaneously Serena and Jackson let out a laugh. Gizmo looking pleased with himself.

"Arff! Arff!"

With a smile on his face, Jackson said, "I think we should take this into the bedroom."

Serena's gaze moved between her two favorite males. "I think you're right."

Once they got Gizmo settled on his dog bed, Jackson took her hand in his. She led him to the bedroom where they could explore these kisses in private.

CHAPTER FOURTEEN

SERENA COULDN'T SLEEP.

She was too wound up—too happy.

For a while now, she'd been watching Jackson sleep. His face was so handsome and he looked so peaceful. He was so much more than the alpha image he projected on television. There was a gentleness to him—a compassion that broke through the wall around her heart.

This evening had been more amazing than she'd ever thought possible. And as she watched Jackson draw in one deep breath after the other, she had a light-bulb moment. She realized the reason she couldn't finish her screenplay.

Her mind started to play over where she'd left her heroine bereft after the black moment with the hero. Until now, everything Serena had tried to bring the couple back together had felt hollow and empty. And that was because she didn't know what it was like to fall in love.

Until now...

She was falling in love with Jackson Bennett—the man who greeted America with a smile and a mug of coffee every weekday.

And he was the inspiration she'd needed to finish the script. Perhaps this was a whole new start to her life. She knew that she was jumping too far ahead and she had to slow down.

After all, Jackson had said that he cared about her—not that he loved her or that he was falling in love with her. Maybe that was the line he handed all his women. She didn't want to believe it because he just didn't seem like the type to go casually from one relationship to the next.

Was that how her heroine would feel? Or would she be confident that they could overcome their biggest obstacle? The questions continued to whirl through her mind, but she kept them relegated to her script. She would figure out where her relationship with Jackson went later—preferably after she got some sleep.

But for now, she had a mission. She gently slipped out of bed. There was a distinct nip in the air. She threw on clothes as fast as she could. All the while she kept glancing over her shoulder to make sure she hadn't disturbed Jackson. His breathing was deep and even.

Holding her breath, she tiptoed out of the room, closing the door behind her. The fire had died off in the great room and a definite chill was in the air. Gizmo lifted his head and looked at her. He didn't make any attempt to move from his oversize cushion with his blue blanket and his stuffed teddy he used for a pillow. She turned on a lamp next to the couch. Gizmo gave her a curious look as she made her way to the fireplace to rekindle the fire. But apparently it was too cold or he was too tired to beg her to take him outside. She couldn't blame him.

With the fire started, she fussed over Gizmo before gathering her laptop and moving to the end of the couch closest to the fireplace. With a throw blanket over her legs, she opened her laptop and set to work. For the first time in quite a while, her fingers moved rapidly over the keyboard. When the words came to her without a lot of effort, it was like magic. It was as though the story had taken on a life of its own. The characters were speaking to her and all she had to do was type out the words.

She didn't know how much time had passed but the sun was just starting to come up when she typed *The End* and pressed Save for the last time. She shut her laptop, set it on the coffee table and then laid her head on the back-rest of the couch with a satisfied smile, her heavy eyelids drooping closed.

Quack. Quack.

Jackson's eyes opened at the sound of his alarm. His assistant, who was fresh out of college, had decided to play a trick on him and had reset his phone to various obnoxious sounds. A duck for his alarm, an old car horn for his phone and other random, off-the-wall sounds. What she didn't count on was him liking them. They were easy to distinguish from everyone else's cell phone. And best of all, it made those around him smile. So he'd left the tones as they were.

He wondered what Serena thought of his quacking alarm. He opened an eye and glanced over to find the bed empty. Serena was gone. He ran his hand over the pillow and mattress, finding her spot cold. Apparently she'd been gone for quite some time.

He sat up and looked around the room, but there was no sign of her. What did her absence mean? Did she regret their lovemaking? Did he regret it?

The reality of their actions sharpened his sleep-hazed thoughts. He'd made love to another woman. He sunk back against the pillows. Maybe it was a good thing that Serena had gone. He wasn't sure he'd be good company right now.

He'd broken his word to himself. He was moving forward—starting something—leaving the memories of his wife behind. Guilt slugged him in the gut. What would June think?

No. He couldn't go there. Right now, he had to straighten things out with Serena. He had to tell her that they'd made a mistake. But if Serena hadn't spent the entire night, did that mean she wasn't looking for a relationship? Could it be that easy?

The only way to find the answer was to find Serena. He quickly showered and dressed. His film crew was picking him up this morning. And while out and about, he'd arranged to rent another vehicle that he'd pick up some time that day.

He exited the master suite and Gizmo came running up to him. "Shh…"

Gizmo moved to the front door. Jackson glanced around, expecting Serena to be hot on Gizmo's heels, but she was nowhere to be found. Jackson grabbed his coat and the leash. Gizmo was so excited that he kept stepping in front of Jackson, almost tripping him.

"Arff!"

A distinct grunt soon followed.

Jackson put his finger to his lips. "Shh…"

Gizmo's tail continued to rapidly swish.

Jackson tiptoed over to the couch and there he found Serena curled up in a ball beneath a little blanket that didn't even completely cover her. She'd rather freeze on the couch than be snug in bed with him?

The thought dug at him as he rushed to the bedroom to grab a blanket from the bed. He draped it over her. With a sigh, she snuggled to it.

Jackson stared down at her very sweet face. She looked almost angelic as she slept. He wondered what she was dreaming about. He doubted that it would be about him. Not that he wanted her to dream of him.

No matter what Serena said, she still didn't trust him. Her sleeping out here was proof of it. And why should she when he acted without thinking? He had nothing to offer her.

"Arff!"

He had to take Gizmo out before Serena woke. It would be so much easier if they didn't speak—not just yet. He had to get his thoughts sorted. He needed time to find the right words to say to her—to salvage their friendship. Serena was a very special person and he hated the thought of completely losing her from his life.

CHAPTER FIFTEEN

THE CABIN WAS QUIET—too quiet.

Serena utilized the printer on the desk in the great room and spent most of the day proofing her script. But the reason she'd rushed in and immersed herself in editing the script had more to do with filling in the silence around her. She was amazed at how quickly she'd gotten used to having Jackson around. And how much she missed him when he was gone.

Warning bells rang in her head. She was getting in deep—perhaps too deep. It wasn't like Jackson was asking for her hand in marriage. Not that she wanted him to drop down on one knee. She just wanted to know that he cared for her—and his feelings for her were more than a passing fancy.

Her gaze moved toward the window. Evening was settling in and snow had begun to fall. Big fat flakes fluttered about before piling on top of the many feet of snow. And Jackson was out there somewhere on these mountain roads. She wished he'd taken the four-wheel drive like she'd insisted. But he'd assured her that he would be fine. If he was so fine—why wasn't he home yet?

She gathered the pages she'd been working on and put a rubber band around them. With a deep breath and a bit of trepidation, she carried the script into the master suite.

Jackson had requested to read it. Why should she resist him? After all, if she wanted it to be produced into a movie, a lot of other people would have to read it.

She stopped in front of the king-size bed. She lowered the pages that she'd been clutching to her chest. The pages still had her corrections on them, but they were clean enough for Jackson to read.

Her gaze moved to the title page. Letting Jackson read this would be more revealing than making love to him—at least that was the way it felt in that moment. They weren't just words on a page, they were an intimate piece of her. Her empty stomach roiled. She swallowed hard.

Without giving it any further thought, she placed the manuscript at the end of the bed. Then she turned and headed for the door as fast as her legs would carry her. She knew that if she didn't leave quickly she would chicken out and take back the pages.

Just then a set of headlights streamed in through the windows. Jackson was home. She smiled and Gizmo ran to the door barking.

"It looks like I'm not the only one anxious to see Jackson, huh, boy?"

Gizmo turned to her and wagged his tail before he turned back to the door to continue barking.

Serena glanced at the clock on the fireplace mantel. She would have to let the little furbaby get the first greeting. She was needed in the kitchen. She'd prepared dinner to the best of her ability and it was just about to come out of the oven.

Time to get it over with.

Jackson had played out this scene in his mind more times than he cared to admit. None of it ended well. But he couldn't put it off any longer.

He opened the door, not sure what to expect. Gizmo jumped up on him with his tail swishing back and forth. Jackson had him get down so that he could step inside and close the door.

Then Jackson bent over to pet Gizmo's fuzzy head. "Hey, boy, I'm happy to see you, too."

Maybe he should reconsider getting a dog. It was really nice to come home to somebody. But it was Serena that he wanted to see. Where was she?

He'd been thinking of what to say to her all day, to the point where he'd been distracted during taping. It'd made for a very long day with many retakes. And he'd ended up frustrating his crew. He'd apologized and blamed it on his ankle. He wasn't ready to tell anyone about Serena. They'd make more of the situation than he wanted.

He'd just shrugged off his coat and hung it near the door to dry when he heard footsteps behind him. He turned and there was Serena looking all down-to-earth in faded jeans, a red sweater and her hair pulled up in a ponytail.

There was something different about her. It took him a moment and then he realized that she'd changed her hair back to its former blond color—at least close to it.

"You changed your hair?"

She smiled and nodded. "I thought it was time that I got back to being me."

He didn't know what that meant. Did it have something to do with her creeping out of his bed during the night? Was she sending him some sort of message? If so, he wasn't sure he understood.

"It looks nice." That was not what he'd planned to say, but he was caught off guard.

"And you are just in time."

"For what?"

"Dinner. I cooked again."

"Oh. Okay." Why was she acting all nice? He thought she would be angry at him for rushing things last night. Instead, she was cooking for him. What had he missed?

"Don't look so worried. It came out of a box and I followed the directions." She sent him a puzzled look as though she didn't understand why he was acting strange. "I set the table in the kitchen, but we can eat in here if you'd prefer."

"Serena, stop it."

Her eyes widened. "Stop what?"

"Acting all nice. Like nothing happened."

"Oh. You mean last night."

"Yes, last night. Don't act like you forgot."

"How could I forget?"

At last, they were getting somewhere. "Well, say it."

"Say what?"

Was she going to make this whole thing difficult? Was he going to have to drag every word out of her mouth? One thing was for sure, if he didn't know it before, he knew it now, Serena was so different from June. When June was angry, he knew it. With the outside world, his wife had been reserved. With him, not so much. Thankfully they hadn't argued much.

But Serena for some reason was masking her displeasure. Instead of telling him the problem, she was hiding behind a friendly but cool demeanor. He didn't like it. He'd rather face the problem and then move on. So if she wasn't going to do something about it, he would.

"Say what you're upset about. Don't hide it."

She worried her bottom lip. "That's strange, because I'm usually a much better actress. It's nothing for you to worry about."

"Of course I'm worried. It involves me." He stopped

himself just short of saying that if there was a way he could make it up to her he would.

That was how he used to handle June. Then again, maybe that was how June handled him. He wasn't so sure anymore. The more time he spent with Serena, the more clarity he was gaining on his past. Maybe it hadn't been as perfect as he wanted to remember.

She sighed. "I don't want it to ruin dinner. We can talk after we eat."

He did not understand this woman. She wanted to eat first and then argue? Who did things like that? Before he could ask her, she'd headed into the kitchen.

He sighed and shook his head. He might as well as get comfortable. This was going to be a long evening. He headed for the master suite to take off his suit jacket and tie.

When he entered the room, he flipped on the overhead light. He kicked off his shoes and loosened his tie. He really didn't have any appetite. He'd been tied up in knots all day.

He sat down on the bed and his hand landed on paper. He glanced down to find a ream of paper. He picked it up and read the top sheet: *Life Atop The Ferris Wheel* by Mae Ellwood.

Jackson removed the rubber band and flipped to the last page. The last line read: *The End*. She'd finished it? But last night she'd said she was stuck.

He dropped the pages to the bed and headed for the kitchen. He plowed through the door and came to a stop when he found the kitchen aglow with a candle in the center. Dishes were set out and dinner was awaiting him. But it was the woman wearing the great big smile that drew and held his attention.

"Dinner's ready. I hope you brought your appetite."

"I, uh, sure." But he couldn't eat, not yet. There was one thing he had to know. "Did you get out of bed last night to go work on your script?"

The smile slipped from her face. "Is that what's bothering you?"

"Of course it is. Imagine how I felt when I woke up alone and the spot next to me was cold, as in you never slept there."

She approached him. "I'm sorry. I didn't think. Well, actually I did a lot of thinking. That's why I couldn't go to sleep. I realized what I was missing for the ending of the script and I had to go write it out while it was fresh in my mind. I was afraid that if I went to sleep I would forget parts of it."

He breathed his first easy breath all day. "So you didn't leave because you regretted what happened between us?"

The smile returned to her face. "No, silly. I don't regret any of it."

He reached out and drew her to him. She melted into his embrace as though they'd been doing it for years. He planted a kiss on her lips. She immediately kissed him back.

As his lips moved over hers, each muscle in his body began to relax. He had no idea until now how worked up he'd been. And it'd all been over a screenplay.

Serena pressed a hand to his chest and pulled back. "Are you ready to eat?"

He really didn't want to eat at the moment. He'd be more than happy to keep kissing her. But he knew this meal was a big deal. And he was proud of her for going outside her comfort zone and cooking dinner—even if it came out of a box.

"Sure. What is it?"

"It's baked mac-'n'-cheese. Is that all right?"

"Sure."

"And there was some bread that I picked up at the market."

"Sounds good to me." After they were settled at the table, Jackson said, "So I saw the manuscript on the bed. Did you leave that for me?"

She nodded. "Did you change your mind about reading it?"

"Definitely not." He took her hand in his. "Thank you for trusting me with it."

"Thank you for caring enough to read it."

Tonight Serena would sleep and he'd stay up. He loved to read and the fact that Serena had penned this script made it all the more special. No matter how much he tried to deny it, Serena was special. He just didn't know what to do about his growing feelings for her and his nagging guilt over letting go of his past.

CHAPTER SIXTEEN

THE FOLLOWING EVENING, Serena paced back and forth in the great room. Gizmo was right behind her, pacing, too. Back and forth they went, from the staircase to the front door. If she stopped, Gizmo stopped. He always did sense when something was bothering her.

She stopped and looked down at the dog, who sat down and looked up at her. "What are we going to do? We can't keep pacing. It's not helping anything."

"Arff!"

"Sorry. I'm too worked up to sit."

If only she had something to take her mind off Jackson's impending critique of her script. But now that the script was done, she didn't have anything else planned for the trip. If only she knew how to knit or crochet, she'd have something to do with her hands.

Instead, all she could do was wonder if Jackson had liked the story line. He'd left that morning while she'd still been asleep. And now he was home, but he hadn't even mentioned one word about the script. He could have at least given her a clue if he liked what he'd read so far.

Jackson exited the kitchen.

Serena stopped pacing. Instead of barraging him with questions about her script, she calmly asked, "Do you need help with dinner?"

"No. It's all under control."

Should she ask the question that was teetering on the tip of her tongue? But what if he didn't like it? What if he hated it? Her stomach plummeted.

Forgetting that he was still in the room, she resumed pacing. In time, hopefully the activity would work out some of her nervous tension. Because she'd resolved not to ask Jackson about the script. She would not. It was for the best.

"Anything on your mind?" Jackson asked.

She stopped and looked at him. Was he reading her mind? Or was this his way of toying with her? Well, she wasn't falling for it.

"No," she said as normally as possible. "Is it time to eat?"

"Actually it won't be ready for a while. I thought we could do something in the meantime."

Her gaze narrowed. "What did you have in mind?"

"You'll see. Dress warm. We're going outside."

She didn't know what he was up to, but it obviously had nothing to do with her script. "Don't you have something else you need to do?"

He paused as though considering her question. "Hmm... the meat is marinating. The potatoes are prepped. And the salad is ready. No. I have everything done."

She frowned at him. How could he forget about her script? Was it that forgettable? Disappointment settled in her chest. "Maybe you have something to read?"

A smile pulled at his very kissable lips. "I don't have anything urgent—"

"Jackson!" Every bit of her patience had been used up.

"Oh. You mean your script?" he said it innocently enough, but the smile on his face said that he'd been playing with her this whole time.

"Of course I mean the manuscript. I thought you wanted to read it."

"I did."

"You did? You mean read the whole thing already? I just gave it to you last night."

"I know. And it's your fault that I didn't get any sleep."

"You stayed up all night and read it?"

He nodded, but he didn't say a word. There was no smile on his face. There was no clue as to what he thought of her script. He was going to make her drag it out of him.

"And…" She waved her hands as though pulling the words from him.

"And…I think…that…"

"Jackson, say it. If you hated it, just say so."

"I love it."

"What?" Surely she hadn't heard him correctly. If he loved it, why did he make it so hard for her to get an answer out of him?

"Serena, you're very talented. Your words are vivid and emotional. I could see the entire story play out in my mind."

Her heart was pounding with excitement. And a smile pulled at her lips. "Really? You're not just saying that to be nice, are you?"

"Do I look like a nice guy to you?"

"Well, yes, you do. So I have to be sure. Because if you didn't like it, you can tell me. I can take it. I might cry myself to sleep, but I can take it."

He laughed. "So much for the calm and cool Serena Winston that graces the covers of all the glossy magazines. This uncertainty and nervousness is a whole new side of you."

"Jackson!"

"Okay." The smile slipped from his face. "Yes, I'm serious. You are a talented writer and I would like to interview you—"

"No." She didn't know how he could take such a nice compliment and ruin it in the next breath, but that was exactly what he'd done.

"You didn't even let me finish."

"You don't need to. I thought you were different. I thought you were my friend. But you're just like the others, you want something from me."

He frowned at her. "I don't know who you spend your time with, but I'm not like that. If you had let me finish, I was going to say that I could do the interview and it would be about your writing. We could start spinning the story of your screenplay and then you'd have producers and directors pounding down your door to get their hands on it."

"Oh." She wanted to believe him. She wanted to think that he wasn't after her to help further his career, but she'd trusted people in the past and they'd turned against her. "I don't think so. I want this screenplay to sell on its own merits and not the fact that I'm famous. I need to know that I can do it on my own."

His eyebrows rose. "You do know what you're turning down, don't you? I can do the interview according to your rules. I don't have to touch upon your personal life… unless you want me to."

"I… I don't know."

"Will you at least consider it?"

She sighed. "I guess. But don't get your hopes up."

"I won't. But don't dismiss the fact that you can present yourself to the world as something more than an accomplished actress."

She nodded. "I hear you. I'll consider it."

"And while you do that, I have a surprise for you. Now, go put on your warmest clothes."

"You were serious about that?" When he nodded, she asked, "What do you have in mind?"

"You'll find out as soon as you change. Hurry."

Sled riding.

Serena felt like a kid again. There was a hill beside the cabin that ended in a small field. They'd been outside for an hour. She hadn't laughed this much in a very long time, if ever. Even Gizmo was having fun riding down the hill. He took turns riding on her lap and then on Jackson's.

At first, she wasn't sure about taking Gizmo on a sled. But the hill wasn't too steep. And her pup seemed perfectly fine with it. Jackson didn't go down the hill as much as her because walking up the incline with the boot on his ankle was a hard and slow process for him. At least he'd thought ahead and had wrapped a bag around his leg to keep it dry.

Serena felt bad that he couldn't enjoy sledding as much as her, but he insisted she keep going and Gizmo had barked his agreement. Jackson had even brought along a thermos of his amazing hot chocolate. And as the sun set, she couldn't think of anyplace she'd rather be.

After they took a seat on an old log, she turned to him. "Thank you for this. Would you believe I've never been sledding before?"

"Never?"

She shook her head.

"I thought you said you went to Tahoe."

"Later. As an adult. By then I spent most of my time in the lodge." She took a sip of hot cocoa. "When I was a kid, I didn't know what snow was. My father hated it. And my mother, well, she had her own life."

"I'm sorry. I grew up in New York, so we had snow often."

"Did your parents take you sledding?"

He shook his head. "My father left when I was seven. And my mother was always working. When she wasn't working, she was blaming me for my father leaving."

"That's awful. It must have been so hard on you. I'm so sorry."

He stared off into the distance. He didn't say anything for the longest time. She didn't push him. Maybe it was time that she opened up more about herself.

She drew in a deep breath to settle her nerves. "I know what it's like to have a rough childhood. Though most people wouldn't guess it because my family had money and fame. A lot of people think that money equates to happiness. I can testify that it doesn't. Sometimes I think the more money you have, the unhappier you are."

She chanced a glance as Jackson to see if he was listening.

Jackson cleared his throat. "My father was a doctor. But when he split, he was terrible at paying my mother what he owed her. She had to fight and beg for every check. And when they did arrive, they were always months late."

"Do you still speak to your parents?"

He shook his head. "I haven't seen my father since I was nine or ten. He remarried and that was that. As for my mother, she never did stop blaming me for her marriage breaking up. I send her a check once a month to make sure she's taken care of."

"You send her money, but you don't visit?"

"It's better that way."

"Where does your mother live now?"

"In New York."

"So you live close to each other, but you never see each other?"

Jackson turned to her. "Why are you making it out like it's all my fault? My mother could just as easily track me down. My address is on every check I send—checks that she promptly cashes."

Serena knew she probably should mind her own business and keep her thoughts to herself, but she knew what it was like to lose a parent—a parent that she had unresolved issues with.

"I understand that it's tough for you, but talking as someone who recently lost a parent, I have regrets. There are so many things that I wish I had told my father. He may have annoyed me and he may not have been the perfect parent, but he was the one that was always there for me. While my mother was off moving from one younger man to the next, my father was home every night. He cared about what I did. I didn't always agree with him—okay, I rarely agreed with him—but I believe that everything he did, he did because he loved me. He just didn't know how to tell me. As a result, I never got to thank him or tell him…" Her voice cracked with emotion. She cleared her throat. "Tell him that through it all…I loved him, too. That chance was stolen away when he had a massive heart attack. Now, all I'm left with are memories and regrets."

Jackson wrapped his arm over her shoulders and pulled her close. He leaned over and pressed a kiss to the top of her head. "Neither of us have had an easy time when it comes to family. But I'm sure your father knew that you loved him."

"Just as your mother knows that each check is your way of saying that you love her?"

"Something like that."

Serena felt as though she was finally getting through to him. She shifted so that she could look into his eyes. "Tell her. Tell your mother how you feel before it's too late."

He shook his head. "It is too late. Anything that was between us ended a long time ago."

"A parent and child's love is forever."

"Maybe in some cases. But not in ours. I'm just a re-minder of how her life went wrong."

"Will you at least think about it?" She knew she had no right to ask it of him, but she didn't want him to end up with nothing but remorse. And when he did realize the error of his ways, she didn't want him to talk to a cold tombstone that couldn't talk back.

"I will, if you'll agree to that interview."

Her lips pressed together into a firm line. One thing had nothing to do with the other. Nothing at all.

"Listen," Jackson said, "I know you don't like hiding who you are. I think the real you is pretty special. Don't let people steal that away from you. Stand up for who you are and what you've created."

He made a good point. It had felt so good washing out that temporary red dye from her hair, even if it all didn't come out. But was what he was asking of her the right move? Could she trust him to do the right thing? She'd heard him talking on his phone when he didn't think she was around, and he was hungry for a big story to propel his career even higher.

The only way to know was to ask. She worried her lip. If he was on the up-and-up, he would take her question as a sign of doubt in him. And if he was stringing her along for a big story, he'd never admit it. So where did that leave her?

Her heart said to trust him. He'd never hurt her. But her mind said to be cautious. She'd been burned before by people that she thought she could trust. She wished there was an easy way to figure out whom she could trust and whom she couldn't. If her past was any indication, she wasn't a good judge of character.

Jackson's gaze met hers. "I can see that you're struggling with the decision. What if we do the interview and I give you the decision of whether to air it or not?"

In his gaze, she found honesty and so much more. Her heart pounded out its decision, overruling her mind. Sometimes she overthought things.

She pulled off her glove and held out her hand. "You have a deal."

He removed his glove and wrapped his warm hand around hers. "It's a date. Tomorrow evening after my last day of filming, I'll have the crew stop by and film it for us."

"And they won't mind? You know, staying late and doing this?"

He smiled. "When they find out who I'll be interviewing, they'll be falling all over themselves to help out."

"But they won't tell anyone?"

"Not if you don't want them to. I've worked with this crew for a long time. They are a good bunch."

Serena thought about it for a moment. "If they could just keep it quiet until after the New Year that would be good."

He lifted her hand to his lips. "It's a deal."

He kissed the back of her hand. And then he leaned over, pressing his lips to hers. She approved of the way he sealed deals. They might have to do a lot more negotiating in the future.

CHAPTER SEVENTEEN

In a strange twist of fate, that car accident had been a blessing.

As the thought crossed his mind, Jackson wondered if he should have had the doctor examine his head as well as his ankle. But if not for the accident, he most likely never would have met Serena. Instead of looking forward to Christmas, he would be looking for ways to avoid the holiday.

Just as promised, the next evening, Jackson's crew showed up at the cabin to film the interview. Jackson wasn't sure what to expect of Serena. He knew that she was professional, but he also knew how nervous she was about her new venture into script writing.

Instead of dressing in the latest fashion and wearing her signature eye makeup, she'd dressed modestly in a cream-colored sweater and matching pants. Her blond hair was twisted in back and pinned up. Wisps of hair surrounded her face, softening the style. And though she did wear makeup, it was light and just enough to accentuate her beauty. She looked perfect.

They'd previously agreed on a list of questions and Jackson followed the script, even though it was in his nature to venture into unknown territory. But out of respect to

Serena, he stuck by their agreement. That was until the very end…

"Why have you decided to make this move from in front of the cameras to a place behind the scenes?"

Serena's green eyes momentarily widened as she realized it wasn't one of the preapproved questions. But he hadn't been able to help himself. He found this question to be paramount.

Like a professional, she had taken the question in stride. "I wouldn't say this is a permanent move. I've already signed on for an upcoming movie."

"That's great. I'm sure your fans will be relieved to hear the news. I know I am." It was the truth. He loved her movies. They'd helped get him through some of the toughest days of his life after his wife died. "But what drove you to try something new?"

"Actually, writing isn't new for me. The part that is new is sharing my words with the world. I think that writing is as close to magic as you can get—bringing life to a page. And I've found that I love putting words on the page."

And now that the interview was over, it was time Jackson worked a little magic of his own. He sent the interview over to his agent. He wanted Fred to have the interview edited and polished just the way it would be done if it were to air on *Hello America*.

His agent immediately phoned. As they talked, Fred got him to admit that if Serena did go through with releasing the interview to the public that it would help not just her but him as well. His agent begged him to release it or let him do it. Fred swore that this was what they needed to rocket Jackson past the other applicants for the national evening news spot.

Jackson told his agent to calm down. This interview

wasn't for him—no matter how much his career could use the boost. He'd truly done the interview with altruistic intentions. And he'd made his agent promise to have the raw footage cut and cleaned up. Then he was to forward it back to Jackson so he could play it for Serena, who still hadn't made her mind up about airing it.

"Phone me as soon as it's finished," Jackson said to his agent.

"Are you sure we can't just use some of it? I mean, come on, she's been missing for almost two weeks now. It's all the media is talking about."

"No. And don't you dare leak her location or you'll be fired."

His agent laughed. "You'd never do that. We've been together since the beginning—"

"Fred, I'm serious. Don't do anything that we'll both regret."

"Don't worry. I've got your back."

"And you'll get the footage back to me by tomorrow night?" Jackson really wanted to present it to Serena for Christmas. He was certain she would be so impressed by the results that she'd gladly release it.

"I'll do my best," Fred said. "But you have to realize that most people are already on Christmas holiday."

"Surely you know someone you can trust to turn this around quickly."

"Well…there is someone, but he's not cheap, especially with this being the holiday."

"Money isn't an issue."

"I'll give him a call."

"Thank you," Jackson said. "I'll owe you."

"And I'll collect." His agent laughed.

As Jackson disconnected the call, he knew that Fred would in fact collect on that favor. Usually it was to get

Jackson to make an appearance at some stuffy dinner that he wouldn't want to attend. But Jackson would deal with the ramifications later.

Right now, he was feeling optimistic about the final cut of the interview. Serena was a natural in front of the camera. Her face had lit up when she was talking about her script. And he'd never had so much fun interviewing anyone.

"What has you smiling?" Serena stepped through the doorway after taking Gizmo for a short walk.

"I'm just happy, is all." He stood next to the window, staring out at the snowy evening. "Do you think it always snows this much?"

"I have no idea, but I like it. It puts me in the holiday spirit." The smile slipped from her face. "I suppose now that your work is done here you'll have to head back to the States."

He reached out and wrapped his arms around her waist. "Are you saying you're already tired of me?"

"I could never get tired of you. I was just wishing you could stay for Christmas. After all, it's just in two days."

"That soon?" When she nodded, he said, "Well, if you were to twist my arm, I might consider staying. After all, my flight isn't until the day after Christmas."

Instead of smiling, she frowned.

"What's the matter?" he asked. "I thought you wanted me to stay."

"I do. That's not it. I just realized that I don't have any-thing for you—you know, Christmas presents." Her eyes reflected her concern. "Do you think it's too late to head into the village to shop?"

"Yes, I do. They close early in the evenings." He could see his answer only compounded her distress. "Hey, look at me." When she glanced at him, he said, "I don't need any presents. I promise. I have everything I want right here."

He drew her close and placed a quick kiss on her lips.

Serena pulled back. Her eyes opened wide and then a big grin filled her face.

"Oh, no," he said.

"What?"

"You have a look on your face that worries me. I have a feeling I'm not going to like what you say next."

"You can stop worrying. I just got an idea for a new screenplay."

"That's what you were thinking about when I kissed you?"

She shrugged and looked a little sheepish. "I can't help when inspiration strikes."

"Uh-huh. And what is this idea?"

She shook her head. "I'm not telling you. You'll have to wait and read it."

"Really? That's all I get for being your inspiration?"

"Well, maybe if you kissed me some more, you might get something you do like."

Now she was talking his language. "How about we take this to the bedroom?"

"I think that would be a good idea."

The next morning, Serena woke up early.

Jackson was still sound asleep, but that wasn't surprising as he'd had a late night—a very late night. Serena smiled as she recalled the night she'd spent in his arms.

She knew their time together was quickly running out. But she was wondering about relocating to New York, once filming for her next movie wrapped up, of course. After all, she could stand to take a break from movies, and she hadn't yet signed up for anything after this next film. If writing screenplays didn't pan out for her, she could try Broadway. Actually, that was another item on her bucket list. Why put off until tomorrow what she could do today?

The more she thought about the idea, the more she liked it. She just wondered what Jackson would think of the idea. After all, it wasn't like they had to move in together. She could get her own place. They could go slow and see where things were headed.

Slow? Like they'd taken things so far? It sure hadn't been very slow, but she wouldn't change any of the events that got them to this point—well, that wasn't exactly true. She could have avoided the whole Shawn debacle. And she was certain that Jackson would have preferred to skip the accident. But at least he was safe and they were happy together.

She slipped out of bed and put on her fuzzy robe. She quietly padded out of the room and headed for the desk. Her mind was buzzing with thoughts of New York and ideas for her next screenplay. She wanted to get started on notes for it. She decided it was going to be a holiday rom-com.

She opened her laptop and typed in the password. She paused as she realized this would be her second romance. What was up with that? She always thought she would work on a serious drama that dealt with tough issues, but for some reason, it was matters of the heart that spoke to her. Jackson's image came to mind and she smiled. He'd definitely had an influence over her.

And then she realized what she could give him for Christmas—herself. She could wrap up a piece of paper that said something about her being New York–bound. She liked the idea. She just hoped that he would, too.

But first, she had to get some writing done. When her computer booted up, it automatically loaded to her email.

It was one thing to skip town and not take calls, but totally sealing herself off from life was another thing altogether. As long as she kept up on her emails and listened to her voice mails, she let herself buy into the illusion that she was on top of things.

The top email in her inbox was from her agent. There was a high-priority flag. Her agent really needed to take some time off and enjoy the holiday. After all, it was Christmas Eve.

The subject line caught and held Serena's attention:

Call me ASAP! Damage control needed!

Damage control? For what? She hadn't been in town for days. There was no way she could have done anything to require such a message. And then she noticed that there was an attachment.

Her agent wasn't an alarmist, so dread was churning in her empty stomach. Her finger hovered over the open button. She knew that once she looked at it that it would cast a cloud over this wonderful holiday season. Was it so wrong for her to want this bit of heaven to last just forty-eight hours more? Besides, who would be looking at the tabloids over the holiday?

She closed her email and opened a new word processing document. She put the email out of her mind and instead concentrated on the idea that had come to her last night while she'd been kissing Jackson.

One of the hardest things for her to write was the opening line. It carried so much weight. It had to snag the viewer's attention. It had to set the tone for the entire movie.

And so Serena typed out a sentence that would be read as part of the heroine's thoughts…

This was to be a Christmas unlike any other.

It was okay. It gave an idea of what was to come. But it didn't pop. It wouldn't stand out and make the viewers forget about their popcorn and soda. Nor would it draw them to the couch to sit down and find out what happened next.

Her mind wandered back to her Christmas present for Jackson. Her mind started playing over all of the various messages that she could write. It could be a long letter, explaining what their time together had meant to her and how she'd been able to regain her trust in her judgment and in men. But that seemed like too much.

Perhaps she should tell him how much fun she'd had with him and that she didn't want it to end. Something like: This wasn't an ending but rather a beginning.

And then she realized the best route was the simplest one. Nine little words would tell him everything he needed to know.

She opened a blank document and started to type. She played with the font size and the color until she ended up with:

My ♥'s in New York...
so I'm moving there.

She made it so the font filled the page and then she printed it. She searched the desk until she found an envelope. Now all she needed was to dress it up. After all, it was a Christmas present of sorts.

But she had no wrapping paper. She would have to be inventive. Her gaze strayed to the Christmas tree and latched on to the red velvet bows attached to the end of random branches. One of those would be perfect.

And so she decorated the envelope and placed it beneath the Christmas tree. Now she couldn't wait for Christmas. She hoped this present would make him as happy as it did her.

CHAPTER EIGHTEEN

ALONE AGAIN...ON Christmas Eve.

Instead of getting upset over finding the spot next to him empty, Jackson just smiled. He knew last night when Serena got her stroke of genius that it wouldn't be long until she headed to the keyboard to start her next screenplay.

He was proud of her for following her dreams, even though she didn't know for sure how they would turn out. She may be famous, but she was known for her acting, not her writing. There was no guarantee that any production company would get behind her screenplays. But he was excited to know that his interview might help pave this new road for her.

He grabbed his phone to see if his agent had sent him the interview. His fingers moved over the screen until he pulled up the email with the attached video. A smile pulled at his lips. After they'd talked on the phone, Jackson had followed up with an email. He made sure to tell his agent to add music at the beginning as well as some visual narrative. Nothing was to be overlooked. This was that important to him.

Jackson played the video. It was just as he'd imagined—no it was better. And the most striking part was Serena Winston. She was a star, even when she wasn't on the big screen. Beyond her undeniable beauty, there was an air about her—the kind that princesses and queens possessed.

The bedroom door creaked as it opened. Jackson pressed Pause on the video. Then he turned off his phone. There was no way that he was letting her see it. Not yet. This was special and it was his Christmas gift to her.

Serena poked her head inside. "Morning, sleepyhead."

Gizmo squeezed past her, ran into the room with his tail wagging, jumped on the cushioned bench at the end of the bed and then hopped on the bed.

"Arff! Arff!"

"He's been waiting for you to get up. It seems that Gizmo approves of you, which is saying something because he doesn't take to many people. Usually he hides."

Gizmo rushed up to Jackson and before Jackson could move fast enough, Gizmo licked his cheek. "Yes, Gizmo. I like you, too. And it's okay, sometimes I want to hide from people, too." After wiping the wet kiss from his cheek, Jackson turned his attention back to Serena. Their gazes met and he smiled. "I don't even have to ask what happened to you. I can see by that glint in your eyes that the writing is going well."

"It is. And this screenplay is going to be even better than the first one."

"It better be."

"Why do you say that?"

"Because I was the inspiration, remember?"

Her cheeks grew rosy. "I remember." And then she pulled a white pastry box from behind her back. "I have a surprise for you."

His empty stomach rumbled its anticipation. "And what have you been up to besides writing?"

"I drove into the village."

"Did you sleep at all?"

She nodded. "But I'm an early riser."

"You couldn't have gotten much sleep."

She shrugged. "That's what coffee is for. And that reminds me. I picked up some more dark chocolate while I was in the village. I don't know if it's as good as what you bought at the Christmas market, but it was all I could get at that hour of the morning."

He arched a brow. "I take it you really like the cocoa?"

"Oh, yes. What could be better? Chocolate and fresh pastries."

He climbed out of bed. "You don't have to convince me." He threw on some clothes and headed for the door. He paused to place a kiss on her lips. "Well, what are you doing standing there? We have some cocoa to make."

It didn't take long until he had the milk warmed and the chocolate melted into it. With two steamy cups and a box of pastries, they returned to the great room. Serena had started a fire while he was taking care of things in the kitchen. And she'd thought to turn on the Christmas tree lights. It was a very cozy setting, even if the cabin was quite large.

She turned to him on the couch. "Do you know what the best part of a chilly morning is?"

"There's a best part?"

She smiled and nodded. "Snuggling together under a blanket."

He reached for the throw on the back of the couch and snuggled it around Serena before draping what was left over his legs. Gizmo decided it was a good idea and joined them on the couch.

"You know I could get used to this," she said.

Jackson leaned toward her and pressed his lips to hers. He didn't say it, but he could get used to this, too. This relationship was so different from the others in his past.

Serena was more than willing to meet him halfway, like her thoughtful trip to the village for breakfast food or her attempt to cook dinner, even though it was a struggle. It didn't matter to him if she'd burned the food, he'd have still loved it, just because she put herself out there for him.

He deepened the kiss. She tasted sweet like chocolate and it had never tasted so good. His hand cupped her face. He never wanted to let her go.

And yes, he knew that their time together was almost at an end. He had a flight back to New York in less than forty-eight hours. When he'd flown to Austria, he hadn't wanted to come. He'd been fully focused on his career and he'd wanted to be any other place but the Alps, where no news ever happened. Instead he'd found something more important—happiness.

He pulled back so that he could look into Serena's eyes. "Do you know how happy you make me?"

She smiled at him. "How happy is that?"

"So happy that I think I want to give you your Christmas present right now." When she frowned, he realized that they'd agreed to forgo presents. "Listen, I know we said that we weren't going to exchange gifts, but this is special. And I hope you really like it—"

"But we can't open gifts."

"Why not?"

"It's not Christmas morning."

"Oh." He hadn't realized that she was a stickler for tradition. And he really didn't want to wait. "Can you make an exception just this once?"

"I suppose." A big grin lit up her face. She looked excited, like a little kid on Christmas morning after Santa left a sled full of presents under the tree. "I got you a present, too."

He struggled to keep from smiling. "You broke the agreement."

"You broke it first."

"True enough." He smiled at her, causing her stomach to dip. "I think you're really going to like my present."

"Open mine first—"

"Not so fast. Maybe we should flip for it."

"Or maybe you should be a gentleman and let the lady go first."

He sighed. "I guess you have me there." He motioned with his hand. "Okay. Go ahead."

She smiled in triumph. "You're really going to like it. The present is under the tree."

He turned but he didn't see anything. "Are you sure?"

"It was right there." She stood and walked over to the tree. She got down on her hands and knees. She looked all around, even under the tree skirt. "It's not here." And then she turned around. "Gizmo."

The dog's ears lowered and he put his head between his paws.

"Don't look so innocent. It's not going to work this time." Serena got to her feet. "Gizmo, how could you do this?"

The pup let out a whine.

Jackson didn't want to see the whole day ruined. "It's okay. It'll turn up. I can give you my present."

"No." And then, as though Serena understood how bad her response sounded, she said, "I'm sorry. I'm just frustrated. I have to find your gift. I can't believe this happened. That dog is such a thief."

Jackson laughed. "I can't argue with that."

"Please help me look for it."

"What am I looking for?"

"You'll know it when you see it. It has your name on the front."

Jackson got down and looked under the couch and then he checked under the armchair. "You know, you could make this a new tradition—hunting for your Christmas present. I'm sure Gizmo would be glad to help."

"Oh, no. When we get back to the States someone is going back to doggy school. Huh, Gizmo?"

He whined and put his paw over his head.

Jackson chuckled. "I'd like to help you, buddy, but I think she means business."

And sadly, he wouldn't be around to see Gizmo's transformation from an ornery puppy to a well-behaved dog. But more than that, Jackson was going to miss Serena. She was a ray of sunshine in his otherwise bland and gray life.

But before all of that, he had his present for her. While Serena was off searching the kitchen, Jackson pulled out his cell phone to forward her the video. Luckily they'd been talking over lunch yesterday about how to keep in touch and she'd given him her email—*GizmoPuppy007@mymail.com*. He smiled at the address. He didn't think he'd ever forget it—or her.

"I have it."

Serena ran into the great room, waving the envelope around.

"Where did you find it?" Jackson asked as he stood next to the Christmas tree.

"Under the bed. I also found my wallet. I didn't even know that it was missing…again. I must have put it down when I got back from the bakery and he found it. I also found my hairbrush and one of your socks. He had quite a collection."

"Well, bring it over here." When she approached him and held out the sock, he smiled. "Not that."

She dropped the sock on the floor. "Did you mean this?"

"Yes." He snatched the envelope from her fingers.

She automatically grabbed for it, but he held it out of her reach. "Hey, that wasn't fair."

"Ah…but see, it has my name on it." He pointed to where she'd scrolled his name with a red pen.

"But…" The protest died in her throat. What was she going to say? That she was having an attack of nerves? How would that sound? "Oh, go ahead."

She didn't have to tell him twice. He jabbed his finger into the corner of the envelope and started to rip the seam open. Talk about an overgrown child.

He pulled out the folded piece of paper. His face was void of expression as he read it. His gaze moved to her and then back to the paper. For the longest time, he didn't say anything.

"I don't understand." His eyes studied hers.

Was he serious? She didn't think it was that hard to understand. But if he really needed her to break it down for him, she could do it in three words. "I love you."

Jackson took a step back as though her admission had dealt him a physical blow. "No, you don't."

AKA, he didn't love her back. And by the horrified look on his face, he didn't want her moving to New York, either. Her heart plummeted down to her toes. She blinked repeatedly. She would not cry in front of him. She moved to retrieve the note from his hand, but he took another step away from her.

With his back against the tree, he said, "You can't love me. It's too soon."

Each denial that passed by his lips was like a dagger stabbing into her fragile heart. Her vision blurred.

She blinked away the unshed tears and then summoned a steady voice. "I think what you mean to say is that you don't love me."

"I… I…"

"Save it. The truth is written all over your face."

"I tried to tell you that I wasn't ready for a relationship."

"Was that before or after we made love? Or perhaps when you offered to do this interview? Because I never heard those words. You made it seem like—well, it doesn't matter because I obviously read everything wrong."

"I never meant to hurt you. You've been great. I really appreciate everything you've done—"

She glared at him. "Stop with the kind words." The last thing she could stand now was him being all nice to her. He was yet another man who took what he needed from her heedless of her feelings. "The truth is you think that the time we've spent together was a mistake. One you wish you could forget."

"Serena, I…" He hesitated as he stared at her, seeing that she meant business. "Okay. You're right. I did things and said things that I shouldn't have done. Our time together was great. You're great. But it can't last. You've got to understand. I still love my wife."

The words were pointed and drove straight into her heart. For a moment, she couldn't breathe. So this was it. There was nowhere to go from there. She struggled to keep it all together. She forced herself to take one breath and then another. The last thing in the world she wanted was for him to see just how deeply his words had hurt her.

Serena reached for the note she'd written him and finally snatched it out of his hand. "Now that we've cleared the air. You should go."

She didn't need him to stay and make this worse. There was no way she could compete with a ghost. The ghost would win every time because he could switch up his memories to make his late wife perfect.

And Serena was anything but perfect. Hence, the misguided note in her hand. She clenched her fingers, crunching up the paper.

"Please don't take this personally." Jackson's voice was low. He took a step toward her. "Your note, it was the sweetest, most generous gesture that anyone has ever done for me. Someday you'll find the right man to share that note with. I'm sorry it wasn't me."

Her heart clenched in her chest as she shook her head. "Don't say any more. You're making it worse. Just go."

"You want me to leave now?"

"Yes." She wasn't sure how much longer she could keep her emotions in check. She'd made such a mess of everything.

"Serena, we don't have to end things like this."

"I don't want to work this out. It's not like we're in love. We need to go our separate ways. Now." And then, because she didn't trust herself to keep her rising emotions in check, she said, "I'll be in the kitchen until you're gone."

Gizmo, as though sensing her distress, had moved to sit at her feet. She bent over and scooped him into her arms. With her head held high, she walked away. After all, she was a Winston—Winstons knew how to maintain their composure—even when their dignity and their hearts had been shredded.

Once in the kitchen with the door shut, she set Gizmo down on the floor. There were no happy barks and no tail wagging. He moved over to the table where Jackson's chair was still pulled out. He settled on the chair and stared at her with those sad puppy eyes.

"Stop looking at me like that," she whispered, feeling

guilty for the mess she'd made of all their lives. "Jackson was never going to stay anyway."

Gizmo whined and covered his head with his paw.

Great. Now even the dog was upset with her. You'd think Gizmo belonged to Jackson instead of her. It looked like she wasn't the only one to let down her defenses and fall for the sexy New Yorker.

Serena moved to the window and stared out at the sunny day. The cheeriness of the weather mocked her black mood. She clung to her dark and stormy emotions. It was so much easier to be angry with Jackson than to deal with her broken heart.

She didn't know how much time had passed when she finally plunked down in a chair opposite Gizmo. By then, the pup had dozed off. She was thankful. She didn't think she could take any more of his sad face.

Her phone buzzed. Certain that it was just a friend wishing her a merry Christmas, she leaned over and retrieved it from the kitchen counter. The screen showed that she had four new emails.

Two from friends, one from her agent and one from Jackson—that was strange. What would he send her?

She checked the time stamp, finding the email from Jackson had been sent some time ago—before she'd made an utter fool of herself. What could it be?

And then she recalled him mentioning something about a Christmas gift. Could this have something to do with it?

She hesitated before opening her email. Maybe it would be best to get it over with now. But when she went to click on the email from him, the screen jumped as more graphics loaded. Instead of Jackson's email, the email from her agent opened. Before she could close it, her gaze skimmed over Jackson's name. How would her agent know anything about Jackson being here with her?

The more she read, the worse she felt. Her stomach churned when she got to the end of the email. Jackson had broken his word and had used her interview to further his career. Here she was throwing herself at a man who felt nothing for her and, worse, had lied to her. Once again, her poor judgment had led her into trouble.

She rushed out of the kitchen to confront Jackson, but he was nowhere to be found. When she moved to the window, she saw his rental car pulling out of the driveway.

She told herself it was for the best. There was no way he could undo the fiasco with the video. Right now, it was out there for all the world to see. But even worse than that was the fact that she was in love with a man who didn't love her back.

So much for a merry Christmas…

CHAPTER NINETEEN

THE OUTLINE OF the cabin filled his rearview mirror.

Jackson turned onto the mountain road and headed for the nearby village, hoping that there would be a vacancy. It was Christmas Eve. The village might be full of people visiting for the holidays. If so, he'd keep driving. There was nothing keeping him here.

He told himself he would be fine, even though he felt anything but fine. After all, he hadn't come to Austria to start a relationship. How dare she accuse him of leading her on? He hadn't. He wouldn't. He had made his situation clear to her. Hadn't he? Suddenly he wasn't so sure those words had made it from his thoughts to his lips. When he held Serena in his arms, it was so easy to forget about everything but kissing her.

Just then his phone rang. It was his agent. He didn't really want to talk to him, but it would be best to tell him that the deal with the interview was off. He put the man on speakerphone.

"Hey, Fred, I was about to call you."

"She loved the video, didn't she?" Before Jackson could respond, Fred said, "I knew she would. That's why I took the liberty of releasing it before people got too distracted with Christmas."

"You did what?" Surely Jackson hadn't heard him correctly. He wouldn't go public with the video after Jackson told him how important Serena's privacy was to her.

"Don't worry. It's trending. It's going to hit a million views anytime now—"

"Fred, I told you not to do this!" He was shouting now and he didn't care.

"Relax. I've got your back."

"You're kidding, right? I told you how important this video was to me."

"Of course it's important. That's why I had the best people in the business polish it up before I released it. And let me tell you, after it aired on your network, the video went viral. People are talking about it on every media platform. You're a hero. You found Serena Winston."

"And what about her? Do you know what you've done to her?"

His agent's voice took on an angry tone. "I didn't do anything to her. She should thank me for her name being on everyone's tongue."

"And did you ever stop to think that if she worked that hard to disappear she might value her privacy?" Serena was going to be so hurt and he'd already done so much damage. He had to do something to fix this.

"Give me some credit. I didn't tell anyone where she is." Fred's voice drew him from his thoughts. "What is up with you? I thought you wanted to do whatever it took to land that evening anchor position? Where is the thank-you?"

"There isn't going to be one. I told you the interview was to be kept under wraps—"

"Wait. You're upset about her, aren't you?"

"No."

"You are. You don't care about the tape being leaked—you care that Serena Winston is upset. What has gotten into you? Where are your priorities?"

"You want to know my priorities? My priority is keeping my word—without it I'm nothing. And I gave Serena my word that I would keep that interview confidential until she decided if or when to go public with her screenplay. And now, thanks to you, everyone and their grandmother knows about Serena's project—a project that she wasn't ready to take public."

"But this will help both of you—believe me, this is all going to work out. And I didn't tell you the best part. The network executives tuned in. They loved the interview and they want you." When Jackson didn't respond, Fred asked, "Did you hear me?"

"I did. And I don't care. This isn't about me. It's about Serena."

"And she's going to thank you—"

"No. She isn't." Jackson's hands clenched the steering wheel until his knuckles turned white.

"Wow! I've never heard you go off the handle like this."

"If you thought I'd be happy using someone I care about to further my career, you don't know me at all."

"I thought I did. You used to always be so calm and take everything in stride. What has happened to you? It's Serena. She's gotten to you."

"No, she hasn't." Besides, he'd messed things up with her. If he'd had any hope of ever making things right with Serena—this was the final straw.

"Oh, I get it. You're in love with her, aren't you? That's why you're so upset."

He may not be able to do anything about Serena's anger toward him, but he could make sure his agent never leaked a video again.

"Fred, you're fired."

Jackson disconnected the call. He pulled off the quiet mountain road. He got out of his vehicle and just started pacing. He had so much pent-up energy and he just needed to wear it off.

Because there was no way Fred was right. He was not in love with Serena. Sure, he thought she was great. And she had opened his eyes to a life without June, but did that constitute love?

Erase. Erase. Erase.

Serena sat at her desk trying to work on her rom-com screenplay but nothing she wrote was the least bit entertaining. Her heroines were snappy and her heroes were being mulish. It was a disaster.

Her muse was on strike.

And worse yet, her heart was broken. Splintered into a million painful shards.

What had she been doing letting herself get so close to a man who was obviously still in love with his late wife? She should have gotten the hint by the amount of times he'd mentioned June—the love of his life.

And then there was the leaked video. Now that she'd calmed down, she realized it wasn't the disaster she'd originally imagined. Her agent had sent a follow-up email letting her know that there had been numerous read requests for her script.

Jackson may not love her—it had been written all over his face when he'd read the note she'd given him for Christmas. And then he'd tried to gently wiggle out of the idea of them continuing their relationship when they returned to the States.

Even so. He never struck her as a liar or a man who went back on his word. She'd been in the industry long enough to know there were a hundred and one different opportunities to leak a video to the public—

Serena drew her thoughts up short. What was wrong with her? Why was she making excuses for him?

Because whether she wanted to admit it or not, she couldn't hate a man for loving his late wife. It wasn't his fault that someone had laid claim to his heart before Serena had met him.

And perhaps she'd read more into things than she should have. There appeared to be plenty of blame to go around. She thought of talking to him—of setting things straight—but she didn't have his phone number. And at this point, she was probably the last person that he'd want to speak to.

Maybe a year or two from now, when this evening was a distant memory, she'd bump into him during one of her business trips to New York. It would be awkward at first, but perhaps they could get coffee. Maybe they could find their way back to being friends.

A tear splashed onto her cheek. Gizmo rushed over and settled on her lap. Her hand automatically stroked his back, but all she could think about was Jackson and how friendship with him would never be enough.

CHAPTER TWENTY

HE LOVED HER.

He loved her laugh, her smile, and her so-so cooking.

He loved everything about her.

Jackson had thought about nothing else since Serena had tossed him out of her life. And though he hated to admit it, his agent was right. His reaction where she was concerned was way over the top. If that interview had been with anyone else, he would have dealt with it in a more businesslike, more restrained manner. But this interviewee was so much more than a pretty face—she was a breath of fresh air in his otherwise stale life.

And because he'd been too busy trying to impress her, he hadn't slowed down long enough to think about how letting her interview out of his possession could end up being a mess. Jackson paced back and forth in his rented room in the village. He raked his fingers through his hair.

He'd made a gigantic mess of everything. But he refused to give up hope on rectifying his relationship with Serena. After all, wasn't Christmas the season of hope and forgiveness?

He loved Serena Mae Winston.

Not the Hollywood star.

Not the up-and-coming screenplay writer.

But he loved the woman who struggled to cook pasta,

who was brave enough to climb in a wrecked car to save a total stranger and who didn't take any gruff from a less than stellar patient.

He grabbed his phone but then realized that he didn't have her phone number. He swore under his breath. What had he been thinking? He should have gotten it a long time ago. Wasn't that one of the first things guys asked for when they were trying to pick up women? It just went to show how long he'd been out of the dating world.

Left with few options, he started typing her a brief email. He had no idea if she would even open it, but he had to try. His thumbs started moving rapidly over the screen of his phone.

Mae. Yes, that's the name of the woman who first caught my attention. It's the name of the person I've come to admire and care a lot about—more than I realized until now.

I guess it's true what they say about not realizing what you've got until it's gone. I made a HUGE mistake and for that I apologize. I wish I could undo so many things, but I can't.

I promise you that I will not take advantage of any opportunities that come my way because of the leaked video. All I want is a chance to show you how sorry I am for not realizing what a precious Christmas present you had given me.

I love—

Erase. Erase.

He didn't want to say too much without seeing her—without being able to gaze into her eyes. He wanted her to see how much she meant to him.

He concluded the email with a simple: Jackson.

His finger hovered over the send button. He reread each

word, evaluating its meaning and wondering if he could do anything to make the email more powerful. He knew he was overthinking everything. But this message was all he had at this point.

He knew that she would see the subject line before she pressed Delete. And he only had two words for it.

I'm sorry.

His gut was telling him that this wasn't the right way to do things. He could do better. The cursor moved back and forth between Send and Delete.

He pressed Delete.

He needed to woo her over and an email wouldn't do it. This was going to take him pulling out all of the stops. He had to show Serena how much she meant to him.

It was still early—before noon. Perhaps there would still be some shops open. With a plan in mind, he rushed out of his rented room, down the steps and out the door. The sidewalks were busy with people bustling around with last-minute shopping before the big day.

A group of young people stopped on the sidewalk to sing to a growing audience. Jackson got caught up in the lurkers. He paused to listen to their harmonious and joyful voices. It wouldn't have been so long ago when he would have walked right past such an exhibition, unmoved and uncaring. But he was beginning to see all the wonderful things around him when he slowed down and paid attention.

After their first song, Jackson continued down the sidewalk. Thanks to his visit here with Serena, he remembered a few of the stores in the town square. He just hoped they were still open.

His first stop was the florist. He picked out every long-stem red rose and for double the usual delivery fee he was able to have them sent to Serena right away. He attached a note:

This is only the beginning...
J

The singers were still entertaining people as Jackson made his way to the jewelry store. He was going to get Serena a real Christmas present. One that was all wrapped in shiny paper and tied up with a red bow. It would be a gift that told her exactly how he felt about her.

The jewelry store had exactly what he had in mind. And his plan was taking shape. On his way out of the store, he knew what else he needed in order to get Serena's full attention.

CHAPTER TWENTY-ONE

READING WAS GOOD.

They said that it could be an escape from reality. And right now, Serena needed to escape from the mess she'd made of her life. After all, no way did an actress and a television journalist belong together. Just the thought of it would have made her father roll in his grave.

Serena focused on the words on the page. Her eyes scanned the sentence and then the next. By the time she got to the third sentence, she'd forgotten what she'd read in the beginning.

And so she returned to the beginning of the paragraph, intent on reading this reference book on writing screenplays. She really did enjoy writing her first screenplay and though her second had hit a snag, she was certain if she kept at it, the story would come together.

Just over the top of the book, she spotted the large bouquet of red roses that Jackson had sent her. She rested the book against her chest as she continued to stare at the beautiful blossoms nestled in a sea of baby's breath. She'd placed them on the coffee table.

She should probably just get rid of them—out of sight, out of mind. But they were so beautiful. It would be a crime to do away with them.

But it was the attached card that had stirred her interest.

What had Jackson meant by saying this was just the beginning? Had he had a change of heart? Were these flowers something that he'd planned before their big blowup? If so, he obviously didn't know that red roses symbolized unconditional love.

Her contemplation came to a halt as she heard not one, but multiple car engines. This was followed by a string of car doors closing. Gizmo awoke from his nap and started his guard dog routine of *bark-bark-howl. Bark-bark-howl.* Repeat. He took off toward the door to defend his home.

Serena tried to hear beyond the dog. It sounded like there was a whole army descending on the cabin—wait, no, not an army.

There was singing.

Christmas carolers?

Serena tossed aside her book and joined the excited Gizmo at the door. She glanced out the window to find the sun had set. Her driveway quickly filled with carolers. They were each holding a candle as they sang. And they were singing in English. Serena was impressed.

She rushed to pull on her coat and boots. Then she attached Gizmo's leash.

She picked up the barking, tail-wagging dog. "Shh…or I'm not taking you outside."

It took a moment, but he quieted down…just until she got outside with him. When he started again, she shushed him. And ran her hand over his back, hoping to calm him.

The singers were amazing. Their voices were beautiful. But what were they doing out here? It wasn't like there were houses lining the road. Dwellings were quite scattered in this particular area. Still, she felt blessed that they would come visit her.

They helped to buoy her flagging spirits. If only Jackson were here with her. She'd bet he'd really enjoy this.

But she didn't know where he was. For all she knew, he could be on a flight back to New York.

And then the group parted. It was hard to make out who was walking between them in the dark. Whoever it was, they were approaching the porch. As the person got closer, Serena recognized Jackson. Her heart jumped into her throat. What was he doing here?

She noticed that he was carrying more flowers. The backs of her eyes stung. His image started to blur. She blinked repeatedly. She couldn't believe he was here.

Gizmo wiggled and barked, anxious to get to Jackson. She wasn't the only one happy to see him. She put the dog down. Gizmo immediately ran over to Jackson, who bent down to pet the dog.

In the background, the choir continued to sing. And then Serena realized this was what Jackson had meant by the note with the flowers. He was responsible for bringing the carolers to her door.

He approached her. Their gazes met and held. Her heart started to pound.

"I'm sorry," they both said simultaneously.

Then they both gave an awkward laugh. He held the flowers out to her and she accepted them.

Serena knew she had to say more. She had to make this right. "I overreacted earlier. I was feeling insecure when you didn't like the idea of me moving to New York and I handled it badly."

"You didn't do anything wrong. I did. I totally messed up everything when you gave me that most amazing Christmas present. I panicked. And then I complicated matters by giving your video to my agent to have him get a team to clean it up and give it a polish. I wanted to surprise you with it for Christmas. But my agent got it into his head to leak the video, even though I told him not to. Anyway, he's no longer my agent."

"He's not? Because of me?" She didn't like the thought that she was responsible for someone losing their job.

"No. I let him go because I can't work with someone I don't trust."

"Do you trust me?"

"I do. It's just that I wasn't being honest with myself."

"How so?" She held her breath wondering what he would say.

"I promised June that I would move on—that I'd make a new life for myself. Before she got sick, we'd talked about having kids—a boy and girl. She wanted me to have that chance. She…she thought I'd make a good father. And so she made me promise to marry again. At the time, I would have said anything to make her happy. I didn't think that I could take a chance on love again—the loss—the pain. I didn't want to love anyone ever again. And then I met you. Do you know what you've taught me?"

Serena shook her head.

"I learned that it's a very lonely life without someone to share it with. And I don't want to hide from the truth."

"What truth would that be?"

He stepped closer to her. He reached out and stroked his fingers over her cheek. "The undeniable truth is that I love you, Serena Mae Winston."

"You do?"

"I do."

She at last drew in a full breath. "I love you, too."

He pulled her close and kissed her. It was the sweetest, most meaning-filled kiss of her life. She didn't know why it took traveling halfway around the globe to find her soul mate, but she'd do it again. At last, she felt as though she was right where she belonged.

When Jackson pulled back, he looked her right in the eyes. "Do you trust me?"

She knew what he was asking. If his career would come between them. "Do you plan to share with the world details of our private lives?"

"Only the pieces that we agree on sharing."

"Then yes, I trust you." She knew in that moment that her father had rolled over in his grave with a very loud groan, but she wouldn't let that stop her. Her father had died alone. She didn't want to end up like him. She wanted to learn from her father's mistakes.

In the background, the carolers had moved on to a slower song in German. Even though she understood only a few words, it was still a beautiful harmony.

Jackson pulled a little box from his pocket. It was wrapped in shiny silver paper with a red bow. It looked like a jewelry box. What exactly had he done?

He held it out to her. "This is for you. It is a proper Christmas present to replace the one that was ruined. I hope you like it."

Her fingers trembled slightly as she undid the ribbon and the paper. It was indeed a little black box from a jeweler's. The breath caught in her throat. When she lifted the lid, she found a black velvet box—a box bigger than one that holds a ring.

Jackson held the wrappings so that she could use her hands to open the last box. Inside was a silver heart locket. It was engraved with a beautiful design. It was delicate and attached to a thin box chain.

"It's beautiful." Tears of happiness filled her eyes. She glanced up at him. "Thank you."

"You have my heart for now and always."

"And you have mine."

"Arff! Arff!"

Jackson stuffed the wrapping paper and empty boxes in his pockets. Then he bent over and scooped Gizmo up in his arms.

Serena leaned forward and hugged her two favorite guys. "We love you, too, Gizmo."

"Arff!"

EPILOGUE

One year later...

"I CAN'T BELIEVE you were able to lease the same cabin."

Jackson carried Serena over the threshold. "I wanted everything to be special for my Christmas bride."

She turned to look into her husband's eyes. "You didn't have to bring me to Austria for it to be special. You do that all by yourself."

Serena leaned forward and pressed her lips to his. She'd never tire of kissing him. Ever.

Jackson was everything she'd never thought she'd have. He was her best friend. He lent her an ear when she needed to vent. He offered a word of reason when she was worked up. And he was the person who filled her life with much laughter and tons of love. And she could only hope she did the same for him.

Their lives had been evolving over the past year. She'd filmed her last contracted movie and was now concentrating on her writing, which meant she could relocate to New York. Jackson had been promoted to the anchor chair of the evening news for the biggest network in the country. He had more control over the content than ever before and he was very happy. They both were deliriously happy.

"Arff! Arff!"

Reluctantly, she pulled back. Jackson gently set her feet on the floor.

Serena knelt down and ran a hand over Gizmo. "You are special, too."

"*Arff!*"

Serena couldn't help but laugh. "I still think Gizmo understands exactly what we say."

"I think you're right."

She straightened and walked into the great room. "I can't believe that yesterday we were with your mother next to the Pacific Ocean where we exchanged vows. And today we are in the Alps. I'm so glad you patched things up with her."

"I'm glad I'm smart enough to listen to my very intelligent wife with her wise advice."

"Aw…" She approached him and wrapped her arms around his trim waist. "You know exactly what to say." She pressed a quick kiss to his lips.

"Look." Jackson gestured toward the window. "The snow I ordered is just starting—"

"It is?" She rushed over to the window. "It is." She turned back to Jackson. "Something tells me if you have any pull with Mother Nature this will turn into a snowstorm."

"You bet. It worked well the first time around."

"You consider a car accident working well?"

He shrugged. "It brought you into my life, didn't it?"

A smile tugged at Serena's lips. "It did, but I'd prefer if you didn't get hurt this time around."

"I'll see what I can do about that. Maybe if we hide away in this cabin, you can keep an eye on me." His eyes had a playful twinkle in them.

"I think you have a good idea." She stepped farther into

the room. "Oh, look, a Christmas tree." She turned back to Jackson. "Did you do this?"

He nodded. "I know how much you enjoy the holiday."

"But it isn't decorated."

"I thought you'd enjoy doing it." Then he pulled something from his pocket. "And I have the first ornament."

He handed it to her. She glanced down at the cake topper from their wedding. It was a winter bride and her dashing groom; the bride was dressed in white with a hood and cape, and holding red roses. The cake topper now had a small brass hook with a red ribbon strung through it.

Serena's gaze rose to meet her husband's. "Did you think of everything?"

"I tried."

She slipped off her coat and rushed over to the tree where the ladder was waiting. She climbed up to find the perfect spot for the ornament. It took her a moment to decide. "There. Isn't it perfect?"

"Yes." And then he started to gently shake the ladder.

"Jackson. Stop." She held on so she didn't fall. "What are you doing?"

"The last time you were up on that ladder, you fell into my arms. I just want a repeat."

She frowned at him. "Stop playing around."

"I won't drop you. I promise."

"That's good, because I have a Christmas present for you. I hope you like it."

He arched a brow. "I thought we agreed not to get each other anything since we were going to be on our honeymoon."

"I didn't go shopping for it. I promise."

"So you made me a gift?" There was a look of intrigue reflected in his eyes.

"In a manner of speaking." Happiness and excitement bubbled up in her chest. "Merry Christmas, Daddy."

His eyes opened wide. "Daddy?"

The breath caught in her throat. This hadn't been planned, but she knew he wanted children. She just didn't know if he wanted them now.

Please be excited. Please. Oh, please.

Why wasn't he saying anything? Was he in shock?

"Jackson?" She snapped her fingers. "Jackson, speak."

"I… I'm going to be a dad?"

A hesitant smile lifted her lips as she nodded. "Does that make you happy?"

At last, his lips lifted at the corners. "Oh, yes. That makes me very happy. Come here, Mrs. Bennett."

She started to climb down the last couple of rungs on the ladder, but her feet never touched the floor as her husband swept her into his arms. His lips pressed to hers. He left no doubt in her mind just how happy he was about this news.

And then he pulled back ever so slightly. "What do you say we trim the tree later?"

"Why, Mr. Bennett, what do you have on your very naughty mind?" She laughed.

"As I recall, you like my naughty mind."

"Mmm-hmm…" She smiled up at him.

And with that he carried her to the master suite to begin their happily-ever-after.

* * * * *

IT STARTED AT
CHRISTMAS...

JANICE LYNN

To Blake Shelton for retweeting me following his Nashville concert and giving me a total fangirl rush moment. Life is good.

CHAPTER ONE

"Okay, who's the hunk that just winked at you?"

At her best friend's question Dr. McKenzie Sanders rolled her eyes at the emcee stepping out onto the Coopersville Community Theater stage. "That's him."

"That's the infamous Dr. Lance Spencer?" Cecilia sounded incredulous from the chair next to McKenzie's.

No wonder. Her best friend had heard quite a bit about the doctor slash local charity advocate. Was there any local charity he wasn't involved with in some shape, form or fashion? McKenzie doubted it.

Still, when he'd invited her to come and watch the Christmas program, she'd not been expecting the well-choreographed show currently playing out before her eyes. Lance and his crew were good. Then again, knowing Lance, she should have expected greatness. He'd put the event together and everything the man touched was pure perfection.

And these days he wanted to touch her.

Sometimes McKenzie wondered if it was a case of women-chasing-him-toward-the-holy-matrimony-altar burnout that had him focusing on commitment-phobic her. She never planned to marry and Lance knew it. She made no secret of the fact she was a good-time girl and was never going to be tied down by the golden band of death to all future happiness. After his last girlfriend had gone a lit-

tle psycho when he'd told her flat out he had no intention
of ever proposing, Lance apparently wanted a break from
tall lanky blonde numbers trying to drag him into wed-
ded "bliss." He'd taken to chasing petite brunettes who got
hives at the mere mention of marriage thanks to unhappily
divorced parents.

Her.

Despite accepting his invitation and hauling Cecilia with
her to watch his show, McKenzie was running as fast as she
could and had no intention of letting Lance "catch" her. She
didn't want a relationship with him, other than their professional one and the light, fun friendship they already shared.
Something else she'd learned from her parents thanks to her
dad, who'd chased every female coworker he'd ever had.
McKenzie was nothing like either of her parents. Still, she
could appreciate fineness when she saw it.

Lance was fine with a capital F.

Especially in his suit that appeared tailor-made.

Lance was no doubt one of those men who crawled out of
bed covered in nonstop sexy. He was that kind of guy. The
kind who made you want to skip that heavily iced cupcake
and do some sit-ups instead just in case he ever saw you
naked. The kind McKenzie avoided because she was a free
spirit who wasn't going to change herself for any man. Not
ever. She'd eat her cupcake and have another if she wanted,
with extra icing, thank you very much.

She'd watched women change for a man, seen her own
mother do that, time and again. Ultimately, the changes
didn't last, the men lost interest, and the women involved
ended up with broken hearts and a lot of confusion about
who they were. McKenzie never gave any man a chance
to get close enough to change her. She dated, had a good
time and a good life. When things started getting sticky,
she moved on. Next, please.

Really, she and Lance had a lot in common in that regard. Except he usually dated the same woman for several months and McKenzie's relationships never lasted more than a few weeks at best. Anything longer than that just gave guys the wrong idea.

Like that she might be interested in white picket fences, a soccer-mom minivan, two point five kids, and a husband who would quickly get bored with her and have flirtations with his secretary…his therapist…his accountant…his law firm partner's wife…his children's schoolteacher…and who knew who else her father had cheated on her mother with?

Men cheated. It was a fact of life.

Sure, there were probably a few good ones out there still if she wanted to search for that needle in a haystack. McKenzie didn't.

She wouldn't change for a man or allow him to run around on her while she stayed home and scrubbed his bathroom floor and wiped his kids' snotty noses. No way. She'd enjoy life, enjoy the opposite sex, and never make the mistake of being like her mother…or her father, who obviously couldn't be faithful yet seemed to think he needed a wife on hand at all times since he'd just walked down the aisle for the fourth time since his divorce from McKenzie's mother.

Which made her question why she'd said no to Lance when he'd asked her out.

Sure, there was the whole working-together thing that she clung to faithfully due to being scarred for life by her dad's office romantic endeavors. Still, it wasn't as if either she or Lance would be in it for anything more than to have some fun together. She was a fun-loving woman. He was a fun-loving man. They'd have fun together. Of that, she had no doubt. They were friends and occasionally hung out in groups of friends or shared a quick meal at the hospital. He managed to make her smile even on her toughest days. But when it had come to actually dating him she'd scurried away faster than a mouse in the midst of a spinster lady's feline-filled house.

"Emcee got your tongue?" Cecilia asked, making McKenzie realize she hadn't answered her friend, neither had she caught most of what Lance had said as she'd gotten lost in a whirlwind of the past and present.

"Sorry, I'm feeling a little distracted," she shot back under her breath, her eyes on Lance and not the woman watching her intently.

"I just bet you are." Cecilia laughed softly and, although McKenzie still didn't turn to look at her friend, she could imagine the merriment that was no doubt sparkling in her friend's warm brown eyes. "That man is so hot I think I feel a fever coming on. I might need some medical care very soon. What's his specialty?"

"Internal medicine, not that you don't already know that seeing as he works with me," McKenzie pointed out, her gaze eating up Lance as he announced the first act, taking in the fluid movements of his body, the smile on his face, the dimples in his cheeks, the twinkle in his blue eyes. He looked like a movie star. He was a great doctor. What else could he do?

McKenzie gulped back the knot forming in her throat as her imagination took flight on the possibilities.

"Yeah, well, Christmas is all about getting a fabulous package, right? That man, right there, is a fabulous package," Cecilia teased, nudging McKenzie's arm.

Snorting, she rolled her eyes and hoped her friend couldn't see the heat flooding her cheeks. "You have a one-track mind."

"So do you and it's not usually on men. You still competing in that marathon in the morning?"

Running. It's what McKenzie did. She ran. Every morning. It's how she cleared her head. How she brought in each new day. How she stayed one step ahead of any guy who tried to wiggle his way into her heart or bedroom. She ran.

Literally and figuratively.

Not that she was a virgin. She wasn't. Her innocence had run away a long time ago, too. It was just that she was choosy about who she let touch her body.

Which brought her right back to the man onstage wooing the audience with his smile and charm.

He wanted to touch her body. Not that he'd said those exact words out loud. It was in how he looked at her.

He looked at her as if he couldn't bear not to look at her.

As if he'd like to tear her clothes off and show her why she should hang up her running shoes for however long the chemistry held out.

She gulped again and forced more of those possibilities out of her mind.

Loud applause sounded around the dinner theater as the show moved from one song to the next. Before long, Lance introduced a trio of females who sang a song about getting nothing for Christmas. At the end of the trio's set, groups of carolers made their way around the room, singing near the tables rather than on the stage. Lance remained just off to the side of the stage and was directly in her line of vision. His gaze met hers and he grinned. Great, he'd caught her staring at him. Then again, wasn't that why he'd invited her to attend?

Because he wanted her to watch him.

She winced. Doggone her because seeing him outside the clinic made her watch. She didn't want to watch him… only she did want to watch. And to feel. And to…

Cecilia elbowed her, and not with the gentle nudge as before.

"Ouch." She rubbed her arm and frowned. No way could her friend have read her mind and even if she had, she was pretty sure Cecilia would be high-fiving her and not dishing out reprimands.

"Just wanted to make sure you were seeing what I'm seeing, because he can't seem to keep his gaze off you."

"I'm not blind," she countered, still massaging the sore spot on her arm.

"After seeing the infamous Dr. Spencer I've heard you talk about so much and that I know you've said no to, I'm beginning to think perhaps you are. How long has it been since you last saw an optometrist?"

"Ha-ha, you're so funny. There's more to life than good looks." Okay, so Lance was hot and she'd admit her body responded to that hotness. Always had. But even if there wasn't her whole-won't-date-a-coworker rule, she enjoyed her working relationship with Lance. If they dated, she didn't fool herself for one second that they wouldn't end up in bed. Then what? They weren't going to be having a happily ever after. Work would become awkward. Did she really want to deal with all that just for a few weeks of sexy Lance this Christmas season?

Raking her gaze over him, she could almost convince herself it would be worth it...almost.

"Yeah," Cecilia agreed. "There's that voice that I could listen to all night long. Sign me up for a hefty dose of some of that."

"Just because he has this crowd, and you, eating out of the palm of his hand, it doesn't mean I should go out with him."

Cecilia's face lit with amusement. "What about you? Are you included in those he has eating out of the palm of his hand? Because I'm thinking you should. Literally."

She didn't. She wouldn't. She couldn't.

"I was just being a smart aleck," McKenzie countered.

"Yeah, I know." Cecilia ran her gaze over where Lance

caroled, dressed up in old-fashioned garb and top hat. "But I'm serious. He could be the one."

Letting out a long breath, McKenzie shook her head. "You know better than that."

Cecilia had been her best friend since kindergarten. She'd been with McKenzie through all life's ups and downs. Now McKenzie was a family doctor in a small group of physicians and Cecilia was a hairdresser at Bev's Beauty Boutique. They'd both grown up to be what they'd always wanted to be. Except Cecilia was still waiting for her Prince Charming to come along and sweep her off her feet and across the threshold. Silly girl.

McKenzie was a big girl and could walk across that threshold all by herself. No Prince Charming needed or wanted.

Her gaze shifted from her friend and back to Lance. He was watching her. She'd swear he'd smiled at her. Maybe it was just the sparkle in his eyes that made her think that. Maybe.

Or maybe it went back to what she'd been thinking moments before about how the man looked at her. He made her want to let him look. It made her feel uncomfortable. Very uncomfortable.

Which was probably part of why she kept telling him no.

Only she was here tonight.

Why?

"I think you should go for it."

She blinked at Cecilia. "It?"

"Dr. Spencer, aka the guy who has you so distracted."

"I have to work with the man. Going for 'it' would only complicate our work relationship."

"His asking you out hasn't already complicated things?"

"Not really, because I haven't let it." She hadn't. She'd made a point to keep their banter light, not act any differently around him.

If she'd had to make a point, did that mean the dynamics between them had already changed?

"Meaning?"

"Meaning I don't take him seriously."

"He's looking at you as if he's serious."

There was that look. That heavenly making-her-want-to-squirm-in-her-chair look.

"Maybe."

"Definitely."

But then suddenly he wasn't looking at her.

He'd rushed over to one of the dinner tables and wrapped his arms around a rather rosy-faced gentleman who was grabbing at his throat. Everyone at the man's table was on their feet, but looking lost as to what to do.

McKenzie's natural instincts kicked in. She grabbed her purse and phone. Calling 911 as she did so, she rushed over to where Lance gave the man a hearty thrust. Nothing happened. The guy's eyes bulged out, more from fear than whatever was lodged in his throat. The woman next to him was going into hysterics. The carolers had stopped singing and every eye was on what Lance was doing, trying to figure out what was going on, then gasping in shock when they realized someone was choking.

Over the phone, McKenzie requested an ambulance. Not that there was time to wait for the paramedics. There wasn't. They had to get out whatever was in the man's throat.

Lance tried repeatedly and with great force to dislodge whatever was blocking the panicking guy's airway. McKenzie imagined several ribs had already cracked at the intensity of his chest thrusts.

If the man's airway wasn't cleared, and fast, a few broken ribs weren't going to matter. He had already started turning blue and any moment was going to lose consciousness.

"We're going to have to open his airway." Lance said what she'd been thinking. *And pray they were able to establish a patent airway.*

She glanced down at the table, found the sharpest-appearing knife, and frowned at the serrated edges. She'd have made do if that had been her only option, but in her purse, on her key chain, she had a small Swiss army knife that had been a gift many years before from her grandfather. The blade was razor sharp and much more suitable for making a neat cut into someone's neck to create an artificial airway than this steak knife. She dumped the contents of her purse onto the table, grabbed her key chain and a ballpoint pen.

As the man lost consciousness, Lance continued to try to dislodge the stuck food. McKenzie disassembled the pen, removed the ink cartridge, and blew into the now empty plastic tube to clear anything that might be in the casing.

Lance eased the man down onto the floor.

"Does he still have a heartbeat?" she asked, kneeling next to where the man now lay.

"Regardless of whether or not he does, I'm going to see if CPR will dislodge the food before we cut."

Sometimes once a choking victim lost consciousness, their throat muscles relaxed enough that whatever was stuck would loosen and pop out during the force exerted to the chest during CPR. It was worth a try.

Unfortunately, chest compressions didn't work either. Time was of the essence. Typically, there was a small window of about four minutes to get oxygen inside the man's body or there would likely be permanent brain damage. If they could revive him at all.

McKenzie tilted the man's head back. When several seconds of CPR didn't give the reassuring gasp of air to let them know the food had dislodged, she flashed her crude cricothyroidotomy instruments at Lance.

"Let me do it," he suggested.

She didn't waste time responding, just felt for the indentation between the unconscious man's Adam's apple and the cricoid cartilage. She made a horizontal half-inch incision that was about the same depth into the dip. Several horrified cries and all out sobbing were going on around her, but she drowned everything out except what she was doing to attempt to save the man's life.

Once she had her incision, she pinched the flesh, trying to get the tissue to gape open. Unfortunately, the gentleman was a fleshy fellow and she wasn't satisfied with what she saw. She stuck her finger into the cut she'd made to open the area.

Once she had the opening patent, she stuck the ballpoint-pen tube into the cut to maintain the airway and gave two quick breaths.

"Good job," Lance praised when the man's chest rose and fell. "He still has a heartbeat."

That was good news and meant their odds of reviving him were greatly improved now that he was getting oxygen again. She waited five seconds, then gave another breath, then another until their patient slowly began coming to.

"It's okay," Lance reassured him, trying to keep the man calm, while McKenzie gave one last breath before straightening from her patient.

"Dr. Sanders opened your airway," Lance continued. "Paramedics are on their way. You're going to be okay."

Having regained consciousness, the man should resume breathing on his own through the airway she'd created for him. She watched for the reassuring rise and fall of his chest. Relief washed over her at his body's movement.

Looking panicky, he sat up. Lance held on to him to help steady him and grabbed the man's hands when he reached for the pen barrel stuck in his throat.

"I wouldn't do that," Lance warned. "That's what's letting air into your body. Pull it out, and we'll have to put it back in to keep that airway open."

"Is he going to be okay?" a well-dressed, well-made-up woman in her mid-to-late fifties asked, kneeling next to McKenzie a little shakily.

"He should be." She met the scared man's gaze. "But whatever is stuck in your throat is still there. An ambulance is on the way. They'll take you to the hospital where a general surgeon will figure out the best way to remove whatever is trapped there."

The man looked dazed. He touched a steady trickle of blood that was running down his neck.

"Once the surgeon reestablishes your airway, he'll close you up and that will only leave a tiny scar," she assured him.

Seeming to calm somewhat the longer he was conscious, the man's gaze dropped to her bloody finger. Yeah, she should probably wash that off now that the immediate danger had passed.

"Go wash up," Lance ordered, having apparently read her mind. "I'll stay with him until the ambulance arrives."

With one last glance at her patient she nodded, stood, and went in search of a ladies' room so she could wash the blood off her hands and her Swiss army knife.

Carrying McKenzie's purse and the contents she'd apparently gathered up, Cecilia fell into step beside her. "Omigosh. I can't believe that just happened. You were amazing."

McKenzie glanced at her gushing friend. "Not exactly the festive cheer you want spread at a charity Christmas show."

"You and Dr. Spencer were wonderful," Cecilia sighed. She shrugged. "We just did our job."

"Y'all weren't at work." Cecilia held the bathroom door open for McKenzie.

"Doesn't mean we'd let someone choke to death right in front of us."

"I know that, I just meant..." Cecilia paused as they went into the bathroom. She flipped the water faucet on full blast so McKenzie wouldn't have to touch the knobs with her bloodstained hands.

"It was no big deal. Really." McKenzie scrubbed the blood from her finger and from where it had smeared onto her hands. Over and over with a generous amount of antibacterial soap she scrubbed her skin and then cleaned her knife. She'd rub alcohol on it later that evening, too. Maybe even run it through the autoclave machine at work for good measure.

Cecilia talked a mile a minute, going on and on about how she'd thought she was going to pass out when McKenzie had cut the man's throat. "I could never do your job," she added.

"Yeah, and no one would want me to do yours. They'd look like a two-year-old got hold of them with kitchen shears."

When she finally felt clean, she and Cecilia returned to the dinner theater to see the paramedics talking to the man who'd choked. Although he couldn't verbalize, the man nodded or shook his head in response.

As he was doing well since his oxygenation had returned to normal, they had him climb onto the stretcher and they rolled him out of the large room. Lance followed, giving one of the guys a full report of what had happened. McKenzie fell into step with them.

"Dr. Sanders saved his life," Lance told them.

He would have established an airway just as easily as she had. It wasn't that big a deal.

The paramedic praised her efforts.

She shook off the compliment. It's what she'd trained for.

"You're going to need to go to the hospital, too," Lance reminded her.

Her gaze cut to his, then she frowned. Yeah, she'd

thought of that as she'd been scrubbing the blood from the finger she'd used to open the cut she'd made. Blood exposure was a big deal. A scary big deal.

"I know. I rode here with Cecilia. I'll have her take me, unless I can hitch a ride with you guys." She gave the paramedic a hopeful look.

"I'll take you," Lance piped up, which was exactly what she hadn't wanted to happen. The less she was alone with him the better.

She arched a brow at him. "You got blood on you, too?"

He didn't answer, just turned his attention to the paramedic. "I'll bring her to the hospital and we'll draw necessary labs."

In the heat of the moment she'd have done exactly the same thing and saved the man's life. After the fact was when one started thinking about possible consequences of blood exposure. In an emergency situation one did what one had to do to preserve another's life.

She didn't regret a thing, because she'd done the right thing, but her own life could have just drastically changed forever, pending on the man's health history.

She didn't have any cuts or nicks that she could see on her hands, but even the tiniest little micro-tear could be a site for disease to gain entry into her body.

Whether she wanted to or not, she had to have blood tests.

"Cecilia can take me," she assured Lance. Beyond being alone with him, the last thing she wanted was to have to have him there when she had labs drawn.

McKenzie hated having blood drawn.

Blood didn't bother her, so long as it was someone else's blood. Really, it wasn't her blood that was the problem. It was her irrational fear of needles that bothered her. The thought of a needle coming anywhere near her body did funny things to her mind. Like send her into a full-blown panic attack. How could she be so calm and collected when she was the one wielding the needle and so absolutely terrified when she was going to be the recipient?

She could do without Lance witnessing her belonephobia. He didn't need to know she was afraid of needles. Uh-uh, no way.

McKenzie gave Cecilia a pleading look, begging for her friend to somehow rescue her, but the grinning hairdresser hugged her goodbye and indicated that she was going to say something to someone she knew, then headed out rather than stay for the remainder of the show. Unfortunately, several of the other attendees seemed to be making the same decision to leave.

"I'm going to the hospital anyway, so it wouldn't make sense for someone else to bring you."

"But I..." She realized she was being ridiculous. One of the local doctors going into hysterics over getting a routine phlebotomy check would likely cause a stir of gossip. Lance would end up hearing about her silliness anyway. "Okay, that's fine, but don't you have to finish your show?"

He glanced back toward the dinner theater. "Other than thanking everyone for coming to the show, I've done my part. While you were washing up, I asked one of the singers to take over. The show can go on without me." A worried look settled on his handsome face. "The show must go on. It's for such a great cause and I don't want what happened to give people a bad view of the event. It's one of our biggest fund-raisers."

McKenzie frowned, hating that the incident had happened for many reasons. "It's not the fault of Celebrate Graduation that the man choked. Surely people understand that."

"You'd think so," he agreed, as they exited the building and headed toward the parking lot. "That man was Coopersville's mayor, you know."

"The mayor?" No, she hadn't known. Not that it would have mattered. She'd done what had needed to be done and would have done exactly the same regardless of who the person had been. A life had been on the line.

"Yep, Leo Jones."

"Is he one of your patients?" she asked, despite knowing he shouldn't answer. He knew exactly why she was asking. Did she need to worry about the man's health history? Did Lance know anything that would set her mind at ease?

"You know I wouldn't tell you even if he was."

Yes, she knew.

"But I can honestly say I know nothing about any mayor's health history." He opened the passenger door to his low-slung sports car that any other time McKenzie would have whistled in appreciation of. Right now her brain was distracted by too many possibilities of the consequences of her actions and that soon a needle would be puncturing her skin.

Was it her imagination or had she just broken a sweat despite the mid-December temperatures?

"Thank you," she whispered back, knowing her question had put him in an awkward position and that he'd answered as best he could. "I guess I won't know anything for a few days."

"Probably not." He stood at the car door for a few seconds. A guilty look on his face, he raked his fingers through his hair. "I should have cut the airway, rather than let you do it."

She frowned at him. "Why?"

"Because then you wouldn't be worrying about any of this."

She shrugged. "It was my choice to make."

"I shouldn't have let you."

"You think you could have stopped me from saving his life?"

His grip tightening on the car door, he shook his head. "That's not what I meant."

"I know what you meant and I appreciate the sentiment, but I'm not some froufrou girl who needs pampering. I knew the risks and I took them." She stared straight into his eyes, making sure he didn't misunderstand. "If there are consequences, I'll face them. I did the right thing."

"Agreed, except I should have been the one who took the risks."

"Because you're a guy?"

He seemed to consider her question a moment, then shook his head. "No, because you're you and I don't want anything bad to happen to you."

His answer rang with so much sincerity that, heart pounding, she found herself staring up at him. "You'd rather it happen to you?"

"Absolutely."

CHAPTER TWO

LANCE DROVE TO the hospital in silence. Just as well. Mc-Kenzie didn't seem to be in the mood to talk.

Was she thinking about what he'd said? Or the events of the evening? Of the risks she'd taken?

When he'd realized Leo Jones had been choking, he'd rushed to the man and performed the Heimlich maneuver. Too bad he hadn't been successful. Then McKenzie wouldn't have any worries about blood exposure.

Why hadn't he insisted on performing the procedure to open Leo's airway? He should have. He'd offered, but precious time had been wasting that could have meant the difference between life and death, between permanent brain damage and no complications.

He'd let her do what she'd competently done with quick and efficient movements. She'd saved the man's life. But Lance would much rather it was him being the one worrying about what he'd been exposed to.

Why? Was she right? Was it because she was female and he was male and that automatically made him feel protective?

Most likely he'd feel he should have been the one to take the risks regardless of whether McKenzie had been male or female. But the fact she was female did raise the guilt factor, with the past coming back to haunt him that he'd failed to protect another woman once upon a time when he should have.

Plus, he'd been the one to invite McKenzie to the show. If he hadn't done so she wouldn't have been at the community center, wouldn't have been there to perform the cricothyroidotomy, wouldn't have possibly been exposed to something life threatening.

Because of him, she'd taken risks she shouldn't have had to take. Guilt gutted him.

If he could go back in time, he'd undo that particular invitation. If he could go back in time, he'd undo a lot of things.

Truthfully, he hadn't expected McKenzie to accept his invitation to watch his show. She'd shot down all his previous ones with polite but absolute refusals.

He glanced at where she stared out the window from the passenger seat. Why had she semiaccepted tonight?

Perhaps the thought of seeing him onstage had been irresistible. He doubted it. She'd only agreed to go and watch and so had technically not been there as his date.

Regardless, he'd been ecstatic she'd said she'd be there. Why it mattered so much, he wasn't sure. Just that knowing McKenzie had been attending the show had really upped the ante.

Not knowing if she'd let him or not, he reached out, took her hand, and gave a squeeze meant to reassure.

She didn't pull away, just glanced toward him in question.

"It's going to be okay." He hoped he told the truth.

"I know. It's not that."

"Then what?"

She shook her head.

"Seriously, you can tell me. I'll understand. I've had blood exposure before. I know it's scary stuff until you're given the all-clear."

She didn't look at him, just stared back out the window. "I don't want to talk about it."

"What do you want to talk about?"

She glanced toward him again. "With you?"

He made a pretense of looking around the car. "It would seem I'm your only option at the moment."

"I'd rather not talk at all."

"Ouch."

"Sorry." She gave a nervous sigh. "I'm not trying to be rude. I just…"

"You just…?" he prompted at her pause.

"Don't like needles." Her words were so low, so torn from her that he wasn't sure he'd heard her correctly.

Her answer struck him as a little odd considering she was a highly skilled physician who'd just expertly performed a procedure to open a choking man's airway.

When he didn't immediately respond, she jerked her hand free from his, almost as if she'd been unaware until that moment that he even held her hand.

"Don't judge me."

How upset she was seemed out of character with everything he knew about her. She was always calm, cool, collected. Even in the face of an emergency she didn't lose her cool. Yet she wasn't calm, cool or collected at the moment. "Who's judging? I didn't say a word."

"You didn't have to."

"Maybe I'm not the one judging?"

She didn't answer.

"If you took my moment of silence in the wrong way, I'm sorry. I was just processing that you didn't like needles and that it seemed a little odd considering your profession."

"I know."

"Yet you're ultrasensitive about it."

"It's not something I'm proud of."

Ah, he was starting to catch on. McKenzie didn't like

to have a weakness, to be vulnerable in regard to anything. That he understood all too well and had erected some major protective barriers years ago to keep himself sane. Then again, he deserved every moment of guilt he experienced and then some.

"Lots of people have a fear of needles," he assured her. They saw it almost daily at the clinic.

"I passed out the last time I had blood drawn." Her voice was condemning of herself.

"Happens to lots of folks."

"I had to take an antianxiety medication to calm a panic attack before I could even make myself sit in the phlebotomist's chair and then I still passed out."

"Not unheard of."

"But not good for a doctor to be that way when she goes around ordering labs for her patients. What kind of example do I set?"

"People have different phobias, McKenzie. You can't help what you're afraid of. It's not like we get to pick and choose."

She seemed to consider what he'd said.

"What are your phobias, Lance?"

Her question caught him off guard. He wasn't sure he had any true phobias. Sure, there were things that scared him, but none that put him into shutdown mode.

Other than memories of Shelby and his immense sense of failure where she was concerned.

Could grief and regret be classified as a phobia? Could guilt?

"Death," he answered, although it wasn't exactly the full truth.

She turned to face him. "Death?"

His issues came more from having been left behind when someone he'd loved had died.

When his high school sweetheart had died.

When it should have been him and not her who'd lost their life that horrific night.

When he didn't answer, she turned in her seat. "You are, aren't you? You're afraid of dying."

Better she think that than to know the horrible truth. He shrugged. "Aren't most people, to some degree? Regardless, it isn't anything that keeps me awake at night."

Not every night as it had those first few months, at any rate. He'd had to come to terms with the fact that he couldn't change what had happened, no matter how much he wanted to, no matter how many times people told him it wasn't his fault. Now he lived his life to help others, as Shelby would have had she lived, and prevent others from making the same mistakes two teenagers had on graduation night.

"The thought of needles doesn't keep me awake at night," McKenzie said, drawing him back to the present. "Just freaks me out at the thought of a needle plunging beneath my skin."

Again, her response seemed so incongruent with her day-to-day life. She was a great physician, performed lots of in-office procedures that required breaking through the skin.

"Is there something in your past that prompted your fear?" he asked, to keep his thoughts away from his own issues. Shelby haunted him enough already.

From the corner of his eye as he pulled into the hospital physician parking area he saw her shake her head.

"Not that I recall. I've just always been afraid of needles."

Her voice quivered a little and he wondered if she told the full truth.

"Medical school didn't get you over that fear?"

"Needles only bother me when they are pointed in my direction."

"You can dish them out but not take them, eh?"

"I get my influenza vaccination annually and I'm up to date on all my other immunizations, thank you very much."

He laughed at her defensive tone. "I was only teasing you, McKenzie."

"If you knew how stressful getting my annual influenza vaccination is for me, you wouldn't tease me." She sighed. "This is the one thing I don't take a joke about so well."

"Only this?" he asked as he parked the car and turned off the ignition.

Picking up her strappy purse, she shrugged. "I'm not telling you any more of my secrets, Lance."

"Afraid to let me know your weaknesses?" he taunted.

"What weaknesses?" she countered, causing him to chuckle.

That was one of the things that attracted him to McKenzie. She made him laugh and smile.

They got out of the car and headed into the hospital.

The closer they got to the emergency department, the more her steps slowed. So much so that currently she appeared to be walking through molasses.

"You okay?"

"Fine." Her answer was more gulped than spoken.

Stupid question on his part. He could tell she wasn't. Her face was pale and she looked like she might be ill. She'd made light of her phobia, but it was all too real.

Protectiveness washed over him and he wanted to scoop her up and carry her the rest of the way.

"I'll stay with you while you have your labs drawn."

Not meeting his eyes, she shook her head. "I don't want you to see me like that."

"You think I'm going to think less of you because you're afraid of needles?"

"I fully expect you to tease me mercilessly now that you know this."

Her voice almost broke and he fought his growing urge to wrap her up into his arms. If only he could.

"You're wrong, McKenzie. I don't want to make light of anything that truly bothers you. I want to make it all better, to make this as easy for you as possible. Let me."

"Fine." She gave in but didn't sound happy about it. "Write an order for blood exposure labs. Get the emergency room physician to get consent, then draw blood on our dear mayor. Let's hope he's free from all blood-borne pathogens."

He definitely hoped that. If McKenzie came to any harm due to having done the cricothyroidotomy he'd never forgive himself for not insisting on doing the procedure, for putting her in harm's way. He'd not protected one woman too many already in his lifetime.

McKenzie counted to ten. Then she counted backward. Next she counted in her very limited Spanish retained from two years of required high school classes. She closed her eyes and thought of happy thoughts. She told her shoulders to relax, her heart not to burst free from her chest, her breath not to come in rapid pants, her blood not to jump around all quivery-like in her vessels.

None of her distraction techniques worked.

Her shoulders and neck had tight knots. Her heart pounded so hard she thought it truly might break free from her rib cage. Her breathing was labored. Her blood jumped and quivered.

Any moment she half expected her feet to take on minds of their own and to run from the lab where she waited for the phlebotomist to draw her blood.

Lance sat with her, telling her about Mr. Jones and that the surgeon was currently with him. "Looks like they're taking him into surgery tonight to remove the stuck food and close the airway opening you made."

Only half processing what he said, she nodded. She tried to focus on his words, but her skin felt as if it was on fire and her ears had to strain beyond the burn.

"The surgeon praised the opening you made. He said it would be a cinch to close and would only leave a tiny scar."

Again, she nodded.

"He also said you'd nicked two main arteries and the guy was going to have to be seen by a vascular surgeon. Shame on you."

As what he said registered, her gaze cut to Lance's. "What? I didn't nick a main artery, much less two. What are you talking about?"

The corner of his mouth tugged upward. "Sorry. I could tell your mind was elsewhere. I was just trying to get your attention back onto me."

"I didn't hit two arteries," she denied again.

"No, you didn't. The surgeon really did praise you, but didn't say a thing about any nicked arteries."

"You're bad," she accused.

Not bothering to deny her claim, he just grinned. "Sometimes."

"All the time."

"Surely you don't believe that? I come with good references."

"You get references from the women you've dated?"

"I didn't say the references were from women or from previous dates. Just that I had references."

"From?"

"My mother."

She rolled her eyes and tried not to pay attention to the man who entered the room holding her lab order. He checked over her information, verifying all the pertinent details.

Her heartbeat began to roar in her ears at a deafening level.

"You should meet her sometime," Lance continued as if she weren't on the verge of a major come-apart.

"Nice penguin suit, Dr. Spencer," the phlebotomist teased, his gaze running over Lance's spiffy suit.

"Thanks, George, I'm starting a new trend."

"Pretty sharp-looking, but good luck with that," the phlebotomist said, then introduced himself to McKenzie. "In case you didn't catch it, I'm George."

He then verified her name and information, despite the fact McKenzie had seen him around the hospital in the past. She imagined he had a checklist he had to perform.

So did she. Sit in this chair. Remain calm. Do not pass out. Do not decide to forget the first three items on her checklist and run away as fast as she could.

She clenched and unclenched her sweaty hands.

"She'd like you," Lance continued as if the phlebotomist hadn't interrupted their conversation about his mother and wasn't gathering his supplies.

Oh, she didn't want anyone else to know of her phobia. Why couldn't she just tell herself everything was going to be fine and then believe it? Everything was going to be fine. People did not die from having blood drawn. She knew that logically. But logic had nothing to do with what was happening inside her body.

"McKenzie?"

Her gaze lifted to Lance's.

"You should go to dinner with me sometime."

"No." She might be distracted, but she wasn't that distracted.

"You have other plans?"

"I do."

"I haven't said which day I wanted to take you to dinner. Maybe I wanted to take you out over the holidays."

"Doesn't matter. I don't want to go to dinner with you. Not now or over the holidays."

"Ouch."

"That's my line," she told him, watching George with growing dread.

The phlebotomist swiped an alcohol pad across her left antecubital space. "Relax your arm."

Yeah, right.

Lance moved closer. "McKenzie, you have to relax your arm or he can't stick you."

Exactly. That's why her arm wasn't relaxed.

Lance took her right hand and gave it a squeeze. "Look at me, McKenzie."

She did. She locked her gaze with his and forced her brain to stay focused on him rather than George. That really shouldn't have been a problem except George held the needle he was lowering toward her arm.

She wanted to pull away but she just gripped Lance's hand all the tighter.

She wanted to run, but she kept her butt pasted into her chair. Somehow.

"Keep your eyes on me, McKenzie."

Her eyes were on him, locked into a stare with him. It wasn't helping. All she could think about was George and his blasted needle.

She was going to pass out.

Lance lifted her hand to his lips and pressed a kiss to her clenched fingers.

McKenzie frowned. "What was that for?"

"You've had a rough evening."

"You shouldn't have done that."

"Sure, I should have. You deserve accolades for everything you've done."

"That's ridiculous. I just did my job."

"You're going to feel a stick," George warned, and she did.

Sweat drenched her skin.

Lance took the man's words as permission to do whatever he pleased. Apparently, kissing her hand again pleased him because he pressed another kiss to her flesh. This time his mouth lingered.

"Stop that." She would have pulled away but she was too terrified to move. Plus, her mind was going dark. "I think I'm going to pass out," she warned as the needle connected with its target.

She gritted her teeth, but didn't move. Couldn't move.

"Stay with me, McKenzie."

"No."

He laughed. "You planning to sleep through this?"

"Something like that." Her gaze dropped to where George swapped one vial for another as he drew blood from her arm.

She shouldn't have looked. She shouldn't have.

"Hey."

Lance's rough tone had her gaze darting back to him.

"Stay with me or I might have to do mouth-to-mouth."

"You wouldn't dare."

"Oh, I'd dare." He waggled his brows. "Do you think I have a shot at dating you?"

"Not a chance." She glowered at him. Really? He was going to ask her that now?

"Then I should go ahead with that mouth-to-mouth while you're in a compromised situation."

"I'm not that compromised," she warned, curling her free-from-George fingers into a fist.

"Don't mind me, folks. I'm just doing my job here," George assured them with a chuckle.

"I'm doing my best not to mind you." Actually, she was doing her best not to think about him and that needle.

"You're doing fine," he praised.

Amazingly, she was doing better than she'd have dreamed possible. She glanced toward Lance.

He was why she was doing better than expected. Because he was distracting her. With threats of mouth-to-mouth.

Her heart was pounding from fear, not thoughts of Lance's mouth on hers, not of him taking advantage of her compromised situation.

George removed the needle from her arm. McKenzie glanced down, saw the sharp tip, and another wave of clamminess hit her.

She lifted her gaze to Lance's to tell him she was about to go out.

"McKenzie, don't do it." He snapped his fingers in front of her face, as if that would somehow help. "Stay with me."

But out she went.

CHAPTER THREE

"Give it a rest, McKenzie. I'm seeing you inside your place." Lance maneuvered his car into the street McKenzie had indicated he should turn at. He'd wanted to punch her address into his GPS, but she'd refused to do more than say she'd tell him where he could go.

Yeah, he had no doubt she'd do exactly that and exactly in what direction she'd point him. He suspected it would be hellish hot there, too.

She crossed her arms. "Just because I passed out, it doesn't give you permission to run roughshod over me."

"Is that what I'm doing?" He glanced toward her. Finally, her color had returned and her cheeks blushed with a rosiness that belied that she'd been as white as a ghost less than an hour before.

Her lips twisted. "Maybe."

"You have had a lot happen tonight, including losing consciousness. Of course I'm concerned and going to make sure you get inside your place, okay?"

"I think you're overreacting."

"I think you're wasting your breath trying to convince me to drop you at the curb and drive away."

"That's not what I said for you to do."

"No, but the thought of inviting me into your place scares you."

"I never said that."

"You didn't have to."

"You're imagining things. I came to your Christmas show."

"You brought a friend." As long as they were bantering she'd stay distracted, wouldn't think about having passed out.

"You were part of the show. It wasn't as if you were going to sit beside me and carry on conversation."

He shot a quick glance toward where she sat in the passenger seat with her arms crossed defensively over her chest.

"Is that what you wanted?" he asked. "For me to be at the dinner table beside you?"

"If I'd been on a date with you, that's exactly what I would have expected. Since I was just there watching your show as a friend and someone who wanted to help support a great cause, it's not a big deal."

"I could take you to a Christmas show in Atlanta, McKenzie. We could go to dinner, or to a dinner show."

"Why would you do that?"

"So I could sit beside you and carry on conversation."

"I don't want you to sit beside me and carry on conversation." She sounded like a petulant child and they both knew it. She was also as cute as all get-out and he couldn't help but smile.

"Isn't that what we're doing right now?"

"Right now you are bringing me home, where you can walk me to my front door, and then you can leave."

"What if I want to come inside?" He couldn't help but push, just to see what she'd say. He had no intention of going inside McKenzie's place, unless it was to be sure she really did make it safely inside.

Her eyes widened. "We've not even been on a date. What makes you think I'd let you stay?"

"You're jumping to conclusions, McKenzie. Just because I said I wanted to come inside, it didn't mean I planned to stay."

"Right," she huffed. She turned to stare out the window.

"Then again, I guess it's a given that I want to stay. I think you and I would have a good time."

She sighed. "Maybe."

"You don't sound enthused about the prospect."

"There is no prospect. You and I are coworkers, nothing more."

"You came to my show tonight."

"Coworkers can support one another outside work without it meaning anything."

"I see how you look at me, McKenzie."

McKenzie blinked at the man driving her home. More like driving her crazy.

How she looked at him?

"What are you talking about? You're the one who looks at me as if you've not seen a woman in years."

"I'm sure I do, but we're not talking about how I look at you. We're talking about how you look at me."

"I don't look at you."

"Yes, you do."

"How do I look at you, Lance?"

"As if you've not seen a man in years."

"That's ridiculous." She motioned for him to make a right turn.

"But nonetheless true. And now that I've had to do mouth-to-mouth to revive you, you know you're dying for another go at these lips." Eyes twinkling, he puckered up and kissed the air.

"You have such an inflated ego," she accused, glad to see him pull into her street. A few more minutes and she'd be able to escape him and this conversation she really didn't want to be having. "Besides, you did not do mouth-to-mouth. I passed out. I didn't go into respiratory arrest."

"Where you are concerned, I didn't want to take any chances, thus the mouth-to-mouth." His tone was teasing. "You were unconscious, so you probably don't recall it. George offered to help out, but I assured him I had things under control."

"Right." She rolled her eyes. She knew 100 percent he'd not taken advantage of her blacking out to perform mouth-to-mouth, even though when she'd come to he'd been leaning over her. She also knew the phlebotomist had offered to do no such thing. "Guess that's something we really do have in common, because I don't want to take any chances either. Not with the likes of you, so you'll understand that there will be no invitations into my house. Not now and not ever."

"Not ever?"

"Probably not."

McKenzie really didn't want Lance walking her to her doorway. Since she'd passed out at the hospital, she supposed she shouldn't argue as it made logical sense that he'd want to see her safely into her home. That was just a common courtesy really and didn't mean a thing if she let him. Yet the last thing she wanted was to have him on her door stoop or, even worse, inside her house.

"You have a nice place," he praised as he drove his car up into her driveway.

"It's dark. You can't really see much," she countered.

"Not so dark that I can't tell you have a well-kept yard and a nice home." As he parked the car and turned off the ignition, he chuckled. "I've never met a more prickly, stubborn woman than you, McKenzie."

She wanted to tell him to not be ridiculous, but the fact of the matter was that he was way too observant.

"I didn't ask you to be here," she reminded him defensively. She was sure she wasn't anything like the yes-women he usually spent time with. "I appreciate your concern, but I didn't ask you to drive me to the hospital or to stay with me while I had my blood drawn or to threaten me with mouth-to-mouth."

He let out an exaggerated sigh. "I'm aware you'd rather have faced George again than for me to have driven you home."

That one had her backtracking a little. "That might be taking things too far."

"Riding home with me is preferable to needles? Good to know."

He was teasing her again, but the thought she was alone with him, sitting in his car parked in her driveway, truly did make her nervous.

He made her nervous.

Memories of his lips on her hand made her nervous.

Because she'd liked the warm pressure of his mouth.

Had registered the tingly pleasure despite the way her blood had pounded from terror over what George had been up to.

At the time, she'd known Lance had kissed her as a distraction from George more than from real desire. She might have been prickly, might still be prickly, but tonight's blood draw had been one of the best she could recall, other than the whole passing-out thing. "Thank you for what you did at the emergency room."

"My pleasure."

"I didn't mean that."

"That?"

"You know."

"Do I?" He looked innocent, but they both knew he was far, far from it.

"Quit teasing me."

"But you're so much fun to tease, McKenzie." Neither of them made a move to get out of the car. "For the record, I was telling the truth."

That kissing her hand had been his pleasure?

Her face heated.

His kissing her hand had been her pleasure. She hadn't been so lost in Terrorville that she'd missed the fact that Lance had kissed her hand and it had felt good.

"I'm sorry tonight didn't go as planned for your Christmas show."

"A friend texted to let me know that they finished the show and although several left following the mayor's incident, tonight's our biggest fund-raiser yet."

"That's great."

"It is. Keeping kids off the roads on graduation night is important."

"Celebrate Graduation is a really good cause." The program was something Lance had helped get started locally after he'd moved to Coopersville four years ago. McKenzie had been away doing her residency, but she'd heard many sing his praises. "Did your school have a similar program? Is that why you're so involved?"

He shook his head. "No. My school didn't. I wish they had."

Something in his voice was off and had McKenzie turning to fully face him. Rather than give her time to ask anything further, he opened his car door and got out.

Which meant it was time for her to get out too.

Which meant she'd be going into her house.

Alone.

It wasn't a good idea to invite Lance inside her place.

She dug her keys out of her purse and unlocked her front door, then turned to him to issue words that caused an internal tug-of-war of common courtesy and survival instincts.

"Do you want to come inside?"

His gaze searched hers then, to her surprise, he shook his head. "I appreciate the offer, but I'm going to head back to the community theater to help clean up."

"Oh."

"If I didn't know better I'd think you were disappointed by my answer."

Was she?

That wasn't disappointment moving through her chest. Probably just indigestion from the stress of having to get blood drawn. Or something like that.

She lifted her chin and looked him square in the eyes. "I'm sorry I kept you from things you needed to be doing."

"I'm sure the crew has things under control, but I usually help straighten things up. Afterward, we celebrate another successful show, which I'm calling tonight despite everything that happened, because you were there and I got to spend time with you."

She glanced at her watch. "You're going out?"

"To an after-show party at Lanette and Roger Anderson's place. Lanette is one of the female singers and who I asked to take over emceeing for me." He mentioned a couple of the songs she'd done that night and a pretty brunette with an amazing set of pipes came to mind.

"She will have their place all decked out with Christmas decorations and will have made lots of food," he continued. "You want to come with me?"

She immediately shook her head. "No, thanks. I ate at the dinner show."

He laughed. "I thought you'd say no."

"You should have said you had somewhere you needed to be."

"And keep you from sweating over whether or not you were going to invite me in? Why would I do that?"

"Because you're a decent human being?"

"I am a decent human being. I have references, remember?"

"Mothers don't count."

"Mothers count the most," he corrected.

When had he moved so close? Why wasn't she backing away from him? Any moment now she expected him to close the distance between their mouths. He was that close. So close that if she stretched up on her tippy-toes her lips would collide with his.

She didn't stretch.

Neither did he close the distance between their mouths. Instead, he cupped her jaw and traced over her chin with his thumb. "You could easily convince me to change my plans."

His breath was warm against her face.

"Why would I want to do that?" But her gaze was on his mouth, so maybe her question was a rhetorical one.

He laughed and again she felt the pull of his body.

"You should give me a chance to make this up to you by taking you to the hospital Christmas party next weekend."

"I can take myself."

"You can, but you shouldn't have to."

"To think I need a man to do things for me would be a mistake. I started wearing my big-girl panties a long time ago."

His eyes twinkled. "Prove it."

"You wish."

"Without a doubt."

Yet he hadn't attempted to kiss her, hadn't taken up her offer to come inside her place where he could have attempted to persuade her into something physical. Instead, he'd said she could convince him to change his plans. He'd given her control, left the power in her hands about what happened next.

"I'll see you bright and early Monday morning, McKenzie."

"Have fun at your party."

"You could go with me and have fun, too."

She shook her head. "I wouldn't want to cramp your style."

His brows made a V. "My style?"

"What if you met someone you wanted to take home with you?"

"I already have met someone I want to take home with me. She keeps telling me no."

"I'm not talking about me."

"I am talking about you."

Exasperation filled her. She wasn't sure if it was from his insistence that he wanted her or the fact that he hadn't kissed her. Maybe both. "Would you please be serious?"

His thumb slid across her cheek in a slow caress. "Make no mistake, McKenzie. I am serious when I say that I'd like to explore the chemistry between us."

Shivers that had nothing to do with the December weather goose-pimpled her body.

"Why should I take you seriously?" she challenged. "We've been standing on my porch for five minutes and you haven't threatened mouth-to-mouth again. Much less actually made a move. I don't know what to think where you're concerned."

That's when he did what she'd thought he would do all along. It had taken her throwing down a gauntlet of challenge to prompt him into action. Lance bent just enough to close the gap between their mouths.

The pressure of his lips was gentle, warm, electric and made time stand still.

Her breath caught and yet he made her pant with want for more. She went to deepen the kiss, to search his lips for answers as to why he made her nervous, why he made her feel so alive, why he made her want to run and stay put at the same time. She closed her eyes and relaxed against the hard length of his body. He felt good. Her hands went to his shoulders, his broad shoulders that her fingers wanted to dig into.

"Good night, McKenzie," he whispered against her lips, making her eyes pop open.

"Unless you text or call saying you want to see me before then, I'll see you bright and early Monday morning. Good luck with your run tomorrow." With that he stepped back, stared into her eyes for a few brief seconds then headed toward his car.

"I wouldn't hold my breath if I were you," she called from where she stood on the porch.

He just laughed. "Thank you for my mouth-to-mouth, McKenzie. I've never felt more alive. Sweet dreams."

"You're not welcome," she muttered under her breath while he got into his car, then had the audacity to wave goodbye before pulling out of her driveway. Blasted man.

McKenzie's dreams weren't sweet.

They were filled with hot, sweaty, passionate kisses.

So much so that when she woke, glanced at her phone and saw that it was only a little after midnight, she wanted to scream in protest. She'd been asleep for less than an hour. Ugh.

She should text him to tell him to get out of her dreams and to stay out. She didn't want him there.

Wouldn't he get a kick out of that?

Instead, she closed her eyes and prayed.

Please go back to sleep.

Please don't dream of Lance.

Please no more visions of Lance kissing me and me begging for so much more instead of watching him drive away.

Please don't let me beg a man for anything. I don't want to be like my mother.

I won't be like my mother.

CHAPTER FOUR

EDITH WINTERS CAME into the clinic at least once a month, always with a new chief complaint. Although she had all the usual aging complaints that were all too real, most of the time McKenzie thought the eighty-year-old was lonely and came in to be around other humans who cared about her.

The woman lived alone, had no local family, and her only relative as far as McKenzie knew was a son who lived in Florida and rarely came home to visit.

"How long have these symptoms been bothering you, Mrs. Winters?"

"Since last week."

Last week. Because when you had severe abdominal pain and no bowel movements for four days it was normal to wait a week to seek care. Not.

"I didn't want to bother anyone."

"Any time a symptom is severe and persistent, you need to be checked further."

"I would have come sooner if I'd gotten worse."

Seriously, she'd seen Edith less than a month ago and it had only been two weeks prior to that she'd been in the clinic for medication refills. Severe abdominal pain and no bowel movement was a lot more than what usually prompted her to come to the clinic. "What made you decide you needed to be seen?"

The woman had called and, although McKenzie's schedule had been full, she'd agreed for the woman to be checked. She'd grown quite fond of the little lady and figured she'd be prescribing a hug and reassurance that everything was fine.

"There was blood when I spit up this morning."

McKenzie's gaze lifted from her laptop. "What do you mean, when you spat up?"

Her nurse had said nothing about spitting up blood.

"It wasn't really a throw-up, but I heaved and there was bright red blood mixed in with the stuff that came up."

Bright red blood. Abdominal pain the woman described as severe.

"Have you ever had an ulcer?"

Edith shook her head. "Not that I know of, but my memory isn't what it used to be."

"I'm going to get some labs on you and will decide from there what our next best step is. I may need to admit you, at least overnight, to see what's up with that bright red blood."

Speaking of labs, she needed to log in and see if her labs from the other night were available online. George had told her they should show up on Monday. She should be notified of the mayor's results today, too.

Although there would still be some risks involved, once she had the mayor's negative ones, she'd breathe much easier. Assuming the mayor's results were negative.

She prayed they would be.

She hadn't allowed herself much downtime to consider the ramifications of her actions. How could she when she'd been so distracted by a certain doctor's kiss? But this morning when she'd run she'd not been able to keep the pending results out of her head. She'd run and run and hadn't wanted to stop when she'd had to turn back or she'd have been late into work.

McKenzie examined the frail little woman in her examination room, then filled out the lab slip. "I'll see you back after your blood is drawn."

She left the room, gave the order to her nurse, then went into the examination room.

An hour later, she was heading toward her office when her cell phone rang. She glanced at the screen and recognized the hospital's number. She stopped walking.

"Dr. Sanders," she answered.

"Hi, Dr. Sanders. This is Melissa from the lab. The ER doc looked over your results and wanted to let you know that all of your labs came back negative, as did those of the subject whose blood you were exposed to. He thought you'd want to know ASAP."

Almost leaning against the clinic hallway wall, she let out a sigh of relief. "He's right and that's great news."

"You know the drill, that you and the person you were exposed to will both need to have routine repeat labs per protocol?"

She knew. She finished the call then clicked off the phone, barely suppressing the urge to jump up and yell, "Yes!"

"Your labs were good?"

She jumped at Lance's voice. She hadn't heard him come up behind her in the hallway.

"Don't do that," she ordered, frowning. Mostly she frowned to keep her face preoccupied because instantly, on looking at him, she had a flashback to the last time she'd seen him.

On her front porch when he'd kissed her and completely rewired her circuitry.

That had to be it because she didn't fantasize about men or kisses or things way beyond kisses, yet that's exactly what she'd done more often than she'd like to admit since Friday night.

"Sorry." He studied her a little too closely for her liking. "I didn't realize I'd startle you or I would have made some noise when walking up."

She stepped into her office and he followed, stomping his feet with each step.

She rolled her eyes.

"So your tests are all negative?"

She nodded without looking at him because looking at him did funny things to her insides.

"Thank goodness." He sounded as relieved as she'd felt. "The mayor's too?"

She nodded again.

"That is great news."

She set her laptop down on her desk then faced him. "Was there something you needed?"

He shook his head. "I was checking to see if you'd heard anything on your labs."

She waved the phone she still held. "Perfect timing."

He waggled his brows. "We should go celebrate."

Not bothering to hide her surprise, she eyed him. "Why?"

"Because you got great news that deserves celebrating."

She needed to look away from those baby blues, needed to not think about his amazing smile that dug dimples into his cheeks, needed to not stare at his magical lips that had put her under some kind of spell.

"My great news doesn't involve you," she reminded him, not doing any of the things she'd just told herself to do.

"Sure it does. I was there, remember?"

How could she ever forget? Which was the problem. So much about that night plagued her mind. Lance acting so protective of her as he'd driven her to the hospital and stayed during her blood draw. Lance taking her home. Lance kissing her.

Lance. Lance. Lance.

Yeah, he had definitely put her under a spell. Under his kiss.

Her cheeks heated at the memory and she hoped he couldn't read her mind. Her gaze met his and, Lord, she'd swear he could, that he knew exactly where her thoughts were.

Don't think of that kiss. Don't think of that kiss. Just don't think at all.

"My news doesn't involve you," she repeated, reminding herself that she worked with him. She wasn't like her father who'd drag any willing member of the opposite sex into his office for who knew what? A relationship with Lance would be nothing short of disastrous in the long run.

Plus, there was how she couldn't get him out of her head. What kind of stupid would she be if she risked getting further involved with someone who made her react so differently from how she did to every other man she'd met? To do so would be like playing Russian roulette with the bullet being to end up like her mother. She was her own person, nothing like her parents.

"You're a stubborn woman, McKenzie." He sounded as if that amused him more than upset him.

"You're a persistent man, Lance," she drily retorted, trying to look busy so he'd take the hint and leave. She wanted out from under those eagle eyes that seemed to see right through her.

Instead, he sat on the desk corner and laughed. "Just imagine what we could accomplish if we were on the same team."

"We aren't enemies." Maybe that was how she should regard him after that treacherous and oh-so-unforgettable kiss.

His gaze held hers and sparked with something so intense McKenzie struggled to keep her breathing even.

"But you aren't willing to be more than my friend."

She wasn't sure if he was making a comment or asking a question. Her gaze fell to her desk and she stared at a durable medical equipment request form she needed to sign for a patient's portable oxygen tanks. Her insides shook and her vision blurred, making reading the form impossible. They did need to just be friends. And coworkers. Not lovers.

"I didn't say that." McKenzie's mouth fell open. What had she just said? She hadn't meant to say anything and certainly not something that implied she'd be willing to share another kiss with him.

She wouldn't, would she?

"You are willing?" He asked what was pounding through her head.

"I didn't say that either." She winced. Poor man. She was probably confusing the heck out of him because she was confusing herself.

Despite her wishy-washiness, he didn't seem upset. Actually, he smiled as if he thought she was the greatest thing since sliced bread. "You want to go get frozen yogurt tonight?"

Totally caught off guard by his specific request, she blinked. "Frozen yogurt? With you?"

Was he nuts? It was December and thirty or so degrees outside. They were having a serious conversation about their relationship and he'd invited her to go get frozen yogurt? Really? That was his idea of celebrating her good news?

Why was she suddenly craving the cold dessert?

"They're donating twenty percent of their take to the Sherriff's Toys for Tots fund tonight. We could sit, eat frozen yogurt. You could tell me about your half marathon on Saturday morning. I heard you won your age division."

Oh.

"You wouldn't say no to helping give kids toys for Christmas, would you?"

No, she wouldn't do that. "You should have gone into sales. Did I mention earlier that you were persistent?"

"Did I mention how stubborn you were?"

A smile played on her lips, then she admitted the truth. "I'll be here until late, Lance. You should go without me, but I can swing by and pick up some frozen yogurt on my way home. That way the kids can get their Christmas toys."

His grin widened, his dimples digging in deep. "You think I won't be here until late?"

"I don't know what you have going on," she admitted. She always made a point to not know what Lance was up to. She hadn't wanted to think about him, hadn't wanted to let his handsome smile and charm get beneath her skin. So much for that. She could barely think of anything else.

"We should correct that."

No, they shouldn't.

"Plus, I plan to go to the hospital to check on a patient." Edith's blood count had come back low enough that McKenzie really was concerned about a gastrointestinal bleed. Hopefully, the gastroenterologist would see her soon. Although she could pull up test results and such remotely from her office, she wanted to put eyes on her patient.

"We could ride to the hospital together, then go get frozen yogurt afterward."

They could, but should they?

"It might cause people to ask questions if we were seen at the hospital together so close on the tails of Saturday night."

"You think my kissing your hand in the lab hasn't caused a few tongues to wag?"

His kissing her hand had caused her tongue to wag when she'd returned his kiss on her front porch.

A sweet kiss that hadn't lasted nearly long enough.

A passionate kiss that had made her want to wind her

arms around him, pull him as close to her as she possibly could and kiss him until she'd had her fill.

"We're already the top story around the hospital. George has told everyone how I saved your life with mouth-to-mouth when you passed out."

Heat flushed her face. "You did not do mouth-to-mouth on me in the lab."

He arched a brow. "You sure? You are still alive."

Very alive. Intensely alive. Feeling more alive by the second beneath his gaze.

"You owe me." His eyes locked with hers. "Say yes."

Needing to break the contact, she rolled her eyes. "I don't owe you."

He let out an exaggerated sigh. "You're right. I'm the one who owes you. Let me make it up to you by taking you out for frozen yogurt."

Her brows made a V. "What do you owe me for?"

"That kiss."

Her cheeks flushed hot and she stared at the durable medical equipment form again, still not able to focus on it. "You don't owe me."

"Sure I do."

"Why?" She refused to glance up at him.

"Because it was an amazing kiss."

It had been an amazing kiss.

"If you said yes to going with me for frozen yogurt, I could repay you."

"With another kiss?"

"Well, I had frozen yogurt in mind, but I like how you think a lot better."

When she didn't immediately answer, he sat down on the edge of her desk and grinned down at her. "But I'm a compromising kind of guy. If you ask nicely, we could do both frozen yogurt and mouth-to-mouth."

McKenzie bit her lower lip. She wanted to say yes.

Way more than she should.

It was only frozen yogurt.

And his lips against hers.

Not giving her breath but stealing hers away.

"You think threatening me with more mouth-to-mouth is going to convince me to say yes?" She made the mistake of looking directly at him.

He stared into her eyes for long moments, that intensity back, then he nodded. "I know it is."

Her eyes widened at his confidence.

"You want me as much as I want you, McKenzie. I'm not sure why you feel you need to say no or not date me, but I'm one hundred percent positive that it's not because you don't want to be with me or that you didn't enjoy that kiss as much as I did."

"That's cocky of you."

"Honesty isn't cockiness."

"Why should I want to be with you?"

He frowned. "We get along well at the clinic and hospital. You make me smile and I make you smile. We have a lot in common, including that neither of us is looking for a long-term relationship," he pointed out. "I'm basically a nice guy."

"Who I work with," she reminded.

"That's really your hang-up? That we work together?"

Sinking her teeth into her lower lip again, McKenzie nodded. It was, wasn't it? It wasn't because he scared her emotionally, that the way she reacted to him emotionally scared her silly, that she was afraid she'd get too attached to him and end up reminding herself of her man-needing mother?

Was fear what was really holding her back?

His gaze bored into her. "If we didn't work together, you'd go out with me? Admit that there was something between us?"

"We do work together so it's a moot point," she said, as much to herself as to him, because she wasn't chicken. She wasn't afraid to become involved with Lance. If she were, that would mean admitting she really was like her mother.

She wasn't.

"But if we didn't work together, you'd go have frozen yogurt with me tonight?"

She closed her eyes then nodded. Lord help her, she would. Probably take some more of that mouth-to-mouth, too. She squeezed her eyes tighter to try to block out the image.

See, she wasn't afraid of Lance. Her reservations were because of their jobs. She heard Lance stir, wondered if he was moving toward her, if he was going to go for more mouth-to-mouth, and, when she opened her eyes, was surprised to see that he was leaving her office.

Seriously, she'd essentially just admitted that she wanted to date him, to share kisses with him, and he was leaving? Not cool.

"Where are you going?" she asked, instantly wishing she could take her question back as she didn't want him to know it bothered her he'd been leaving. *Why had he been leaving?*

"To leave you alone. We're both adults, neither of whom wants a long-term relationship. When we'd both be going in with no long-term expectations and there's no company policy against dating, that you'd use that as your reason doesn't make sense unless the truth is that I've misread the signs that you return my attraction or you're scared. Either way doesn't work for me. Sorry I've bothered you, McKenzie."

CHAPTER FIVE

McKENZIE BOLTED OUT of her office chair and took off after Lance. She grabbed hold of his white lab coat and pulled him back into her office.

He couldn't just leave like that.

She pushed her office door closed and leaned against it, blocking his access to leave until she was ready to let him go.

"Does that mean we aren't going to be friends anymore?" Did she sound as ridiculous as she felt? He'd asked her out. She'd turned him down. Repeatedly. He'd told her he'd leave her alone. She'd stopped him. What did that say about her?

Dear Lord, she was an emotional mess where this man was concerned. She should have let him go. Why hadn't she?

"You want to just be my friend?" His blue eyes glittered with steeliness. "I'm sorry, McKenzie, but I want more than that. After our kiss, it's going to take time before I can re-wire my brain to think of you as just a friend. We can't be 'just friends.' At least, I can't think of you that way."

"Stop this," she ordered, lifting her chin in defiance at him and the plethora of emotions assailing her. "All this because I won't go get frozen yogurt with you? This is ridiculous."

"Not just frozen yogurt, McKenzie, and you know it. I want to date you. As in you and me acknowledging and embracing the attraction between us. As in multiple episodes of mouth-to-mouth and wherever that takes us. I've been honest with you that although I'm not interested in something long term, I'm attracted to you. Isn't it time you're honest with yourself and me? Because to say our working in the same building is why you won't date me is what I find ridiculous."

"But..." She trailed off, not sure what to say. Way beyond her excuse of not wanting to date a coworker, McKenzie was forced to face some truths.

She liked Lance.

She liked seeing glimpses of him every day, seeing his smile, hearing his voice, his laughter, even when it was from a distance and had nothing to do with her. She liked catching sight of him from time to time and seeing his expression brighten when he caught sight of her. She liked the way his eyes ate her up, the way his lips curved upward. She didn't want him to avoid her or not be happy when he saw her. She didn't want to stop grabbing a meal with him at the hospital or hanging out with him at group functions. She enjoyed his quick wit, his easy smile, the way he made her feel inside, even if she'd never admitted that to herself. If he shut her out of his life, she'd miss him. She'd miss everything about him.

"You can date other women," she pointed out, wondering at how her own heart was throbbing at the very idea of seeing him with other women. Not that she hadn't in the past. But in the past she'd never kissed him. Now she had and couldn't stand the thought of his lips touching anyone else's. "You can date some other woman," she continued in spite of her green-flowing blood. "Then we could still be friends."

He shook his head. "You're wrong."

"How am I wrong?"

He bent his head and touched his lips to hers.

McKenzie's heart pounded so hard in her chest she was surprised her teeth weren't rattling. But her thoughts from moments before had her kissing him back with a possessiveness she had no right to feel.

She slid her hands up his chest and twined her arms around his neck, threading her fingers into his dark hair. She kissed him until her knees felt so weak she might sag to the floor in an ooey-gooey puddle. Then she kissed him some more because she wanted him to sag to the floor in an ooey-gooey puddle with her.

The thought that he might cut her out of his life completely gave desperation to how she clung to him.

Desperate. Yep, that was her.

When he pulled slightly away he rested his forehead against hers and stared into her eyes. "That's some mouth-to-mouth, McKenzie."

She shook her head. "Mouth-to-mouth restores one's breath. That totally just stole mine."

Why was she admitting how much he affected her?

He cupped her face in a caress. "I can't pretend that doesn't exist between us. I don't even want to try. I want you, McKenzie. I want to kiss you. Your mouth, your neck, your breasts, all of you. That's not how I think of my 'friends.'"

Fighting back visions of him kissing her all over, she sighed. "You don't play fair."

His fingers stroking across her cheek, he arched his brow. "You think not? I'm being honest. What's unfair about that?"

She let out an exasperated sigh, which had him touching his lips to hers in a soft caress.

Which had her insides doing all kinds of crazy somersaults and happy dances. Okay, so maybe she'd wanted to say yes all along, but that didn't mean everything about him wasn't a very bad idea. Just as long as she kept things simple and neither of them fell under false illusions or expectations, she'd be fine.

When he lifted his head, she looked directly into his gaze.

"I will go to the hospital with you and get frozen yogurt afterward with you, but on one condition."

"Name it."

She should ask for the moon or something just as elaborately impossible. Then again, knowing him, he'd find a way to pluck it right out of the sky and deliver on time.

"No more mouth-to-mouth at work," she told him, because the knowledge that she'd dropped to her father's level with making out at work and to her mother's level of desperation already cut deep.

He whistled softly. "Not that I don't see your point, McKenzie, but that might be easier said than done."

She stepped back, which put her flat against the door. With her chin slightly tilted upward, she crossed her arms. "That's my condition."

"Okay," he agreed, but shook his head as if baffled. "But I'm just not sure how you're going to do it."

Her momentary triumph at his *Okay* dissipated. She blinked. "Me?"

Looking as cool as ever, he nodded. "Now that you know how good I am at mouth-to-mouth, how are you going to keep from pulling me behind closed doors every chance you get for a little resuscitation?"

Yeah, there was that.

"I'll manage to restrain myself." Somehow. He was very, very good at kissing, but there was that whole self-respect thing that she just as desperately clung to. "Now leave so I can work."

And beat herself up over how she'd just proved her parents' blood ran through her veins.

McKenzie looked over Edith's test results while she waited for Lance to come to her office. Her hemoglobin and hematocrit were both decreased but not urgently so. Her abdominal and pelvic computerized tomography scan didn't show any evidence of a perforated bowel or a cancerous mass, although certainly there was evidence of Edith's constipation.

Had the woman really spit up blood? If she had, where had the blood come from? Had she just coughed too hard and had a minor bleed in her bronchus? It wasn't likely, especially as Edith had said it hadn't been like throwing up.

McKenzie had ordered the gastroenterology consult. She suspected Edith would be undergoing an endoscopy to evaluate her esophagus and stomach soon. Then again, it was possible the specialist might deem that, due to her age, she wasn't a good candidate for the procedure.

"You look mind-boggled," Lance said, knocking on her open office door before coming into the room. "Thinking about how much fun you're going to have with me tonight?"

"Not that much fun," she assured him, refusing to pander to his ego any more than she must have done earlier. "I'm trying to figure out what's going on with a patient."

"Want to talk about it?"

"Not really." At his look of disappointment, she relented. "One of my regulars came in today with a history of abdominal pain, constipation, and spitting up blood that she described as not a real throw-up, but spitting up."

"Anemic?"

"Slightly, but not enough to indicate a major bleed. She always runs borderline low, but her numbers have definitely dipped a little. I'm rechecking labs in the morning."

"Have you consulted a gastroenterologist or general surgeon?"

"The first."

"Any other symptoms?"

"If you named it, Edith would say she had it."

"Edith Winters?"

Her gaze met his in surprise. "You know her?"

"Sure. I used to see her quite a bit. She's a sweet lady."

"She has me a bit worried. It's probably nothing. Maybe she drank grape juice with breakfast and that's what she saw when she spat up. I don't know. I just feel as if I'm missing something."

"You want me to have a look at her for a second opinion?"

"Would you mind?"

"I wouldn't have offered if I minded. I'll be at the hospital with you anyway."

"Good point." She got her purse from a desk drawer, then stood. "You ready to go so we can get this over with?"

"'This' as in the hospital or the night in general?"

She met his gaze, lifted one shoulder in a semishrug. "We'll see. Oh, and if you think you're going to get away with just feeding me frozen yogurt, you're wrong. I'm not one of those 'forever dieting and watching her carbs' chicks you normally date who doesn't eat. I expect real food before frozen yogurt."

Lance grinned at the woman sitting next to him in his car. Twice in less than a week she'd been in his car when he'd begun to wonder if she was ever going to admit there was something between them.

He understood her concerns regarding them working together, but it wasn't as if they worked side by side day in and day out. More like in the same office complex and caught glimpses of each other from time to time with occasional prolonged interaction. With other women he might be concerned about a "work romance," but not with Mc-

Kenzie. She was too professional to ever let a relationship interfere with work.

Thinking back over the past few months, really from the time he'd first met her a couple years ago when she'd moved back to Coopersville after finishing her medical training, he'd been fascinated by McKenzie. But other than that he'd catch her watching him with a curious look in her eyes, she hadn't seemed interested in anything more than friendship and was obviously not in a life phase where she wanted a serious relationship.

Not that he wanted that either, but he also didn't want to become last month's flavor within a few weeks. She didn't seem interested in dating anyone longer than a month. It was almost as if she marked a calendar and when thirty days hit, she moved on to the next page of her dating life.

Although he had no plans of marriage ever, he did prefer committed relationships. Just not those where his partner expected him to march her down the aisle.

He owed Shelby that much. More. So much more. But anything beyond keeping his vow to her was beyond his reach.

Since his last breakup he definitely hadn't been interested in dating anyone except McKenzie. If he was being completely honest, he hadn't been interested in dating anyone else for quite some time.

Oddly enough, since she dated regularly and routinely, she'd repeatedly turned him down. Which, since she was obviously as attracted to him as he was her, made no sense. Unless she truly was more a stickler for not dating coworkers than he believed.

"Have you ever dated a coworker in the past?"

At his question, she turned to him. "What do you mean?"

"I was just curious as to why going on a date with me was such a big deal."

"I didn't say going on a date with you was a big deal," she immediately countered.

"My references say that going on a date with me is a very big deal."

"Yeah, well, you might need to update that reference because I'm telling you Mommy Dearest doesn't count."

He grinned at her quick comeback. He liked that about her, that she had an intelligence and wit that stimulated him. "Did you think about our kiss?"

"What?"

He grinned. He knew that one would throw her off balance. "I was just curious. Did you think about our kiss on your porch this weekend?"

"I'm not answering that." She turned and stared out the window.

Lance laughed. "You don't have to. I already know."

"I don't like how you think you know everything about me."

"I wouldn't presume to say I know everything about you by a long shot, but your face and eyes are very expressive so there's some things you don't hide well."

"Such as?"

"Your feelings about me."

"Sorry. Loathing tends to do that to a girl."

There went that quick wit again. He grinned. "Keep telling yourself that and you might convince yourself, but you're not going to convince me. I've kissed you, remember?"

"How could I forget when you keep reminding me?"

He laughed again. "I plan to keep reminding you."

"I have a good memory. No reminders needed."

"I'm sure you do, but I enjoy reminding you."

"Because?"

"You normally don't fluster easily, yet I manage to fluster you."

"You say that as if it's a good thing," she accused from the passenger seat.

Seeing the heightened color in her cheeks, hearing the pitch-change to her voice, watching the way her eyes sparked to life, he smiled. "Yes, I guess I do. You need to be flustered, and flustered good."

"Why am I blushing?"

"Because you have a dirty mind?" he suggested, shooting her a teasing look. "And you liked that I kissed you today in your office and Friday night on your porch."

"Let's change the subject. Let's talk about Edith and her bowel movements."

He burst out laughing. "You have a way with words, McKenzie."

"Let's hope they include *no*, *no* and *no* again."

"Then I just have to be sure to ask the right questions, such as, do you want me to stop kissing you, McKenzie?"

She just rolled her eyes and didn't bother giving a verbal answer.

There really wasn't any need.

They both already knew that she liked him kissing her.

CHAPTER SIX

EDITH DIDN'T LOOK much the worse for wear when McKenzie entered her hospital room. The elderly woman lay in her bed in the standard drab hospital gown beneath a white blanket and sheet that were pulled up to beneath her armpits. Her skin was still a pasty pale color that blended too well with her bed covering and had poor turgor, despite the intravenous fluids. Oxygen was being delivered via a nasal cannula. Edith's short salt-and-pepper hair was sticking up every which way about her head as if she'd been restless. Or maybe she'd just run her fingers through her hair a lot.

"Hello, Edith, how are you feeling since I last saw you at the office earlier today?"

Pushing her glasses back on her nose, the woman shrugged her frail shoulders. "About the same."

Which was a better answer than feeling worse.

"Any more blood?"

Edith shifted, rearranging pillows. "Not that I've seen."

"Are you spitting up anything?"

She shook her head in a slow motion, as if to continue to answer required too much effort. "I was coughing up some yellowish stuff, but haven't since I got to the hospital."

"Hmm, I'm going to take a look and listen to you again,

and then one of my colleagues whom you've met before will also be checking you. Dr. Spencer."

"I know him. Handsome fellow. Great smile. Happy eyes."

Lance did have happy eyes. He had a great smile, too. But she didn't want thoughts of that happy-eyed handsome man with his great smile interfering with her work, so she just gave Edith a tight smile. "That would be him."

"He your fellow?"

McKenzie's heart just about stopped.

Grateful she'd just put her stethoscope diaphragm to the woman's chest, McKenzie hesitated in answering. Was Lance her fellow? Was that what she'd agreed to earlier?

Essentially she had agreed to date him, but calling him her fellow seemed a far stretch from their earlier conversation.

She made note of the slight arrhythmia present in the woman's cardiac sounds, nothing new, just a chronic issue that sometimes flared up. Edith had a cardiologist she saw regularly. Perhaps McKenzie would consult him also. First, she'd get an EKG and cardiac enzymes, just to be on the safe side.

"Take a deep breath for me," she encouraged. Edith's lung sounds were not very strong, but really weren't any different from her usual shallow and crackly breaths. "I'm going to have to see why your chest X-ray isn't available. They did do it?"

The woman nodded. "They brought the machine here and did the X-ray with me in bed."

Interesting, as Edith could get up with assistance and had walked out of the clinic of her own free will with a nurse at her side. Plus, she'd had to go to the radiology department for the CT of her abdomen. They would have taken her by wheelchair, so why the bedside X-ray rather than doing it in Radiology?

There might be a perfectly logical reason why they'd done a portable chest X-ray instead of just doing it while she'd been there for her CT scan, McKenzie told herself.

"Is there something wrong?" Edith asked.

"You're in the hospital, so obviously everything's not right," McKenzie began. "It concerns me that you saw blood when you spat up earlier. I need to figure out where that blood came from. Your esophagus? Your stomach? Your lungs? Then there's your pain. How would you rate it currently?"

"My stomach? Maybe a two or three out of ten," Edith answered, making McKenzie question if she should have sent the woman home and just seen her back in clinic in the morning.

Maybe she'd overreacted when Edith had mentioned seeing the blood. No, that was a new complaint for the woman and McKenzie's gut instinct said more was going on here than met the eye. Edith didn't look herself. She was paler, weaker.

"Does anywhere else hurt?"

"Not really."

"Explain," she prompted, knowing how Edith could be vague.

"Nothing that's worth mentioning."

Which could mean anything with the elderly woman.

"Edith, if there's anything hurting or bothering you, I need to know so I can have everything checked out before I release you from the hospital. I want to make sure that we don't miss anything."

McKenzie listened to Edith's abdomen, then palpated it, making sure nothing was grossly abnormal that hadn't shown on Edith's CT scan.

"I'm fine." The woman patted McKenzie's hand and any moment McKenzie expected to be called *dearie*. She finished her examination and was beginning to decide she'd truly jumped the gun on the admission when Lance stepped into the room.

"Hey, beautiful. What's a classy lady like you doing in a joint like this?"

McKenzie shook her head at Lance's entrance. The man was a nut. One who had just put a big smile on Edith's pale face.

"What's a hunky dude like you doing wearing pajamas to work?"

McKenzie blinked. Never had she heard Edith talk in such a manner.

Lance laughed. "They're scrubs, not pajamas, and you and I have had this conversation in the past. Good to note your memory is intact."

"That your fancy way of saying I haven't lost my marbles?"

"Something like that." He turned to McKenzie. "I'm a little confused about why they did a portable chest X-ray rather than do that while she was in Radiology for her CT."

"I wondered that myself. I'll talk to her nurse before we leave the hospital."

"We?" Edith piped up.

Before Lance could say or reveal anything that McKenzie wasn't sure she wanted to share with the elderly woman, McKenzie cleared her throat. "I suspect Dr. Spencer will be going home at some point this evening, and I certainly plan to go home too."

After real food and frozen yogurt.

And mouth-to-mouth.

Her cheeks caught fire and she prayed Edith didn't notice because the woman wouldn't bother filtering her comments and obviously she had no qualms about teasing Lance.

"After looking over everything, I'm thinking you just needed a vacation," Lance suggested.

To McKenzie's surprise, Edith sighed. "You know it's bad when your husband's doctor says you need a vacation."

Edith's husband had been gone for a few years. He'd died about the time McKenzie had returned to Coopersville and started practicing at the clinic. Edith and her husband must have been patients of Lance's prior to his death. Had the woman changed doctors at the clinic because McKenzie hadn't known her husband and therefore she'd make no associations when seeing her?

No wonder he'd been so familiar with Edith.

"What do you think is going on, Edith?" Lance asked, removing his stethoscope from his lab coat pocket.

"I think you and my doctor are up to monkey business."

McKenzie's jaw dropped.

Lance grinned. "Monkey business, eh? Is that what practicing medicine is called these days?"

"Practicing medicine isn't the business I was talking about. You know what I meant," the older woman accused, wagging her finger at him.

"As did you when I asked what you thought was going on," Lance countered, not fazed by her good-natured fussing.

The woman sighed and seemed to lose some of her gusto. "I'm not sure. My stomach has been hurting, but I just figured it was my constipation. Then today I saw that blood when I spit up, so I wasn't sure what was going on and thought I'd better let Dr. Sanders check me."

"I'm glad you did."

"Me, too," the woman admitted, looking every one of her eighty years and then a few. "I definitely feel better now than I did earlier. I think the oxygen is helping."

"Were you having a hard time breathing, Edith?"

"Not really. I just felt like air was having trouble getting into my body."

More symptoms Edith had failed to mention.

"Any weight gain?"

"She was two pounds heavier than at her last office visit a couple of weeks ago," McKenzie answered, knowing where his mind was going. "Her feet and ankles have one plus nonpitting edema and she says her wedding band," which Edith had never stopped wearing after her husband's death, "isn't tighter than normal."

While Lance checked her over from head to toe, McKenzie logged in to the computer system and began charting her notes.

"Chest is noisy." Lance had obviously heard the extra sounds in Edith's lungs, too. They were difficult to miss. "Let's get a CT of her chest and maybe a D-dimer, too."

She'd already planned to order both.

"I've added the chest CT and a BNP to her labs, and recommended proceeding with the D-dimer if her BNP is elevated." McKenzie agreed with his suggestions. "Anything else you can think of?"

He shook his head. "Maybe a sputum culture, just in case, but otherwise I think you've covered everything."

Not everything. With the human body there were so many little intricate things that could go wrong that it was impossible to cover every contingency. Especially in someone Edith's age when things were already not working as efficiently.

They stayed in Edith's room for a few more minutes, talking to her and trying to ascertain more clues about what was going on with her, then spoke with Edith's nurse to check on the reason for doing the portable chest X-ray rather than having it done in the radiology department. Apparently, the machine had been having issues. Edith's nurse was going to check with the radiologist and text McKenzie as soon as results were available.

"Anyone else you need to see before we go?" she asked Lance.

He shook his head. "I went by to check on the mayor prior to going to Edith's room."

"Oh," McKenzie acknowledged, glancing his way as they crossed the hospital parking lot. The wind nipped at her and she wished she'd changed from her lab coat into her jacket. "How is he doing?"

"He's recovering from his surgery nicely. The surgeon plans to release him to go home tomorrow as long as there are no negative changes between now and then."

"That's good."

"You saved his life."

"If I hadn't been there, you would have done so. It's really no big deal."

"He thinks it is a big deal. So does his wife. They are very grateful you were there."

McKenzie wasn't sure what Lance expected her to say. She'd just been at the right place at the right time and had helped do what had needed to be done.

"He wants us to ride on his float in the Christmas parade."

"What?"

"He invited us to ride on his float this Saturday."

"I don't want to be in the Christmas parade." Once upon a time she'd have loved to ride on a Christmas parade float.

"You a Scrooge?"

"No, but I don't want to ride on a Christmas float and wave at people who are staring at me."

Ever since her fighting parents had caused a scene at school and her entire class had stared at McKenzie, as if she had somehow been responsible, McKenzie had hated being the center of attention.

"That's fine," he said, not fazed by her reticence. "I'll do the waving and you stare at me."

"How is that supposed to keep them from staring at me?"

"I'm pretty sure everyone will be staring at the mayor and not us."

"I hope you told him no."

The corner of his mouth lifted in a half grin. "You'd hope wrong."

She stopped walking. "I'm not into being a spectacle."

She'd felt that way enough as a child thanks to her parents' antics. She wouldn't purposely put herself in that position again.

"How is participating in a community Christmas parade being a spectacle?"

She supposed he made a good point, but still…

"Besides, don't people stare at you when you run your races?"

"Long-distance running doesn't exactly draw a fan base." She started toward his car again.

"That a hint for me to come cheer you on at your next run?"

She shook her head. "I don't need anyone to cheer me on."

"What if I want to cheer you on?"

She shook her head again. She didn't want him or anyone else watching her run. She didn't want to expect someone to be there and then them possibly not show up. To run because she loved running was one thing. To run and think someone was there, supporting her, and them not really be, well, she'd felt that disappointment multiple times throughout her childhood and she'd really prefer not to go down that road again.

Some things just weren't worth repeating.

"I tell you what, if you want to come to one of my races, that's fine. But not as a cheerleader. If you want to come," she challenged, stopping at his car's passenger side, "you run."

He opened the car door and grinned. "You're inviting me to be on your team? I like the sound of that."

"There are no teams in the races I run."

"No? Well, maybe you're running in the wrong races."

"I'm not." She climbed into the seat and pulled the door to. She could hear his laughter as he rounded the car.

"You have yourself a deal, McKenzie," he said as he climbed into the driver's seat and buckled his seat belt. "I'll run with you. When's your next race?"

"I just did a half marathon on Saturday morning." She thought over her schedule a moment. "I'm signed up for one on New Year's Day morning. You should be able to still get signed up. It's a local charity run so the guidelines aren't strict."

"Length?"

"It's not a real long one, just a five-kilometer. Think you can do that?" she challenged. He was fit, but being fit didn't mean one could run. She'd learned that with a few friends who'd wanted to go with her. They'd been exercise queens, but not so much into running. McKenzie was the opposite. She was way too uncoordinated to do dancing, or anything that required group coordination, but she was a boss when it came to running.

His lips twitched with obvious amusement at her challenge. "You don't have the exclusive on running, you know."

"I've never seen you out running," she pointed out.

"You've never seen me take a shower either, but I promise you I do so on a regular basis."

Lance. In the shower. Naked. Water sluicing over his body. She gulped. Not an image she wanted in her head. "Probably all cold ones."

Maybe she needed a cold one to douse the images of him in the shower because her imagination was going hot, hot, hot.

He chuckled. "Only lately."

That got her attention. "You're taking cold showers because of me?"

"What do you think?"

"That we shouldn't be having this conversation." She
stared at him, unable to help asking again. "I'm really why
you need to take cold showers lately?"

He grinned. "I was only teasing, McKenzie. I haven't
taken a cold shower in years."

"That I believe."

"But not that I might be rejected and need cold water?"

"I doubt you're rejected often."

"Rarely, but it does happen from time to time."

"Is that why you're here with me?"

"Because you rejected me?" He shook his head. "I'm
here with you because you were smart enough to say yes
to getting frozen yogurt with me."

"And real food," she reminded him as he put his car into
reverse. "Don't forget you have to feed me real food before
plying me with dessert."

McKenzie closed her mouth around her spoonful of frozen
birthday-cake yogurt and slowly pulled the utensil from her
mouth, leaving behind some of the cold, creamy substance.

"Good?"

Her gaze cut to the man sitting across the small round
table from her. "What do you think?"

"That watching you eat frozen yogurt should come with
a black-label warning."

"Am I dangerous to your health?"

"Just my peace of mind."

McKenzie's lips twitched. "That makes us even."

They'd gone to a local steak house and McKenzie had
gotten grilled chicken, broccoli and a side salad. She'd been
so full when they'd left the restaurant that if not for Lance's
insistence that they do their part to support the Toys for

Tots, she'd have begged off dessert. She'd been happy to discover the old adage about there always being room for ice cream had held true for frozen yogurt. She was enjoying the cold goodness.

She was also enjoying the company.

Lance had kept their conversation light, fun. They'd talked about everything from their favorite sports teams, to which McKenzie had had to admit she didn't actually have favorites, to talking about medical school. They'd argued in fun about a new reality singing television program she'd been surprised to learn he watched. Often she'd sit and have the show on while she was logged in to the clinic's remote computer system and working on her charts. He did the same.

"I'm glad you said yes, McKenzie."

"To frozen yogurt?"

"To me."

Taking another bite, she shook her head. "I didn't say yes to you."

His eyes twinkled. "That isn't what I meant. We can take our time in that regard."

"Really?"

For once he looked completely serious. "As much time as you want and need."

"What if I never want or need 'that'?"

"Then I will be reintroduced to cold showers," he teased, taking a bite of his yogurt and not seeming at all concerned that she might not want or need "that," which contrarily irked her a bit.

"I'm not going to jump into bed with you tonight."

"I don't expect you to." He was still smiling as if they were talking about the weather rather than his sex life, or potential lack thereof.

"But if I said yes, you would jump into my bed?"

"With pleasure."

Shaking her head, she let out a long breath. "This morning, had someone told me I'd go out to dinner with you, go for dessert with you, I'd have told them they were wrong. It's going to take time to get used to the idea that we are an item."

"Does it usually take a while to get used to the idea of dating someone?"

"Not ever," she admitted.

"Why me?"

She shrugged. "I don't know. Maybe because for so long I've told myself I'm not allowed to date you."

"Because of work?"

"Amongst other things."

"Explain."

"I'm not sure I can," she admitted. How could she explain what she didn't fully understand herself? Even if she could explain it to him, she wasn't sure she'd want to. "Enough serious conversation. Tell me how you got started in community theater."

CHAPTER SEVEN

LANCE WALKED MCKENZIE to her front door, and stood on her porch yet again. This time he didn't debate with himself about whether or not he was going to kiss her.

He was going to.

What he wasn't going to do was go inside her place.

Not that he didn't want to.

He did.

Not that he didn't think there was a big part of her that wanted him to.

He did.

But she was so torn about them being together that he'd like her to be 100 percent on board when they made that step.

Why she was so torn, he wasn't sure. Neither of them were virgins. Neither of them had long-term expectations of the relationship. Just that his every gut instinct told him to take his time if that's what it took.

Took for what?

That's what he couldn't figure out.

He just knew McKenzie was different, that for the first time in a long time he really liked a woman.

Maybe for the first time since Shelby.

Guilt slammed him, just as it always did when he thought of her. What right did he have to like another woman? He didn't deserve that right. Not really. He took a deep breath and willed his mind not to go there. Not right now, although maybe he deserved to be reminded of it right now and every other living, breathing moment. Instead, he stared down into the pretty green eyes of the woman looking up at him with a thousand silent questions.

"Well?" she asked. "Are we back to my having to ask for your next move? Seriously, I gave you more credit than this."

He swallowed the lump forming in his throat. "If that were the case, what move would you ask me to make?"

McKenzie let out an exaggerated sigh. "Just kiss me and get it over with."

He tweaked his finger across her pert, upturned nose. "For that, I should just go home."

She crossed her arms. "Fine. Go home."

"See if you care?"

Her brows made a V. "What?"

"I was finishing your rant for you."

"Whatever." She rolled her eyes. "Go home, Lance. Have your shower. Cold. Hot. Lukewarm. Whatever."

Despite his earlier thoughts, he couldn't hold in his laughter at her indignation. "I intend to, but not before I kiss you good-night."

"Okay."

Okay? He smiled at her response, at the fact that she closed her eyes and waited for his mouth to cover hers, though her arms were still defensively crossed.

She was amazingly beautiful with her hat pulled down over her ears and her scarf around her neck. The temperature was only in the upper fifties, so it wasn't that cold. Just cold enough to need an outside layer.

And to cause a shiver to run down Lance's spine.

It had probably been the cold and not the anticipation of kissing McKenzie that had caused his body to quiver.

Maybe.

"Well?" She peeped at him through one eye. "Sun's going to be coming up if you don't get a move on. Time's a-wasting."

She closed her eye again and waited.

Smiling, he leaned down, saw her chin tilt toward him in anticipation, but rather than cover her lips he pressed a kiss to her forehead.

Her eyes popped open and met his, but she didn't say anything.

Her lips parted in invitation, but he still didn't take them. He kissed the corner of each eye, her cheekbones, the exposed section of her neck just above her scarf. He kissed the corners of her mouth.

She moaned, placed her gloved hands on his cheeks and stared up at him. She didn't speak, though, just stood on tiptoe while pulling him toward her, taking what she wanted.

Him.

She covered his mouth with hers and the porch shifted beneath Lance's feet. They threatened to kick up and take off on a happy flight.

Unlike their previous kisses, where he'd initiated the contact, this time it was her mouth taking the lead. Her lips demanding more. Her hands pulling him closer and closer. Her body pressing up against his.

Her wanting more, expressing that want through her body and actions.

Lance moaned. Or growled. Or made some type of strange noise deep in his throat.

Whatever the sound was, McKenzie pulled back and giggled. "What was that?"

"A mating call?"

"That was supposed to make me want to rip off your clothes and mate?"

His lips twitched. "You're telling me it didn't?"

Smiling, she shook her head. "Better go home and practice that one, big boy."

"Guess I'd better." He rubbed his thumb across her cheek. "Thank you for tonight, McKenzie."

"You paid for dinner and dessert. Everything was delicious. I'm the one who should be thanking you, again."

"You were delicious."

She laughed. "Must have been leftover frozen yogurt."

He shook his head. "I don't think so."

She met his gaze and her smile faded a little. "Tell me this isn't a bad idea."

"'This'?"

She gnawed on her lower lip. "I don't do long-term relationships, Lance. You know that. We've talked about that. This isn't going to end with lots of feel-good moments."

"I do know that and am fine with it. I'm not looking for marriage either, McKenzie. Far from it."

"Then we both understand that this isn't going anywhere between us. Not anywhere permanent or long lasting."

"We're clear." Lance wasn't such a fool that he didn't recognize that he'd only kissed her and yet he wanted McKenzie more than he recalled wanting any woman, ever.

Even Shelby.

Then again, he'd been a kid when he and Shelby had been together, barely a man. Old enough to enter into adulthood with her only to lose her before either of them had experienced the real world. Typically, when he dated, Shelby didn't play on his mind so much. Typically, when he dated, he didn't feel as involved as he already felt with McKenzie.

"I'll see you in the morning?" she asked, staring up at him curiously.

"Without a doubt."

Her smile returned. "I'm glad."

With that, she planted one last, quick kiss on his mouth then went into her house, leaving him on her front porch staring at her closed front door and wondering what the hell he was getting himself into and if he should run while he still could.

McKenzie ran as fast as she could, but her feet weren't co-operating. Each time she tried to lift her running shoe–clad foot, it was as if it weighed a ton and she didn't have the strength to do more than lean in the direction she wanted to go. She stared off into the distance. Nothing. There was nothing there. Just gray-black nothingness.

Yet, desperately, she attempted to move her feet in that direction.

Fear pumped her blood through her body.

She had to run.

Had to.

Yet, try as she might, nothing was happening.

Run, McKenzie, run before...

Before what?

She wasn't sure. There was nothing to run to. Was she running from something?

She turned, was shocked to see Lance standing behind her.

Again, she tried to move her feet, but nothing happened. Desperation pumped through her. She had to get away from him. Fast.

She glanced down at her running shoes and frowned. Gone were her running shoes and in their place were con-crete blocks where her shoes and feet should be.

What was going on?

She glanced over her shoulder and saw that Lance was casually strolling toward her. He was taking his time, not in any rush, not even breaking a sweat, but he was steadily closing the gap between them.

Grinning in that carefree way he had, he blew her a kiss and panic filled her.

People were all around, watching them, gawking, pointing and staring.

Run, McKenzie, run.

It's what she did.

What she always did.

But she'd never had concrete blocks for feet before.

Which really didn't make sense. How could her feet be concrete blocks?

Somewhere in the depths of her fuzzy mind she realized she was dreaming.

Unable to run?

People everywhere staring at her?

That wasn't a dream.

That was a nightmare.

Even if it was Lance who was closing in on her and he seemed quite happy with his pursuit and inevitable capture of her.

"The radiologist just called me with the report on Edith's CT and D-dimer." McKenzie stood in Lance's office doorway, taking him in at his desk. His brown hair was ruffled and when his gaze met hers, his eyes were as bright as the bluest sky.

"She has a pulmonary embolism?" Lance asked.

"He called you, too?"

"No, I just figured that was the case after listening to her last night and the things you said."

"That doesn't explain the blood she spat up. She shouldn't have spat up blood with a clot in her lungs. That doesn't make sense."

"You're right. Makes me wonder what else is going on. Did they get the sputum culture sent off?"

"Yes, with her first morning cough-up. Her pulmonologist is supposed to see her this morning. Her cardiologist, too."

"That's good."

Suddenly, McKenzie felt uncomfortable standing in Lance's doorway. What had she been thinking when she'd sought him out to tell him of Edith's test results?

Obviously, she hadn't been thinking.

She could have texted him Edith's results.

She'd just given in to the immediate desire to tell him, to see him, to share her anxiety over the woman's diagnosis. She really liked Edith and had witnessed Lance's affection for her, too.

"Um, well, I thought you'd want to know. I'll let you get back to work," she said, taking a step backward and feeling more and more awkward by the moment.

"Thank you, McKenzie."

Awkward.

"You're welcome." She turned, determined to get out of Dodge as quickly as possible.

"McKenzie?"

Heart pounding in her throat, she slowly turned back toward him. "Yes?"

His gaze met hers and he asked, "Dinner tonight if I don't see you before then?"

Relief washed over her.

"If you do see me before, what then? Do I not get dinner? Just dessert or something?"

He grinned. "You do keep me on my toes."

Since he was sitting down, she didn't comment, just waited on him to elaborate.

"Regardless of when we next see each other, I'd like to take you to dinner tonight, McKenzie. As you well know, I'm also good for dessert."

"Sounds like a plan," she answered, wondering why she felt so relieved that he'd asked, that they had plans to see each other after work hours. He'd been asking her for weeks and she'd been saying no. Now that she was willing to say yes, had she thought he wasn't going to ask?

"Great." His smile was bigger now, his dimples deeper. "We can discuss what we're going to wear for the Christmas parade. I'm thinking you should be a sexy elf."

"A sexy elf, hmm?" she mused, trying to visualize what he was picturing in his mind. He'd make a much sexier Santa's helper than she would. Maybe he should do the sexy-elf thing. "I haven't agreed to be in the Christmas parade," she reminded him.

"It'll be fun. The mayor's float is based on a children's story about a grumpy fellow who hates Christmas until a little girl shows him the true meaning of the holidays. It's a perfect float theme."

"I get to do weird things to my hair and wear ear and nose extensions that make me look elfish for real?" she asked with false brightness.

"You do. Don't forget the bright clothes."

She narrowed her gaze suspiciously. "And you're going to do the same?"

"I'm not sure about doing weird things to my hair." He ran his fingers through his short brown locks. "But I can get into the colorful Christmas spirit if that makes you happy."

This should be good. Seeing him in his float clothes would be worth having to come up with a costume of her own. After all, she had a secret weapon: Cecilia, who rocked makeup and costumes.

"Well, then. Sign me up for some Christmas float happiness."

Cecilia really was like a Christmas float costume secret weapon. A fairy godmother.

She walked around McKenzie, her lips twisted and her brow furrowed in deep thought.

"We can use heavy-duty bendable hair wires to wrap

your hair around to make some fancy loops." Cecelia studied McKenzie's hair. "That and lots of hair spray should do the trick."

"What about for an outfit?"

"*K-I-S-S.*"

"What?"

"Keep It Simple, Stupid. Not that you're stupid," Cecilia quickly added. "Just don't worry about trying to overdo anything. You've got less than a week to put something together. The mayor may not be expecting you to be dressed up."

"Lance says we are expected to dress up."

Cecilia's eyes lit with excitement, as if she'd been patiently waiting for the perfect opportunity to ask but had gotten distracted at the prospect of having her way with McKenzie's hair and costume makeup. "How is the good doctor?"

"Good. Very good."

Cecilia's eyes widened. "Really?"

McKenzie looked heavenward, which in this case was the glittery ceiling of Bev's Beauty Boutique. "I've kissed the man. That's it. But, yes, he was very good at that."

Cecilia let out a disappointed sight. "Just kissing?"

Her lips against Lance's could never be called "just kissing," but she wasn't going to point that out to Cecilia.

"What did you think I meant when I said he was very good?"

"You know exactly what I thought, what I was hoping for. What's holding you back?"

McKenzie shrugged. "We've barely been on three dates, and that's if you count the community Christmas show, which truly shouldn't even count but since he kissed me for the first time that night, I will." Why was she sounding so breathy and letting her sentences run together? "You think I should have already invited him between my sheets?"

"If I had someone that sexy looking at me the way that man looks at you, I'd have invited him between my sheets long ago."

McKenzie shrugged again. "There's no rush."

"No rush?" Shaking her head, Cecilia frowned. "I'm concerned."

"About me? Why?"

"For some reason you are totally throwing up walls between you and this guy. For the life of me I can't figure out why."

McKenzie glanced around the salon. There was a total of five workstations. On the other side of the salon, Bev was rolling a petite blue-haired lady's hair into tight little clips, but the other two stylists had gone to lunch, as had the manicurist. No one was paying the slightest attention to Cecilia and McKenzie's conversation. Thank goodness.

"How many times do I have to say it? I work with him. A relationship between us is complicated."

Cecilia wasn't buying it. "Only as complicated as the two of you make it."

McKenzie sank into her friend's salon chair and spun around to stare at the reflection of herself in the mirror. "I am creating problems where there aren't any, aren't I?"

"Looks that way to me. My question is why. I know you don't fall into bed with every guy you date and certainly not after just a couple of dates, but you've never had chemistry with anyone the way you do with Lance. I could practically feel the electricity zapping between you that night at the Christmas show," she pointed out. "You've never been one to create unnecessary drama. So, as your best friend, that leaves me asking myself, and you, why are you doing it now?"

True. She hadn't. Then again, she never dated anyone very long. Not that three dates classified as dating Lance for a long time. She'd certainly never dated anyone like

Lance. Not even close. He was...different. Not just that he worked with her, but something more that was hard to define and a little nerve-racking to contemplate.

"You really like him, don't you?"

At her best friend's question, McKenzie's gaze met Cecilia's in the mirror. "What's not to like?"

Cecilia grinned. "What? No argument? Uh-oh. This one has you hooked. You may decide you want to keep him around."

"That's what I'm afraid of." Then what? Eventually, he'd be ready to move on and if she were more vested in an actual relationship, she'd be hurt. Being with someone so charismatic and tempting was probably foolish to begin with.

She toyed with a strand of hair still loose from its rubber band. "So, on Saturday morning you're going to make me look like Christmas morning and then transform me into a beautiful goddess for the hospital Christmas party that evening?"

"Sure. Just call me Fairy Godmother." Cecilia's eyes widened again. "Does that mean you're going to go to the hospital Christmas party with Lance?"

McKenzie nodded. She'd just decided that for definite, despite his having mentioned it to her several times. Even if she did insist on them going separately, what would be the point other than that stubbornness he'd mentioned?

Lance stared at the cute brunette sitting on a secured chair on the back of a transfer truck flatbed that had been converted into a magical winter wonderland straight out of a children's storybook.

As was McKenzie with her intricate twisted-up hair with its battery-powered blinking multicolored minilights that were quite attention gathering for someone who'd once said she didn't want anyone staring at her, her elaborate makeup done to include a perky little nose and ear tips, and a red velvet dress fringed with white fur, white stockings and knee-high black boots that had sparkly bows added to them.

She fit in with the others on the float as if she'd been a planned part rather than a last-minute addition by the mayor. Lance liked her costume best, but admitted he was biased. The mayor and his wife stood on a built-up area of the float. They waved at the townspeople as the float made its way along the parade route.

"Tell me this isn't the highlight of your year."

"Okay. This isn't the highlight of my year," she said, but she was smiling and waving and tossing candy to the kids they passed. "Thank you for bringing candy. How did you know?"

"My favorite part of a Christmas parade was scrambling to get candy."

"Oh."

Something in her voice made him curious to know more, to understand the sadness he heard in that softly spoken word.

"Didn't your parents let you pick up candy thrown by strangers?" He kept his voice light, teasing. "On second thought, I should talk to my parents about letting me do that."

"Well, when there are big signs announcing who is on each float, it's not really like taking candy from strangers," she conceded. "But to answer your question, no, my parents didn't. This is my first ever Christmas parade."

"What?"

She'd grown up in Coopersville. The Christmas parade was an annual event and one of the highlights of the community as far as he was concerned. How could she possibly have never gone to one before?

"You heard me, elf boy."

He smiled at her teasing.

"How is it that you haven't ever gone to a Christmas parade before when I know you grew up here and the parade has been around for more decades than you have?"

She shrugged a fur-covered shoulder. "I just haven't. It's not a big deal."

But it was. He heard it in her voice.

"Did your parents not celebrate the holidays?" Not everyone did. With his own mother loving Christmas as much as he did, he could barely imagine someone not celebrating it, but he knew those odd souls were out there.

"They did," McKenzie assured him. "Just in their own unique ways."

Unique ways? His curiosity was piqued, but McKenzie's joy was rapidly fading so he didn't dig.

"Which didn't include parades or candy gathering?"

"Exactly."

"Fair enough."

"You know, I've seen half a dozen people we work with in the crowds," she pointed out. "There's Jenny Westman who works in Accounting, over there with her kids."

She smiled, waved, and tossed a handful of candy in the kids' general direction.

"I see her." He tossed a handful of individually wrapped bubble gums to the kids, too, smiling as they scrambled around to grab up the goodies. "Jenny has cute kids."

"How can you tell with the way she has them all bundled up?" McKenzie teased, still smiling. "I'm not sure I would have recognized them if she wasn't standing next to them."

"You have a point. I think she just recognized us. She's waving with one hand and pointing us out to her husband with the other."

Still holding her smiling, waving pose, McKenzie nodded.

"I imagine everyone is going to be talking about us being together on this float."

"We've had dinner together every night this week. Everyone is already talking about us."

"You're probably right."

"And the ones who aren't will be after tonight's office Christmas party."

"Why? What's happening tonight?"

"You're going as my date. Remember?"

"I remember. I just thought you meant something more."

"More than you going as my date? McKenzie, a date with me is something more."

"Ha-ha, keep telling yourself that," she warned, but she was smiling and not just in her waving-at-the-crowds way of smiling. Her gaze cut to him and her smile dazzled more than any jewel.

"You look great, by the way," he said.

"Thanks. I owe it all to Cecilia. She worked hard putting this together and got to my house at seven this morning to do my hair and makeup. She came up with the lights and promised me that my hair, the real and the fake she brought with her to make it look so poufy and elaborate, wouldn't catch fire. I admit I was a bit worried when she told me she was stringing lights through my hair."

"Like I said, you look amazing and are sure to help the mayor win best float. Cecilia's good."

"Yep. Works at Bev's Beauty Boutique. Just in case you ever need a cut and style or string of Christmas lights dangled above your head on twisted-up fake hair."

"I'll keep that in mind." He reached over and took her gloved hand in his and gave it a squeeze. "I'm glad you agreed to do this."

She didn't look at him, but admitted, "Me, too."

When they reached the final point of the parade, the driver parked the eighteen-wheel truck that had pulled the float. Lance jumped down and held his hand out to assist McKenzie. The mayor and his wife soon joined them. He'd just been discharged from the hospital the day before and probably shouldn't have been out in the parade, but the man had insisted on participating.

"Thank you both for being my honored guests," he praised them in a hoarse, weakened voice. He shook Lance's hand.

"It was our pleasure," Lance assured the man he'd checked on several times throughout his hospital stay despite the fact that he wasn't a patient of their clinic. He genuinely liked the mayor and had voted for him in the last election.

The mayor turned to McKenzie. "Thank you for saving my life, young lady. There'd have been no Christmas cheer this year in my household if not for you."

McKenzie's cheeks brightened to nearly the same color as her plush red dress. "You're welcome, but Dr. Spencer did just as much to save your life as I did. He's the one who did the Heimlich maneuver and your chest compressions."

"You were the one who revived me. Dr. Spencer has told me on more than one occasion that your actions are directly responsible for my still being here."

McKenzie glanced at him in question and Lance winked.

"If there's ever anything we can do." This came from the mayor's wife. "Just let us know. We are forever indebted to you both. You're our Christmas angels."

"We're good, but thank you," Lance and McKenzie both assured them.

"Amazing costume," the mayor's wife praised McKenzie further.

They talked for a few more minutes to those who'd been on the mayor's float, then walked toward the square where the rest of the parade was still passing.

"If it's okay, I'd like to swing by to see Cecelia at the shop."

"No problem," he assured her. "I need to thank her for making you look so irresistibly cute."

McKenzie grimaced. "Cute is not how a woman wants to be described."

"Well, you already had beautiful, sexy, desirable, intelligent, brilliant, gorgeous, breathtaking—"

"You can stop anytime," she interrupted, laughing.

"Amazing, lickable—"

"Did you just say *lickable*?" she interrupted again.

He paused, frowned at her. "Lickable? Surely not."

"Surely so."

"I said *likable*. Not lickable."

"You said lickable."

He did his best to keep a straight face. "You'd think with those elongated ears you'd have better hearing."

She touched one of her pointy ears. "You'd think."

"So maybe I'll just thank her for your costume that's lit up my day so far."

McKenzie reached up and touched her hair. "That would be accurate, at least."

"All the other was, too." Before she could argue, he grabbed her hand and held it as they resumed walking toward Bev's Beauty Boutique.

The wind was a little chilly, but overall the weather was a fairly mild December day in mid-Georgia.

"Oh, goodness, look at you two," Bev gushed in her gravelly voice when McKenzie and Lance walked up to the shop. Lance had met her at a charity function a time or two over the years he'd been in Coopersville. A likable woman even if he did always have to take a step back because of her smoky breath.

Bev and a couple other women were outside the shop, watching the remainder of the parade pass.

"Cecilia, you outdid yourself, girl! McKenzie, you look amazing." Bev, a woman who'd smoked her way to looking older than she was, ran her gaze over Lance's trousers, jacket, and big Christmas bow tie. He'd borrowed some fake ears and a nose tip from the community center costume room from a play they'd put on several years before. "I'm pretty sure you're hotter than Georgia asphalt in mid-July."

McKenzie laughed out loud at the woman's assessment of him. Lance just smiled and thanked her for her hoarse compliment.

"You do look amazing," Cecelia praised her friend. "Even if I do say so myself." She pulled out her cell phone. "I want a picture."

"You took photos this morning," McKenzie reminded as her friend held her cell phone out in front of her.

"Yeah, but that was just you," Cecilia pointed out. "I want pictures of you two together, too. Y'all are the cutest Christmas couple ever."

Reluctantly, McKenzie posed for her friend, then seemed to loosen up a little when she pulled Lance over to where she stood. "Come on, elf boy. You heard her. She wants pictures of us both. If I have to do this, so do you."

Lance wasn't reluctant at all. He wrapped his arm around McKenzie and smiled for the camera while Cecilia took their first photos together.

Their first. Did that mean he thought there would be other occasions for them to be photographed together? Did that imply that he wanted those memories with her captured forever?

"Do something other than smile," Cecilia ordered, looking at them from above her held-out phone.

Lance turned to McKenzie to follow her lead. Her gaze met his, and she shrugged, then broke off a sprig of mistletoe from the salon's door decoration. She held up the greenery, then pulled him to her, did a classic one-leg-kicked-up pose, and planted a kiss right on his cheek with her eyes toward her friend.

No doubt Cecilia's phone camera flash caught his surprise.

He quickly recovered and got into the spirit of things by pointing at the mistletoe McKenzie held and giving an *Oh, yeah* thumbs-up, then posed for several goofy shots and laughed harder than he probably should have at their antics.

All the women and a few spectators laughed and applauded them. A few kids wanted to pose for photos with them, especially McKenzie.

"Is your hair real?" a little girl asked, staring at the twisted-up loops of hair and string of minilights.

"Part of it is real, but I don't normally wear it this way. Just on special days."

"Like on Christmas parade days?" the child asked.

"Exactly."

When they'd finished visiting with her friends, McKenzie hugged Cecilia and thanked her again.

"Don't forget to forward me those pictures," she requested with one last hug.

"I may be calling on you to help with some of our charity events. We're always needing help with costumes and you're good," Lance praised.

Cecilia beamed. "Thank you."

The parade ended and the crowd began to disperse. Customers came to the shop to have their ritual Saturday morning hair appointments and the stylists went back into the salon.

"Now what?" McKenzie asked, turning to face him. Her cheeks glowed with happiness and she looked as if she was having the time of her life.

"Anything you want."

She laughed. "If only I could think of something evil and diabolical."

He took her gloved hand into his. "I'm not worried."

"You should be."

She tried to look evil and diabolical, but only managed to look cute. He lifted her hand to his mouth and pressed a kiss to her fuzzy glove.

"You wouldn't hurt a fly."

"I definitely would," she contradicted. "I don't like flies."

"Okay, Miss Evil and Diabolical Fly-Killer, let's go grab some hot chocolate and see what the Christmas booths have for sale that we can snag."

"Sounds wonderful."

CHAPTER EIGHT

"You looked amazing today," Cecilia told her as she ran a makeup pencil over McKenzie's brow with the precision of an artist working on a masterpiece.

"Thanks to you and the fabulous work you did getting me ready for the mayor's float," McKenzie agreed, trying to hold perfectly still so she didn't mess up what her friend was doing to her face.

"I have to admit, I had fun. Then again, I had a lot to work with."

"Yeah, right," McKenzie snorted. "Let's just hope you can pull off another miracle for tonight, too."

"For your work Christmas party?"

"Yes." She cut her eyes to her friend. "What did you think I meant?"

"You've never asked me to help doll you up in the past for a mere work party."

"This one is different."

"Because of Lance?"

Because of Lance. Yes, it seemed that most everything this week had been because of Lance. Lots of smiles. Lots of hot kisses. Lots of anticipation and wondering if tonight was the night they'd do more than "mouth-to-mouth."

"I suppose so. Can't a girl just want to look her best?"

"Depends on what she's wanting to look her best for."

"For my party."

"And afterward?"

"Well, I'm hoping not to turn into a pumpkin at midnight, if that's what you're asking."

"No pumpkins," Cecilia promised. "Wrong holiday. But what about that mistletoe this morning?"

"What about it?"

"You've gone to dinner every night this week, ridden on a Christmas float with him, and you are going as his date to the Christmas party. That's big, McKenzie. For you, that's huge. What changed?"

"Nothing."

"Something has to have changed. You were saying no to the guy left and right only a week ago."

"You were the one who said I was crazy for not going out with him."

"You *were* crazy for not going out with him. He seems like a great guy. Lots of fun, hot, and crazy about my bestie. I like him."

"You've only been around him twice," McKenzie reminded.

"During which times he helped save a man's life and made you laugh and smile more than I've seen you do in years."

There was that.

"I was in character."

"Yeah right." Cecilia threw McKenzie's words back at her. "If I'd been you, I'd have used that mistletoe for more than a kiss on the cheek."

"I'm sure you would have."

"But you didn't need to, did you?"

"I'm not the kind of girl to kiss and tell." Which was hilarious because Cecilia had been her best friend since before her first kiss and she'd told her about pretty much all her major life events. Plus, she had already told Cecilia that she and Lance had kissed.

Cecilia leaned back, studied McKenzie's face, then went back to stroking a brush across her cheeks. "Even if you hadn't already told me that you kissed Lance on the night of the Christmas show, I'd know you had."

"How would you know that?"

"I can tell. The same as I can tell that, despite our conversation the other day, what you still haven't done is have sex with him."

Could Cecilia see inside her head or did her friend just know her that well?

"And how is it you know that?"

Cecilia's penciled on brow arches. "Am I wrong?"

"No," she admitted. "I've not had sex with him."

Not that he'd made any real plays to get into her bed. He hadn't. Which surprised her.

"The tension between you two is unreal."

"Tension? We weren't fighting today."

"Sexual tension, McKenzie. It's so thick between you two that you could cut it with a knife."

There was that. Which made his lack of pushing beyond their nightly kisses even more difficult to understand.

"I see you're not denying it."

"Would there be any point?"

"None." Cecilia leaned back again and smiled at what she saw. She held a hand mirror up for McKenzie to see what she'd done. "Perfect."

McKenzie stared at her reflection. Cecilia had done wonders with her face. McKenzie rarely wore more than just mascara and a shiny lip gloss that she liked the scent of. Cecilia had plucked, brushed, drawn and done her face up to the point where McKenzie barely recognized the glamorous woman staring back at her. "Wow."

"How much do you want to bet that when Lance sees

you he'll want to forget the party and just stay here and party with you?"

"Not gonna happen." Not on her part and, based on the past week, not on his part either. But anticipation filled her at the thought of Lance seeing her at her best. "Help me into my dress?"

"Definitely. I want to see what underwear you're wearing."

McKenzie's face caught on fire. Busted. "What?"

"You heard me," Cecilia brooked no argument. "I'll know your intentions by your underwear."

McKenzie sighed and slipped off her robe.

Grinning, Cecilia rubbed her hands together. "Now that's what I'm talking about."

"This doesn't mean a thing, you know."

"Of course it doesn't. That's why you aren't wearing granny panties."

McKenzie stuck her tongue out at her friend. "I never wear granny panties."

"Yeah, well, you don't usually wear sexy thongs either, but you are tonight."

"Works better with the material of my dress. No unsightly panty lines that way."

Cecilia had the audacity to laugh. "Keep telling yourself that."

"Fine. I will. Think what you like."

Cecilia laughed again. "Here, let's get you into your dress, let me do any necessary last-minute hair fixes, and then I'm out of here before Dr. Wonderful shows up."

"He's not that wonderful," McKenzie countered.

"Sure he's not. That's why you're a nervous wreck and wearing barely-there panties and a matching bra."

Cecilia laughed and slid McKenzie's sparkly green dress over her head and tugged it downward.

"A real best friend wouldn't point out such things," Mc-

Kenzie pointed out to the woman who'd been a constant in her life since kindergarten. "You know, it's not too late to trade you in for a less annoying model."

Cecilia's loud laughter said she was real worried.

"Have I told you how beautiful you look?"

"Only about a dozen times." McKenzie ran her gaze over Lance. He had gone all out and was wearing a black suit that fit so well she wondered if it was tailor-made. He'd washed away all traces of his Christmas parade costume. His hair had a hint of curl, his eyes a twinkle, and his lips a constant smile. "Have I mentioned how handsome you look in your suit?"

"A time or two." He grinned. "I'm the envy of every man in the building."

"Hardly."

"It's true. You look absolutely stunning."

"Cecilia gets all the credit. She's the miracle worker. I sure can't pull off this…" she gestured to her face and hair "…without her waving her magic wand."

"Your fairy godmother, huh?"

"That's what I've called her this week."

"She's definitely talented," he agreed. "Then again, she had a lot to work with because on your worst day, you're beautiful, McKenzie."

"That does it. No more spiked Christmas punch for you." She made a play for his glass, but he kept it out of her reach.

"Is the punch really spiked?"

"It must be," she assured him, "for you to be spouting so many compliments."

He waggled his brows and took another drink. "I don't think so."

The Christmas party was being held in a local hotel's conference room. There were about two hundred employees in total who worked for the clinic. With those employees and their significant others, the party was going full swing and was full of loud commotion from all directions.

Several of their coworkers had commented on how great they looked tonight, how great they'd looked in the Christmas parade, how excited they were that they were a couple.

Those comments made McKenzie want to squirm in her three-inch heels. All their coworkers now knew without a doubt that they were seeing each other as more than friends.

She'd known this would happen. She'd allowed this to happen.

Several of her female coworkers stared at her with outright envy that she was with Lance. She couldn't blame them. He was gorgeous, fun, intelligent and charming. He didn't seem to notice any of their attention, just stayed close to McKenzie's side and tended to her every need.

Well, almost every need.

Because more and more she'd been thinking of Cecilia's teasing. Yeah, her green dress fit her like a glove right down to where it flared into a floaty skirt that twirled around her thighs when she moved just right. But she hadn't had to wear teeny-tiny underwear because of the dress. She'd worn them because...

"That's the first time I've not seen a smile on your face all evening," Lance whispered close to her ear.

"Sorry," she apologized, immediately smiling. "I was just thinking."

Which, of course, led to him asking what she'd been thinking about.

She just smiled a little brighter, grabbed his hand, and tugged him toward the dance floor. "Dance with me?"

"I thought you'd never ask," he teased, leading her out onto the crowded dance floor. "I've been itching to have you in my arms all evening."

"All you had to do was ask."

"Well, part of me was concerned about the consequences of holding you close."

"Consequences?" She stared into his eyes, saw the truth there, then widened her eyes. "Oh."

"Yeah, oh."

"I guess it's a good thing girls don't have to worry about such things."

His eyes remained locked with hers, half teasing, half serious. "Would that be a problem for you, McKenzie?"

A problem?

Her chin lifted. "I'm not frigid, if that's what you're asking."

"It wasn't, but it's good to know." He pulled her close and they swayed back and forth to the beat of the music.

"You smell good," she told him, trying not to completely bury her face in his neck just to fill her senses totally with the scent of him.

"I was just thinking the same thing about you. What perfume are you wearing?"

"Cecilia sprayed me with some stuff earlier. I honestly don't know what it's called, just that she said it was guaranteed to drive you crazy. Of course, she didn't tell me that until after she'd hit me with a spray."

He nuzzled against her hair. "She was right."

"Feeling a little crazy?"

"With your body rubbed up against mine? Oh, yeah."

She laughed. "I'll let her know the stuff works."

"Pretty sure if you had nothing on at all I'd be feeling just as crazy. Actually, if you had nothing on at all, my current level of crazy would be kid's stuff in comparison."

She wiggled closer against him. "Well, that makes sense. We're both just kids at heart."

"True, that." His hands rubbed against her low back. "Were you thinking about our coworkers just a few minutes ago?"

She knew when he meant and at that time it hadn't been thoughts of their coworkers that had robbed her of her smile. No, it had been thoughts of what she was anticipating happening later in the evening. Not that she was sure that's what would happen, but she'd questioned it enough that she'd shaved, lotioned, powdered, perfumed and dressed in her sexiest underwear.

Because all week Lance had kissed her good-night, deep, thorough passionate kisses that had left her longing for more. She hadn't invited him in and he hadn't pushed. Just hot good-night kisses night after night that left her confused and aching.

Mostly, she just didn't understand why he hadn't attempted to talk his way into her bed. Or at least into her house. He'd still not made it off the front porch.

He might not push for more tonight either. She was okay with it if he didn't. It was just that something had felt different between them today on the Christmas float, and afterward when they'd weaved their way from one booth to another. All week she'd felt as if she was building up to something great. From the moment he'd picked her up at her house this evening and had been so obviously pleased with the way she looked and how she'd greeted him—with lots of smiles—the feeling had taken root inside her that tonight held magical possibilities that she wasn't sure she really wanted in the long run, but in the short term, oh, yeah, she wanted Lance something fierce, thus the itsy-bitsy, barely-there thong.

"Should I be concerned about how quiet you are?" he asked.

"Nope. I'm just enjoying the dance."

"Any regrets?"

His question caught her off guard and she pulled back enough to where she could see his face. "About?"

"Coming to the party with me."

"Not yet."

He chuckled. "You expecting that to change?"

"Depends on your behavior between now and the time we leave."

"Then I guess I better be on my best, eh?"

"Something like that."

Not that she could imagine Lance not being on his best behavior at all times. He was always smiling, doing something to help others. Never had she met a man who volunteered more. It was as if his life's mission was to do as much good as he possibly could in the world. Or at least within their small community.

The music changed to an upbeat number and they danced to a few more songs. The emcee for the evening stopped the music and made several announcements, gave away a few raffle items.

"Now, folks." The emcee garnered their attention. "I'd like to call Dr. Lance Spencer to the stage."

Lance glanced at her. "Do you know anything about this?"

McKenzie shook her head. She didn't have a clue.

Pulling McKenzie along with him, he headed up toward the makeshift stage. She managed to free her hand just before he stepped up onto the stage. No way was he taking her up there with him. Who knew what was about to happen? Maybe he had won a raffle or special door prize or something.

"Dr. Spencer," the emcee continued, "I'm told you make a mean emcee."

"I wouldn't say 'mean,'" Lance corrected, laughing.

"Well, a little birdie tells me you've been known to rock a karaoke machine and requested you sing to kick off our karaoke for the evening."

Lance glanced at McKenzie, but she shook her head. That little birdie wasn't her.

Always in the spirit of things, Lance shrugged, and told the emcee the name of a song. As the music started, microphone in hand, he stepped off the stage and took McKenzie's hand again.

"I need a singing partner."

Her heart in her nonsinging throat, McKenzie shook her head. He wasn't doing this. She didn't want to make a spectacle of them by pulling her hand free of his, but her feet were about to take off at any moment, which meant he was either coming with her, hands clasped and all, or she'd be doing exactly that.

"Come on," he encouraged. "Don't be shy. Sing with me, McKenzie. It'll be fun."

By this time, the crowd was also really into the spirit of things and urging her onto the stage. She heard a female doctor whose office was right next to hers call out for her to go for it.

McKenzie's heart sank. She wasn't going to be able to run away. Not this time. She was surrounded by her coworkers. Her hand was held by Lance.

She was going to have to go onstage and sing. With Lance. Nothing like a little contrast to keep things interesting.

A singer she was not.

She closed her eyes.

What had been a great night had just gone sour. Very, *very* sour.

She blamed Lance.

Lance realized he'd made a mistake the moment he'd put McKenzie on the spot. Unfortunately, his request wasn't something she could easily refuse with their coworkers now cheering for her to join him. She could either sing or be seen as a total party pooper—which she wasn't and he knew she'd resent being labeled as one.

McKenzie's eyes flashed with fear and he wasn't sure what all else.

He'd messed up big time.

Faking a smile, she stepped up onto the stage with him. He still held her hand. Her palm was sweaty and her fingers threatened to slip free. He gave her a reassuring squeeze. She didn't even look at him.

Lance sang and McKenzie came through from time to time, filling the backup role rather than taking a lead with him, as he'd initially hoped. Mostly, she mumbled, except during the chorus. With almost everyone in the crowd singing along, too, maybe no one noticed.

McKenzie noticed, though. The moment the song was over, she gave him the evil eye. "For the record, I don't sing and if you ever do that to me again, it'll be the last time."

"That's funny," he teased, planning to keep their conversation light, to beg her forgiveness if he needed to. "I just heard you do exactly that."

"Only a tone-deaf lunatic would call what I just did singing."

"I thought you sounded good."

"You don't count."

"Ouch." He put his hand over his heart as if she'd delivered a fatal blow. "My references say I count."

She flashed an annoyed look his way. "You're really going to have to get over those references."

"Or use them as a shield against the walloping you seem determined to deliver to me."

"Not everyone enjoys being the center of attention."

"Tell me the truth. You didn't have fun onstage just then? Not even a little?" he coaxed.

McKenzie stared at him as if he was crazy. He *was* crazy.

"I detested being onstage in front of my coworkers." She frowned as they moved onto the dance floor. Her body remained rigid, rather than relaxing against his like it had during their earlier dances. "For the record, I really don't like people staring at me. Put it down to bad childhood memories of when my parents thrust me into situations where I got a lot of unwanted attention."

When he'd gone after her to sing with him, he'd never considered that she might not enjoy being onstage. He'd just selfishly wanted her with him.

"I'm sorry, McKenzie. If I'd known how you felt, I wouldn't have put you in the spotlight that way. I definitely would never intentionally upset you. It was all in fun, to kick off the night's karaoke. That's all."

"I know you didn't intentionally pull me up there to upset me," she admitted. "I just prefer you not to put me in situations where all eyes are on me. I have enough bad childhood flashbacks as it is."

"What kind of childhood flashbacks?"

"Just situations where my parents would yell and scream at each other regardless of where we were and no matter who was around. Way too often all eyes would be on me while they had a knock-down, drag-out. When people stare at me, it gives me that same feeling of humiliation and mortification."

"I'm sorry your parents did that to you and that I made those negative feelings come to surface. But, for the record, maybe you're finally getting past those old hang-ups because you were smiling." She had been smiling. Mumbling and smiling.

"I was faking it."

"Ouch." His hand went to his chest and he pretended

to receive another mortal blow. "Not good when a man's woman has to fake it."

"Exactly. So you should be careful what situations you put me into where I might have to fake other things," she warned with a half smile. "I don't sing. I barely dance. Take note of it."

He pulled her to him, his hand low on her back, holding her close. "You dance quite nicely when you aren't in rigor mortis. However, I'll make a note. No more singing and barely dancing. Got it."

"Good."

"Also, for the record, when I put you in a certain situation, there will be no need for faking it."

Her chin tilted up and she arched a brow in challenge. "How can you be so sure?"

"Because I'll use every ounce of skill, every ounce of sheer will, every ounce of energy I have to make sure I blow your mind," he whispered close for her ears only. "My pleasure will be seeing your pleasure. Feeling your pleasure."

"That sounds…fun. Maybe you should have tried your hand at that instead of pulling me onstage with you."

He swallowed. Was she saying…?

"I want you, McKenzie. I haven't pushed because I know you still have a lot of mixed emotions about being with me, but when you're ready I want to make love to you. I've made no pretense about that."

"Sex. You want to have sex with me," she corrected, resting her forehead against his chin. "I'll let you know when I'm ready."

Lance's heart beat like a drum against his rib cage. "I'll be waiting."

"Don't hold your breath."

"I'd rather hold yours."

That had her looking up.

"Kiss me, McKenzie."

"Here? Now? On the dance floor? Around our coworkers? Are you crazy?"

He glanced around the dim room. The dance floor was crowded with couples, some of them stealing kisses. There were some single women who were dancing in a circle off to one side of the dance floor. One of the admin girls currently had the microphone and was belting out a tune. No one was paying them any attention.

McKenzie's gaze followed his, no doubt drawing the same conclusions, but she shook her head anyway. "No. I'm not one of those girls who is into public displays of affection."

"You kissed me in front of Bev's Beauty Boutique."

"That was different."

"How was that different? Other than it being in broad daylight and in the middle of the square with half the town in the near vicinity?"

"I can't explain how that was different, but it was." Her lower lip disappeared between her teeth. "Don't push me on this, please."

He sighed. "It would probably have been a bad idea for you to kiss me here, anyway."

"Why is that?"

Did she really not know how much she affected him? How much he was having to fight sweeping her up into his arms and carrying her out of the ballroom and straight to the first private place he could find where he could run his fingers beneath her sparkly green dress?

"I think I've already mentioned how much I want you and the effect you have on me."

"But... Oh." Her eyes widened as she moved against him.

"Yeah. Oh."

To his surprise, her body relaxed and he'd swear the

noise that came out of her mouth was a giggle. Not that McKenzie seemed the giggling type, but that's what the sound had most resembled.

Regardless, her arms relaxed around his neck and just to prove how ornery she was and to his total surprise her lips met his in a soft kiss that only lasted a few seconds but took his breath and made his knees weak.

"There," she taunted. "I kissed you in public."

"Not sure what made you change your mind, but thank you." He studied her expression and he'd swear there was a mischievous glint in her eyes. "I think. Because if I didn't know better I'd think you were trying to set me up for embarrassment."

There was the sound again. Definitely a giggle. "Would I do that after our conversation, with you pointing out the obvious differences in the way our bodies react?"

A grin tugged at his lips. "Yeah, you would."

Her eyes sparkled. "Did it work?"

He pulled her close and let her feel for herself that his body was indeed reacting to her, making him uncomfortable in the process. Then again, he'd left her front porch this way every night the past week.

She tilted her face toward him. "I think it did."

"You think?" He shook his head, then stroked his finger across her cheek.

He held her close until the slow dance ended then they moved to a couple of fast songs. Despite what she'd said, McKenzie could dance. She could definitely sing too if she wouldn't let her own self-doubt get in the way.

Laughing, McKenzie fell into his arms. "Hey, Lance?"

"Hmm?" he asked, kissing the top of her head just because he could, because it felt right and wonderful.

"I'm ready."

"Already?" He'd figured they'd be one of the last to

leave, not one of the first. Still, if she was done partying, he'd take her home. Then he met her gaze and what she meant glittered brightly in her emerald eyes. "Really?"

She nodded. "Let's get our coats, please."

"Yes, ma'am."

"Such good manners," she praised.

Lance grinned. "Just wait until I show you what else I'm good at."

CHAPTER NINE

YES, IT HAD been a while since she'd had sex, but McKenzie wasn't a virgin. She enjoyed sex, was athletic enough to have good stamina and a good healthy drive so she felt she was decent in the sack. So why was she suddenly so nervous?

Because she'd essentially agreed to have sex with Lance.

With Lance!

Wasn't that what the dress, the hair and makeup, *the sexy undies* had all been about? Leading up to his taking them off her, kissing her body, running his fingers though her hair, making her sweat from the intensity of their coming together?

Sex with Lance.

Lance, who did everything perfectly.

He looked perfect.

Danced perfectly.

Doctored perfectly.

Made love perfectly?

That was the question.

She gulped and had to fight to keep her eyes on the road and off the man driving his car toward her house. He hadn't looked at her and seemed to have no desire to make small talk, which she appreciated. He was as lost in his thoughts as she was.

What was he thinking?

About sex? With her?

Sometimes she wondered why he even bothered. He'd been asking her out for weeks before she'd agreed to go to the Christmas show at the community center. Why hadn't he just moved on to someone else who was more agreeable?

Ha. She was agreeable tonight. She was practically throwing herself at him.

When he'd realized what she'd meant, he'd taken her hand and, with a determined gleam in his eyes, had made a beeline for their coats, not stopping to chat with any of their coworkers and friends as they'd left.

She took a deep breath.

Lance asked, "Second thoughts?"

She glanced toward him. "No, but I feel like a teenager sneaking off from a high school dance to mess around."

He wasn't looking at her, but she'd swear Lance's face paled, that his grip on the steering wheel tightened to the point his skin stretched white over his knuckles.

When he didn't comment, she asked, "You?"

"No regrets, but we don't have to do this if you're not sure."

"I'm sure." He still looked way tenser than she felt a man on his way to getting what he'd been supposedly wanting for weeks should look. Which made her uneasy. Maybe they were talking too much and not having enough action.

Maybe she was boring him with all her conversation.

They were still another ten minutes from her house. What were they supposed to do during the drive?

Then again, she wasn't the one driving so the possibilities were only limited by her imagination.

She'd always had a good imagination. A vivid imagination.

She wiggled in the seat, enjoying the car's seat warmers. "Nice seaters you've got here."

His gaze flicked her way. "Seaters?"

"Seat heaters. Yours are awesome." Seat belt still in place, she twisted as best she could toward him and wiggled her hips. "I'm feeling all toasty warm."

He kept his eyes on the road, but his throat worked and his fingers flexed along the steering wheel. "Things getting hot down there?"

Yes, this was much better than their terse silence. This was fun. As fun as she wanted to make it.

As fun as she could imagine it.

With Lance her imagination was working overtime.

Odd because even though the thought of sex with him made her nervous, she felt no hesitation in unbuttoning her coat and slipping her arms free, and running her palms down her waist, hips, thighs, letting her fingers tease her skirt hem.

"Maybe. Give me your hand and I'll let you check for yourself."

"McKenzie." Her name came out as half plea, half groan. "I need to concentrate on the road. I don't want to wreck."

"You won't. I only need one hand. You keep your eyes on the road and your other hand on the steering wheel. No worries. I'll take good care of you."

"You think I can touch your body and not look?" His voice sounded strained.

She liked it that his voice sounded strained, that what she was doing was having a profound effect on him. "Can't you?"

"I'm not sure." He sounded as if he really wasn't.

Which made McKenzie giddy inside. He wanted her. Really wanted her. She knew this, but seeing the reality of his desire was something more, was the cherry on top.

"Let's find out." She reached for him and he let her pull his right hand to her thigh. "See, I have faith in your ability to let your fingers have some fun. You've got this."

"Fun? Is that what you call between your legs?"

Excited from how much she could see he wanted her, she reached her free hand out and ran her fingers over his fly. "It had better be what I'm calling between your legs by morning."

"McKenzie." This time her name was a tortured croak.

She smiled, liking the hard fullness she brushed her fingertips over. That was going to be hers before the sun came up. Oh, yeah. He really was perfect.

"You're testing my willpower," he ground out through gritted teeth when her fingers lingered, exploring what she'd found and become fascinated by.

That made two of them. Her willpower was in a shambles. How she'd gone from teasing to totally turned on she wasn't sure, but she had. So much so that she wiggled against the seat again, causing his hand to shift on her thigh and make goose bumps on her skin.

"I have no doubt that you've never failed a test." She placed her free hand over his and guided him beneath the hem of her dress.

"There's always a first."

"Not this time," she told him, gliding his hand between her thighs to where she blazed hotly, and not from the car's seat warmers.

"You sure about that?"

"Positive," she assured him, "because if you lose your willpower we have to stop, and where's the fun in that?"

"Fun being where my fingers are?"

"Exactly." She shifted, bringing him into full contact with those itty-bitty panties she'd put on earlier.

"If I get pulled over for speeding to get us home quicker?"

She squeezed her buttocks together in a Kegel, pressing against his fingers. "Not sure how you'd explain to the officer why you were going so fast."

"I'd tell him to look in my passenger seat and he'd understand just fine."

For all his talk, the speedometer stayed at the speed limit, which she kind of liked. Safety mattered. Even when your passenger was seducing you. That he wasn't gunning the engine of the sports car surprised her, though. She'd have bet money he'd be a speed demon behind the wheel, but she couldn't think of a time she'd been in his car when he'd been going too fast or pulling any careless stunts.

His thumb brushed lightly over her pubic bone and she moaned, forgetting all about safety.

She gripped his thigh and squeezed. "That feels good."

"I couldn't tell."

He didn't have to look at her for her to know he was smiling, pleased with her body's reaction to his touch. She heard his pleasure in his voice, felt it in the way his fingers toyed over the barely-there satin material.

"Might be time to turn that seater off since you're already steamy down there."

She tilted her hips toward his touch. "Might be, but I'm sure I could get hotter."

"You think?"

"I'm hoping."

He slowed the car and turned into her street. "Thank God we're almost there."

"Not even close," she teased. "But if you move those fingers just so, maybe."

"McKenzie." Her name was torn from deep within him. "You're killing me."

His fingers said otherwise. His fingers were little adventurers, exploring uncharted territory, staking claims in the wake of his touch.

She closed her eyes, holding on to his thigh, spreading her legs to give him better access. Gentle back-and-forth movements created cataclysmic earthquakes throughout her body.

Yearnings to rip off her clothes hit her. To rip off *his* clothes, right then, in the car, to give him free access to touch with no material in the way.

Why couldn't she?

Why couldn't she take her panties off?

That wasn't something she'd ever done before, but she was an adult, a responsible one usually. If she wanted to suddenly go commando, she could do that, right?

She hiked her dress up around her thighs, looped her fingers through the tiny straps of her thong and wiggled them down her legs. She probably looked ridiculous raised up off the seat to remove them, but who cared?

His eyes were on the road and now there was nothing to keep him from touching her. Not her panties, but her, as in skin to skin. She needed that. His skin against hers. His touch on her aching flesh.

"If I were a stronger man, I'd make you wait until we're at least in your driveway before I touched you for real," he warned.

"Good thing you're not a stronger man," she replied as his fingers slid home. "Very good thing."

His touch was light, just gentle strokes teasing her.

"This isn't fair," he complained.

"Life isn't fair. Get over it."

He laughed. "No sympathy from you."

"Hey, you've been trying to get in my pants for weeks now. Why would I feel sympathetic toward you when you're getting what you want?"

"I want more than to get into your pants, McKenzie. I want a relationship with you."

"Here's a news flash for you—if you're in my pants, you're in a relationship with me."

"For thirty days or less?" he asked.

"I'm not putting a time limit on our relationship. Move your fingers faster."

"Not until you promise you'll give me two months."

Two months? Why two months?

"This isn't as business negotiation."

"True," he agreed. "But if you want my fingers to do more than skim the surface, you'll give me your word. I want two months. Not a day less. Not a day more."

She moved against him, trying to get the friction she craved. "Two months?"

"Two months."

Ugh. He was pushing for more than she usually gave. It figured. Then again, what was two months in the grand scheme of life?

"I don't have to agree to this to get what I want. It's not as if you're going to turn down what I'm offering."

He chuckled. "Confident, aren't you?"

"Of that? Yes, you're a man."

"I won't be used for sex, McKenzie."

"Isn't that usually the woman's line?"

"These are modern times and you're a modern woman."

She arched further against his hand. "Not that modern."

"Two months?" He teased her most sensitive area with the slightest flick of his finger.

"Fine," she sighed, moving against his fingers. "You can have two months, but I won't promise a day more."

He turned into her driveway, amazing since she hadn't even realized they were that close to her house. Hadn't even recalled that they were in her street or even on the planet, for that matter. All that existed was the two of them inside his car.

He killed the engine, turned toward her, and moved her thighs apart, touching where she ached.

"I knew you could find it if you tried hard enough," she teased breathlessly.

"Oh, I'm definitely hard enough."

She reached out and touched him again. He was right. He definitely was.

Lance leaned toward her, taking her mouth as his fingers worked magic. Sparkles and rainbows and shooting-stars magic.

Her inner thighs clenched. Her eyes squeezed tight then opened wide.

Her body melted in all the right places in a powerful orgasmic wave that turned her body inside out. Or it felt like it at any rate.

Sucking in much-needed oxygen, she met his smug gaze.

Two months might not be nearly enough time if that was a preview of the main event.

Bodies tangled, Lance and McKenzie tossed a half dozen pillows off her bed and onto the floor with their free hands. A trail of clothes marked their path from the front door to her bed. His. Hers.

"I want you, McKenzie," he breathed, his hand at the base of her neck as his mouth took hers again. Long and hard, he kissed her.

McKenzie was positive she'd never been kissed so possessively, never been kissed so completely.

Even when his mouth lifted from hers, she didn't answer him verbally. She wasn't sure her vocal cords would even work if she tried.

Her hands worked, though. As did her lips. She touched Lance and kissed him, exploring the strong lines of his neck, his shoulders, his chest.

"So beautiful."

Had she said that or had he? She wasn't sure.

His hands were on her breasts, cupping her bottom, everywhere, and yet not nearly all the places she wanted to be touched.

"More," she cried, desperation filling her when it was him she wanted, him she needed. "Please. Now, Lance. I want you now."

Maybe her desperation was evident in her tone or maybe he was just as desperate because he pushed her back onto the bed, put on the condom he'd tossed onto the nightstand when they'd first entered the room, then crawled above her.

With his knee he spread her legs, positioned himself above her. "You're sure?"

What was he waiting for?

She arched her hips, taking him inside, then moaned at the sweet stretching pleasure.

That was what she had been wanting for a very long time.

Breathing hard, Lance fell back against the bed.

She'd been amazing.

Beautiful, fun, witty, sexy, actively participating in their mating, urging him on, telling him what she wanted, what she needed. Showing him.

The chemistry between them was unparalleled. Never had he experienced anything like what they'd just shared.

"That. Was. Amazing."

He grinned at her punctuated words. "My thoughts exactly."

He turned onto his side and stared at her. "You are amazing."

"Ha. Wasn't me."

"I think it was."

"Right. I assure you that I've been there every time I've had sex in the past and it's never been like that so it must be you who is amazing."

His insides warmed at her admission. "For the record, it's never been like that for me either."

Her expression pinched and she scooted up on a pillow.

Shaking her head, she went for the sheet that was bunched up at the foot of the bed. When she'd covered her beautiful body, she turned to him.

"I don't really think I need to say this, not with a man like you, but I'm going to, just in case. I don't want there to be any confusion."

He knew from her words, her tone what she was going to say. He was glad. He felt the same, but hearing the reminder was good and perhaps needed.

"Despite your amazing orgasm-giving ability, I'm not looking for a long-term relationship."

"Me, either," he assured her, trying not to let his ego get too big at her praise.

"I guess that's crude of me, to talk about the end when we're still in bed and I feel wonderful. But we work together so we need to be clear about the boundaries of our relationship so work doesn't become messy."

The thought of ending things with her, not being able to touch her, kiss her, make love to her and experience what they'd just shared, because it might make things messy, wasn't a pleasant thought, but it should be.

He didn't want marriage or kids, didn't want that responsibility, that weight on his heart, that replacing of Shelby. He'd made a vow to his first love. He owed Shelby his heart and more. McKenzie was right to remind them both of the guidelines they'd agreed to. Setting an end date and clear boundaries was a smart move.

Two months for them to enjoy each other's bodies, then move on with their lives. Him with his main focus being his career and charity work in memory of Shelby. McKenzie with her career and her running and whatever else filled her life with joy.

Two months and they'd call it quits. That sounded just right to him.

* * *

Staring at the oh-so-hot naked man in her bed, McKenzie hugged the sheet tighter to her.

Please agree with me, she silently pleaded.

She'd just had the best sex of her life and couldn't fathom the idea of not repeating the magic she'd just experienced.

But she would do just that if he didn't agree.

Already she was risking too much. That's why she usually ended her relationships after a month, because she didn't want pesky emotional attachments that might lead her down the paths her parents had taken. She didn't want a future that held multiple marriages and multiple divorces like her father. Neither did she want the whiny, miserable, man-needing life her mother led.

Bachelorettehood was the life for her, all the way.

Hearing Lance agree that they'd end things in two months was important, necessary for them to carry on. She simply wouldn't risk anything longer. Already she was giving him double the time she usually spent with a man.

He deserved double time.

Triple time.

Forever.

No, not forever. She didn't do forever. Two months, then adios, even if he was an orgasm-giving god.

"Promise me," she urged, desperately needing the words.

"Two months sounds perfect."

Relief flooded her, because she hadn't wanted to tell him to leave. For two months she didn't have to.

CHAPTER TEN

"YOU CAN'T BE working the entire Christmas holiday," Lance insisted, following McKenzie to the hospital cafeteria table where she put down her food tray.

She'd gotten a chicken salad croissant and a side salad. He'd gone for a more hearty meal, but had ended up grabbing a croissant as well.

Sitting down at the table, she glanced at him. "I'm not, but I am working at the clinic half a day on Christmas Eve and then working half a day in the emergency room on Christmas morning." She'd done so the past few years so the regular emergency room doctor could have the morning off with his kids and she liked filling in from time to time so she kept her emergency care skills sharp.

"When will you celebrate with your parents?"

Bile rose up in her throat at the thought of introducing Lance to her parents. Her mother would probably hit on him and her dad would probably ask him what he thought about wife number five's plastic surgeon–constructed chest. No, she wouldn't be taking Lance home for the holidays.

Actually, when she'd talked to her mother a few days ago, Violet had said she was going to her sister's for a few days and spending the holidays with her family. She hadn't mentioned Beau, the latest live-in boyfriend, so McKenzie wasn't sure if Beau was going, staying or if he was history. Her father had planned a ski trip in Vermont with his bride and a group of their friends.

"We don't celebrate the holidays like other folks."

"How's that?"

"We'll meet up at some point in January and have dinner or something. We just don't make a big deal of the day. It's way too commercialized anyway, you know."

"This coming from the winner of the best costume in the Christmas parade."

She couldn't quite keep her smile hidden. The call from the mayor telling her she'd won the award had surprised her, as had the Christmas ornament he'd dropped by the clinic to commemorate her honor.

"Cecilia is the one who should get all the kudos for that. She put my costume together."

"But you wore it so well," he assured her, giving her a once-over. "You wear that lab coat nicely, too, Dr. Sanders."

She arched a brow at him and gave a mock-condescending shake of her head. "You hitting on me, Dr. Spencer?"

"With a baseball bat."

She rolled her eyes. "Men, always talking about size."

He laughed.

"Speaking of size, you should see the tree my mother put up in her family room. I swear she searches for the biggest one on the lot every year and that's her sole criterion for buying."

"She puts up a live tree?"

"She puts up a slew of trees. All are artificial except the one in the family room. There, she goes all out and insists on a real tree. There's a row of evergreens behind my parents' house, marking Christmases past."

McKenzie couldn't even recall the last Christmas tree her mother had put up. Maybe a skimpy tinsel one that had seen better days when McKenzie had still been young enough to ask about Santa and Christmas. Violet had never been much of a holiday person, especially not after Mc-Kenzie's father had left.

"She wants to meet you."

McKenzie's brow arched. "Why would she want to do that? For that matter, how does she even know about me?"

"She asked if I was seeing anyone and I told her about you."

Talking to his mother about her just seemed wrong.

"She shouldn't meet me."

"Why not?"

"Mothers should only meet significant others who have the potential for being around for a while."

"Look, telling her I was dating someone was easier than showing up and there being some single female there eager to meet me and plan our future together. It's really not as big a deal as you're making it for you to come to my parents' at Christmas."

Maybe not to him, but the thought of meeting his family was a very big deal to her. She didn't meet families. That implied things that just weren't true.

"Obviously you haven't been paying attention," she pointed out. "I'll be here on Christmas, working."

"The shifts are abbreviated on the holidays. What time will you get off?"

"Oh, no. You're not trapping me that way."

He gave her an innocent look. "What way?"

"The way that whatever time I say you're going to say, 'Oh, that's perfect. Just come on over when you're finished.'"

"Hey, McKenzie?"

She frowned at him, knowing what he was about to say.

"The time you get off from the emergency room is perfect. Just come to my parents' house when you're finished."

"Meeting parents implies a commitment you and I don't have," she reiterated.

"There'll be lots of people there. Aunts. Uncles. Cousins. People even I've never met. It's a party. You'll have fun and it's really not a big deal, except it saves me from my mother trying to set me up with every single nonrelated female she knows."

How in the world had he talked her into this? McKenzie asked herself crossly as she pushed the Spencers' doorbell.

She didn't do this.

Only, apparently, this year she did.

Even to the point she'd made a dessert to bring with her to Lance's parents. How corny was that?

She shouldn't be here. She didn't do "meet the parents." She just didn't.

Panic set in. She turned, determined to escape before anyone knew she was there.

At that moment the front door opened.

"You're here."

"Not really," she countered. "Forget you saw me. I'm out of here."

Shaking his head, he grinned. "Get in here."

"I think I made a mistake."

His brows rose. "McKenzie, you just drove almost an hour to get here and not so you could get here and leave without Christmas dinner."

"I've done crazier things." Like agree to come to Christmas dinner with Lance's family in the first place.

"Did you make something?" He gestured to the dish she held.

"A dessert, but—"

"No buts, McKenzie. Get in here."

She took a deep breath. He was right. She was being ridiculous. She had gotten off work, gone home, showered, grabbed the dessert she'd made the night before and typed his parents' address into her GPS.

And driven almost an hour to get here.

"Fine, but you owe me."

He leaned forward, kissed the tip of her nose. "Anything you want."

"Promises. Promises."

He grinned, took the dish from her, and motioned her inside. "I'm glad you're here. I was afraid you'd change your mind."

"I did," she reminded him as she stepped into his parents' foyer. "Only I waited a bit too late because you caught me before I could escape."

"Then I'm glad I noticed your headlights as your car pulled into the driveway, because I missed you last night."

He'd driven to his parents' home the afternoon before when he'd finished seeing his patients. It had been the first evening since their frozen yogurt date that they'd not seen each other.

She'd missed him too.

Which didn't jibe well, but she didn't have time to think too much on it, because a pretty woman who appeared to be much younger than McKenzie knew she had to be stepped into the foyer. She had sparkly blue eyes, dark brown hair that she had clipped up, black slacks and the prettiest Christmas sweater McKenzie had ever seen. Her smile lit up her entire face.

Lance looked a lot like his mother.

"We are so glad you're here!" she exclaimed, her Southern drawl so pronounced it was almost like something off a television show. "Lance has been useless for the past hour, waiting on you to get here."

"Thanks, Mom. You just called me useless to my girl." Lance's tone was teasing, his look toward his mother full of adoration.

McKenzie wanted to go on record that she wasn't Lance's girl, but technically she supposed she was. At least for the time being.

"Nonsense. She knows what I meant," his mother dismissed his claim and pulled McKenzie into a tight hug. She smelled of cinnamon and cookies.

Christmas, McKenzie thought. His mother smelled of Christmas. Not McKenzie's past Christmases, but the way Christmas was supposed to smell. Warm, inviting, full of goodness and happiness.

"It's nice to meet you," McKenzie said, not quite sure what to make of her hug. Lance's mother's hug had been real, warm, welcoming. She couldn't recall the last time her own mother or father had given her such a hug. Had they ever?

"Not nearly as nice as it is to finally meet one of Lance's girlfriends."

Did he not usually bring his girlfriends home? He'd said her being there was no big deal. If he didn't usually bring anyone home, then her presence was a big deal. She wanted to ask, but decided it wasn't her place because really what did it matter? She was here now. Whatever he'd done with his past girlfriends didn't apply to her, just as what he did with her wouldn't apply to his future girlfriends.

Future girlfriends. Ugh. She didn't like the thought of him with anyone but her. His smile, his touch, his kisses, they belonged to her. At least for now, she reminded herself.

"I'm glad you're here." Lance leaned in, kissed her briefly on the mouth, then took her hand. "I hope you came hungry."

Her gaze cut to Lance's and she wondered if he'd read her thoughts again?

"Take a deep breath. It's time to meet the rest of the crew," he warned.

"Be nice, Lance. You'll scare her off. They aren't that bad and you know it," his mother scolded.

Lance just winked at her.

Two hours later, McKenzie had to agree with Lance's mother. His family wasn't that bad. She'd met his grandparents, who were so hard of hearing they had everyone talking loudly so they could keep up with the conversation, his aunts and uncles, his cousins, and a handful of children who belonged to his cousins.

It was quite a bunch: loud, talking over one another, laughing, eating and truly enjoying each other's company.

The kids seemed to adore Lance. They called him Uncle Lance, although technically he was their second cousin.

"You're quiet," Lance observed, leaning in close so that his words were just for her ears.

"Just taking it all in," she admitted.

"We're something else, for sure. Is this similar to your family get-togethers?"

McKenzie laughed. "Not even close."

"How so?"

"I won't bore you with my childhood woes."

"Nothing about you would bore me, McKenzie. I want to know more about you."

She started to ask what would be the point, but somehow that comment felt wrong in this loving, warm environment, so she picked up her glass of tea, took a sip, then whispered, "I'll tell you some other time."

That seemed to appease him. They finished eating. Everyone, men and women, helped clear the table. The kids had eaten at a couple of card tables set up in the kitchen and they too cleared their spots without prompting. McKenzie was amazed at how they all seemed to work together so cohesively.

The men then retired to the large family room while

the women put away leftovers and loaded the dishwasher. All except Lance. He seemed reluctant to leave McKenzie.

"I'll be fine. I'm sure they won't bite."

He still looked hesitant.

"Seriously, what's the worst that could happen?"

What indeed? Lance wondered. He had rarely brought women home and never to a Christmas function. His entire family had been teasing him that this must be the one for him to bring her home to Christmas with the family. He'd tried to explain that he and McKenzie had been co-workers and friends for years, but the more he'd talked, the more he reminded them that he'd already met and lost "the one," the more they'd smiled. By the time McKenzie arrived, he'd been half-afraid his family would have them walking down the aisle before morning.

He didn't think she'd appreciate any implication that they were more than just a casual couple.

They weren't. Just a hot and heavy two-month relationship destined to go nowhere because McKenzie didn't do long-term commitment and his seventeen-year-old self had vowed to always love Shelby, for his heart to always be loyal to her memory.

What was the worst that could happen? He hesitated.

"Seriously, Lance. I'm a big girl. They aren't going to scare me off."

"I just…" He knew he was being ridiculous. "I don't mind helping clean up."

"Lance Donovan Spencer, go visit with your grandparents. You've not seen them since Thanksgiving," his mother ordered. "That will give me and your girl time to get to know each other without you looming over us."

"Looming?" he protested indignantly.

"Go." His mother pointed toward the door.

Lance laughed. "I can tell my presence and help is not

appreciated or wanted around here, so I will go visit with
my grandmother who loves me very much."

"Hmm, maybe she's who you should list on your references," McKenzie teased him, her eyes twinkling.

"Maybe. Mom's been bumped right off."

"I heard that," his mom called out over her shoulder.

He leaned in and kissed McKenzie's cheek. "I'm right
in the next room if their interrogation gets to be too much."

"Noted." McKenzie was smiling, like she wouldn't mind
his mother's, aunts' and cousins' questions. Lord, he hoped
not. They didn't have boundaries and McKenzie had boundaries that made the Great Wall of China look like a playpen.

"Lance tells me you two have only been dating for a
few weeks," his mother said moments after Lance left the
kitchen.

"You know he's never brought a woman home for Christmas before, right?" This came from one of Lance's cousins' wives, Sara Beth.

"He seems to be head over heels about you," another
said. "Told us you two work together and recently became
an item."

"We want the full scoop," one of his dad's sisters added.

"Um, well, sounds like you already know the full scoop,"
McKenzie began slowly. She didn't want to give Lance's
family the wrong idea. "We have been friends since I returned to Coopersville after finishing my residency."

"So you're from Coopersville originally? Your family
is still there?"

"My mother is. My dad lives here in Lewisburg."

His mother's eyes lit up with excitement. "We might
know him. What's his name?"

She hoped they didn't know him. Okay, so he was a
highly successful lawyer, but personally? Her father was
a mess. A horrible, womanizing, cheating mess. If Lance's
mother knew him, it probably meant he'd hit on her. Not

the impression McKenzie wanted Lance's mother to have of her.

Avoiding the question, she said instead, "I don't have any brothers or sisters but, like Lance, I do have a few cousins." Nice enough people but they rarely all got together. Really, the only time McKenzie saw them was when one of them was sick and was seen at the clinic. "My parents divorced when I was four and I never quite got past that."

She only added the last part so Lance's family would hopefully move on past the subject of her parents. Definitely not because she wanted to talk about her parents' divorce. She never talked about that. At least, not the nitty-gritty details that had led up to her world falling apart.

"Poor thing," Lance's mother sympathized. "Divorce is hard at any age."

"Amen," another of Lance's aunts said. "Lance's Uncle Gerry is my second husband. The first and I were like gasoline and fire, always explosive."

The conversation continued while they cleaned up the remainder of the dishes and food, jumping from one subject to another but never back to McKenzie's parents. She liked Lance's noisy, warm family.

"Well, we're just so happy you're here, McKenzie. It's about time that boy found someone to pull him out of the past."

McKenzie glanced toward the aunt who'd spoken up. Her confusion must have shown because the women looked back and forth at each other as if trying to decide how much more to say.

Sara Beth gave McKenzie an empathetic look. "I guess he never told you about Shelby?"

Who was Shelby and what had she meant to Lance? "No."

The woman winced as if she wished she could erase

having mentioned the woman's name. "Shelby was Lance's first love."

Was. An ominous foreboding took hold of McKenzie.

"What happened?"

"She died." This came from Sara Beth. Every pair of eyes in the room was trained on McKenzie to gauge her reaction, triggering the usual reaction to being stared at that she always had.

Lance's first love had died and he'd never breathed a word.

"Enough talk about the past and anything but how wonderful it is to have McKenzie with us," Lance's mother dried her hands on a towel and pulled McKenzie over to the counter for another of her tight, all-encompassing hugs. "Truly, we are grateful that you are in my son's life. He is a special man with a big heart and you are a fortunate young woman."

"Yes," McKenzie agreed, stunned at the thought someone Lance had loved had died. Was he still in love with Shelby? How had the woman died? How long ago? "Yes, he is a special man."

CHAPTER ELEVEN

"YOU SURE ABOUT THIS?" McKenzie asked the man stretching out beside her. He wore dark running pants that emphasized his calf and thigh muscles and a bright-colored long-sleeved running shirt that outlined a chest McKenzie had taken great pleasure in exploring the night before as they'd lain in bed and "rung in" the New Year.

Lance glanced at her and grinned. "I'll be waiting for you at the finish line."

She hoped so. She hoped Lance hadn't been teasing about being a runner. He was in great shape, had phenomenal endurance, but she'd still never known him to run. But the truth was he hadn't stayed the whole night at her place ever, so he could do the same as her and run in the early morning before work. They had sex, often lay in bed talking and touching lightly afterward, then he went home. Just as he had the night before. She hadn't asked him to stay. He hadn't asked to. Just, each night, whenever he got ready to go, he kissed her good-night and left.

Truth was, she'd have let him stay Christmas night after they'd got back from his parents'. He'd insisted on following her back to her place. Despite the late hour, he'd come in, held her close, then left. She hadn't wanted him to go. She'd have let him stay every night since. He just hadn't wanted to. Or, if he had wanted to, he'd chosen to go home anyway.

Why was that? Did it have to do with Shelby? Should she tell him that she knew about his first love? That his family had told her about his loss? They just hadn't told her any of the details surrounding the mysterious woman Lance had loved.

Maybe the details didn't matter. They shouldn't matter.

Only McKenzie admitted they did. Perhaps it was just curiosity. Perhaps it was jealousy. Perhaps it was something more she couldn't put her finger on.

She'd almost asked him about Shelby a dozen times, but always changed her mind. If he wanted her to know, he'd tell her.

Today was the first day of a new year. A new beginning.

Who knew, maybe tonight he'd stay.

If not, she was okay with that, too. He might be right in going, in not adding sleeping together to their relationship, because she didn't count the light dozing they sometimes did after their still phenomenal comings together as sleep. Sleeping together until morning would be another whole level of intimacy.

"You don't have to try to run next to me," she advised, thinking they were intimate enough already. Too intimate because imagining life without him was already becoming difficult. Maybe they could stay close friends after their two months were up. Maybe. "Just keep your own steady pace and I'll keep mine. We'll meet up at the end."

Grinning, he nodded. "Yes, ma'am. I'll keep that in mind."

They continued to stretch their muscles as the announcer talked, telling them about the cause they were running for, about the rules, etc. Soon they were off.

McKenzie never tried to take the lead early on. In some races she never took the lead. Not that she didn't always do her best, but sometimes there were just faster runners for that particular distance. Today she expected to do well, but perhaps not win as she was much more of an endurance runner than a speed one.

Lance ran beside her and to her pleased surprise he didn't try to talk. In the past when she'd convinced friends to run with her, they'd wanted to have a gab session. That was until they became so breathless they stopped to walk, and then they often expected her to stop and walk with them.

McKenzie ran.

Lance easily kept pace with her. Halfway in she began to wonder if she was slowing him down rather than the other way around. She picked up her pace, pushing herself, suddenly wanting distance between them. Without any huffing or puffing he ran along beside her as if she hadn't just upped their pace. That annoyed her.

"You've been holding out on me," she accused a little breathily, thinking it was bad when she was the one reverting to talking. Next thing you knew she'd be stopping to walk.

"Me?" His gaze cut to her. "I told you that I ran."

"I've never seen you at any of the local runs and yet clearly you do run."

"I don't do organized runs or competitions."

Didn't do organized runs or competitions? McKenzie frowned. What kind of an answer was that when he clearly enjoyed running as much as she did? Well, maybe almost as much.

"That's hard to believe with the way you're into every charity in the region," she said. "Why wouldn't you participate in these fund-raisers when they're an easy way to raise money for great causes? For that matter, why aren't you organizing races to raise money for all your special causes?"

McKenzie was a little too smart for her own good. Lance was involved with a large number of charities and helped support many others, but never those that had to do with running.

He did run several times a week, but always alone, always to clear his head, always with someone else at his side, mentally if not physically.

High school cross-country had been where he'd first met Shelby. She'd been a year older than him and had had a different set of friends, so although he'd seen the pretty brunette around school he hadn't known her. She'd have been better off if he never had.

"No one can do everything," he answered McKenzie.

"I'm beginning to think you do."

"Not even close. You and I just happen to have a lot in common. We enjoy the same things."

She shook her head. "Nope. I don't enjoy singing."

"I think you would if you'd relax."

"Standing onstage, with people looking at me?" She cut her gaze to him. "Never going to happen."

Keeping his pace matched to hers, he glanced at her. "You don't like things that make people look at you, do you, McKenzie?"

"Nope."

"Because of your parents?"

"I may not have mentioned this before, but I don't like talking while I run. I'm a silent runner."

He chuckled. "That a hint for me to be quiet?"

"You catch on quick."

They kept up the more intense pace until they crossed the finish line. The last few minutes of the race Lance debated on whether or not to let McKenzie cross the finish line first. Ultimately, he decided she wasn't the kind of woman who'd appreciate a man letting her win.

In the last stretch he increased his speed. So did McKenzie. If he hadn't been a bit winded, he'd have laughed at her competitive spirit. Instead, he ran.

So did she.

They crossed the finish line together. The judge declared Lance the winner by a fraction of a second, but Lance would have just as easily have believed that McKenzie had crossed first.

She was doubled over, gasping for air. His own lungs couldn't suck in enough air either. He walked around, slowly catching his breath. When he turned back, she was glaring.

"You were holding out on me," she accused breathlessly, her eyes narrowed.

"Huh?"

"You were considering letting me win." Her words came out a little choppy between gasps for air.

"In case you didn't notice…" he sucked in a deep gulp of air "… I was trying to cross that finish line first."

"You were sandbagging."

He laughed. "Sandbagging?"

"How long have you been running?"

"Since high school." Not that he wanted to talk about it. He didn't. Talking about this particular subject might lead to questions he didn't want to answer.

"You competed?"

He nodded.

"Me, too." She straightened, fully expanding her lungs with air. "I did my undergraduate studies on a track scholarship."

Despite the memories assailing him, the corners of Lance's mouth tugged upward. "Something else we have in common."

McKenzie just looked at him, then rolled her eyes. "We don't have that much in common."

"More than you seem to want to acknowledge."

"Maybe," she conceded. "Let's go congratulate the guy who beat us both. He lives about thirty minutes from here.

His time is usually about twenty to thirty seconds better than mine. He usually only competes in the five-kilometer races, though. Nothing shorter, nothing longer."

They congratulated the winner, hung out around the tent, rehydrating, got their second and third place medals, then headed toward McKenzie's house.

They showered together then, a long time later, got ready to go and eat.

The first day of the New Year turned into the first week, then the first month.

McKenzie began to feel panicky, knowing her time with Lance was coming to an end as the one-month mark came and went. Each day following passed like sand swiftly falling through an hourglass.

Then she realized that the day before Valentine's Day marked the end of the two months she'd promised him. Seriously, the day before Valentine's?

Why did that even matter? She'd never cared if she had a significant other on that hyped-up holiday in the past. Most years she'd been in a casual relationship and she'd gotten a box of chocolates and flowers and had given a funny card to her date for the evening. Why should this year feel different? Why did the idea of chocolates and flowers from Lance seem as if it would be different from gifts she'd received in the past? Why did the idea of giving him a card seem to fall short?

She'd be ending things with Lance the day before every other couple would be celebrating their love.

She and Lance weren't in love. She wasn't sure love even truly existed.

A vision of Lance's grandparents, married for sixty years, his parents, married for forty years, ran through her mind and she had to reconsider. Maybe love did exist, but not for anyone with her genetic makeup. Already her dad was complaining about his new wife and had flirted outrageously with their waitress when they'd had their usual belated Christmas dinner a few weeks back. Hearing that his new marriage would be ending soon wouldn't surprise McKenzie in the slightest. Her mother, well, her mother had taken up the vegan life because Beau was history and her new "'love" was all about living green. Her mother was even planning to plant out her own garden this spring and wanted to know if McKenzie had any requests.

McKenzie had no issue with her mother trying to live more healthily. She was glad of it, even. But the woman enjoyed nothing more than a big juicy steak, which was what she ordered on the rare occasions she met McKenzie for a meal—usually in between boyfriends or at Christmas or birthdays.

McKenzie had managed both meals with her parents this year without Lance joining them. Fortunately, his volunteer work oftentimes had him busy immediately following work and she had scheduled both meals with her parents on evenings he had Celebration Graduation meetings.

"You've been staring at your screen for the past ten minutes," Lance pointed out, gesturing to her idle laptop. "Problem patient?"

He'd come over, brought their dinner with him, and they'd been sitting on her sofa, remotely logged in to their work laptops and charting their day's patients while watching a reality television program.

McKenzie hit a button, saving her work, then turned to him. "My mind just isn't on this tonight."

"I noticed." He saved his own work, set his laptop down on her coffee table and turned to her. "What's up?"

"I was just thinking about Valentine's Day."

His smile spread across his face and lit up his eyes. "Making plans for how you're going to surprise me with a lacy red number and high heels?" He waggled his brows suggestively.

Despite knowing he was mostly teasing, she shook her head. "We won't be together on Valentine's Day. Our two months is up the day before. The end is near."

His smile faded and his forehead wrinkled. "There's no reason we shouldn't be able to spend Valentine's Day together. I have the Celebration Graduation Valentine's Day dance at the high school that I'll be helping to chaperone. It ends at ten and it'll take me another twenty to thirty minutes to help clean up. But we can still do something, then we'll call it quits after that."

She shook her head. "You already had plans for that evening. That's good."

She, however, did not and would be acutely aware of his absence from her life, and not just because of the holiday.

"I hadn't really thought about it being the end of our two months. You could volunteer at the dance with me."

She shook her head again. "Not a good idea."

"Think you'd be a bad influence on those high schoolers?" Even though his tone was teasing, his eyes searched hers.

"I probably would," she agreed, just to avoid a discussion of the truth. They would be finished the night before. There would be no more charting together, dining together, going to dances or parties together, no more running together, as they'd started doing every morning at four. Lance would be gone, would meet someone else, would date them, and, despite what he claimed, he would very likely eventually find whatever he was looking for in a woman and marry her.

Was he looking for someone like Shelby?

What was Shelby like?

Why had he still not mentioned the woman to her?

Then again, why would he mention her? He and McKenzie were temporary. He owed her nothing, no explanation of his past relationships, no explanation of his future plans.

Yet there were things about him she wanted to know. Suddenly needed to know.

"Do you want kids?" Why she asked the question she wasn't sure. It wasn't as if the answer mattered to her or was even applicable. She and Lance had no future together.

To her surprise, he shook his head. "I have no plans to ever have children."

Recalling how great he was with his cousins' kids, that shocked her. Then again, had she asked him the question because she'd expected a different answer? That she'd expected him to say he planned to have an entire houseful, and that way she could have used that information as one more thing to put between them because, with her genetics, no way could she ever have children.

"You'd make a fantastic dad."

His brow lifted and he regarded her for a few long moments before asking, "You pregnant, McKenzie?"

Her mouth fell open and she squished up her nose. "Absolutely not."

"You sure? You've not had a menstrual cycle since we've been together. I hadn't really thought about it until just now, but I should have."

Her face heated at his comment. They were doctors, so it was ridiculous that she was blushing. But at this moment she was a woman and he was a man. Medicine had nothing to do with their conversation. This was personal. Too personal.

"I rarely have my cycle. My gynecologist says it's because I run so much and don't retain enough body fat for proper estrogen storage. It's highly unlikely that I'd get pregnant. But even if that weren't an issue," she reminded him, "you've used a condom every single time we've had sex. I can't be pregnant."

Not once had she even considered that as a possibility. Truth was, she questioned if her body would even allow her to get pregnant if she wanted to, which she didn't. No way would she want to bring a baby in to the world the way her parents had.

"Stranger things have happened."

"Than my getting pregnant?" She shook her head in denial. "That would be the strangest ever. I'm not meant to have children."

His curiosity was obviously piqued as he studied her. "Why not?"

"Bad genetics."

"Your parents are ill?"

How was she supposed to answer that one? With the truth, probably. She took a deep breath.

"Physically, they are as healthy as can be. Mentally and emotionally, they are messed up."

"Depression?"

"My mother suffers from depression. Maybe my dad, too, really. They both have made horrible life choices that they are now stuck living with."

"Your dad is a lawyer?"

She nodded.

"What does your mom do?"

"Whatever the man currently in her life tells her to do."

Lance seemed to let that sink in for a few moments. "She's remarried?"

McKenzie shook her head. "She's never remarried. I think she purposely stays single because my father has to pay her alimony until she remarries or dies."

"Your father is remarried, though?"

"At the moment, but ask me again in a month and who knows what the answer will be."

"How many times has he remarried?"

She didn't want to answer, shouldn't have let this conversation even start. She should have finished her charts, not opened up an emotional can of worms that led to conversations about her menstrual cycle, pregnancy and her parents. What had she been thinking?

"McKenzie?"

"He's on his fifth marriage."

Lance winced. "Hard to find the one, eh?"

"Oh, he finds them all right. In all the wrong places. He's not known for his faithfulness. My guess is that he's to blame for all his failed marriages. Definitely he was with his and my mother's."

"There's always two sides to every story."

"My mother and I walked in on him in his office with his secretary."

"As in…"

Feeling sick at her stomach, McKenzie nodded. She'd never said those words out loud. Not ever. Cecilia knew, but not because McKenzie had told her the details, just that she'd figured it out from overheard arguments between McKenzie's parents.

"How old were you?"

"Four."

CHAPTER TWELVE

LANCE TRIED TO imagine how a four-year-old would react to walking in on her father in a compromising situation with a woman who wasn't her mother. He couldn't imagine it. His own family took commitment seriously. When they gave their word, their heart to another they meant it.

His own heart squeezed. Hadn't he given his word to Shelby? Hadn't he promised to love her forever? To not ever forget the young girl who'd taught him what it meant to care for another, who'd brought him from boyhood to manhood?

He had. He did. He would. Forever.

He owed her so much.

"That must have been traumatic," he mused, not knowing exactly what to say but wanting to comfort McKenzie all the same. Wanting not to think of Shelby right now. Lately he'd not wanted to think of her a lot, and had resented how much he thought of her, of how guilty he felt that he didn't want to think of her anymore.

How could he not want to think of her when it was his fault she was no longer living the life she had been meant to live? When if it wasn't for him she'd be a doctor? Be making a difference in so many people's lives?

"It wasn't the first time he'd cheated."

Lance stared at McKenzie's pale face. "How do you know?"

"My mother launched herself at them, screaming and yelling and clawing and…well, you get the idea. She said some pretty choice things that my father didn't deny."

"You were only four," he reminded her, trying to envision the scene from a four-year-old's perspective and shuttering on the inside at the horror. "Maybe you misunderstood."

She shook her head. "He doesn't deserve you or anyone else defending him. He doesn't even bother defending himself anymore. Just says it's genetic and he can't help himself."

"Bull."

That had McKenzie's head shooting up. "What?"

"Bull. If he really loved someone else more than he loved himself then being faithful wouldn't be an issue. It would be easy, what came naturally from that love."

McKenzie took a deep breath. "Then maybe that's the problem. No one has ever been able to compete with his own self-love. Not my mother, not his other wives or girlfriends and certainly not me."

There was a depth of pain in her voice that made Lance's heart ache for her. "Did he have more children?"

McKenzie shook her head. "He had a vasectomy so that mistake would never happen again."

"Implying that you were a mistake?"

McKenzie shrugged.

"He's a fool, McKenzie. A stupid, selfish fool."

"Agreed." She brushed her hands over her thighs then stood. "I'm going to get a drink of water. You need anything?"

"Just you."

She paused. "Sorry, but the discussion about my parents has killed any possibility of that for some time."

"Not what I meant."

She stared down at him. "Then what did you mean?"

Good question. What had he meant?

That he needed her?

Physically? They were powerful in bed together. But it was more than sex. Mentally, she challenged him with her quick intelligence and wit. Emotionally...emotionally she had him a tangled-up mess. A tangled-up mess he had no right to be feeling.

He'd asked her to give him two months. That's all she planned to give him, that's all he'd thought he'd wanted from McKenzie.

Usually he had long-lasting relationships even though he knew they were never going anywhere. He'd always been up-front with whomever he'd been dating on that point. When things came to an end, he'd always been okay with it, his heart not really involved.

With McKenzie he'd wanted that time limit as much as she had, because everything had felt different right from the start.

She made him question everything.

The past. The present. The future. What had always seemed so clear was now a blurred unknown.

That they had planned a definite ending was a good thing, the best thing. He had a vow to keep. Guilt mingled in with whatever else was going on. Horrible, horrible guilt that would lie heavily on his shoulders for the rest of his life.

"I'll take that glass of water after all," he said in way of an answer to her question. Not that it was an answer, but it was all he knew to say.

"Yeah, this conversation has left a bad taste in both our mouths."

Something like that.

"Edith came in to see me this morning."

Lance glanced up from his desk. "How is she doing?"

McKenzie sank down in the chair across from his desk.

"Quite well, really. She had a long list of complaints, of course. But overall she looked good and the latest imaging of her chest shows that her pulmonary embolism has resolved."

"That's fantastic. She's a feisty thing."

"That she is."

He studied her a moment then set down the pen he held, walked around his desk, shut his office door, then wrapped his arms around her.

"What are you doing?"

"Shh…" he told her. "Don't say anything."

Not that his arms didn't feel amazing, but she frowned up at him. "Don't tell me what to do."

He chuckled. "You're such a stubborn woman."

"You're just now figuring that out, Mr. Persistence?"

"No, I knew that going in."

"And?"

"I can appreciate that fact about you even if it drives me crazy at times."

"Such as now?"

He shook his head. "Not really because for all your protesting, you are still letting me hold you."

"Why are you holding me? I thought we agreed we wouldn't do this at work? You promised me we wouldn't."

"This is a hug between friends. A means of offering comfort and support. I never promised not to give you those things when you obviously need a hug."

"Oh." Because really what could she say to that? He was right. She obviously had needed a hug. His hug.

Only being in his arms, her body pressed close to his, her nostrils filled with his spicy clean scent, made her aware of all the other things she needed him for, too.

Things she didn't need to be distracted by at work.

She pulled from his arms and he let her go.

"Sorry I bothered you. I just wanted to let you know about Edith and that I'd be at the hospital during lunch."

"I'll see you there."

"But—"

"I'll see you there," he repeated.

"You're a persistent man, Lance."

"You're a stubborn woman, McKenzie."

A smile tugged at her lips. "Fine, I'll see you at the hospital at lunch."

Lance had a Celebration Graduation meeting for last-minute Valentine's Day dance planning that he'd tried to convince McKenzie to attend with him. She didn't want to get too involved in his pet projects because their days together as a couple were dwindling. The more entangled their lives were the more difficult saying goodbye was going to be.

McKenzie's phone rang and she almost didn't answer when she saw that it was her mother. When she heard what her mother had to say she wished she hadn't.

"I'm getting married."

Three little words that had McKenzie dropping everything and agreeing to meet her mother at her house.

Violet's house was the same house where McKenzie had grown up. McKenzie's father had paid for the house where they'd lived when he'd first been starting his law career. He'd also provided a monthly check that had apparently abdicated him of all other obligations to his daughter.

"Whatever is going through your head?" McKenzie asked the moment she walked into her mother's living room. She came to a halt when she saw the man sitting on her mother's sofa. The one who was much younger than her mother. "How old are you?"

"What does it matter how old he is?" her mother interrupted. "Age is only a number."

"Mom, if I'm older than him, I'm walking out of this house right now."

Her mother glanced at the man and giggled. *Giggled.* "He's eight years older than you, McKenzie."

"Which means he's ten years younger than you," McKenzie reminded her. She wasn't a prude, didn't think relationships should be bound by age, except for when it came to her mother. Her mother dating a man so much younger just didn't sit well.

"Yes, I am a lucky woman that Yves has fallen for me in my old, decrepit state," her mother remarked wryly. "Thank goodness I'll have him around to help me with my walker and picking out a nursing home."

"Mom…" McKenzie began, then glanced back and forth between her mother and the man she was apparently engaged to. She sank down onto her mother's sofa. "So, maybe you should tell me more about this whole getting-married bit since I know for a fact you were single at the beginning of the year."

She was used to her father marrying on a whim, but her mother had been single since the day she'd divorced McKenzie's father almost three decades ago. Violet dated and chased men, but she didn't marry.

"I met Yves at a New Year's Eve party."

"You met him just over a month ago. Don't you think it's a little quick to be getting engaged?"

"Getting married," her mother corrected, holding out her hand to show McKenzie the ring on her finger. "We're already engaged."

The stone wasn't a diamond, but was a pretty emerald that matched the color of her mother's eyes perfectly.

"When is the wedding supposed to take place?"

"Valentine's Day."

Valentine's Day. The first day McKenzie would be without Lance and her mother was walking down the aisle.

She regarded her mother. "You're sure about this?"

"Positive."

"Why now? After all this time, why would you choose to marry again?"

"The only reason I've not remarried all these years is because I hadn't met the right person, McKenzie. I have had other proposals over the years, I just haven't wanted to say yes until Yves."

Other proposals? McKenzie hadn't known. Still, her mother. Married.

"Does Dad know?"

"What does it matter if your father knows that I'm going to remarry? He has nothing to do with my life."

"Mom, if you remarry Dad will quit sending you a check every month. How are you going to get by?"

"I'll take care of her," Yves popped up, moving to stand protectively by Violet.

"And how are you going to do that?"

"I run a health-food store on the square."

McKenzie had read about a new store opening on the square, had been planning to swing by to check out what they had.

"He more than runs it," Violet bragged. "He owns the store. Plus, he has two others that are already successful in towns nearby."

So maybe the guy wasn't after her mother for a free ride.

"You know I don't need your permission to get married, McKenzie."

"I know that, Mother."

"But I had hoped you'd be happy for me."

McKenzie cringed on the inside. How was she supposed to be happy for her mother when she worried that her mother was just going to be hurt yet again? She'd seen her devastation all those years ago, had watched the depression take hold and not let go for years. Why would she want her mother to risk that again? Especially with a man so much younger than she was?

She must have asked the last question out loud because her mother beamed at Yves, placed her hand in his and answered, "Because for the first time in a long time, maybe ever, I know what it feels like to be loved. It's a wonderful feeling, McKenzie. I hope that someday you know exactly what I mean."

Lance hit McKenzie's number for what had to be the dozenth time. Why wasn't she answering her phone?

He'd driven out to her place, but she wasn't home. Where would she be? Cecilia's perhaps? He'd drive out there, too, but that made him feel a little too desperate.

Unfortunately, he was the bearer of bad news regarding a patient she'd sent to the emergency room earlier. The man had been in the midst of a heart attack and had been airlifted to Atlanta. When the hospital hadn't been able to reach McKenzie they'd called him, thinking he might be with her.

He would like to be with her. He should be with her. Instead, he'd sat through the last meeting before the Valentine's Day dance. They had everything under control and the event should be a great fund-raiser.

But where was McKenzie?

He was just getting ready to pull out of her driveway when her car came down the street and turned in.

"What are you doing here?" she asked, getting out of her car. "It's almost ten."

Yeah, he should have gone home. He didn't have to tell her tonight. Nothing would have been lost by her not finding out about the man until the next morning.

"I was worried about you."

"I'm fine."

"I'll go, then. I was just concerned when you didn't answer your phone."

"Sorry. I had my ringer turned off. I was at my mother's."

Her mother that he'd not met yet.

"She's getting married."

"Married?"

"Seems after all this time she's met the man of her dreams."

"You don't sound very happy about it."

She shrugged. "He's growing on me."

"Someone I know?"

"Unlikely. He just opened up the new health-food store on the square."

"Yves St. Claire?"

Her brows veed. "That's him. You know him?"

"I met him a few days after he opened the store. Great place he has there. Seems like a nice enough fellow."

"And?"

"And what?"

"Doesn't he seem too young for my mother?"

"I've never met your mother so I wouldn't know, but age is just a number."

"That's what she said."

"If I were younger than you, would it matter, McKenzie?"

"For our intents and purposes, I suppose that depends on how much younger. I don't mess with jailbait."

He laughed, leaned back against his car. "Glad I have a few years on you, then."

"Do you want to come inside?"

Relief washed over him. "I thought you'd never ask."

February the thirteenth fell on a Friday and McKenzie was convinced that the day truly was a bad-luck day.

Today was it. The end of her two months with Lance.

She'd promised herself there would be no fuss, no muss, just a quick and painless goodbye. He had his dance tomorrow night and no doubt by next week he'd have a new love interest.

But she couldn't quite convince herself of that.

Something in the way Lance looked at her made her think he wouldn't quickly replace her but might instead take some time to get over her.

Unfortunately, she might require that time, too.

Lots and lots of recovery time, though perhaps not the three decades' worth her mother had taken to blossom into a woman in love.

Her mother was in love. And loved.

Over the past several days McKenzie had been fitted for a maid-of-honor dress and had met Yves's best friend for his tux fitting. Her mother was getting married at a local church in a small, simple ceremony the following day.

"You're not planning to see me at all tonight?" Lance asked.

She shook her head. "My mother's wedding-rehearsal dinner is tonight."

"I could go with you."

"That would be a bad idea."

"Why?"

"Our last night together and we go to a wedding rehearsal? Think about it. That's just all kinds of wrong. Plus, I don't want you there, Lance."

He winced and she almost retracted her words. Part of her did want him there. Another part knew the sooner they parted the sooner she could get back to the regularly scheduled program of her life. Her time with Lance had been a nice interlude from reality.

"I should tell you that Yves invited me to the wedding."

"I don't want you there," she said.

"I'll keep that in mind." Without another word, he left her office.

McKenzie's heart shuddered at the soft closing of her office door as if the noise had echoed throughout the building.

She went to her mother's rehearsal dinner, smiled and performed her role as maid of honor. Truth was, watching her mother and Yves left her heart aching.

Feeling a little bereft at the thought she was soon to be single again.

Which was ridiculous.

She liked being single.

She thrived on being single.

She didn't want to be like her parents.

Only watching her mother glow, hearing her happy laughter, maybe she wouldn't mind being a little like her mother.

McKenzie got home a little after eleven. She'd not heard from Lance all evening. She'd half expected him to be waiting in her driveway.

No, more than half. She had expected him to be there.

That he wasn't left her feeling deflated.

Their last night together and they weren't together.

Would never be together again.

Sleep didn't come easily but unfortunately her tears did.

This was exactly why she should never have agreed to more than a month with him. Anything more was just too messy.

Lance sat in the fourth pew back on the groom's side. There were only about fifty or so people in the church when the music started and the groom and his best man joined the preacher at the front of the building. The music changed and a smiling McKenzie came down the aisle. Her gaze remained locked on the altar, as if she was afraid to look around. Maybe she was.

Maybe she had been serious in that she really hadn't wanted him to attend. Certainly, she hadn't contacted him last night. He'd checked his phone several times, thinking she might. She hadn't. He'd told himself that was a good thing, that McKenzie sticking to their original agreement made it easier for him to do so too.

Their two months was over.

The music changed and everyone stood, turned to watch the bride walk down the aisle to her groom.

Lance had never met McKenzie's mother, but he would have recognized the older version of McKenzie anywhere. Same green eyes. Same fine bone structure.

Seeing McKenzie made his insides ache.

Part of him wanted to ask her for more time, for another day, another week, another month.

But he couldn't.

Wouldn't.

He'd vowed to Shelby that he'd remain committed to her memory.

To spend more time with McKenzie would be wrong.

He wasn't free to be with her and never would be.

"You invited Dad?" McKenzie whispered, thinking her knees might buckle as she took her mother's bouquet from her.

Her mother's smile was full of merriment, but she didn't answer, just turned back to her groom to exchange her vows.

The exchange of wedding vows was brief and beautiful. McKenzie cried as her mother read the vows she'd written for a man she'd known for less than two months.

Less than the time McKenzie had been dating Lance.

McKenzie outright wept when Yves said his vows back

to her mother. Okay, so if the man loved her mother all his days the way he loved her today, he and McKenzie would get along just fine and her mother was a lucky woman.

The preacher announced the happy couple as Mr. and Mrs. Yves St. Clair and presented them to their guests.

A few photos were taken, then the reception began. McKenzie spotted Lance talking to a tall blonde someone had told her earlier was Yves's cousin. A deep green pain stabbed her, but she refused to acknowledge it or him. She headed toward her father, who was downing a glass of something alcoholic.

"I can't believe you are here."

He frowned into his empty glass. "She invited me."

"You didn't have to come."

His gaze met hers. "Sure I did. Today is a big day for me, too."

"Freedom from alimony?" she said drily.

For the first time in a long time her father's smile was real and reached his eyes. "Exactly."

"She seems really happy."

That had her father pausing and glancing toward her mother. "Yeah, she does. Good for her."

"What about you? Where is your wife?"

He shrugged. "At home, I imagine."

He excused himself and went and joined the conversation with Lance and the blonde. No doubt he'd have the blonde cornered in just a few minutes.

He must have because Lance walked up shortly afterward to where McKenzie stood.

"You look very beautiful," he said quietly.

Okay, so a smart girl wouldn't let him see how his words warmed her insides. A smart girl would play it cool. McKenzie tried. "Cecilia works wonders."

"She is indeed talented."

Their conversation was stilted, awkward. The conversation of former lovers who didn't know what to say to each other.

"I see you met my father," she said to fill the silence.

Shock registered on Lance's face. "That was your father?"

McKenzie laughed at his surprise. "Yes. Sorry he moved in on Yves's cousin while you were talking her up."

"I wasn't talking her up," he replied. "And, for the record, had I been interested in her no one would have moved in, including your father." He glanced around until his gaze lit on where her father still chatted with the blonde, who laughed a little too flirtatiously. "Isn't he married?"

She nodded. "Fidelity isn't his thing. I've mentioned that before."

Lance's expression wasn't pleasant. "Seems odd for him to be here, at your mother's wedding."

"I thought the same thing, but my mother invited him and he came. They are a bit weird that way. Something else I've mentioned."

Lance's gaze met McKenzie's and locked for a few long seconds before he glanced at his watch as if pressed for time. "Sorry to rush off, but I've got to head out to help with the Valentine's Day dance tonight."

"Oh. I forgot." Had her disappointment that he wasn't going to stay for a while shown? Of course it had.

He reached out, touched her cheek. "McKenzie, there's so much I could say to you."

"But?"

"But you already know everything I'd say."

"Not everything."

His brow rose and she shook her head. Now wasn't the time to ask him about Shelby. That time had come and gone.

Apparently he agreed because he said, "It's been fun."

She nodded, hoping the tears she felt prickling her eyes didn't burst free.

"Your car door was unlocked and I left something for you in the front seat of your car."

Her gaze lifted to his. "What? Why would you do that?"

"Just a little something for Valentine's Day."

He'd gotten her a gift for Valentine's Day? But they'd ended things the day before. She had not bought him the standard card. "I didn't get you anything."

"You didn't need to. Our two months is finished, just as we are." He glanced at his watch again. "Goodbye, Mc-Kenzie." Then, right there in the reception hall in front of her mother, her father and her brand-new stepfather, Lance kissed her.

Not a quick peck but a real kiss. Not a dragged-out one but one jam-packed with emotion all the same. One that demanded the same emotion back from her.

McKenzie blinked up at him. He looked as if he was about to say something but instead shook his head and left.

"Who was that man, McKenzie?" her mother asked, immediately joining her as Lance exited the building.

"That's what I want to know," her father practically bellowed. "Why was he kissing you?"

"Why is he leaving?" Her mother asked the more pressing question.

"He's just someone I work with," she mumbled, not wanting to discuss Lance.

"She gets that from you," her mother told her father. "The idea she's supposed to kiss people she works with."

"Violet," her father began, crossing his arms and giving her a sour look.

But her mother seemed to shake off her thoughts and smiled. "Come, let me introduce you to your much younger, more virile and loyal replacement."

"Sure took you long enough," her father gibed.

"Some of us are more choosy than others."

McKenzie watched her parents walk away together, bickering back and forth. It wasn't even six in the evening and exhaustion hit her.

Much, much later, after she'd waved sparklers at her mother and Yves's exit, McKenzie gathered up her belongings from the church classroom where the bridal party had gotten ready.

When she got into her car, her gaze immediately went to the passenger floorboard where she saw a vase full of red roses. On the passenger seat was a gift box. Chocolates?

She doubted it due to the odd box size. She ripped open the package, and gave a trembling smile at what was inside.

A new pair of running shoes.

CHAPTER THIRTEEN

"YOU'RE NOT RIGHT, you know."

McKenzie didn't argue with her best friend. Cecilia was correct and they both knew it. Then again, one didn't argue with a person streaking hair color through one's hair.

"I think you should talk to him."

"Who said this was about him?" Okay, so maybe she was feeling more argumentative than she should be.

Cecilia's gaze met McKenzie's in the large salon mirror in front of her styling chair. "You're still upset about your mother getting hitched? I thought you were over that."

"I am over that." How could she not be when her mother was happier than McKenzie recalled her ever being? When she'd morphed into an energetic, productive person who suddenly seemed to have her act together?

Yves had taken her to South America to a bird-watching resort for their honeymoon. Since they'd returned her mother seemed as happy as a lark, working at the health-food store with her new husband.

This from a woman who'd never really held a job.

"Then it has to be Lance."

"Why does it have to be Lance?"

"The reason you're lost in your thoughts and moping around like a lovesick puppy? Who else would it be?"

"I'm not," she denied with way too much gusto.

"Sure you are."

"I meant I'm not a lovesick puppy," she countered, because at least that much was true.

Cecilia laughed. "Keep telling yourself that, girlfriend, and maybe you'll convince one of us."

McKenzie didn't say anything, just sat in the chair while Cecilia dabbed more highlight color onto her hair, then wrapped the strand in aluminum foil.

"Have you tossed out the roses yet?"

What did it matter if she still had the roses Lance had given her on Valentine's Day? They still had a little color to them.

"I'm not answering that."

"It's been a month. They're dead. Let them go."

"I thought I might try my hand at making potpourri."

"Sure you did." Cecilia had the audacity to laugh as she tucked another wet strand of hair into a tinfoil packet. "What about the shoes?"

"What about them?"

"Don't play dumb with me. I've known you too long. Have you worn them yet?"

That was the problem with best friends. They had known you too long and too well.

"I've put them on," she admitted, not clarifying that she'd put them on a dozen times, staring at them, wondering what he'd meant by giving her running shoes. "They're a perfect fit."

"I wouldn't have expected otherwise. He pays attention to details."

Lance did pay attention to details. Like the fact she ran away when things got sticky. Then again, he hadn't tried to convince her not to. Not once had he mentioned anything beyond their seeing each other on Valentine's Day. If she'd agreed, would he have asked for more? No matter how many times she asked herself that question, she couldn't convince herself that he would have. She wasn't the only one who ran.

Maybe she should have gotten him a pair of running shoes, too.

She bit the inside of her lower lip. "You think I messed up letting him go, don't you?"

Cecilia's look was full of amusement. "If you were any quicker on the uptake I'd have to call you Einstein."

"It wasn't just my choice, you know. He walked away that night at my mother's rehearsal."

"He gave you roses and running shoes."

Yeah, he had.

"Running shoes? What kind of a gift is that anyway?"

"The kind that says he knows you better than you think he does. You're a runner—physically, mentally, emotionally. He also gave you red roses. What does that say?"

"Not what you're implying. He never told me that he loved me."

"Did you want him to?"

"I don't know."

"Sure you do." Cecilia pulled another strand of hair loose, coated it in dye, then wrapped it.

"He was in love with a woman who died. I can't compete with a ghost."

"She's gone. She's no longer any competition."

"Cecilia!"

"I don't mean to be crude, McKenzie, but if he's in love with a woman who is no longer around, well, she's not a real threat. Not unless you let her be."

"He never even mentioned her to me."

"There are lots of things you still haven't told him. That's what the rest of your lives are for."

"He and I agreed to a short-term relationship."

"You didn't have a signed contract. Terms can change."

"Ouch!" McKenzie yelped when Cecilia pulled a piece of hair too tightly.

"Sorry." But the gleam in her eyes warned that she might have done it on purpose. "You could have kept seeing him. You should have kept seeing him."

"He didn't want to go beyond our two months any more than I did."

"Sure you didn't. That's why you're miserable now that you're not with him anymore."

"I'm not miserable," McKenzie lied. "Besides, I see him at work."

"How's that?"

"Awkward. Strange. As bad as I was afraid it would be. I knew I shouldn't become involved with a coworker."

"So why did you?"

"Because…because I couldn't not."

Cecilia's face lit with excitement that McKenzie had finally caught on. "Exactly. That should tell you everything you need to know about how you feel about the man. Why you are so intent on denying that you miss him makes no sense to me."

"I miss him," she admitted. "There, does that make you happy? I miss Lance. I miss the way he looks, the way he smiles, the way he smells, the way he tastes. I miss everything about him."

Cecilia spun the chair to face her straight on, her eyes full of sympathy. "Girl, how can you not see what is so obvious?"

McKenzie's rib cage contracted tightly around everything in her chest. "You think I'm in love with him."

"Aren't you?"

McKenzie winced. She wasn't. Couldn't be. She shouldn't be.

She was.

"What am I going to do?"

"Well, you are your mother's daughter. Maybe you should grab the happiness you want instead of being afraid it's always going to be just outside your grasp."

All these years she'd not wanted to be like her mother, but her mother had been happy, had been choosing to be single, but not out of fear of love. If her mother, who'd borne the brunt of so much hurt, could love, could trust, why couldn't McKenzie?

If her mother could put her heart out there, be in a committed relationship, find happiness, why couldn't McKenzie?

Maybe she wasn't like her father. Maybe she wasn't like her mother either.

Maybe she was tiny pieces of both, could learn from their mistakes, learn from their successes and be a better person.

Right now, she wasn't a better person. Right now, she didn't even feel like a whole person. She felt like only half a person, with the other half of her missing.

Lance.

"I want him back," she admitted, causing Cecilia's eyes to widen with satisfaction.

"Good. Now, how are you going to make it happen?"

"He didn't want more than our two months, Cecilia. He was as insistent on our ending point as I was," she mused. "I wasn't the only one who let us end at two months. He didn't fight to hang on to me." He hadn't. He'd walked away without a backward glance. "His heart belongs to another woman."

"Another woman who can't have him," Cecilia reminded her. "If you want Lance back, then you don't worry about whether or not he's fighting for you. You fight for him. You show him you want him in your life. Show him how much he means to you."

She did want Lance back and, Lord help her, she wanted

to fight for him, to show him she missed him and wanted him in her life.

"How am I supposed to do that?"

Cecilia's gaze shifted to the back of a flyer posted on the salon's front door. A flyer someone from Celebration Graduation had dropped by a week or so ago, advertising a St. Patrick's Day show at the Senior Citizen Center.

"I have the perfect idea."

McKenzie could see her friend mentally rubbing her hands together in glee. "Why do I get the feeling I'm not going to like this?"

Lance shoved the giant four-leaf clover to the middle of the stage, trying to decide if the light was going to reflect off the glittery surface correctly or if he should reposition the stage prop.

"That looks great there," one of the other volunteers called out, answering his silent question.

He finished arranging props on the stage, then went to the room they were using as a dressing room to get ready for the actual show. He was emceeing.

The event hadn't been a planned Celebration Graduation fund-raiser, but the Senior Citizen Center had approached him with the idea and the earnest desire to help with the project. How could he say no?

Besides, he'd needed something to focus on besides the gaping hole in his chest.

He should be used to having a gaping hole in his chest.

Hadn't he had one since he'd been a seventeen-year-old kid and the love of his life had been killed in a car accident?

Only had Shelby really been the love of his life? Or had she just been his first love and their relationship had never been able to run its natural course to its inevitable conclusion?

Which was his fault.

He winced at his thoughts. Why was he allowing such negativity into his head?

It had been his fault Shelby was no longer alive. He'd promised her that her death wouldn't be in vain, that her life wouldn't be forgotten. He'd vowed to keep her alive in his heart and mind. Wasn't that why he did the volunteer work?

Wasn't that why he headed up Celebration Graduation?

So that no other teen had to go through what he and Shelby had gone through?

So that there were other options in teens' lives besides making bad choices on graduation night?

If only their school had offered a Celebration Graduation program. If only he and Shelby had gone to the event rather than the party they'd been at. If only he hadn't given in to peer pressure and drunk. If only he'd not let her drink, not let her get into that car for him to drive them home that night.

If only.

If only.

If only.

Hadn't he spent a lifetime playing out if-onlys in his head? What good had they ever done? He couldn't go back to that night, couldn't bring Shelby back. All he could do was carry on and make a difference in other teens' lives.

He did make a difference in other teens' lives. Both at his job where he counseled and encouraged teens to make good decisions and with Celebration Graduation.

Shelby would be proud of the man he'd become.

At least, he thought she would.

That's what kept him going, knowing that he was living his life to make a difference for others.

He couldn't let anything, anyone get in the way of that.

"There's a full house out there already," one of the other cast members told him, taking one last look in the mirror before moving to the doorway. "This was a great idea, Dr. Spencer."

"I can't take the credit. The Senior Citizen Center approached me," he admitted.

"Well, I'd say they've sold out the show," Lanette said, peeping through a curtain to look at the crowd. "There's only a few seats left and it's still a good fifteen minutes before showtime."

Lance had called the cast members from the Christmas show and gotten them on board to do a St. Patrick's Day show. They'd kept it simple, doing numbers that they all already knew, but that would be fun for the audience. Lance had even convinced a magician to come in and do a few tricks between sets. If the guy worked out, Lance hoped to have him perform on graduation night at the kids' lock-in to help pass their time in a fun way.

Seven arrived and Lance went out onto their makeshift stage. He welcomed the crowd, apologized to the ones standing in the back of the room, but applauded them on participating in something that was for such a worthy cause.

He moved to the side of the stage. Four of the female performers came out onstage, holding sparkly four-leaf clovers the size of dinner plates. The performers changed and a male singer crooned out a love ballad that had Lance's throat clogging up a little.

He didn't want to think about Shelby. He didn't want to think about McKenzie.

He couldn't stop thinking about either.

The crowd cheered each performance.

They finished the first half of the show, went to the back to grab a drink and change costumes while the magician did his show. Lance found himself laughing at some of the tricks and trying to figure out how a few others were done. The crowd loved the show. Soon the singers were back onstage and sang a few more songs. Lanette had the lead in the next number and took the stage with a bright smile.

"Okay, folks, this is a little different from what's on your program, but sometimes the best performances are the unexpected, impromptu ones," Lanette began, causing Lance to frown.

He was unaware of any changes to their schedule and certainly there weren't any planned impromptu performances that he knew of.

That's when he saw her.

McKenzie, wearing her sparkly green dress that she must have had hidden beneath a jacket for him to have not noticed her before because she glimmered with every step she took toward the stage.

What was she doing?

But even before Lanette handed her the microphone, he knew.

McKenzie was going to sing.

The question was why.

And why was his heart beating so crazily in his chest with excitement over what she was about to do when he had no right to feel that excitement?

To feel that joy that McKenzie was there?

Any moment McKenzie expected her heels to give way and she would fall flat on her face. Definitely she was more comfortable in her running shoes than the three-inch heels she'd chosen to wear because Cecilia had told her they made her legs look phenomenal.

Who cared how good her legs looked if she was flat on her butt from her feet going out from under her?

Or maybe it was because her knees were shaking that she feared falling.

Her knees were shaking, knocking together like clackers. Why was she doing this? Wouldn't a simple phone call or text message have sufficed? No, she'd had to go along with Cecilia's idea that she had to do something big, something totally out of character to convince Lance she was playing for keeps.

Cecilia had arranged a voice coach who'd worked with McKenzie every night that week. Cecilia had called a client who happened to be one of the female singers in the show and arranged for McKenzie's surprise performance. Lanette had been thrilled to help because she'd seen McKenzie and Lance save the mayor's life and had thought them a perfect couple even back then.

Now it was all up to McKenzie.

She hated people looking at her and the entire room's eyes were all trained on her, waiting to see what she was going to do. To see if she was going to cry or scream out like her parents.

No, that's not why they were here. That's not why they were looking at her. They were here for entertainment. Entertainment she was about to add to, and perhaps not in a good way.

She couldn't sing.

A week with a voice coach wasn't going to fix that. A year with a voice coach couldn't.

But she'd learned what her voice's strengths were and what her weaknesses were. Her performance wasn't going to have any agents lining up to sign her, but hopefully her putting herself out there for him would impress a certain man enough for him to rethink two months, for him to open up his heart and let her inside, to at least give her, give them, a chance.

The music started up as she made her way up the steps to the stage. One step. Two steps. Three steps. On the stage without falling. Yes, now, if she could just stay upright during her song, she totally had this.

She made her way over to Lance, smiled at him suggestively as she ran her finger along his shirt collar. His body heat lured her in, making her want to touch him for real, but common sense said she was on a stage, everyone was watching, the show must go on and this wasn't that kind of show.

Taking a deep breath first that she hoped the microphone didn't pick up, she broke into a song about going after what she wanted and making it hers.

If he walked away from her, she'd look a fool.

She'd feel a fool.

But, even more, he might not forgive her for interfering in his show.

Still, she agreed with Cecilia. She had to make a grand gesture to show Lance that she was serious about wanting him in her life, that she was willing to take risks where he was concerned, that she'd fight for him.

That she'd sing for him.

So she sang.

His eyes searched hers and she couldn't quite read his expression.

Fine. She was going to do this, was going to put her heart into it, and whatever happened happened.

She played her eyes at him, did her best to be sultry and seductive without being trashy, and felt a huge weight lift off her when Lance grinned.

Thank God. At least he wasn't going to have her look a fool on the stage.

To those in the audience he looked believable. To McKenzie he looked more beautiful than anything she'd ever seen.

She finished the song.

Shaking his head, he wrapped her into his arms, spun her around, and kissed her forehead.

"Ladies and gentlemen, give it up for Dr. McKenzie Sanders."

The room filled with applause.

"Bow," Lance whispered, squeezing her hand.

Feeling a bit silly, she did so.

He led her off the stage and round to the back as Lanette took to the stage again to perform another song.

"What are you doing here?" he asked the second they were out of sight of the audience.

Ouch. Not exactly what she'd hoped to hear him say. Then again, what had she expected? For him to immediately know what her song had meant? He was a man. Sometimes men had to be hit over the head with the obvious for them to recognize the truth, or so her best friend had told her repeatedly.

"I'm here to sing for you."

His brow lifted. "I thought you didn't like singing?"

"I don't."

"Then why?"

"Because I want to be a part of the things you enjoy. Two months wasn't enough time. I want more. I need more."

He considered her a moment, glanced at the other crew members who were backstage, then pulled her toward the back. "Obviously we need to talk, but this isn't the time or the place."

"Obviously," she agreed, knowing the other cast members were watching them curiously.

"I have to be there for the last song. All the cast members will be onstage for it. I give my thanks to the cast and the Senior Citizen Center, and then we'll take our bows."

"I can wait."

The others lined up to take the stage as soon as Lanette's number ended. Lance glanced toward her and looked torn.

"Go. I'll be here when you're finished."

"You're sure?"

"In case you haven't figured it out just by my being here, I'm planning to stick around, Lance. Two months wasn't

enough time. At least, not for me. Unless... You're not seeing anyone else, are you?"

She'd not even considered that he might already be seeing someone else. She couldn't imagine it. Not with the way
he looked at her. But sometimes people did stupid things.

"There's no one else, McKenzie. Just you."

Although his face went a ghostly white at his own words,
they put such joy into her heart that she threw her arms
around him and kissed him, letting every bit of feeling inside her show in her kiss.

One of the other singers cleared his throat, reminding
them that Lanette's number was coming to an end.

"Sorry," McKenzie apologized, then took it back. "No,
I'm not sorry. Not that I kissed you anyway. Just that I
haven't kissed you every night for the past month. I've
missed you."

Lance pulled away from McKenzie without saying anything.

He'd already said enough.

He'd said there was no one else.

Just her.

How could he have said that?

His insides shook.

A crushing weight settled onto his chest.

One that made breathing difficult, much less saying anything as he took to the stage.

He went through the motions, had the cast bowing at the
appropriate times, the crowd applauding, and the cast applauding the Senior Citizen Center. But he couldn't keep his
mind on what he was doing, no matter how much he tried.

Just her. Just McKenzie.

Not Shelby.

How could he have said *Just McKenzie*?

How could he feel that?

He owed Shelby his dedication, his life, because he'd taken hers.

Then it was time for Lance to thank everyone for attending and for their donations to Celebration Graduation.

Only when he went to thank them did more words spill out than he'd meant to say. Words he'd never spoken out loud. Not ever.

"I've had people ask me in the past why I'm so passionate about Celebration Graduation," he began, staring out into the audience without really seeing anyone. "Most of the time I come up with an answer about how I believe in the cause and want to do my part. The truth goes much deeper than that. The truth is that I'm the reason programs such as Celebration Graduation need to exist. At the end of my junior year my girlfriend, who'd just graduated from high school, was killed in a car crash because I made the bad decision to drive while under the influence of alcohol. I lost control of the car and hit a tree. We were both airlifted to a trauma hospital. She died later that night."

McKenzie covered her mouth with her hand.

Oh, God. She should have known, should have figured out the truth behind Shelby's death. Only how could she have?

"So the truth is that my passion about Celebration Graduation, which gives teenagers an alternative to how they spend their graduation night, comes from my own past mistakes. I lived through what I hope to prevent from ever happening again." Lance's voice broke and for a moment McKenzie didn't think he was going to be able to say more, but then he continued.

"Through Celebration Graduation I hope to keep Shelby's memory alive, to make her life, her death matter, for her to make a difference in others' lives because she was a very special person and would have done great things in the world had she gotten the chance."

Tears ran down McKenzie's face. Dear Lord, she was devastated by the pain inside him. By the guilt inside him. She could hear it wrenched from him. He had loved Shelby.

He did love Shelby.

Lance's heart belonged to another. Irrevocably.

"Thank you for being here today, for helping me keep Shelby alive in my heart, and for making a difference in our youth's lives through this wonderful program."

At first there was a moment of silence, as if the audience wasn't sure whether to applaud or just sit there, then a single person clapped, then the room burst into applause.

McKenzie watched Lance say something to Lanette. She nodded, and he disappeared off the opposite side of the stage.

McKenzie waited at the side of the stage, but Lance didn't reappear. After they'd mingled with the crowd, the other performers returned.

"He told me to tell you he was sorry but that he had to leave," Lanette told her in a low voice so the others couldn't hear.

"He left?" McKenzie's heart pounded. He'd left. How could he do that, knowing she was backstage? Knowing she'd come to fight for him?

But she knew.

She recognized exactly what he'd done, because it was something she excelled at.

He'd run.

CHAPTER FOURTEEN

LANCE KNELT BESIDE the grave, thinking himself crazy for being at a cemetery at this time of night. The show hadn't ended until after nine, and by the time he'd realized where he'd been headed it had been almost eleven.

He hadn't consciously decided to go to Shelby's grave, but it's where his car had taken him. Maybe it was where he needed to go to put things into proper perspective.

Because for a few minutes he'd allowed himself to look into McKenzie's eyes while she'd sung to him and he'd acknowledged the truth.

He was in love with her.

Right or wrong, he loved her.

And she loved him. Perhaps he'd always known she felt that way, had seen the truth in her eyes when she'd looked at him, had felt the truth in her touch, in her kiss.

She looked at him the way her mother looked at Yves. The way his mother looked at his father. The way his grandmother looked at his grandfather.

Tonight, while she'd sung to him, McKenzie had looked at him with her heart shining through every word.

In the past she'd fought that feeling, had been determined not to allow herself to be hurt by making the mistakes her parents had made. Tonight she'd put everything on the line and he'd felt exhilarated to realize she was there for him, that she loved him and wanted him.

Then reality had set in.

He wasn't free to accept her love, to return her love. He'd vowed his love to another he owed everything to.

And he'd resented his vow. He'd resented Shelby.

The guilt of that resentment sickened him.

"Forgive me, Shelby. Forgive me for that night. Forgive me for not keeping you safe," he pleaded over the grave, much as he had many times in the past.

"Forgive me for still being here when you're not."

Wasn't that the crux of the matter?

He'd lived and Shelby hadn't.

How many times had he wished he could give his life for hers?

Standing at this very graveside, he'd vowed that his heart would always belong to her, that he'd never love another, never marry another. Even at seventeen he hadn't been so naive as to think he'd spend his life alone, so he had dated over the years, had been in relationships, but not once had he ever been tempted to sway from his promise to Shelby.

Until tonight.

Until McKenzie.

With McKenzie everything had changed.

With McKenzie he wanted everything.

Because he really did want McKenzie.

"Forgive me, Shelby. Forgive me for the way I feel about McKenzie. You'd like her, you know. She's a lot like what you might have been at her age. She loves to run, just as you did. And she's a doctor, just as you always planned to be. And I love her, just as I planned to always love you."

Guilt ripped through him.

He swiped at moisture on his face.

This was crazy. Why was he here? Then again, he felt crazy. He'd told everyone at the Senior Citizen Center his most guarded secret. He'd told them he'd essentially murdered Shelby.

The authorities hadn't seen it that way. Neither had Shelby's parents or his own family. She'd been eighteen to his seventeen. She'd been caught drinking in the past, he'd been a stupid kid trying to fit in with her older friends, but he knew that he shouldn't have been drinking or driving.

Memories of that night assailed him. For years he'd blocked them from his mind, not wanting to remember.

Shelby dancing. Shelby smiling and laughing. Shelby so full of life. And liquor. She'd been full of that, too.

She'd wanted more, had been going to take his car to get more, and he'd argued with her.

Even with being under the influence himself, he'd known she'd been in no shape to drive. Unfortunately, neither had he been and he'd known it, refusing to give her his keys.

She'd taken off running into the darkness, calling out over her shoulder that if he wouldn't take her, she'd just run there.

He should have let her. She'd have run herself sober.

Instead, to the teasing of her friends that he couldn't control his girlfriend, he'd climbed into his car and driven down the road to pick her up.

But he hadn't been taking her to the liquor store when he'd wrecked the car.

He'd been taking her home.

They'd been arguing, her saying she should have known he was a baby, rather than a man.

He'd been mad, had denied her taunts, reminded her of just how manly she'd said he was earlier that evening, and in the blink of the eye she'd grabbed at the steering wheel and he'd lost control of his car and hit the tree.

The rest had come in bits and pieces.

Waking up, not realizing he'd wrecked the car. The smells of oil, gas and blood.

That was the first time he'd realized blood had such a

strong odor. His car had been full of it. His blood. Shelby's blood.

He'd become aware of people outside the car, working to free them from the crumpled metal, but then he'd lost consciousness again until they'd been pulling him from the car.

Shelby had still been inside.

"I can't leave her," he'd told them.

"We've got her, son," a rescue worker had said. "We're taking you both to the hospital."

"Tell her I love her," he'd said. "That I will always love her."

"We will, son. They're putting her in the helicopter right now, but I'll see to it she gets the message."

"Tell her now. Please. Tell her now." He'd tried to get free, to go to her, but his body hadn't worked, and he'd never got to tell her. He had no idea if the rescue worker had carried through with his promise or not.

But as soon as Lance had been released from the hospital, he'd told Shelby himself.

Kneeling exactly where he currently knelt.

He'd been guilt-ridden then. He was just as guilt-ridden now.

"I'm so sorry, Shelby. I love her. In ways I didn't know I could love, I love McKenzie."

He continued to talk, saying all the things that were in his heart.

For the first time peace came over Lance. Peace and self-forgiveness. Oh, there was a part of him that would never completely let go of the guilt he felt that he'd made such bad choices that night, but whether it was the late hour or his own imagination he felt Shelby's presence, felt her forgiveness, her desire for him to let go and move on with his life.

Was he being self-delusional? Believing what he wanted to believe because he wanted McKenzie?

"I need a sign, Shelby. Give me a sign that you really do forgive me," he pleaded into the darkness.

That was when he looked up and saw a ghost.

McKenzie couldn't stay in the shadows any longer. For the past half hour she had leaned against a large headstone, crying, not knowing whether to make her presence known or not. She hadn't purposely tried to keep her presence from him initially. He just had been so lost in his thoughts, in his confessions that he hadn't noticed her.

Lance had run away from her.

Only he loved her. She'd known he loved her even before she'd heard his heart-wrenching words, and she hadn't been willing to give him up without a fight. Especially not to someone who'd been gone for over fifteen years.

She'd listened to him, cried with him and for him from afar, and had prayed for him to find forgiveness, to be able to let his guilt go.

When he'd asked for a sign she'd swear she'd felt a hard shove on her back, making her stumble forward, almost falling in the process.

"Shelby?"

Her heart broke at the anguish in his voice. "It's McKenzie, Lance."

Wiping at his eyes, he stood. "McKenzie? What are you doing here?"

"I followed you."

"You followed me from the Senior Citizen Center?"

"It wasn't difficult as slowly as you drive." Which she now finally understood. He liked his fast sports car, but never got it up over the speed limit.

"I didn't see you."

"I didn't think you had. I sat in my car for a few minutes after you first got here. I realized where you were going and was going to give you privacy, but it's after midnight and we're at a cemetery and I'll admit I got a little freaked out, sitting in my car by myself."

"You shouldn't be here, McKenzie."

Yeah, he might think that.

"You're wrong. This is exactly where I should be. Right beside you."

"I don't understand."

"You love me," she told him. "And I love you. And maybe you love her, too, but she isn't here anymore." At least, McKenzie didn't think she was. That had been her imagination playing tricks on her when she'd felt that shove. "I am here, Lance. I used to be terrified that I'd make all the same mistakes my parents made, but I'm not anymore. I'm not like my father, although I may be more like my mother than I realized. You told me that my father did those things because he loved himself more than my mother or me."

"I shouldn't have said that, McKenzie."

"Sure you should have. You were right. But guess what, Lance Donovan Spencer? I love you that much. I love you enough to know that you are who I want, that you are the man I admire above all others, that you are the person I love enough to know that being faithful won't be a problem because I don't want anyone but you."

"Don't admire me, McKenzie. I'm not worthy. You heard what I admitted to back at the Senior Citizen Center."

"I heard and I love you all the more for it."

In the moonlight, she saw the confusion on his face. "How can you love me for something I detest myself for?"

"Because in the face of adversity you learned from the lessons life threw at you and you became a wonderful man who is constantly doing things for others, who is constantly trying to save others from the agony he suffers every day, from Shelby's fate."

"You make me sound like a hero. I'm not."

"To me, you are a hero. You are my hero, Lance. You're

the man who made me know what love is, both to feel and to receive it."

He closed his eyes.

"Don't try to tell me you don't love me, because I heard you say it," she warned. "But I already knew, deep down, I knew. That's why I sang to you, why I followed you. Because of love and my trust in that love."

"I don't deserve you."

"I'm stubborn and prideful and prone to run when things get sticky, but take a look at these." She raised one foot up off the ground. While she'd been sitting in her car, waiting for him to come back to his, she'd changed out of her heels and into the pair of running shoes he'd given her. "See these? My man gave them to me for Valentine's Day so I could run to him. He doesn't know it yet, but I have a pair for him in my car so, that way, the next time he runs, he can run to me, too."

"You knew I was going to run away tonight?"

"My singing is pretty bad. I wasn't expecting you to swoon with the sudden realization that everything was going to be perfect."

"Your singing was beautiful."

"I've heard of being blinded by love, but I'm pretty sure you must be tone-deaf from love."

"I do love you, McKenzie."

"I know."

"I made Shelby a promise."

"One you've kept all these years. It's time to let go. You asked Shelby to give you a sign, Lance. I'm that sign. The way we feel about each other." She wrapped her arms around him and leaned her forehead against his chin. "I don't need you to forget Shelby. She's part of what's made you into the man you are, the man I love, but you have to let the guilt go. You can't change the past, only the future. I want to be your future."

"What are you saying, McKenzie?"

"That I want a lot more than two months to see what the future holds for us."

Lance held the woman in his arms tightly to him. He couldn't believe she was here, that they were standing by Shelby's grave at midnight.

He couldn't believe McKenzie was laying her heart on the line, telling him how much she cared.

"If we do this," he warned, his heart pounding in his chest, "I'm never going to let you go, you do realize that?"

She snuggled closer to him and held on tight. "Maybe you weren't paying attention, but that's the idea."

EPILOGUE

"THE EMCEE JUST winked at you."

McKenzie nodded at her mother. "Yep, he did."

"He has a disgusting habit of doing that," Cecilia accused with a shake of her head.

"You're just jealous," McKenzie teased her friend.

"Ha. I don't think so. My hunky boyfriend is Santa, baby," Cecilia countered, making McKenzie laugh.

"Yeah, yeah. Quit pulling rank just because Santa has the hots for you."

"I could dress as Santa if you're into that kind of thing," Yves offered Violet.

"Eww. Don't need to hear this." McKenzie put her fingers over her ears. "La-la-la. I'm finding my happy place, where I *didn't* just hear my stepdad offer to dress up as Santa to give my mom her kicks."

Yves waggled his brows and gave Violet a wink of her own. McKenzie's mother giggled in response. McKenzie just kept her hands over her ears, but she couldn't keep the smile from her face at how happy her mother was or how much in love the two newlyweds were.

"Ahem." Cecilia nudged her arm. "The emcee is trying to get your attention."

"He has my attention." And her heart. The past nine months had been amazing, full of life and happiness and embracing her feelings for Lance, with him embracing his feelings for her. Sure, there were moments when her old insecurities slipped through, but they were farther and farther apart. Just as Lance's moments of guilt were farther and farther apart.

He'd even been asked to speak at the local high school the week before graduation to talk to the kids about what had happened with Shelby. McKenzie had been so proud of him, of the way he'd opened up and shared with the kids his tragedy, how he'd lived his life trying to make amends, but one never really could. The Celebration Graduation committee had surprised Lance by setting up the Shelby Hanover Scholarship in her honor and had made the award to its first recipient following Lance's talk at the high school.

"Yeah, well, he's motioning for you to join him onstage," Cecilia pointed out. "He gonna have you croon for him again?"

"I hope not." McKenzie still didn't enjoy singing or having everyone's eyes on her, but the emcee aka the most wonderful man in the world truly was motioning her to come up onto the stage.

She got onto the stage. "Please tell me I'm not about to embarrass myself by singing some Christmas ditty."

Grinning, he shook his head. "You're not about to embarrass yourself by singing."

"Phew," she said. "That's a relief to everyone in the audience."

One of the performers brought over a chair and set it down behind where McKenzie stood next to Lance. She glanced around at the chair, then looked at Lance in question.

"Have a seat, McKenzie."

She eyed him curiously. "What's going on?"

The look in his eyes had her concerned. His grin had faded and he actually looked nervous.

"Lance?"

"Sit, please."

McKenzie sat, which must have cued the music because it started up the moment her bottom hit the seat.

When she caught the tune, she smiled.

All the performers came out onto the stage and began singing. Lance stood in front of her, his eyes full of love. When the song ended, she got to her feet and kissed him.

The crowd cheered.

"You have me, you know," she whispered, for his ears only.

"I sure hope so or I'm about to look like the world's biggest fool."

She arched a brow at him. "Lance?"

"Have a seat, McKenzie."

Her gaze met his and her mouth fell open as she sat back down.

A big smile on his face, Lance dropped to one knee, right there on the Coopersville Community Center's stage, with half the town watching.

"McKenzie, at this show last year you saved the mayor's life," Lance began. "But without knowing it, you saved mine, too."

McKenzie's eyes watered.

He wasn't doing this.

He *was* doing this.

"This past year has been the best of my life because I've spent it with you, but more than that you've helped me to be the person I was meant to be, to let go of things that needed to be let go of, and to embrace the aspects of life that needed to be embraced."

"Lance," she whispered, her hand shaking as he took it in his.

"I can't imagine my life without you in it every single day."

"You'll never have to," she promised.

"I'd like to make that official, get it in writing," he teased, drawing a laugh from their audience. "McKenzie, will you do me the honor of becoming my wife?"

McKenzie stared into the eyes of the man who'd taught her what it meant to love and be loved and felt her heart expand even further, so much so that she felt her chest bursting with love.

"Oh, yes." She nodded, watching as he slipped a diamond ring onto the third finger of her left hand.

He lifted her hand, kissed her fingers. "I love you, McKenzie."

"I love you, too, Lance."

Lance lifted her to her feet, kissed her.

The curtain fell, closing them off from the applauding audience.

"Merry Christmas, McKenzie."

"The merriest."

* * * * *

MILLS & BOON

THE HEART OF ROMANCE

A ROMANCE FOR EVERY READER

MODERN

Prepare to be swept off your feet by sophisticated, sexy and seductive heroes, in some of the world's most glamourous and romantic locations, where power and passion collide.

HISTORICAL

Escape with historical heroes from time gone by. Whether your passion is for wicked Regency Rakes, muscled Vikings or rugged Highlanders, awaken the romance of the past.

MEDICAL

Set your pulse racing with dedicated, delectable doctors in the high-pressure world of medicine, where emotions run high and passion, comfort and love are the best medicine.

True Love

Celebrate true love with tender stories of heartfelt romance, from the rush of falling in love to the joy a new baby can bring, and a focus on the emotional heart of a relationship.

Desire

Indulge in secrets and scandal, intense drama and plenty of sizzling hot action with powerful and passionate heroes who have it all: wealth, status, good looks…everything but the right woman.

HEROES

Experience all the excitement of a gripping thriller, with an intense romance at its heart. Resourceful, true-to-life women and strong, fearless men face danger and desire - a killer combination!

To see which titles are coming soon, please visit

millsandboon.co.uk/nextmonth

GET YOUR ROMANCE FIX!

Get the latest romance news,
exclusive author interviews, story
extracts and much more!

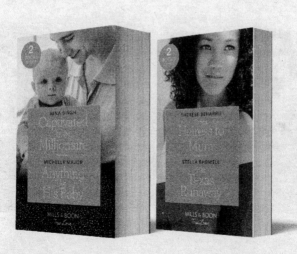

MILLS & BOON
MEDICAL
Pulse-Racing Passion

Set your pulse racing with dedicated, delectable doctors in the high-pressure world of medicine, where emotions run high and passion, comfort and love are the best medicine.